The Gears of Madness

Iain Grant

The Collected Sedgewick Papers,
edited and revised with additional notes of a
historical nature.

Pigeon Park Press

Paperback ISBN: 978-0-9930607-7-9
Ebook ISBN: 978-0-9930607-6-2

Cover artwork and design Copyright © Mike Watts 2015 (www.bigbeano.co.uk)

Published by Pigeon Park Press

www.pigeonparkpress.com
info@pigeonparkpress.com

The Sedgewick Papers by Iain Grant
(available as individual e-chapbooks)

The Angels of the Abyss
The Pearl of Tharsis
The Well of Shambala
The Bridge to Lemuria
The Shadow under London
The Herald of the Ancients

1902 – The Angels of the Abyss

From the memoirs of Mr J. Cadwallander

1.

Within two days of our departure from Plymouth Thermospheric Station I had decided that I did not much care for space travel. In all fairness, Captain Treadaway was a pleasant enough host and our quarters aboard the *Wakefield* were far more spacious than those Professor Sedgewick and I had occupied aboard the submarine *HMS Serpentine* the year previously. Nonetheless, there was something disquieting to the bowels in interplanetary travel, a certain *mal de mer* arising from the subtle tides and currents of the æther.

However, in the light of what would follow over the next several years, it is such a small thing that I wonder now at my lack of character. Indeed, looking back, it is clear the events on board the *Lady Henshall* would be a precursor of such profound terrors that a little digestive distress might be considered a more than welcome alternative.

I could find little relief, above decks or below. Promenading on deck (possible without breathing apparatus whilst we still travelled in the solar ætheric plane), I found myself uncontrollably drawn to the gunwales and the sight of the abysmal black pit of stars beneath the iron hull and propellers of our ship. I would stand there, torn between sublime awe and the trembling fear that I might, in a moment of animalistic madness, cast myself overboard and into the dark. Below decks, I had to endure the company of Lieutenant Moore's men, a platoon of the Queen's Armoured Hussars, who travelled with us. I did not once doubt their devotion or bravery, or the terror their modern weaponry might strike into the hearts of any enemies we encountered, but they were too *earthy* for my sensibilities and I found myself embarrassed and belittled whenever I was privy to their barrack-room ribaldry.

And yet I did not regret having agreed to accompany Professor Sedgewick on this journey. Ever since that fearsome business on Kinder Scout, I had sworn to be his batman and companion for as long as he had need of me and neither seasickness nor uncouth soldiers were going to make me break that oath. I had, at that time, known the good professor for six or seven years. In that time he had been as constant as any man I know. He remained resistant to the portliness, baldness and irascibility that come with approaching middle-age (although he has taken to carrying a walking cane of late, purely for aesthetic reasons). He remained a free-thinker, resistant to the homocentric theology and conservative politics of his academic peers. He remained, thankfully, unmarried.

Professor Erskine Sedgewick read theology and natural sciences at Cambridge before going on to become a Fellow of Trinity College. In a successful career (one not untouched by controversy) he devoted himself equally to science and God. Much of his spiritual and scientific enquiry was beyond my understanding. I possessed the benefits of both education and faith but not to the same degree as the good professor. Imagine if you will that my faith, my spirit, is a stout chapel of grey stone nestling in the green hills of my homeland. The professor's, by comparison, is a soaring cathedral of faith and will, white and indomitable.

In recent months he had become embroiled in a war of letters with Flowers, Chambers and their ilk regarding the possibility of life emanating from outside our Earthly sphere. The nub of their argument was, as I understand it, that as Our Lord has only incarnated on Earth and thus died for *our* sins alone; alien beings, if they did exist, could not expect to receive God's grace and redemption. The professor's viewpoint was that each encountered example of alien life would be further evidence of a universe designed by a benign deity for the proliferation of life.

And so when the professor learned of the message received from the *Lady Henshall* transætheric space-lock, he made use of every favour due him to secure places for us both on the *RMS Wakefield* as the investigative expedition's science officers. The Morse code message, having passed through various ætheric planes back to Earth via innumerable signal lamp operators, had a certain nonsensical quality to it, much as one might experience in the parlour game, Chinese Whispers but there were certain phrases that inspired a great deal of excitement in my companion: *"astral being ... unearthly light ... foreign form..."*

6

We had ample opportunity to contemplate and discuss the meaning of the words *en route*. While the *Wakefield* might have been a speedy packet ship, its engines powered by the purest Yorkshire chthonic coal, our journey was not a short one.

The *Lady Henshall,* stationed almost directly above the orbit of Venus, held a position between the fourth and fifth superætheric planes. As every educated schoolboy knows, the æther that fills the void between all worlds is not of a uniform pressure. Just as sea pressure diminishes as one ascends from the ocean floor, so the ætheric pressure diminishes as one moves, upwards or downwards, away the solar ætheric plane. This, depending upon one's scientific viewpoint, is either a product or cause of the gravitational force we experience on any of the worlds of our solar system. However, unlike the ocean, the change in ætheric pressure is not a gradual one. The ætheric realm is divided into a series of distinct bands or planes, much like the great belts of atmosphere visible on Jupiter (which perhaps, because of the Jovian giant's size, follow the same hitherto unexplained law that governs the ætheric planes).

The pressure differences between the planes and the frequently contrary currents which stir them made naked passage from one plane to the next impossible for all but the most sturdy and securely enclosed ships. Thus, with necessity the mother of invention (and British ingenuity the father), the transætheric space-locks were created. Though the principle behind the space-locks was simply a three-dimensional extrapolation of the two-dimensional canal locks built by our forebears, yet they were mighty works of engineering which, as we passed from the solar ætheric to the first superætheric plane (and thence into three subsequent planes), I had an opportunity to observe at first hand. In shape they resembled a child's drawing of a bone: a long shaft with great protuberances at each end. But what mighty giant could hope to cast such a bone into the heavens! The shaft housed a pressurised lock that in width and height could accommodate the full length of any of Her Majesty's ships. The spiral staircases running the length of the shaft, and by which the space-navvies could carry out their servicing and repair work, would take even the fittest of men a full hour to climb. The protuberances contained the furnaces and engines which powered the lock doors and turbines.

These turbines, a series of huge, enclosed rotors, served a threefold purpose: pumping æther to and from the lock to allow ships' safe and gentle passage between the planes; holding the space-lock in position *laterally* with relation to the solar plane; and preventing the external ætheric pressure from ejecting the space-lock into the lower pressured plane much like a cork fired from a champagne bottle.

Beyond the first superætheric plane one required breathing apparatus if spending long above deck. Beyond the second, the lack of air induced an irritation to the eyes and nose that caused both to water within seconds of exposure. I made the final days of our voyage trapped below deck.

After dinner one evening, I said to my table companions (Captain Treadaway, his first mate Campbell, Lieutenant Moore and, of course, Professor Sedgewick), "We are a long way from Earth."

Lieutenant Moore barked with laughter. "Are you homesick, Cadwallander?"

"No, Lieutenant," I replied, which was true in many ways and false in others. "I am ... mindful of this strange and unsympathetic medium beyond the portholes. Should man have to reach out so far from his home?"

"There are great fields of asteroids in the fifth superætheric," said Treadaway. "Gold and iron, sir. Gold and iron."

"And the *Lady Henshall* is one of how many space-locks providing our ships with access to those fields?" asked Sedgewick, although I imagine he already knew the answer and was simply redirecting the conversation.

"Four," said Moore. "Thus making it of significant strategic value to the empire." He puffed out his chest grandiosely, unsubtly asserting the importance to our mission of both him and his men. He fixed me with a stare and bristled his moustaches. "I would not care if there were no asteroids, no gold or iron out there."

"I doubt the Treasury would agree," spoke Campbell, but was ignored.

"We reach out to the heavens because we can," Moore continued. "It is divine providence and our duty. What did Sir Cecil Rhodes say to his men at Nix Olympus? *You had the fortune to be born Englishmen and as such have won first place in the lottery of life*. Such a birth right comes with duties, yes?"

"Alas," I said. "I am a Welshman. Does that mean I have won second place?"

Treadaway and his mate burst into laughter and the professor allowed himself an indulgent smile.

"Third place perhaps," said Campbell, a Scotsman, and slapped me comradely on the back.

Moore remained unimpressed but the conversation moved on and the evening passed well.

We sighted the *Lady Henshall* on our seventy-third day out. Treadaway signalled to the space-lock. Receiving no response he ordered the *Wakefield* to make a slow, circumspect approach. Lieutenant Moore had his hussars take up their arms and man the *Wakefield's* chase-gun in readiness. The platoon, fifteen men in all, consisted of Moore, his sergeant, an ironclad mortar-man, plus a dozen assorted corporals, lance-corporals and privates, armed with sabres and repeating Webley rifles of Birmingham manufacture. The mortar-man's suit, with its integral helmet and air-cowl, its galvanic joints and gyroscopic movements, had a Maxim gun mounted upon his left shoulder and a traditional mortar on his right. Seeing the mortar-man striding about the hold, seven-feet tall in that powered suit, I understood then why the Fenian rebels had fled the streets of Limerick when confronted with such giants.

Only as we came within the last few miles of the space-lock did its signal lamp begin flashing at us. Both myself and the professor could understand Morse code well enough.

"*Stay away...*" I read. "*French ship fired... Survivors—*" I stopped. The signal was erratic but until that point sufficiently clear. "What do you make that word to be?" I asked the professor.

"Pook?" he suggested. "Pook survived?"

We had not come under fire of any sort and Moore and Treadaway had concurred that if we were to face any danger, we would be better doing it within the thick walls of the space-lock than aboard a mail-service packet ship. The *Wakefield* would be unable to enter the shaft of the space-lock without assistance from within, so Treadaway had the ship dock against a bulkhead hatch and, with the hussars leading the way, Professor Sedgewick, First Mate Campbell and I went aboard.

The inner corridors and companionways of the space-lock, pressurised to Earth-normal, were much like those I experienced aboard the *HMS Serpentine* during our exploration of the Southern Ocean. Everything appeared much as one might expect, but there was not a sign of a single soul! Following the rearmost hussars, I paused to inspect the walls, floors, doorways and such instrumentation that we saw, in hope of a clue. There were no rends, scorch marks or bloodstains that might hint at the untoward. I stopped at one of the many telephonic communication points about the space-lock and listened to the trumpet. It was silent.

"Yes, deserted but without sign of foreign assault or other emergency," said the professor softly, entirely cognisant of my thoughts.

Sergeant Troutbeck gave a shout from up ahead. The hussars had located the signal room.

Shortly, there came the sound of hammering and we hurried to see what the commotion was. We found Troutbeck, battering the door with his fist and demanding that the occupants open up. There was some response, too muffled for me to make out, but the door remained firmly shut.

"He's not opening up," said Troutbeck with a tone of angry finality.

"Then we force the hatch," said Moore.

"Is he alone in there?" asked Sedgewick.

Moore turned on the professor, displeased by the interruption, but Sedgewick expounded calmly. "If there is a lone man in there, he may be the sole survivor of whatever has befallen this place, alone for many weeks. That would be enough to unnerve any man. In such circumstances, who could blame him for refusing to accede to the demands of raised voices and fists?"

"If the space-lock has been virtually unmanned for that long," said Campbell, "then we ought to be concerned about the turbines. Those furnaces don't feed themselves."

Moore nodded in grim understanding and sent Campbell and a small party of men back to the *Wakefield* to collect the ship's engineer and escort him to the *Lady Henshall's* engine rooms to assess the situation. Meanwhile, the professor approached the locked signal room door and rapped on it with the brass lion's head of his cane. "Are you alone in there?" he called.

"Yes, I am," was the reply and in those three words I recognised the lilt of one of my own countrymen.

The professor made some brief introduction, explaining the purpose of our mission, and asked that the man do the decent thing and open the hatch. The man, who had identified himself as Able Seaman Llewellyn, refused to open it.

"Why ever not, man?" asked Sedgewick.

"It's not safe," Llewellyn replied. "They're still out there!"

"What are still out there?"

"We fired the French ship that brought them here but it was too late!"

"Too late? Tell us, what was it?"

"The *pwca*," cried Llewellyn. "Don't look at them!"

"Pooka?" said Sedgewick, frowning, but I had understood the man.

"*Pwca*," I said. "It's Welsh."

"If you look at them, you're lost!" wailed Llewellyn.

"Welsh for what?" demanded Moore.

"Goblins," I said. "Shape-shifters. Demons."

2.

The able seaman's words and what had befallen the *Lady Henshall* became somewhat clearer when we gained access to the shaft of the space-lock. We let the able seaman stew in his cupboard and, whilst Campbell and the *Wakefield's* engineer ensured the furnaces and turbine engines were going to keep us held betwixt the planes, the professor and I, along with the bulk of Moore's men, entered the space-lock shaft.

If you have stood in the open mouth of a huge factory chimney, even if you have stood in the Bazalgette Tunnel that runs under the North Sea to the Low Countries, you still would not have grasped the scale of the space-lock. As we entered via an access hatch and stepped onto the lower lock doors (a mere one foot of iron separating our feet from the fourth superætheric), I looked up and saw, *eight hundred feet above us*, an iron frigate wedged in the shaft. The ship, two hundred feet in length, was not longer than that massive shaft's width but had become grounded with its prow lodged in a *V* of support girders and its stern ensnared in a mangled stairway a quarter turn further round the shaft.

The ship's hull was streaked with black marks. Soot-covered wreckage lay strewn about our feet. The fire which had taken the ship seemed completely burned out. I thought I glimpsed drifting sparks about the wreck although, at the time, I surmised these were peculiar reflections from the lamps marking out the spiral stairways. Moore had Troutbeck lead half of the men up the staircase nearest the prow whilst he led the rest of us up one terminating by the ship's stern.

Rather than shout incoherently at each other across the shaft, Troutbeck and Moore made use of the space-lock's numerous telephonic points, speaking to one another as we progressed. The mortar-man brought up the rear behind the professor and I. The stairway was solidly built, not moving under that metal ogre's weight as we climbed, but the clanging of his cacophonous footsteps reverberated in a way that played evilly upon my imagination.

I focused on our destination above us and soon enough was able to make out the ship's name: *Astrolabe*. The drifting sparks of light persisted in my vision as we approached, slowly resolving into be something entirely unexpected.

"The lights, sir!" called one of the privates with us, pointing. They were neither sparks nor reflections but living creatures! One drifted nearer to us and I had a chance to observe it well.

At its centre was a lump of pale translucent flesh, big as a human fist and within that, a pair of bright golden lights: stars the size of plums. A series of glistening tendrils dangled from this glowing heart. They reminded me of the trailing fronds of a deadly Portuguese Man O' War yet, at the same of time, I was put in mind of the lengths of pig intestine which the local butcher uses to encase his sausages. The creature was kept aloft by a large pair of almost invisible, bird-like wings, delicate and gauzy as a fly's, the imperceptible grey of spider silk.

"In God's name, what are those things?" yelled Moore, betraying a slight quiver of unease.

"Alien beings," said the professor, enraptured.

"What is that glow?" asked Moore.

"Bioluminescence, A trait exhibited by numerous Earth creatures."

"They're beautiful," said the corporal immediately above me, reaching out a hand to touch it. The being seemed to recognise the gesture: with a thrust of its wings it drifted closer.

"Notice, the effort it must exert to fly," said the professor. "May I suggest that this is a creature from a plane of much lighter æther, perhaps several planes above us. Its body is fragile and struggles in our atmosphere. See how—"

The professor's voice trailed off as the creature's lustre took up his full attention. We were all entranced. Perhaps each of us experienced something different but, in those golden orbs, I saw the fire in the hearth on a cold winter's evening, the sunset over Cardigan Bay, the soft lamplight by which my maternal uncle would tell me stories when I was a lad. In sum, I saw peace, comfort and all that I had ever desired in life.

And in recalling my uncle, I remembered something of his stories, and of the *pwca*. Although the lion's share of my mind was ensorcelled by the creature, one small piece of it screamed out in warning just as the alien being began to wrap its tendril around the unresisting corporal's throat.

The screech of the telephonic point nearest us broke the spell entirely.

I came to my senses and, at once, leapt to the corporal's aid. I dug my fingers in between the tendrils and the corporal's neck and pulled. Although cold, slippery and yielding to the touch, the tendrils were remarkably tough. The man was choking but, mesmerised, did nothing to help himself. Fortunately a number of the hussars, fully awoken from the creature's spell, aided me in the struggle. We unwrapped the asphyxiating coils and, each of us holding a section, cast it out into the shaft.

Moore drew his revolver and, with praiseworthy marksmanship, put two shots in the vile thing's radiant body. Its wings folded in on themselves and it tumbled lifelessly towards the lower space-lock doors. I sat heavily on the stairs, and stared at my hands. The stinging cold of the beast's tendrils continued to cling. "The *pwca*," I heard myself say.

"Here, my friend," said Sedgewick and pressed his open hipflask into my hand.

I took a swallow of the professor's whiskey and offered him my thanks. "In some stories," I told him, "the *pwca* carry ghostly lights to lead travellers off the path and to their doom. I should have remembered sooner."

"Better late than never, dear Cadwallander."

Moore gave the order for his men to take up their rifles. A number of the gossamer-winged creatures were descending on Troutbeck's troops across the way and it was clear, even from this distance, that they were subject to the same bewitchment from we had barely escaped.

"Fire at will!" he shouted and the men let loose a volley of shots.

Such fine shots, the Queen's Armoured Hussars! They removed the creatures from the air with speed and accuracy, saving their comrades who, soon enough, were coming round and opening fire themselves.

"O'Bannen!" yelled Moore. "Clear the skies!"

The mortar-man pushed past the professor and I, took position on the outermost step and aimed his Maxim gun at the creatures still circling about the *Astrolabe*.

"Wait!" cried Sedgewick. "Do not slaughter them all! I wish to examine them. They may be intelligent beings!"

The lieutenant's lip curled with distaste. "If you wish to examine them then go back to the entrance. Soon you will find all the samples you may want down there. O'Bannen!"

The mortar-man began firing. The Maxim gun, with its revolving barrel, spat out bullet after bullet. And the noise! It was not the retort of a rifle or even the boom of a cannon; it produced a continuous roar, the deep, hellish blare of some unholy bugle.

The creatures, perhaps twenty in all, rained down from the heights, their wings tattered and their bodies shredded by bullets. A minute later, the firing had stopped, all the winged creatures were dead and my ears were ringing. It took me some time to realise that the telephonic point was making its screeching call once more.

Professor Sedgewick picked up the ear trumpet. He spoke into the device some moments before replacing the trumpet on the cradle. "That was Campbell," he informed us all. "The furnaces and engines are in fine working order and in no short supply of fuel."

"Well, that's all right then," I said and, wiggling a finger in my ear to clear it of the persistent ringing, found myself chuckling despite, or perhaps because of, our recent ordeal.

The corporal who had been attacked by the first creature (a young fellow called Childers) was still dazed and seated upon the stairs. Hands to his neck, he stroked the glistening marks which the creature's tendrils had left as though they were still around him. The professor knelt beside Childers and inspected his wounds, such as they were.

"I don't know what came over me," said the corporal. "It was like a dream."

"I am reminded of the sea-devil, Cadwallander, the angler fish of the bathypelagic zone. Do you recall it from our submarine expedition?"

"The one that draws in its prey with a glowing lure?"

"The same."

"How can I forget?" I said, getting to my feet and readjusting my tie. "Huge mouth of razor sharp teeth. Damned ugly fish, I recall."

"Do you recall anything of its mating habits?" he asked.

I was surprised by the question. "Can't say I do. Is it important?"

The professor shook his head, though it might have been a gesture symbolising regret rather than disagreement. "There are theories," he said, "regarding the transmutation of species, convergent transmutation and symbiosis. Perhaps irrelevant here."

He said no more on the matter.

The wreck of the *Astrolabe* was not far above us and, once Moore had conferred with his sergeant telephonically, both groups continued to climb.

3.

15

In the collision the *Astrolabe* had wrenched the staircase away from the space-lock wall, even contriving to wrap a banister railing around its starboard propeller. However, though the staircase now slanted most alarmingly where it had been pulled free, the entwinement of staircase and propeller, coinciding with a gash in the aft section of the ship's hull, enabled us to make entry with relative ease.

As we explored inward and forward with Davy lamps to guide us, so Troutbeck's group clambered onto the foredeck and made their way aft. We progressed through unlit, fire-damaged holds and discovered nothing of note until we neared the centre of the ship. Our grisly discovery was foreshadowed by a powerful stench: of cooked flesh and fœtid corruption which the faint miasma of smoke could not conceal.

The leading corporals found it first. Holding their noses against the stink, they shone lamps on the wide mound of bodies; bodies that the fire had only partly consumed.

"Look," said Moore. He tugged at an exposed jacket cuff, making the red raw claw of a hand jiggle like a marionette limb. "French Navy."

French they might have been but my heart was moved by their deaths.

"The poor men," I said.

"Men?" said Professor Sedgewick. He stepped forward, took a lamp from one of the corporals, lowering it to more closely inspect one of the corpses. The dead man lay on his front. His shirt had been all but burned from his back; the flesh, scorched and glazed by the fire, was already turning grey with decomposition. What had drawn Sedgewick's eye was the thing fused to his back. A bubbling line of flesh ran up the length of his spine, culminating in a rotted lump at his neck. The delicate wings had been burned away in the fire but the stumps still protruding from just above his shoulders identified the thing as one of the glowing creatures which had attacked us.

"What happened to him?" asked Moore.
"The same thing that happened to these other fellows," I said. In the lamplight I discerned that more creatures, or the remains of them,

were attached to other dead men. "They rounded them up here and killed them!" I cried.

"Chimeras," said the professor. "Like the sea-devil of Earth. A fish," he stated when Moore gave him a blankly uncomprehending stare. "They live in the pitch-black depths of the ocean. The male of the species is tiny compared to the female: mere inch or two in length. It's astounding that such a miniscule and uncommon fish can find a mate in that Stygian gloom."

"Why are you babbling about fish, man?" demanded Moore.

"The female releases a pheromone," continued the good professor, blithely ignoring Moore's rudeness. "A chemical scent which draws the male in from the distance of many miles. Once he finds her, the tiny male bites into her flesh and secretes a chemical which melts and fuses his face into her skin. From that moment on, he draws all his needs from her, as an unborn child draws its sustenance from its mother. No longer has he need for stomach, heart or brain as, one by one, these are absorbed into his mate's body. Eventually, he is entirely consumed by her, but for his reproductive organs, which remain attached to her side, ready to fertilise her when needed."

Several of the men had made expressions of disgust.

"A devil indeed," spat Moore.

"And yet one of God's creatures." Sedgewick spoke lightly. "I hope the analogy I am making is not lost on you."

There was a sudden banging of a hatch from the far side of the hold. The hussars raised their rifles as two shapes stumbled into the hold. I was both surprised and relieved that our men did not shoot them, for the two figures revealed themselves to be from Troutbeck's group. They stopped abruptly, staring at the pile of partially incinerated corpses. One of them remembered himself and saluted.

"Lieutenant Moore, sir. Sergeant Troutbeck has found a ... a creature."

"So have we," replied the lieutenant with a sweep of his arm.

The man glanced at the remains. "No, sir. This one is alive," said he. "Alive and talking."

Without another word, we followed the young soldiers out through the hatch, along a companionway and onto a higher deck

17

where, in what transpired to be the galley stores, Troutbeck and the rest of his men stood in a rough circle, rifles raised, around a peculiar figure.

At first glance, I merely took the figure to be a young woman, in a daring ankle-length skirt which revealed her high-buttoned boots. There was soot on her very pale face, her blouse was askew and several strands of hair had escaped her elaborate chignon. But, in noting those aspects of her appearance, I had failed to grasp the most significant details. The woman bore a pair of wings: gauzy and ephemeral things, six feet from tip to tip even when not fully extended. A light shone around her head: a golden corona emanating from some point on the back of her neck.

The angel (for no one could deny she resembled one, and I saw more than one man cross himself in her presence) took us all in with a benign glance, her eyes and mouth composed in an expression of beatific contentment. *"Encore de beaux messieurs!"* said she in a voice no louder than a whisper.

"She's French!" exclaimed Lieutenant Moore, appalled to realise that this alien being also had the impudence to be a foreigner.

"She *was*," said the professor grimly. "This is the chimerical creature composed of what once was woman and winged creature. *Qu'est-ce que vous êtes, Mademoiselle?"* This last was, of course, directed to the angelic being. *"Un femme, ou une entité étrangere? Qui parle avec votre voix?"*

She replied sweetly. *"Je suis ce qui je suis."*

The professor did not like this at all. He took a step back, shaking his head.

"Is it dangerous?" asked Moore.

I could see Sedgewick was torn between honesty and preventing the lieutenant from killing the creature prematurely. "There may be others," he said eventually.

Moore split his men into two groups to scour the rest of the ship. "We lock this thing in here and decide what to do with it later," he said.

"Please," said the professor, "I would value the chance to interview this creature. It could be the scientific find of the century."

Moore vacillated for a moment and then relented. He ordered that Corporal Childers stay with us to guard the creature and "Shoot the bloody thing if it so much as looks at you funny." Once the remaining hussars had departed, Childers took up a position that allowed him a clear shot of the angel. We too kept a wary distance.

Throughout all of this, the angelic Frenchwoman waited patiently. She seemed in no hurry.

Sedgewick seated himself on a short flour barrel, hands resting on his cane before him, and spoke to the angel. I only know as much French as a decent British gentleman ought but I did my best to follow their conversation.

"Where are you from?" he asked in mellifluous and unhesitant French.

"The highest world," she replied gesturing upwards.

"And yet you speak French."

"I have recently learned much," said she Once I had grasped the meaning of those words, I shuddered.

"Then you will be familiar with the word *angel*. Are you an angel?"

She smiled demurely.

"Have you visited our world before?" demanded the professor.

"Do you have an æther ship?" she asked.

"Why do you ask that? Do you need a ship? Why? You have wings."

"Professor," I interrupted, an agitation bubbling within me. "Are you suggesting that this creature, these creatures, are the angels spoken of in scripture?"

Sedgewick sighed. "I am not about to sully holy writ with those accusations, dear fellow. But the coincidence should not be ignored. What bothers me most is that this alien fauna is able to bond with human beings with such ease – as though our species exist in some sort of symbiotic relationship. And yet we are planes apart. Is our compatibility a matter of chance, of some convergent transmutation, or of design?"

I looked at the angel. She continued to smile. The young woman whose body the creature had possessed was a handsome girl and I found myself unconsciously returning the smile. "But," I said to the professor, "I have heard you say that all transmutation, the evolution of species, is towards a higher form. The extinction of past species, discarded as inferior, is evidence of this."

"I have said as much."

"But is this b_____ creation then meant to be our successor; the next step towards the divine?"

"Calm yourself," said the professor. "I do not presume to understand the mind of God. If you accept the Babbage Hypothesis that all species come into existence not only through the act of transmutation but also according to some divine plan, then this creature does exist for a reason. But to replace us or to test us? Who can say?"

A flicker of some unhappy emotion passed over the angel's face and she put both hands to her stomach.

"*Vous avez un mal d'estomac?*" said the professor standing.

"*C'est l'heure—*" she began but then a spasm came over her and, doubling up, she vomited. Her neck strained and bulged as she disgorged a grey mass of wet tissue onto the storeroom floor. In that first shocking instant I saw what appeared to be a single expelled object. A moment later, I realised it was in fact not unlike the frogspawn one finds in English ponds: a large number of small round things, bound together in a bilious slime. Her body heaved again and she added to the spreading pool.

The mucous covered objects were the colour and size of an uncooked suet dumpling (I was not able to contemplate dumplings or pork faggots for years after the incident). I could not comprehend what they were until a dull golden light began to emanate from within each of them. In that moment Professor Sedgewick and I understood the complete life cycle of these abhorrent parasites and the threat they presented to all humanity.

"Childers!" cried the professor.

The corporal, who had been struck dumb and immobile by the vile spectacle, looked at us and then the angel. As the eggs or nascent creatures, however one must describe them, began to glow brighter, the slime about them rapidly cooked, cracked and evaporated. One of them rolled near to Childer's feet and unfurled two small but perfectly formed gossamer wings. Instead of shooting the angelic woman, Childers raised a boot and stamped on the angel's young, crushing it like over-ripe fruit.

"*Mes enfants!*" screamed the angel. With the slime of afterbirth still clinging to her lips, she leapt at the corporal.

Childers attempted to raise his rifle but she trapped the weapon between them at an unusable angle. Sedgewick swung his cane at her but she was just beyond his reach. I sprang forward to grapple with the angelic woman with the hope of pinning her arms to her side and pulling her off. Before I even had hold of her, she plunged the fingers of her right hand *into the corporal's neck* with an ease that seemed beyond physical possibility. Childers made a dry, rasping sound and struggled feebly.

I took hold of the angel with one hand. Seeing Childers' sabre at his belt within easy reach, I instinctively drew the blade, brought it up and round and sliced down into the angel's right arm, The limb came away between elbow and shoulder and Childers, poor dead Childers, dropped to the floor with the hand still embedded in his neck.

The angel, wounded and angry, turned on me. I should explain at this point that I was no military man and that fencing is not a common sport of the Welsh. So it was that I attacked the angel much as a drunken lumberjack might attack a tree. I swung in a guileless but powerful arc and, with that blow, sliced the creature in twain; in a horizontal line just beneath where her ribcage ought to have been.

I use the words *ought to have been* because the woman no longer possessed ribs, nor indeed any bones, nor most of the vital organs one would expect to find inside the human body. She fell in two, graceless and as lifeless as a window-dresser's mannequin, hollow as a dried gourd. In cross-section, her surface layer, her skin and flesh, was little more than an inch thick. The rest of her insides, a dark recess into which I did not willingly stare, was void but for a mesh of interconnecting divides which supported the outer shell. The mesh, that pith, put me uncomfortably in mind of certain sponge corals or, perhaps because of the pattern of scaffolding, the internal structure of a fungus. There was no stomach or heart, no liver or intestine to be seen. And not a single drop of blood.

No wonder she had been so pale!

It was then that I also saw that where the angel's fingers had pierced Childer's throat there was similarly no blood. The rent in his neck, narrow though it was, revealed a section of bloodless flesh.

I was transfixed, and it was only when Professor Sedgewick shouted my name that I saw what transpired at my feet. The now dry dumplings of alien flesh had all unfurled their wings and, like fledgling chicks, were taking falteringly flight. The lights within them were growing too. Glowing embers became larger, brighter and, as my gaze was sickeningly pulled towards one like a compass needle drawn to the north, more hypnotically alluring.

I thrust my arm over my eyes and, with the good professor, stumbled out into the corridor. I turned to pull the door to behind us but gave a wordless exclamation at finding one of the flying creatures already there, its intestine-like tendrils half-raised to seize me.

"Back!" cried Sedgewick. "To the next hatch! We'll trap them in this section of the ship."

We ran. As we did so, we heard the sharp retort of gunfire from elsewhere within the ship. The shots, more than a score of them, echoed throughout the metal corridors in a manner that made its source impossible to pinpoint. It was patently obvious to us that elsewhere on the ship things were not going well.

4.

The professor and I slammed and sealed every hatch we passed through (we assumed the aliens' slimy fronds surely wouldn't have the strength to open them) until we were once again stepping through the gash in the *Astrolabe*'s side and onto the space-lock stairway. The sound of repeating Webley rifles was equally loud outside the ship and, once I was able to gain a suitable vantage point, I could see there were soldiers on the *Astrolabe*'s deck. I was unable to discern who or what they were fighting but when one gave a cry and pitched over the gunwales, I saw him fall past and the bloody puncture wound in his leg looked very much like a gunshot injury. He screamed all the way down: eight hundred feet, seven whole seconds. The distance he fell and the speed of sound meant that his death cry went on for a moment or two after he impacted with the lower space-lock doors, a chilling echo of a departing life.

"Some of the men have been bewitched," said Sedgewick, a conclusion I had also reached. He hurried to the nearest telephonic point.

A band of men, seven in all, were fighting a retreat down the far staircase. The mortar-man, O'Bannen, came last, his Maxim gun blasting at intervals, his mortar flinging the occasional ballistic charge onto the *Astrolabe*. One such explosion catapulted two men off the deck and into the shaft. Light wings fluttered as they plummeted past, the glowing creatures on their back dead as the men they had possessed.

"Campbell!" shouted the professor into the mouthpiece. "Are the space-lock pumps working? Turn them on! Pump æther into the shaft!" There was a pause as Sedgewick listened to the Wakefield's first mate and then he said (or rather, shouted over the noise of battle), "Just turn them up to their maximum, man! And then return to the *Wakefield* with all haste!"

Sedgewick, replaced the trumpet. As he turned to face me he froze, looking at something behind me.

I spun on my heel. Hovering in the shaft was Lieutenant Moore, his wings flapping hard and fast just to keep the big man aloft. There was an alien halo of light about his head and on his face was an expression that seemed, if I can use such words without offending, to be one of amorous desire.

I still had Childer's sabre in my hand and raised it inexpertly to strike him. However, he too had his sabre and pistol drawn and parried my blow with a turn of his sword arm.

"We'll take the professor alive," he said, aiming his pistol at my heart. "But we don't need you—"

Something flashed past my ear: Sedgewick's cane, which he had thrown like a javelin. The surprisingly powerful throw ripped a sizeable hole in the delicate membrane of Moore's wing and the lieutenant dropped at once. Eyes wide with surprise, still he took a shot at me as he fell. I have no idea where the bullet went for it certainly failed to strike me. Moore descended to the ground in a slow but uncontrollable spiral, like that of one of those dare-devil *parachutists* one sees at aeronautic shows.

"And now we must go," said Sedgewick.

"Quite," I agreed and together we hurried down the stairs.

As we descended, I could hear the increased roar of the space-lock's great engines underlining the sounds of the fighting retreat taking place on the other stairway. A warm breeze pressed against my face. "Why did you ask Campbell to pump æther into the shaft?" I called out to my companion.

"I suspect it might be our best chance of killing the alien creatures, or at least slowing them down."

"How so?"

"You noticed as well as I how much effort it took for them to fly in this higher pressure æther. And what did you make of the changes wrought to that poor mademoiselle's body?"

"Abhorrent!" I said emphatically.

"Of course, but more than that, Cadwallander. The parasite had destroyed her skeleton and vital organs, replacing it with a honeycomb-like structure. Why? To make her lighter. Did you see how Corporal Childer's neck, where one of the flying devils had grabbed him, had already started to change?"

"I did."

The professor's expression was grim. "I am concerned that you have also touched those dangling tendrils with your hands."

I looked at my fingertips. The tingling numbness I had felt after my contact with the creature had gone, but there remained a lingering sensation: a faint tightness of the skin. A subtle feeling of horror overcame me. ."Professor..." I said.

"Don't panic now," said he curtly. "Let us deal with one problem at a time. The observable facts lead me to believe that the creatures are adapted, and will adapt their hosts, to life in lighter ætheric planes. Their bodies are fragile things and cannot possibly cross between ætheric planes unaided. They need the space-lock to descend into the fourth superætheric. As the pressure rises they will find it harder to fly and the more vulnerable their bodies will become."

"So even if they reach Earth, they will be too ungainly to be a threat."

"That is not a gamble I am willing to make," said the professor.

I was beginning to feel an uncomfortable pressure in my ears and, although I was already exerting myself in our race down the stairs, the air I was breathing felt strangely thick and soupy. "Professor, if the first mate and engineer have left the pumps on and returned to the *Wakefield*..."

"Yes," said he, fully comprehending my thoughts. "We don't wish to share the creatures' fate, do we?"

We reached the lowest point of the space-lock, observing the carnage which had rained down from above. The space-lock doors were littered with the smashed bodies of innumerable flying creatures and, I am sad to report, more than a few young men of the Queen's Armoured Hussars. Seeing a uniformed man walking towards us, I raised my hand to greet him before I saw who it was.

Lieutenant Moore had injured his leg in his fluttering descent but was otherwise whole. I was grateful to see that he had lost his revolver, although he still retained his sabre. Moore said something to us but the distance and the roar of the pumping turbines swallowed his words. I hefted my sabre and, because he stood between us and the door leading to the *Wakefield*, had little choice but to walk forward and meet him.

"Lieutenant," said Sedgewick, "we are not your enemies."

Moore shook his head, although at what I could not say.

"Whatever manner of being has latched onto you, I am sure that the real Lieutenant Moore resides within."

"I am not Moore's gaoler," said the lieutenant with a peculiar wiggle of his moustaches. "I am his liberator."

"Lieutenant Moore would not willingly submit to you," said the professor. "He's an Englishman and hardly likely to go native so quickly."

The lieutenant, or the thing that had once been the lieutenant, stumbled and stopped. He turned his head to one side, an alarming procession of strange twitches distorting his features. I wondered what internal conversation or battle of wills was going on between man and astral being. "No!" he suddenly cried. I wasn't sure whether it was man or alien who gave that shout until Moore fixed on us and charged with sabre raised.

I lifted my own blade but too slowly.

There was the sudden violent blare of O'Bannen's Maxim gun; Moore's head burst apart in bloodless ruin. His jaw and the tatters of his moustaches clung to the top of the neck but the rest of his head was gone. Within (how I wish I had averted my gaze!) was nought but the supporting structure of fungal pith and a pair of questing tendrils with one of the lieutenant's eyes attached to the end of each.

Moore's knees gave way and the shocking corpse crumpled to the floor.

"Come on!" bellowed O'Bannen from the far staircase.

We joined O'Bannen and the two lance corporals with him. Some distance above on the stairway, I saw a third soldier walking dreamily to meet one of the unattached alien beings, arms outstretched as though to embrace a loved one.

A lance corporal pulled on the hatch through which we had first gained access to the shaft, but it resisted his efforts. The second lance corporal and I leant our efforts to the doorway and, as it was inched open, a powerful stream of air forced its way out into the corridor. Opening the hatch fully the pressure on either sides of the door equilibrated and the wind lessened.

"We must make for the *Wakefield*," said Sedgewick.

O'Bannen, the mortar-man, shook his head within his Goliath-like suit. "I'm waiting for Sergeant Troutbeck." With an arm of brass and steel he pointed skyward to a point on the stairs above. Four tiny figures with rifles held off the circling enemy: a dozen angelic creatures, some with human hosts, some without.

As we looked up, the *Astrolabe* gave a great metallic groan.

"We don't have time!" Sedgewick exclaimed.

O'Bannen gave my companion a cold, furious stare. "Get the professor to the ship," he ordered the lance corporals. "I will wait for the sarge." The mortar-man turned away, raised his Maxim gun and opened fire.

A soldier put a guiding hand on my elbow and I allowed myself to be escorted through the hatch, where the roar of the *Lady Henshall's* engines was dampened.

The mounting pressure within the entire structure made our passage difficult as we fought to open and close the hatches behind us and the *Wakefield*, but within a few minutes we were through the last of them and into the interior of a packet ship which felt very much like home.

Campbell was there to meet us. "Are you the last of them?" he asked, his voice coloured by a hope that we might leave and a polite grief that we were all that remained of the expeditionary unit.

"There are at least five men still in there," I said.

Campbell made an unhappy murmur. "The pressure is increasing in there."

"Surely the *Lady Henshall* is of sturdy construction," I said.

"But if you put a tin of bully beef on a fire..." He left the thought uncompleted.

"I'm more concerned about the *Astrolabe*," said the professor. "Those sealed holds and chambers. If the ship is compromised and drops from its present position then the results may be utterly catastrophic."

In my mind, I pictured the French ship falling. I thought back to the mathematics of my school days. From eight hundred feet, it would take a mere seven seconds for it to plummet to the lower space-lock. But at what speed? With what weight? What force!

As those thoughts and figures passed through my mind, there came a juddering sound, more felt than heard, from within the *Lady Henshall*. A breeze immediately sprung up around us but Campbell was already throwing his own weight against the hatch and bellowing to the crew to release them from the space-lock.

A second later we were rolling away and I slammed into a painfully solid upright beam. There were shouts and the sound of girders and inch-thick sheets of metal tearing apart. How I prayed that it was the *Lady Henshall* and not us!

I tried to pick myself up from the floor; blood trickled into my eyes from a cut on my brow. A hand gripped me, hoisting me to my feet, and I found myself supported by my fine companion. There was a smear of dirt on the professor's day cravat, but he was otherwise unharmed.

"To the wheelhouse," said he. "I must see this."

Avoiding the crew of the *Wakefield*, who were busily securing their own vessel and distancing it from the *Lady Henshall*, we made our way through the hold and up to the wheelhouse. There, with

Captain Treadaway taking personal control of the tiller, we were able to gaze out of the wide windows at the ruin of the space-lock.

A twisted mass of metal – the *Astrolabe* – was drifting not far from our present position. Beyond it was the space-lock. The lower doors were peeled back, ripped open by the force of escaping æther and the falling French ship. The downward explosion had propelled the space-lock upwards and, although an object of such massive size can only be perceived to be moving slowly, the *Lady Henshall* was on an undeniable course for the fifth superætheric plane and the deep space beyond.

"What the blazes happened in there?" demanded Treadaway.

"That is a matter to be explained at length, captain," said Sedgewick. "Over a large brandy."

A light began to flash on the underside of the space-lock. *Dot dot dot dash dash dash dot dot dot.*

"SOS," I said needlessly.

"Able Seaman Llewellyn," said Sedgewick. "The poor fool."

We watched the *Lady Henshall* climb away from us, spewing debris into the æther: glittering shards against the abysmal black pit of stars.

There was the shout of "Man overboard!" and one of the crew pointed at something that I could not instantly recognise. Evidently, the professor saw it clearly for he turned to the captain and told him to get his crew to the chase-gun.

O'Bannen, the mortar-man, was floating in the æther, perhaps two hundred feet off our bow. The air cowl of his powered suit was over his face, keeping him alive in the rarefied atmosphere. The cowl was suffused with a beautiful golden light that, in the blackness of space, extended as a bright halo around his head and illuminated his outstretched web-like wings.

"What do we do?" asked Treadaway.

The professor did not respond to the captain's question. He was murmuring something to himself and perhaps I was only close enough to hear it and recognise it as quotation from the Book of Daniel.

"*Then I lifted up my eyes and beheld an angel whose loins were girded with fine gold. His body was of brilliant metal and his face as the appearance of lightning and his eyes as lamps of fire and his arms and feet like polished brass."* There was wonder and dismay in his voice.

"Sedgewick!" shouted the captain. "What do we do?"

"Shoot it down, captain," said he. "Destroy it utterly."

5.

On the third day of our homeward journey, the professor agreed to investigate the matter than had been plaguing my thoughts and dreams since our return to the *Wakefield*. Those three days had been busy for the ship's signalman, who was sending ceaseless messages out to all possible recipients, warning of the dangers aboard the *Lady Henshall* and requesting immediate help from any forces loyal to the British Empire.

The professor and I spent the time recording the observations we had made of the creatures. Pencil sketching is one of my few talents and, although my efforts have more of the draughtsman than the artist about them, I was able to draw a number of accurate anatomical diagrams. However, when it came to detailing what we had seen in the Frenchwoman's torso, Childer's neck and Lieutenant Moore's ravaged skull, my fingers shook so much that I had to put my pencil down.

On that third day, the professor had me lie down on my bunk and extend my arm across the flat-topped chest at its side. I looked at my fingertips and rubbed my thumb across them, feeling the strange tautness of the skin which remained there. He gave me a tincture of laudanum then placed a few drops of Simpson's Chloroform on his handkerchief and bade me hold it over my mouth and nose with my free hand.

I inhaled deeply, beginning to feel myself drift away. My good friend took a firm hold of my wrist and, with his other hand, flipped open his leather surgeon's wallet and removed a scalpel. "Fear not, Cadwallander," he said gently, bringing the blade down to the flesh of my hand.

Fighting the encroaching unconsciousness I watched that scalpel dip into the tip of my index finger and, with the slightest pressure, slice it away. A shallow cone of skin and flesh rolled across the flat-topped chest. The interior of my finger was bloodless and hollow, much like the angel's innards.

And, with that, I slipped into a deep sleep, black and starless.

1903 – The Pearl of Tharsis

From the memoirs of Mr J. Cadwallander

I have seen Miss Mina Saxena described as a freedom fighter, a spy, an anarchist, an explorer and an adventuress. It is a documented fact that Professor Sedgewick and I have met her on a number of occasions. I have been asked about our mutual encounters so often it feels as though our own not inconsiderable achievements are but footnotes in her undeniably sensational story (one most likely exaggerated beyond all veracity by the woman herself).

Our first meeting with Miss Saxena was in a stone labyrinth beneath the surface of Mars. I remember her vividly, for her ability to make a lasting impression on a fellow is perhaps one of her primary talents. She was undoubtedly beautiful, in that savage and unruly way certain foreign types have, but she was far from lady-like in her appearance. I recall her standing among the obscene carvings of the maze in flickering yellow lamplight, a pistol in her hand and a bandolier of dynamite slung over her shoulder. A pair of goggles rested on her forehead and she wore a leather jacket that might have previously belonged to a cavalry officer or a helipteron pilot. Her only concession to womanhood were her skirts: too short for my liking, whilst her frilly petticoats, smeared with red Martian dust, were all too visible.

Deep beneath the desert, in that ancient and lifeless place, my companions and I stood with Miss Saxena's pistol aimed at us. I am sure she would have killed us – or at least some of us – there and then (thereby erasing us as even the tiniest of footnotes) if I hadn't voiced a matter which had been bothering me for some moments.

"Excuse me. Can anyone else hear music?"

The four of us fell silent. For a moment, I could no longer hear anything; then I heard it once more: the echoing tinkle of piano keys, the suggestion of a clarinet or oboe and, if I'm not mistaken, the chorus music of *In the Good Old Summertime*.

Miss Saxena's eyebrows rose as she gave me a look that was wantonly unbecoming in the fair sex. Nonetheless, our lives were spared for the time being because Mina Saxena, above all else, is governed by insatiable curiosity...

I have always been a man of modest desires and not fond of new and strange experiences and yet, as we passed high above the mountains of Tharsis, I found myself quite taken by the view. The peaks rising from the soil of Mars were, thanks to the fourth planet's mild gravity, taller and grander than any range an educated man might hope to see elsewhere. Nix Olympus, the largest of them was several hundred miles distant and yet dominated the landscape more completely than any stubby hill of my green homeland.

I pressed my face close to the window like an eager schoolboy, and peered down at the vast mines almost directly beneath us. Plumes of smoke obscured much of the industry but here and there my eye was drawn to one of the monstrous digging machines, variants of the chthonic tunnellers used to extend the London Underground to Oxford, Northampton and beyond. Amassed around the machines, like ants at a discarded cucumber sandwich, I saw the black dots that were individual miners.

"The miners are all immigrant workers?" I asked of Reverend Champney without looking up at him.

"Surely, all men are immigrants here," rumbled Professor Sedgewick genially.

The Reverend Champney gave a bark of laughter. "I say, you can take the Welshman out of the coal mine but you cannot take the coal mines out of the Welshman, eh, Cadwallander?" He punched me playfully me in the shoulder across the table,.

His fist audibly met the brass casement of my false arm through the tweed of my suit jacket. Champney, a young and unworldly soul (even for a university chaplain), winced at the possible social *faux pas* he had committed. "That is a remarkable limb you have there, sir," he mumbled, a burbled compliment to cover his embarrassment.

I placed my metal hand on the table and flexed my fingers in turn, the minute pneumatic joints clicking and hissing in succession. "A gift from Her Majesty's War Office," I said. "Recompense for our involvement in a nasty piece of business in the fifth superætheric plane."

"Fourth, Cadwallander," said the professor.

"I seem to recall something in the papers," said Champney. "It sounded terribly exciting."

Champney's foolish response annoyed me deeply, but I smiled at him politely and looked out of the window once more, focusing on the clouds of Martian dust that seemed to be gathering in the distance. I would never describe the loss of a platoon of the Queen's Armoured Hussars, the death of unknown others along with the loss of my arm to a horror I might not speak of ever again as *exciting*. The professor, sat next to me, made a sound in his throat which I, as his companion and batman of eight years, interpreted as a gentle and avuncular approval of my silence on the matter.

Professor Sedgewick, had been invited by his former student, Champney, to deliver a series of lectures at Barnato University on Mars. In the weeks prior to our voyage to the Red Planet, the professor had drafted a number of lecture essays: on the varieties of native flora on Mars and their earthly equivalents, on the social and economic advantages of introducing selected Earth animals to Mars, and, most interestingly, on the possible effects of Mars' low gravity and rarefied atmosphere on the transmutation of Earth species in the millennia to come. Those same lectures were edited and revised several times over on our six week interplanetary journey from Waterloo Terminus to the Phobos Skylift only for Champney to tell the professor upon meeting us at the Skylift ground station that he hoped the lectures would be religious in nature.

The professor, without hesitation, assured Champney that if that was what was desired then he would gladly deliver. It was clear that Champney, with a zeal unbecoming an Anglican clergyman, was concerned for the spiritual well-being of his fellow ex-patriots. Indeed, as the chartered dirigible carried us further from the ground station to the city of Barnato, Professor Sedgewick raised the matter openly.

"Yes, of course," said Champney brightly. "The salvation of one's flock is of paramount importance." Then his face darkened and he seemed weary, no longer such a young and naïve man. "This is an unsettled world," he said. "As your man pointed out, decent white Christians are outnumbered by African workers and by the hordes of Indians labouring in our mines."

"God's salvation is open to all, is it not?" said the professor.

"But they do not want it," said Champney. "They talk only of pay rises and equal rights under law."

Professor Sedgewick rumbled. "One hears that Cecil Rhodes' Tarsis Company has used and abused them as little more than slaves."

"Sir Cecil is a great man, a servant of Mars."

A chuckle escaped my lips. "What does that American writer, Twain, say about Rhodes? *I admire him, I frankly confess it, and when his time comes I shall buy a piece of the rope as a keepsake.*"

"Twain is a man who has not seen Mars," said Champney with some venom. "Who has not ventured beyond his own back yard, I would wager!"

"Come now, dear fellow," soothed the professor, but Champney would not be calmed.

"You do not understand. This is a dark world. We are far from England. Surely, only at such a distance would the Indian speak openly of rebellion, declaring themselves *citizens* of an independent Mars; a republic no less." He shook his head. "No, it is more than that. I fear a spiritual darkness. We are not just far from England; we are far from Jerusalem, from the cross, from Christ."

"Tarsis," said the professor. "Named for the Biblical land of Tarshish, the edge of the known world."

"Quite," said Champney. "The Hindoo workers worship their numberless gods and, like the Romans of old, will not hesitate to add any new idol to their blasphemous pantheon."

"New gods?" said I, intrigued.

"There is foolish and wild speculation aplenty. What hands dug the great Schiaparelli canals? What feet walked on Martian soil when the Lord himself stood on the shores of Galilee? What bloody altars and vile totems lie buried beneath the desert sands?"

I looked out at the Martian landscape once more. I noted that the clouds of pinkish dust that I had sighted ahead of us had not dissipated but grown in size and density. "Is that a sandstorm?" I asked.

Champney looked and grunted. "I am sure the pilot will steer us straight," he said, returning to his earlier theme. It was clear that having tapped the source of the man's anxiety, there was no stopping him. "Mars is a magnet for all manner of heretics, gurus and mystics, come to find, refine and spread their harmful nonsense."

"And you are expecting some of them to attend my lectures?" asked the professor with a smile.

"I have invited them all!" Champney declared. "And reserved a front row seat for the worst of them. He calls himself Chioa Khan."

"An Asiatic?" asked the professor.

"Nothing of the sort. He is an Englishman, I am sad to say, and his name an invented title. He is the son of a Warwickshire brewer, a foolish dilettante with too much money and not enough learning."

"He sounds like an entirely forgettable fellow," said the professor.

"Oh, he is a wasp! He has a following of sorts and, just the other month, declared he had heard the voice of God in the wilderness! He would have himself as the prophet of a new unholy age. Such behaviour would not be tolerated in England."

"A prophet is not without honour except in his own country," I quoted. It was about the limit of my scriptural knowledge.

This did not please Champney and he replied with a Biblical verse of his own. "Beware of false prophets which come to you in sheep's clothing, but inwardly they are ravening wolves."

Across the table, Professor Sedgewick patted Champney's hand kindly. "Wolves? Wasps?" he smiled. "I am sure we will find this Chioa Khan to be a sheep in wolf's clothing, a striped hoverfly doing its best to appear as a wasp."

At that moment, something flashed upwards past the window. I had the distinct impression of a slender object with a tail of fire, trailing behind it a line like a fishing wire. Before I had time to exclaim, it connected loudly with the airship's gas-filled envelope and our entire world gave a sickening downward lurch.

2.

Our descent to the mountainside was long and terrifying, a matter which, on later reflection, I judged as preferable to the faster and deadlier descent we might otherwise have made. With the envelope punctured on one side, we went down in a wide spiral, the floor pitching. While the pilot and his mate barked orders and readings to one another, we three passengers clung to the chair arms and table tops for dear life and, although it must have taken a minute or more for us to reach the ground, not a word passed between us; for what was there to be said?

Our impact was bone-jarring but I would admit that I'd fallen harder from horses and toboggans in my youth. However, the dirigible gondola had taken quite a hammering, with several struts bent or broken and most of the windows thoroughly smashed. I must also say that, in my state of alarm, the fingers of my powerful artificial hand had driven four deep depressions into the top of the table and my thumb a fifth in the underside. As I worked my metal fingers free, Champney clutched his chest, breathing fast and hard and Professor Sedgewick, climbing unsteadily to his feet, was peering into the dusty murk beyond the window.

"Was that a wire-guided rocket?" he asked.

"Bandits," said the pilot, stumbling over broken fittings into the passenger compartment.

"Or rebels," said Champney.

"Whatever the case, sirs," said the pilot, "we must either abandon ship or prepare to defend it." To make his point all the clearer, he unclipped his holster, removed his revolver and checked that it was loaded.

"Can we not send for help?" I asked.

"We were able to send off a signal before we crashed but help is more than an hour away, and in this weather we may be quite invisible to any rescuers."

The pilot's mate, a lad of no more than sixteen, came through from the control room and, with the pilot's help, wrestled open the cabin door, letting in a shrill and a painful howl of wind which stung the face with a thousand grains of sand. We hastily fashioned scarves to cover our mouths and followed the pilot and his mate out.

I noted with some jealousy but not ill will, that the air company men not only had their Beaumont-Adams pistols with which to defend themselves but also had the advantage of stout knee-length boots and aviator goggles. There were no spares to be offered to us and we did not ask, instead following behind them in near blindness, like clumsy children behind their governess.

The pilot led us up the slope and away from the downed ship, across a generally even terrain which was still littered with lumps of jagged stone. Although I was sure the pilot had a better grasp of things, in truth, our mad descent and the obscuring storm made it impossible to know if we were striking off away from our attackers or towards them.

The pilot spied a wide fissure in the ground ahead and directed us towards it. In our exposed and wind-battered state, it seemed most inviting, both as a place to hide from our enemies and as a shelter from the storm. The pilot waved us on and then, hearing something that I did not, turned to take several shots at shapes which trailed after us through the storm. There was return fire and the pilot's mate also drew his pistol for to defend our retreat.

I scrambled down into the channel-like fissure behind the professor and Reverend Champney. The fissure was steep-sided and flat-bottomed, not unlike the kind of ha-ha excavated along the end of some stately garden to keep wandering sheep and peasants off the lawns, although its ability to protect us from the wind and Martian malcontents was yet to be proven. Professor Sedgewick was already scurrying along the channel, deeper into the hills, with a speed impressive for a man in his middle years. Champney followed, his black cassock whipping around his thighs. I ran after them, spurred onwards by images of some rifle-bearing rapscallion taking careful aim at my exposed back.

I did not see the archway until we were upon it. It was rough-hewn and the same square shape as the channel we had run along. Without pause, I dashed into the tunnel and felt an immediate sense of relief in its gloomy shelter. I loosened the handkerchief tied over my mouth and looked back the way we had come.

"No sign of anyone," said I. We had lost not only our pursuers but the dirigible pilot and his mate also.

"There's light ahead," said Champney.

The dishevelled reverend was correct. Some distance down the tunnel was the yellow glow of a naked flame. With our attackers possibly close behind and this peculiar light ahead of us, we quickly decided to proceed further into the tunnel.

The walls became smoother and straighter the deeper we progressed; when we reached the light source – a shallow bowl of burning oil mounted to the wall – further curiosities were revealed.

"Carvings!" Champney exclaimed.

"Ancient carvings," said the professor, running his fingertips over the worn edges.

It would not be true to say I had not seen carvings like these before. Truth told, I had seen many carvings *similar* to these but none exactly like them. There were carved inscriptions but not in any alphabet I had seen before. There was a symbol or two which appeared vaguely recognisable, but nothing I could identify for sure.

"It's not Egyptian or Cretan," said Champney, peering closely. "The Cambodians had a system of hieroglyphs."

"Not like this," said the professor with certainty. "And it's not ancient cuneiform."

"But it looks so familiar," said Champney, echoing my unspoken thoughts.

"And look at these images—" The professor's voice trailed off, leaving us to silently regard and digest the pictures carved into relief in the stone.

I have known images to inspire trepidation and unease in a man before. All but the most blessed of men have glimpsed scenes in their nightmares that awaken them with an unconquerable sense of fear. The images presented by the lamp's light filled me with a form of dread that I had never before experienced. Just as the inscriptions on the walls were like earthly writing, but unlike any writing on Earth, so the figures in these carvings were very much like human beings, but nonetheless something quite *other*.

I am sure that, from the moment we entered the tunnel, Champney and the professor had, like myself, entertained the notion that this subterranean structure was of Martian – by which I mean *alien* – construction but I did not regard these figures as aliens. These were undeniably carvings of humans and yet were quite amiss. Imagine if you will a person who, having never seen another human soul or indeed a mirror, attempted to sketch an image of himself. There was not one specific aspect of these images that was incorrect, not the eyes or the mouth or the limbs, but a terrible *wrongness* suffused them all.

"I have never seen such profanity," said Champney. "Like Sodom and Gomorrah."

"But the people of those cities were guilty of one particular sin," said the professor. "Here—"

The tableaux in which these stony figures appeared were as odd as the figures themselves. Again, their actions and poses were *almost* like those of normal folk. It was impossible to say for certain what any of them were doing. Were they eating? Were they fighting? Were they engaging in carnal acts? I could not have said then as I cannot describe now what was sinful about any one obscene posture or gesture, but I felt I was gazing at the most perverse of all behaviour and, to be sure, it made me feel damnably queer.

"There are more lights," I said, pointing down the tunnel to further wall-mounted lamps.

"This tomb is clearly inhabited," said the professor.

"Perhaps it is the bandits' lair."

"Then we have indeed leapt out of the frying pan and into the fire."

We moved on, from lamp to lamp, among inscriptions and stone representations that were nauseating in their strangeness. There were turnings and forks at various points and, at each, we listened and looked intently before making our decisions. At one time, we heard gunfire and a booming roar that might have been an explosion or possibly the sound of falling masonry. These noises echoed around us, making pinpointing their origins impossible.

We moved in search of an exit or answers, whichever came first. To be blunt, we moved because it was better than the alternative. If we stayed put then we were simply waiting, like quivering prey, for someone or something to find us. The act of movement alone gave us purpose.

The air in this seemingly endless excavation was cool and dry and I was put in mind of the visit to the Pyramids of Egypt and Cheops tomb the professor and I had made some years before: the variance in external and internal temperatures and humidity. I mentioned as much to my companions.

"A tomb, you think?" said the professor. "I am put in mind of something completely other."

We stopped at another junction and considered our options. Briefly, I fancied I heard a strange sound akin to distant, reedy music but dismissed it as a trick of sound and distance.

"I am rather reminded of Ovid and Plutarch," said the professor softly as he looked back and forth, "and a labyrinth beneath the palace of King Minos."

"I think I was unnerved enough already," said Champney with forced jollity, "without you positing some monster at the centre of—"

He stopped speaking and gave a small gasp of alarm. I turned and saw the woman standing behind Champney, the muzzle of an automatic pistol pressed to his ribcage. This was Miss Mina Saxena, although I did not learn her name until much later. What I saw then was her slight frame, her young face with those large dark eyes of hers, the belt of explosives over her shoulder and her indecently short skirts. She was also, I noticed, quite alone.

"Your weapons," she said. Her Indian accent was laced with something else: a touch of English education and also something altogether Mediterranean.

"We are unarmed," the professor replied.

"You fired on us," she accused.

"In retaliation," said Champney hotly, despite the gun in his side.

"We seem to have mislaid our pilot," said the professor.

I watched her closely and surmised that our pilots were still alive and free, somewhere.

"And your people, your bandit troupe?" I said.

Miss Saxena smiled brightly. "Mislaid in the storm, also. And I am no bandit."

"Oh?" said the professor.

"I'm a treasure-seeker."

Champney, who was either a fool or far braver than I had previously thought him, scoffed. "See?" said he. "Tomb robbers, guarding their blasted trove."

She gave the reverend chaplain a filthy look. "Not all treasure is buried," she said, turning her gaze deliberately on Professor Sedgewick.

"You mean to kidnap me?" said the professor. He could not prevent a modicum of self-satisfaction entering his voice.

"The imperialist dogs of London hold you in very high esteem, professor."

"So you will hold him to ransom," said Champney.

She shook her head. "Is your mind full of nothing but money and gold? The professor can serve the cause of Martian independence in any number of ways." She pulled back the hammer on her pistol and raised it to Champney's head. "You, on the other hand—"

I frowned as I heard once again a high, wavering melody, just on the cusp of sensation. "Excuse me," I interrupted. "Can anyone else hear music?"

3.

Miss Saxena paused, lowering her gun a degree or two. We all listened and heard. It was far off and faint, but there was the sound of piano and woodwind and a tune that had been very popular in the music halls the previous summer.

Miss Saxena gave me the most impertinent and mischievous look. "Music," she said in agreement.

"Your friends?" I suggested.

"I am not in the habit of travelling with a light orchestra in tow, if that's what you're asking," she said. "You will lead the way."

The professor frowned at her.

"I think a mystery such as this demands investigation," she said, "and if there are any ghouls or monsters, I would have you run into them first."

And so it was. The professor, Champney and I proceeded as before but now with an armed woman driving us. Though some might say that we were foolish to fear a woman, armed or not, I felt then as I do now: like a child with a box of luciferous matches, a woman with a loaded gun is capable both of great intentional and unintentional harm to others. That maxim might apply doubly so to one who is also a member of Her Majesty's foreign subjects.

"These images remind me of statues in a temple to Shiva, in Thanjavur," said Miss Saxena.

"Then the Hindoo is more depraved and base than I had previously thought," Champney whispered aside to me.

"But this language is not Sanskrit," said the professor.

"Or the *Prakrit* found in that temple," Miss Saxena agreed, "and yet I am still reminded of it."

I interrupted them to point out a light ahead. We had been following a trail of lamps for a good while but the light that shone from an archway ahead to the left was of a different quality: brighter and more steady. The music too was louder now, although beneath there was another noise: the hubbub of human voices.

At Miss Saxena's direction we edged forward to the archway and looked in. The chamber beyond the archway was as spacious and as high as any ballroom in Europe and that was the very use it had been put to. Tall potted plants and fan-shaped screens of white and green glass lined the dark, stone walls. Hoop-backed chairs and tables with pristine white cloths were arranged to the side of open space on the tiled floor. Four chandeliers hung above the dance floor, casting sparkling electric light all around. However, neither the dance floor nor the chandeliers dominated the room: that role was taken by a huge stone spire, rising up from among the tables and tapering to a point shortly below the high ceiling. It bore some resemblance to Cleopatra's Needle, which the Royal Air Force's helipterons had ferried from Egypt to the banks of the Thames, although this was a far larger and more rough-hewn affair.

Dumbfounding though this room was, the scene was made all the more astonishing by the occupants. There were in excess of a hundred men and women in the room, every one of them dressed for the occasion: elegant high-collared evening gowns for the women and black tail coats with white bow ties over wing collar shirts for the men. There was laughter, gaiety and dancing aplenty.

"This is impossible," said Champney breathlessly.

"I certainly feel a shade underdressed," said Miss Saxena.

"Well, there's no minotaur here," I said.

"But there is a wasp!" growled Champney.

A man was striding across the floor to us, his arms outstretched and a wide close-lipped smile on his face. He had thick dark hair, a heavy jaw and a sheen in his eyes which reminded me of a stage mesmerist I had once seen on Brighton Pier.

"Reverend Champney!" he exclaimed, forcibly taking Champney's hand and pumping it hard. "You've finally decided to join us." He regarded the professor with feigned surprise. "And can it be...? Professor Erskine Sedgewick! Such a pleasure to meet you!"

Champney, bound by good social etiquette despite his extreme discomfort made the introductions through gritted teeth. "Professor Sedgewick, this is Aleister Cr—"

"Chioa Khan," interrupted the brash fellow. "A title bestowed on me by a foreign potentate."

"Ah," said I. "The brewer's son."

The look he gave me was not one of anger or irritation but amused indifference. "And you are?"

"Cadwallander," I said and shook the man's hand, giving him a meaningful squeeze with my artificial hand.

Chioa Khan's smile was weary. "Ah, a latter day Talos, in cheap tweed and a bowler hat." He looked over my shoulder at Miss Saxena. "And a beautiful bandit Queen. What an astonishing entourage you have, professor! But this party is open to all. Mademoiselle, you may even find some of your similarly mutinous compatriots here."

He was right. This was not a gathering of the social élite. There were Indians and Asiatics among the white faces, even a Negro or two, mingling and even dancing together in a manner likely to have the Ladies Anti-Miscegenation League in apoplectic fits. The social divisions within the party went beyond race. Many of the men present were unshaven and rough-skinned and, despite their fine clothes, had the distinct bearing of the working classes.

"Unlike Christ's Kingdom," said Chioa Khan, "which has all the hallmarks of an exclusive gentleman's club, these revelries are open to all."

"The Kingdom of God is open to all," replied the professor firmly.

"Really? But what about *None shall get to the Father except through me*? Jesus stands at the door as gatekeeper and expellant. The doors to the court of Aiwass stand open and unguarded."

"I don't understand," said Miss Saxena. "Who are these people?"

"Pilgrims," replied Chioa Khan. "Wanderers. Outlaws. Explorers. "Many came here by accident. Indentured labourers on the run. Travellers lost in the desert. Some sought it out."

"Sought it out?" asked the professor.

"I heard the voice of Aiwass calling me," he said grandiosely, puffing out his chest like the hammiest of actors in a music hall melodrama. "My disciples and I listened and we came. And that is all he asks of us."

"Who is this Aiwass?" demanded Champney.

"Aiwass. Harpocrates. Horus as a man. God on Earth. Our host."

"Oh," said the professor. "I thought this was *your* party."

Chioa Khan shook his head humbly. "Merely a guest. This is his gathering and it began long before I came."

He turned and gestured with a sweeping arm to a table beneath the stone spire and to the giant of a man sat at the head of that table. I must confess that I cannot adequately describe the one Chioa Khan named Aiwass. I perceived him as an enormous man, at least seven feet tall, and yet he sat among ordinary folk and did not seem out of place. He, like the other men, wore formal evening attire and yet, part of my mind perceived his clothing as something else, something ancient and ecclesiastic. He was quite clearly a man and yet if I was to say he had the head of a savage animal or a bird of prey, I would sound like a fool but I would not be lying. To look at Aiwass was to look through a film of running water in which images were distorted and out of all proportion. He wavered like a phantasmagorical magic lantern trick.

The professor coughed uncomfortably. "I would very much like to speak to him," he said.

"I am sure an audience can be arranged," said Chioa Khan. "I shall ask." With a tiny, mocking bow, he backed away, turned and strode over to the central spire, and the unfathomable figure of Aiwass.

45

A young slip of a thing came by with a tray of champagne flutes. Thirst overcoming my disdain for the man and his party, I took one and drained it. It was cold to my lips but did nothing to ease the dryness in my throat. Professor Sedgewick, who had snagged a sprig of grapes from a platter and was chewing thoughtfully on one, passed them to me. They were as equally tasteless and as unsatisfying as the champagne.

"Who or what is that unholy thing?" Champney hissed.

"A god?" said the professor.

"There is only one God," Champney declared.

"And he doesn't look like that," added Miss Saxena in agreement.

The professor smiled. "Miss, I would have thought that you, as a Hindoo, would be more open to the idea. The universal spirit of Brahman could incarnate in any form it chooses. Why is this not an avatar of the gods?"

"Because the gods have better taste than this. You can almost taste the desperation in this place. We're leaving. Now."

"Not until I've spoken to this Aiwass character," said the professor.

Miss Saxena cleared her throat pointedly. "Have you forgotten which of us is holding the gun?"

"Not at all," said the professor. "However, I think there are certain matters you have failed to comprehend."

"Really?"

"First is the impossibility of our situation. How far is it to the nearest town, reverend?"

"Eighty miles or more," replied Champney.

"Yet here we are, at a veritable banquet of fresh food and drink, surrounded by people in the finest tailored garb. And tell me, reverend, have they laid electricity cables through this part of the region? Or perhaps there is a Tesla energy transmitter nearby?"

"Neither," said Champney.

"And yet there is electric lighting. But, more than that, miss, you have perhaps failed to look in the corners."

"The corners?" said Miss Saxena.

"The dark corners of this room and the shadows behind the screens. In the alcoves and the secluded spots."

At the professor's words, I looked about and saw what we meant. On chaise-longues, not well hidden from sight, individuals writhed together, their limbs interlocked. In the alcoves behind the screens, the gloom did not manage to completely conceal men and women in more intimate embraces. And in the darkest nooks, there were suggestions of movement, half-light reflecting on teeth and wet skin. I was suddenly put in mind of the carvings we had seen: I could not discern whether those people were men or women or whether they were coupling or fighting or—

"And there is that being on his high throne and this sordid little kingdom quite entirely in his thrall. In short, miss," said the professor, turning to address Miss Saxena directly, "you are by no measure the most dangerous thing in this room. If I were you, I would be good and scared and considering that we three men might be your only allies."

"All the more reason for us to leave now," she replied.

"Oh," said the professor reproachfully. "We might all be good and scared, miss, but aren't we all a little curious also?"

Miss Saxena held his gaze levelly and, although she did not smile, there was now a playful glint in her eye. I would have gladly shared with the pair of them a certain adage about the fatal consequences of feline curiosity but the professor spoke first: "Look, the odious brewer's boy is returning."

"You are to be honoured with an audience," called Chioa Khan grandly.

"Wonderful," said the professor. "My companions and I were just commenting on the secretive and licentious behaviour of some of your fellow guests."

"And you are offended?" said Chioa Khan with hopeful glee. "Aiwass would not have us bound by stupid prudery and meaningless social convention."

"Morality, you mean."

"These degenerates are offending all of God's laws," said Champney.

"Do what thou will shall be the whole of the law," said Chioa Khan darkly. "This carnival of liberation began before time had a name and it will continue forever."

"Forever?" said Champney.

47

At that moment I saw something I had not seen before and understood why Miss Saxena had noted an air of desperation in the room. In the corner of Chioa Khan's wide eyes was a minute yet constant twitching, a line of tension, a pink rawness, as though Chioa Khan had been awake for days, with only willpower and strong coffee to keep him from sleep. I saw clear and noticeable variations of that feverish wakefulness in the eyes of every partygoer I spied.

"How long have you been here, man?" I asked.

"Two or three days? I couldn't possibly say. Day and night, time itself, have no meaning in this sacred hall. I heard Aiwass calling me and left Barnato that day. We found this great temple on our fourth day of looking."

"That was over two months ago," said Champney.

"No," said Chioa Khan faintly. "No, that's not possible."

"A party that lasts forever," said the professor. "I may be knocking on in years now, but that sounds not just wearying but downright hellish."

"Repeating the same thing, day and night, forever," I agreed. The celebrations earlier that year for the sixty-fifth anniversary of Her Majesty's coronation went on for ten days and that was, no unpatriotic feeling intended, more than this man could bear.

"A hell indeed," said Miss Saxena, "although perhaps not one of monotonous repetition."

"No?" I said.

"Human imagination knows no bounds," she said. "Nor human depravity."

The professor's eyes flicked to those dark and disturbing recesses of the room once more. "There were certain medieval theologians who wrote at length on the subject of time and repetition of acts. Some suggested that when the universe dies, it is recreated and, the laws of nature being what they are, every event of the old universe be repeated. We would be born again to the same parents and live out our lives exactly as before. That would suggest I have already said these words an infinite number of times and will reiterate them an infinite number of times more. The tiniest moral act of goodness will be repeated and amplified until it is equal to the greatest act of charity imaginable. Likewise, even the tiniest sin, repeated infinitely, will be equal to the disobedience of Adam and Eve or the betrayal of our Lord by Judas Iscariot."

"Fascinating," said Chioa Khan, neither comprehending nor interested. "Aiwass awaits."

"However," said the professor as we followed Chioa Khan through the merrymaking to Aiwass' table, "there were other theologians who, considering God's omniscience, argued that God has no need for reminders and would therefore abhor repetition. There would only be need for one universe, all its acts recorded in God's infinite mind. Some suggested that God would only bring the world to an end once all possible acts, good and evil, had occurred. To take this viewpoint to its logical conclusion, all acts, though not necessarily good, are valid because they will hasten the coming of God's Kingdom."

"A vile perspective," said Champney.

"But look around us," said the professor. "A party of endless duration in which anything and everything is permissible. We are seeing, in those dark corners, the accumulation of sins." He mumbled deeply to himself and then said, "I see some link with those carvings, that mysterious language. There is a gathering here, almost mindless. Almost..."

Chioa Khan had come to a stop at a large circular table. Party guests sat in a semi-circle on the other side of the table, clustered around the enormous yet not enormous figure of Aiwass.

"Lord Aiwass," said Chioa Khan, bowing deeply to his host, "may I introduce Reverend Philbin Champney, chaplain of Barnato University, the esteemed Professor Erskine Sedgewick of Trinity College, Cambridge, and his travelling companions."

My eyes briefly met those of Miss Saxena and I took some small pleasure in seeing that she was far more disgruntled than I at not being introduced by name.

"Professor, this is Aiwass, the voice in the wilderness, who in this manifestation is Ra-Hoor-Khuit, the conqueror and the vengeful, Lord of the Aeon, and also Harpocrates, god of silence."

The professor gave a curt if polite nod.

Aiwass raised arms which, in the manner of the impossible illusion of his body, seemed both to be quite ordinary and yet reached across the full breadth of the table. When he spoke, his voice was not of one pitch but many. At its core was a man's voice, clear and without accent, but around it was a vast rumbling, like a volcanic eruption echoing from some dark seabed.

"Welcome," he said.

As before, a true understanding of Aiwass's physical appearance was beyond my grasp. Here was a dark-haired man, of aristocratic bearing like the finest of Englishmen, although possessing the relaxed and self-assured mannerisms of some nouveau-riche American. Here also was the high priest of some lost civilisation, wrapped up in robes and the dust of ages. Here too was something more bestial and dangerous: the shadow of an eagle against the high sun; the slink of a lion in tall grass. Like a spinning thaumatrope, like the flickering image in the corner of a picture flip book, like the multitude of names and titles Chioa Khan had piled on his master, Aiwass was all of these things at once: Aiwass, a fox in a silk bow tie, sat at the base of a vast and rugged obelisk.

"This is a surprising party," said Professor Sedgewick. "It is quite astonishing that we should stumble upon it by chance."

"Chance?" said Aiwiss with a genial smile. "A fool can be surprised by the rising of the sun or the change of the seasons."

"You planned for us to be here," said the professor. It was neither a statement or a question. "Chioa Khan said he heard you calling to him."

"As a voice in the corner of my hotel room," said Chioa Khan.

"And I have also heard him twice name you as Harpocrates. You are the god of silence, Horus as a child?"

Aiwass nodded. "Not a child in form," he grinned, and the woman cosied up at his side giggled, ran a hand across his chest and inside his jacket. "But a child of the new aeon that I have come to herald."

"The age of Horus," said Chioa Khan obsequiously. "A time of self-realisation, when the will to achieve wisdom and power shall be rewarded."

"Ah, so you are a prophet," said the professor to Aiwass. "Earlier today, the reverend and I were discussing the Sermon on the Mount and Christ's warning against false prophets."

Who come as wolves in sheep's clothing, I thought, seeing the utter aptness of the professor's words.

Aiwass laughed and a waft of his scent, a discordant blend of fine cologne and foetid animal musk, reached my nostrils. "The

Christ was not referring to myself," he said. "Why would he denounce his master?"

"Master?" spluttered Champney. "You claim to be God."

"Foremost of the gods," Aiwass corrected him. "The Hebrews knew me as Yahweh, the sun god, the bringer of the lightning and of battle."

"Blasphemy!" spat Champney.

"There is no such thing," said the would-be god flatly. "All worship is knowingly or unknowingly directed to me. All curses are an invocation of my names. The Aztecs worshipped me with blood sacrifices. Ascetic monks worshipped me with meditations and flagellation. The gambler's dice and the priest's communion wafer are as one to me. To breathe is to worship me. Eating, praying, fighting, fornicating are all acts of worship."

My flesh crawled at this. My faith, like a cottage hearth, is a small thing but stoutly built and at the heart of my very being. His words were an assault on that stone redoubt and I quite clearly saw why Champney was fearful of these foul new faiths of Mars; particularly when the heart and hearth of our Christian faith was worlds away. A thought struck me at this point.

"Why is a god of Earth here on Mars?" I asked.

"A good question!" said the professor. "This temple of yours appears ancient. Are you a god of Mars too?"

"The kingdom of the gods is not conscribed in terms of geography," said Aiwass.

"But who built this grand edifice?" asked the professor.

"It was fashioned by ancient hands," replied Aiwass.

"Oh? Martian hands or human?"

Aiwass, for a reason I did not understand, hesitated a second and the professor plunged on.

"The imagery in this temple has been confusing and disturbing us since our arrival." Both Champney and I made involuntary noises of agreement. "We felt that some of the writing on the walls is very familiar. Some of it is almost like ancient cuneiform, some of it almost like Cambodian inscriptions. Almost like Egyptian cartouches, almost like Sanskrit—"

"Prakrit," Miss Saxena corrected him.

"—Cretan, Mayan. Almost, almost, almost."

"Perhaps you begin to realise that all human languages have a common root," suggested Aiwass. "Perhaps on Mars?"

Professor Sedgewick laughed which, even in the face of a false god, was surprisingly rude and unlike him. "No, Aiwass, I don't. The writing on the walls is a simulacrum of human language and so very nearly successful. Similarly, the pictures carved into the walls are simulacra of humans and, like the writing, are almost perfect. We all felt there was something vulgar in their attitude and posture and I now suspect it is the *almost* nature of these images that preys on us. If they had been crude cartoons we would not have felt the same unease, but this uncanny near-verisimilitude unnerves us deeply."

"If you have a point to make, professor," said Aiwass impatiently, "I fail to see it."

"A wolf in sheep's clothing."

"Me?"

"This temple. At least that was what I had thought for a moment. In the study of nature, it is called aggressive mimicry. For example, the grey shrike bird has been heard to sing the mating call of the passerines upon which it preys. The golden orb weaver spider spins golden webs which passing bees, mistaking them for flowers, are entrapped therein."

"My temple was built as a trap?" said Aiwass.

"No," said the professor. "I don't believe it was built at all or, if it was, it was constructed by an imbecile."

This remark provoked Aiwass to anger at last. He pushed away the woman who clung to his side and cast a finger at the professor. I trusted the professor with my life and would never have let him see me doubt him but even I felt that he had kicked a metaphorical hornets' nest and that we might soon reap the rewards of that transgression.

"You are a madman," Aiwass thundered. "You see the wondrous artifice of my temple and deny the evidence of your senses. An imbecile? At whom do you fling this accusation?"

The professor calmly held his ground. Quite an audience had built up around us. Although the dance music played on, the dancing had stopped and the merrymakers had all turned to observe the confrontation between Aiwass and the professor.

"The humble termite," said the professor blithely. "It is an almost entirely mindless creature and, yet, in Her Majesties Australian colonies they build ornate towers taller than a man. Order and structure from imbecility."

"This is not a termite mound," countered Aiwass. "Consider the artistry, the scale, the proportions. Look upon my works, Sedgewick!"

"I do," said the professor, "and I see it bears more than one similarity to a termite mound. They are built as a home for the termites but, more than that, as a place to hide from a world that is hostile to them. Layer upon layer is accreted around their nest, sheltering their fragile bodies. This is not a trap, Aiwass. This is your shell."

"A shell?" said Aiwass. "You think I am hiding here, like a quivering and defenceless mollusc."

The professor nodded. "You are not a wolf in sheep's clothing but a sheep in wolf's clothing. A hoverfly masquerading as a wasp."

"Steady on, dear chap," said I to my good friend. "Let's not anger him."

"We have nothing to fear from this—" He gesticulated in his search for a word, failed and then addressed the pulsating form of the god in a gentle and sympathetic tone. "You are not a god, Aiwass. I suspect you are not even alive."

"Our wine has gone to your head," declared Aiwass loudly and the assembled partygoers laughed, finding some relief from the mounting tension. "You accuse me of being nothing and yet you must argue the point with me. If I am not here, to whom are you talking?"

"A mirage," said the professor. "A beautiful mirage. A pearl. You do know where pearls come from, Aiwass?"

"How can I? I don't exist!" said Aiwass to fresh laughter.

"A pearl is formed when a speck of dirt becomes trapped in an oyster's mantle. The oyster attacks the invading dirt with layer upon layer of secretions until the beautiful pearl is formed. It is done without purpose or intelligence and yet a man, or indeed a woman, can be lost in the pearl's lustre."

"So I am now a pearl?" Aiwass smiled. "Be assured that you will pay for your blasphemies, professor, but your madness amuses me for the moment."

"I thought you said there was no such thing as blasphemy," interjected Champney.

"A pearl is built around a molecule of dirt," mused the professor, quite possibly to himself. "An accretion around an incongruence. Something similar is afoot here." He looked up at the chamber's high ceiling. "A confluence of energies, perhaps?"

"Speak English, professor," muttered Miss Saxena.

"Have you heard of Black Holes?"

"Like the one in Calcutta?" she asked.

"I was thinking of the astronomical variety. They are pearls in their own way. They are massive stars which, drawing planets and other stars in with their enormous gravitational pull, collapse under their own mass to become something entirely monstrous and inscrutable. An accretion through physical forces. Yes."

This last was spoken as though he had come to a decision. "Aiwass," he said, "this must come to an end."

"Our conversation?" said Aiwass. "I think I agree. Your ramblings begin to bore me. Seize them."

Without hesitation, Chioa Khan leapt forward and grabbed Professor Sedgewick's arm. Others swiftly followed suit and took hold of Champney and myself. Even the women, with shameless impropriety, laid their satin-gloved hands on us. An outburst of protest behind me indicated they had seized Miss Saxena also. Someone leaned heavily on my back, pushing me down to one knee. The professor and Champney were still upright, their arms pinned roughly behind their backs.

I coughed, struggling to breathe. "I say, professor, it's a good job that we have nothing to fear from this mirage or I might start to worry."

"My dear Cadwallander," he replied, "I believe I might have miscalculated."

"Oh, good," said I with desperate sarcasm.

"We have absolutely nothing to fear from Aiwass," said my friend. "But these people could kill us at any time they choose."

The Reverend Champney began to recite a prayer and some way off the piano and woodwind struck up with another lively dancing tune.

5.

It was ever rare for me to hear the professor admit he had made an error, not because of any arrogance but because it was very unlike him to be mistaken in any matter. Refreshing though it might have been to glimpse the man's fallibility, I wished fervently that an opportunity to rectify that mistake might present itself.

The sycophantic Chioa Khan dug his fingers into the professor's shoulder, eliciting a grimace of pain. "You will pay for your conceited comments, Sedgewick," he said. "Aiwass is a generous god but not a merciful one."

"He's no god," gasped the professor. "No more than is the sun or the wind."

"Harpocrates is the sun, fool. The god who dies not, nor is reborn but goes radiant ever upon his way."

"Nothing lasts forever," said the professor insisted.

I considered once more the professor's musings on time and eternity. He had spoken of pearls and Black Holes and earlier of the accumulation – accretion even – of sins. For how long had Aiwass' orgy been proceeding? If Chioa Khan and his naïve followers had spent months here and thought it only days, how long ago had the earliest merrymakers arrived? Could it be years, even as far back as the first human settlements on this red world?

"These four will pay with their lives," announced Aiwass, "but their deaths must serve our entertainments. What novel dooms will we have them suffer as a retributive offering to your god?"

Several people shouted out: wild, improbable and perverted tortures for us to undergo. My mind was elsewhere, careening around the lip of an epiphany.

I recalled the desperate fatigue I had seen on the partygoers' faces. Deluded, ensorcelled into believing time was passing far more slowly; they had perhaps not slept nor taken sufficient victuals to sustain them. But, I reasoned against myself, the people did not seem malnourished and food was plentiful. And yet the wine had failed to quench my thirst and the grapes had been as tasteless as air. I suddenly understood a new truth and I vocalised it in the form of a question: "Where is the band?"

No one heard me over the clamour of taunts and threats. I raised my voice. "Professor! Where is the band? From where comes the music ?"

"You noticed too?" he called back.

From behind, Saxena shouted. "There isn't one!"

The music was an illusion, a mirage. And the food and the drink were illusions too. The men and women who had hold of me were not just tired; unless Aiwass offered them some sustenance beyond human comprehension, they must have been the most wretched bags of skin of bone. The realisation gave me the conviction to exert my strength against them. What opposition could they possibly present to a stout fellow well-fed on meat and bread? I stood upright, throwing the person from my back and, with a backward swing of my mechanical arm, cleared the rest from me.

The crowd gasped and pointed but also laughed. My retaliation was only part of their entertainments. To them, I was a baited animal in their pit, and none anticipated my next act: I charged at Aiwass. My fist was drawn back as I leapt forward and I rammed it at him with all the force my pneumatic limb could muster.

I cannot say whether Aiwass dodged my blow or whether my punch went *straight through his body* as though it were as insubstantial as fog. Whichever the case, my metal fist did not connect with Aiwass but with the stone spire behind him. My knuckles pounded against the stone with the force of a hammer and I half felt, half saw the polished finger coverings buckle and twist under the blow.

A disturbance in the air rippled out from the point of impact, as though the spire was nothing but a reflection in still water. The strange phenomenon changed all it touched, disrupting the chimeric reality of Aiwass' temple. The music stopped. The fine furniture and food were gone. The figure of Aiwass stuttered and froze, the string of his thaumatrope snapped, a thumb paused in his picture flip book illusion. The people around me were, in that moment, not dressed in fine evening wear but all manner of clothes, all caked with red dust; some so ragged that it was impossible to tell what they had originally been. And the people themselves were transformed too: become filthy, pale and more emaciated than any famine victim.

Within moments, the disruptive wave had passed and Aiwass was there again and the gay music picked up once more.

"Kill him!" Aiwass shrieked but the men and women, who had just seen themselves for what they really were, were too shocked to move.

"Hey, Aiwass!" cried out Miss Saxena. "Here's an offering for you!"

I looked back in time to see a stick of dynamite spin up and over my head, its lit fuse describing glittering loops in the air. The explosive charge landed on the ground in the small space between Aiwass and myself.

"Help me!" cried Aiwass, unable to either move or toss the dynamite aside.

None came to his aid. As soon as the dynamite struck the tiled floor (which had been uneven sand seconds before) I ran for my life. My hand caught Champney's elbow and I dragged him along with me, in the wake of Professor Sedgewick and Miss Saxena, who were already hastening to find cover.

The explosion was quite deafening, its awful blast throwing smoke and sand into the air and flinging shards of stone in every direction. Our little party was lucky to escape injury, although a piece of flying rock did cut an irreparable gash in my favourite jacket.

A number of Aiwass' guests – victims all – were not so fortunate: splinters of the great stone obelisk cut through them like cannon-fired shrapnel. The explosion cut a large wedge in the stone spire and driven fat cracks along its full height. Whereas my wild blow had only momentarily interrupted Aiwass's illusion, the dynamite dispelled it completely. Those poor souls cut down by the explosion may have stood in tail coats and finest gowns but they fell lifeless in the shredded remains of whatever clothes they had arrived in weeks, months or years before.

In the ear-ringing silence following the explosion, there was a moment in which all was still; those yet alive looked round to survey the former opulent ballroom. We stood in a dim natural cavern with what I now perceived to be a huge stalagmite of glistening black stone at its centre. I had but a second to stare in wonder before the silence was broken by a scream from the corner of the chamber. Where, in Aiwass' illusions, there had been secluded cushion-strewn alcoves in which people had abandoned themselves to their basest urges, there were now bedraggled, sore-ridden wretches rutting like beasts among the bones and filth of those long dead. I saw – and fervently wished I had not – a man frozen in terror, his naked body wrapped around a rotting corpse, his fingers slick with the brown juices of its decomposition.

A chorus of screams and cries rose up at once from all over. Several persons collapsed to the floor, some with hands clasped over their eyes in horror, some overcome by the abuse and neglect that they had heaped upon their bodies and from which I suspected they would never recover. However, among the crashing tide of fear and disgust, there were other voices raised in anger.

"What have you done?" called Chioa Khan, his voice dry and reedy. The brewer's son cum mystic had lost all of his stage mesmerist suaveness and was now reduced to a filthy tramp with wild, bed-tossed hair and a scraggly beard.

"It was all fantasy," said the professor, brushing dust from his jacket. "It was never real."

Chioa Khan was not interested in talk, not least of all the truth, and broke into a staggering run towards the professor, his fists clenched and ready to strike. There was the loud report of gunfire and Chioa Khan fell writhing in the dirt, a bloody wound in his shoulder.

The professor gave Miss Saxena a furious look. "There was no need for that, woman!" he snapped.

Leisurely, she aimed the pistol at my good friend. "Careful, professor," said she. "I do believe that I am once again the most dangerous thing in the room."

As if in response to her assertion of power, a fresh strangeness swept through the room. It was as though a wind had picked up, swirling through the chamber and around the fractured monolithic stalagmite at the room's centre but *the air was quite still*. It was as though a great humming sound, like a mighty cathedral organ, had begun to emanate from that great black spire, although there was, in truth, *no sound at all*. Through senses other than the conventional five, we could all feel a power and energy circulate around and pulsate from the mysterious stone.

"The speck of dirt in the oyster's mantle," said the professor. "The stone is channelling energies of some sort."

"The devil's work," cried Champney.

"No," the professor insisted. "A natural phenomenon."

Devil's work or scientific mystery, the fearsome anomaly meant us ill. From its heart, a voice that was not a voice and an entity that was neither visible nor palpable, lunged at us. Its meaning and desires were clear enough. I could imagine but not hear Aiwass's voice screaming, *"Kill them! Destroy them!"*

Inaudible though the voice was and nonsensically paradoxical it might be to say it, the professor, Champney and Miss Saxena heard it well enough too.

"And now it's time to leave," said Miss Saxena, stepping back towards the cavern's single exit.

"I concur," the professor swiftly agreed.

6.

We turned on our heels and in a most un-British manner, ran from that pit of horrors. Many of Aiwass's disciples were soon following after us, shambling and lurching in pursuit. I could not rightly say if they, like us, were fleeing that dire place, perhaps hoping that we might lead them to the light of day, or if they were still under Aiwass's sway and meant us harm. It mattered not. Even battered and dazed, we four were far swifter than those starved, half-dead objects of pity.

However, we were not out of danger. The cursing, shrieking spirit of Aiwass hounded us through the tunnels. Though no physical force was laid against us, it took an effort of will to press on, as though the floor was a boggy mire; as though a great and insensible hand was trying to claw us back.

I am sincerely grateful that Professor Sedgewick and Miss Saxena appeared to know exactly where they were going. Champney and I brought up the rear, sometimes linking arms to help one another against the treacherous tide of Aiwass's will. Even in our flight I noted that the carvings and inscriptions on the walls had entirely vanished, yet another illusion destroyed. In their place were the uneven walls of a natural cave, marbled with veins of a glistening black rock that, in a very poor light, might have been mistaken for writing.

In time, the cries of our ragged pursuers faded, as did the unearthly power that had been exerted against us. As it drained completely, we emerged into cold air and rosy light. We were in the deep channel we had followed to the cave entrance. I caught my breath and looked up. The sun was *rising* over the mountains of Tharsis.

"It's morning," I declared. "Tomorrow morning!"

"Impossible," said Miss Saxena. "We had only been in there an hour or two."

"Time," mused the professor, "is perhaps more malleable than we realise."

Together, we climbed out of the channel and onto the mountainside. The cool air felt good in my lungs, nourishing and wholesome. The sandstorm we had sought shelter from had passed – perhaps many hours earlier – and the skies were clear. Two airships, one to the north, one to the south, neither more than a mile distant, turned slow circles in the sky. I saw the Union Jack and the insignia of Her Majesty's Air Corps painted on their helium envelopes.

"It seems we have been missed," I said.

Miss Saxena murmured something to herself and holstered her pistol.

"The odds have turned against you again," suggested the professor.

She smiled. It was a lop-sided and roguish thing and not the kind of expression one would ever catch an English lady making. "Another time, gentlemen," she said loudly, gave the briefest of curtseys, and set off at a sprint down the mountain slope.

We watched her go.

"I don't believe I understand half of what happened in there," I said, mopping my perspiring brow with a handkerchief.

"This is not Earth," said the professor. "Who knows what natural wonders of Mars we have yet to fully comprehend?"

"There was nothing natural about any of that," said Champney curtly, although despite his tone, the man was actually smiling.

"So, tell me," I asked the professor, "when did you realise it was all just a trick of the senses?"

"The grapes," my friend replied. "Tasteless things. False prophets. By their fruits shall you know them."

High above, one of the airship turned towards us and then, shortly afterwards, the other did likewise. I found a fair-sized boulder and sat myself down to await rescue. The cave, which we had previously mistaken for a carved archway, stood a short way off to my side. I stared at its dark mouth and thought about the wilful fools who were still in there.

It took the airships a quarter of an hour to descend to our position. In that time, no one else emerged from the cave. I felt no compunction to go and look for them.

1904 – The Well of Shambala

From the personal journal of M.S.

If there are higher levels of Being among the stars, it may well be that the successive rise to higher levels on this Earth – from inorganic to organic, from organic to mental and from the mental to the spiritual – have come about through the interaction between the parts and the whole. Conditions on this Earth may be more affected than we are aware of by the Universe in its ensemble and by the action of higher Beings in other Earths.

Sir Francis Younghusband:
Life in the Stars: An Exposition of the View that on some Planets of some Stars exist Beings higher than Ourselves, and on one a World Leader, the Supreme Embodiment of the Eternal Spirit which animates the Whole. (1927)

1.

Looking down from the seventh tier of the Temple of One Hundred Thousand Deities, a stereoscopic camera in my gloved hands, I reflected, quite unoriginally, that height and distance gives one a certain degree of perspective and clarity. The epiphany which my rarefied position granted me concerned the British soldiers in the courtyard far below and their orderly ransacking of the temple complex. As the line of men emerged, each carrying a Buddhist statuette, gilded artefact or sacred scroll, I concluded (once again with no pretence of originality) that the British imperialists were not the lions of their heraldry and national mythology. They were not even wolves: a tightly organised pack of ravening predators. No, these tiny figures were locusts, mindless and indiscriminate consumers of that which did not belong to them.

To understand why there was a British invasion force of over three thousand soldiers occupying the Tibetan town of Gyantse (and why I was therefore half-frozen and wind-blown, documenting their military and cultural trespasses) requires the logic and imagination available only to the inbred English aristocracy. Suffice to say, we were barely a handful of years into the new century, the

Great Game between the imperial nations of Britain and Russia was still being played out in central Asia, whilst in Calcutta the delusional Lord Curzon (he of the steel corset and pudding brain) had mystically intuited that Tibet was ripe for Russian invasion and thus the British had best seize it first, for the benefit of all.

Colonel Younghusband's British forces had crossed into Tibet from the northern Indian province of Sikkim in the April and, a month later, had made Gyantse its camp, taking the townsfolk's homes for themselves, confiscating its produce and idly stealing or destroying its religious treasures much like an infant rooting around in its parents' finest porcelain. What little Tibetan resistance they had encountered had been swiftly quashed. What good were muzzle-loading rifles and swords against Maxim guns and repeating mortars?

While Younghusband smoked and played cards in the town's finest mansions, the Dalai Lama cowered in his palace in Lhasa, refusing to come south to negotiate terms with the invaders. Meanwhile, young Tibetans lay dead on the mountainsides, their families bewildered as to why the protective amulets given out by the lamas had failed to save their husbands, fathers and sons.

I carried a Webley automatic pistol beneath my layers of warm clothes. From my vantage point near the top of the *stupa*, I could have easily picked off a couple of the vile invaders before they spotted me; even more before they had the wits to return fire. It would have been a small act of revenge but I had not followed the British forces here from my native India in order to make a small gesture of symbolic martyrdom. My stereoscopic daguerreotype camera was my primary weapon. The British people's support for their armed forces abroad relied on a willing blindness to the truth, a naïve acceptance of the image of the soldier as patrician and protector; of the subjugated as grateful recipient of British governance. Any photographic image of imperial abuse I could smuggle out to the news agencies in Calcutta, or even London, would be a dent in that rose-tinted dream and a small but poisonous cut in the hide of the imperial beast.

Among the soldiers below, I spotted a face I recognised: Captain Walton. He had drawn my eye some days ago; there was something about his bearing and his manner that set him apart from the others. He was a clean-shaven and pale fellow who carried himself with a peculiar aloofness, as though he wanted to mentally and physically distance himself from the other Englishmen. I had also seen him visiting the houses of the townsfolk on a number of occasions, a black leather case in his hand, always knocking softly before entering.

I had spent the last five days sitting on high chilly stone with only the occasional eagle for company and would have known no more about Captain Walton if that had been all. However, I spent my nights down in the military camp, warming myself at their stoves, swiping their food when I could and blending easily with the Pathans, the Sikh Pioneers, the Automated Ghurkhas and the innumerable camp followers. It was there that I heard that Captain Walton was the company doctor and had taken it upon himself to freely dispense his services and medicines to the local people. If rumours were true, he had even performed corrective surgery on a number of local children afflicted with hare lips.

I determined that I would like Captain Herbert Walton or, at least, not hate the man. It was warming to find someone I might observe with something other than repugnance.

Down on the ground, Captain Walton was in conversation with another officer and gesturing off towards the town and the hills beyond. I lifted my *pagri* headscarf away from my ears and strained to hear the subject of their conversation. The chilly wind carried few words my way, but there were two words which Captain Walton uttered clearly enough to compel me to pack away my camera and begin my descent.

"Falling star."

2.

There had been flames in the sky the night before, and distant booming sounds that were not thunder. It had been no natural phenomenon and I suspected it was some British weapon of terror. That Captain Walton spoke of it as a falling star suggested otherwise and so, as he requisitioned half a dozen troops from the temple-raiding party and a further dozen Indian pack-bearers from the camp, I followed discreetly, slipping in among the other Indians as we walked.

At a narrow gully a mile north of the town, we met with a smaller party led by a tall, bewhiskered major. They stood around a steam-horse, one of the British transportation platforms, which was tilted at a steep angle with one of its crooked legs wedged in the gully. A scratched and scorched iron canister, longer than a man, with the remains of a parachutist's canopy tied to it, was lashed to the table-shaped walking machine's back. The canister looked ready to slip off and onto the rocks at any moment.

"Dashed gyroscopes are shot," said the major. "I had to turn it off."

"Then we'll do it the old fashioned way," said Captain Walton. Together the two officers directed the pack-bearers, myself included, to untie the ropes and carry the canister to more level ground. All went well until one man slipped and the weight of the canister dragged the others down. The canister struck a pointed rock and a panel in its side came away.

A waft of chemical fumes washed over us and I reacted without thinking, leaping between the men and throwing myself bodily over the opening in the canister.

"Get that man off!" barked the major.

"Photographic plates!" I shouted back. "Light will destroy them!"

The major paused. Walton stepped forward and sniffed. "I think the boy's right."

I lay there, straddling the fat iron tube while a thick blanket was produced and bound over the opening. The officers had us abandon the steam-horse completely and instead carry the canister back to camp in a cradle of ropes. Captain Walton fell in beside me as we walked. "Tell me, lad. How did you know there were photographic plates in there?" he asked.

"The smell of mercury fumes," I said in the north Indian accent I had cultivated of late. "Also iodine and, I think, William's Fixative Fluid."

"And how would you know such things?"

"I helped in the offices of a British photographer in Patna."

66

Captain Walton laughed. "Then you are probably the finest chemist on the entire expedition. What's your name, boy?"

"Nitish, sir," I lied. "Nitish Paswan."

"I think I might need your help in developing the images in that canister."

"But where did it come from?" I asked.

Captain Walton pointed straight up.

"From space, Nitish."

*

Captain Walton was true to his word and insisted that I help him convert an emptied farmhouse into a dark room in which we might properly open the canister and remove its contents. The major, one Wallace Roxborough, didn't approve of me as photographer's assistant, principally on the grounds that I might be privy to military secrets above my station, but I played up my imbecilic native routine, much to Captain Walton's amusement, and the captain was soon able to usher his superior from the house.

Alone, Captain Walton and I worked on the plates stored on racks inside the canister. Some were already developed, although improperly fixed. Others we developed ourselves with such salts and fixing agents we could derive from the quartermaster's supplies. Once done, we arranged the silver-faced copper plates on a table and inspected them. They were, without exception, incomprehensible patchworks of black and white irregular shapes.

"What are they?" I asked.

Captain Walton leaned over my shoulder and touched one gently. "In space, hundreds of miles above us, just at the point where the Earth's *inward* gravity gives way to the *downward* pull of the solar ætheric plane, is an orbiting space platform, the *Gloriana*, an island in the heavens. The *Gloriana* is manned by twenty-odd men of Her Majesty's Space Corps who watch over us, like angels. They took these pictures of the mountainous regions around us."

"And is this space platform armed?"

Captain Walton gave me a peculiar look. Not for the last time, I thought he might have seen through my disguise. "A single eighteen-hundred pound gun aimed straight down at us, boy," he said. "A man-made hammer of vengeance!"

"Those sounds I heard in the night...?"

Captain Walton nodded. "Firing on suspected Russian positions. Perhaps these plates can show us the truth of the matter." He peered closely, running his fingers over shrouded craters that might have been the impact points of the heaven-sent artillery. "But what's this?" he said.

I looked at where he indicated. Within a patch of darkness was a structure of adjoined and concentric squares.

"I think the colonel will want to see this," he said and called for a messenger at once.

And that was how it came to be that, within the hour, I was standing in the hall of a fine house as Captain Walton's manservant at the court of Colonel Francis Younghusband. I constantly fought against the urge to fiddle with the *pagri* that bound my long hair to my scalp and to rearrange the deliberately loose clothing which hid my camera, pistol and more besides. I should not have worried; Colonel Younghusband – a round-faced man with a moustache that resembled a sleeping vole – had eyes only for the daguerreotypes and the leather wallet of documents which had also come down in the space canister.

While Captain Walton and Roxborough crowded round the dining table and helped the colonel interpret the images, I did my best to both listen and appear utterly inconspicuous. The men were perhaps as surprised as I to discover that there were troop formations, albeit small ones, in the mountains to the east and that the Russians might have indeed made their own military incursions into Tibet. The pictures were taken from such a height that troop numbers and the exact ordnance they carried were hard to make out. The officers spent a considerable time puzzling over these and the successes of the *Gloriana*'s orbital bombardment before contemplating the square formations Captain Walton had noted.

"Are these buildings?" asked Younghusband.

"If so, they don't appear on any maps we have access to, sir," answered Captain Walton.

"Abandoned farm buildings?"

"Not that high in the mountains, sir," said Roxborough. "And, if we have the scale correct, those outer walls are more than a hundred yards long. This is a large complex of buildings. I have a theory."

Younghusband's moustache twitched in amusement, the little vole shifting in its sleep. Captain Walton suppressed a small smile also. "I've heard of your theories," said Younghusband. "You'll have us believe that this is the Olympus of the Himalayas. The magical land of Shambala."

"There's nothing magical about it," said Roxborough stiffly. "And I have no theories concerning the homes of the gods. What I do subscribe to is Laurence Waddell's theory of hyperdiffusionism."

Younghusband grunted. "*From one man, He made all the nations*, eh? No, Roxborough. Lieutenant Colonel Waddell is a fine Orientalist. His book on the birds of Sikkim was a delight. But, believing that all human civilisation originated with a single master race? No."

Roxborough angrily cleared his throat. "With the greatest of respect, sir, do you believe that all men are created equal?" He cast about and suddenly pointed at me. "You believe the Indian is as advanced as the European? You think the dark-skinned Asian, with his weaker frame, his smaller skull, his child-like brain, has the wherewithal to harness the power of steam, to reach out and create an empire that stretches from the ocean floor to the Jovian moons?"

"I believe there were great civilisations and cultures of old, major," said Younghusband. "But a single wellspring of civilisation seems incredible. And even you wouldn't be foolish enough to suggest that our Aryan ancestors trace their lineage back to some ruins in the Himalayas!"

"Waddell thought so and he is the man who conclusively proved the existence of Ashoka's Hell. Perhaps this place is Shambala, the pure source of humanity. Sir, I would like to make an expedition to this location—"

Younghusband was shaking his head before Roxborough had even finished speaking. "That region is more than five days' hike from here, major. It's too high up for our helipterons and the winds too treacherous for airships. There's bad weather closing in from the north. I would not risk a contingent of our men."

Roxborough stood ramrod straight. "Sir, I ask but for a single platoon of regular troops."

"Led by you? And a dozen Sherpas too, no doubt."

"Whatever you may spare, sir."

Younghusband gave Roxborough a long stare and then, hands held behind his back, strolled over to one of the hall's large windows. He peered out through the shutter's slats. "I've known other men risk their lives and the lives of others in pursuit of wild fantasies among these mountains."

"Not fantasies, sir," said Roxborough. "We explore in the name of science and knowledge."

Younghusband held up a hand for silence and the major pressed his lips together obediently. "What do you say, captain?"

"Me, sir?" said Captain Walton. "I'm not sure my opinion is important."

"Then why did I ask for it, man?" snapped the colonel.

Captain Walton uncomfortably cleared his throat. "If these images are to be believed, sir, then our rivals may already have troops in that region. Both the Russians and the weather pose a considerable threat."

"You are saying that the British Army should fear peasants with rifles and the possibility of snow?"

"Sir. Two years ago, Lindsworth lost his entire party of forty men in his expedition to find the white ape-men of the mountains, the Himalayan Orang Utan."

Younghusband turned, his heels clicking on the stone floor. "Do you see?" he said to Roxborough. "Forty men lost on some fool's quest for a mythical mountain creature. And you want to take a platoon on some archaeological beano?"

"If you suspect the Russians are moving into that area, sir," Roxborough countered. "then that is an argument to scout it out, not hide here in the comfort of our camp."

Younghusband gave the major a scowl, although there was a degree of levity in his expression. "Hide, eh?" he said softly. "Very well. One platoon, under your command, Somersets and Pathans."

"I would rather take some of the Automated Ghurkhas than the *Forty Thieves*," said Roxborough.

"If you don't value the 40th Pathans, you can go without," said Younghusband plainly.

"Pathans it is," said Roxborough. "Thank you, sir."

"And Walton here will go with you as your second in command."

"Sir?" said Captain Walton.

"As my eyes and ears. And as the voice of reason."

It was clear that Captain Walton was deeply displeased by this news but did not argue with his commanding officer.

"And you will need to hurry," said Younghusband. He tapped at the documents in the leather wallet. "The *Gloriana* has orders to shell that region in eight days' time."

3.

Major Roxborough had his expeditionary platoon ready by the following morning: twenty-five men of the First Somerset Regiment, led by the ruddy-faced Lieutenant Kingsley and his steel-eyed sergeant, Bishop, plus ten sepoys of the 40th Pathans, riflemen from the Afghan borders who would also double as trackers and pack bearers. Convincing Captain Walton to take me along in the continuing capacity of his manservant (my curiosity in this matter required sating) was surprisingly easy. Walton seemed unaccountably happy to make use of me even though Roxborough had rounded up ten further Sherpas to carry supplies. There were no steam-horses in the party: the walking platforms struggled on the most rugged terrain and there was no easier path between Gyantse and our destination.

We made good distance on the first day, even though the skies whited over completely and the threat of snow hung in the air. We made camp beneath a huge, protective overhang. Captain Walton had me pitch his tent and make him tea on his phlogiston Ever-Heat stove as he sat on his spring-loaded camp bed and wrote in his journal. Outside, Roxborough, Lieutenant Kinglsey and Kingsley's sergeant, Bishop, sat around a fire, talking and laughing loudly.

"Will you not be joining the other officers, sir?" I asked eventually.

Captain Walton put his fountain pen down in the crease of his journal and smiled at me. "I will check on the sentries and report to the major before I retire, Nitish," he said. "But I have no desire to squat at the fireside like a caveman and swap boorish tales of seduction and impropriety." He returned to his note-making but

71

only for a moment or two. "If you have not yet realised it, Major Roxborough is a man with a clearly stratified view of life, with himself at the top." Captain Walton used his pen as a bar to indicate the top and the bottom. "The major regards the Indian native as far below the European. His views on women are no more enlightened, and that will be both the substance of their talk and source of their current laughter."

"And your views of women?" I asked, pouring the captain another cup of tea.

Captain Walton laughed at this. "There you have me, Nitish. I must sadly report that my knowledge of the gentler sex is all but non-existent. I have only the most circumspect of opinions. I understand the woman's desire for personal emancipation and suffrage and they have my tacit support in that. But apart from my own mother, I could hardly say I know a single woman. I am the eternal bachelor and confess that, all told, I am content with the company of bright young fellows such as yourself."

I passed Captain Walton his tea. "What is this hyperdiffusionism that the major spoke of?"

"Waddell's pet theory, wholly unsubstantiated. While most educated people accept that, over millennia, species – ourselves included – transmute towards a state of perfection, the mechanism of this is much debated. Those Cambridge chaps tell us that this process is gradual, slow and imperceptible, like the movement of the hour hand on a clock. But others propose that life moves forward in great leaps, in response to cataclysmic events. Waddell and Roxborough would have us believe the same of mankind's origins: that every great civilisation on earth, from the Egyptians to the Mayans, sprang suddenly from one single location; from one master race."

"The Aryans."

"Exactly. He would convince us that, if not for the master race, we'd all be like the ape-men they say walk these mountains."

"Are not all races and cultures reaching forward towards their own perfection?"

Captain Walton gave me a curious look. "It's only in recent times that man has ever considered the possibility of biological and cultural transmutation as an upward path," he said. "We've spent

72

centuries celebrating the achievements of the ancient civilisations – the Egyptians, the Romans, the Greeks – to such an extent that most thought we later peoples were nothing more than degenerate dwarf-like descendants, doomed to stumble in the shadow of ancient giants. I am sure that racial purists and their ilk would have us believe that the Asiatics and the Negro either never raised themselves up to the Aryan's height or are leading the descent back into the mire."

Perhaps realising the harshness of his words, Captain Walton patted my shoulder tenderly. "Although I don't believe such things, Nitish, and am glad you are here, you will find that some of my countrymen hold you in low esteem, regarding you as an entirely expendable asset." He reached past me and turned down the Ever-Heat stove until its glow was diminished to a dark orange. "You should watch your back, young man."

*

Three days later, I witnessed Roxborough's disregard for human life at first-hand. We had risen through the mountains to a point above the snow line. The promised storms had not yet reached us, though we passed through cloud and a haze of drifting flakes. I walked with the Sherpas and Pathans, my slight frame weighed down with Captain Walton's belongings.

Up ahead, two privates were chatting, one pointing up to the cliff face to our left. The other laughed, joking that his comrade had seen a mountain man, one of the fabled *yeti*. A few of us looked up as we walked but saw nothing. It was only when the Russians opened fire that we realised the true danger above our heads.

Lieutenant Kingsley was the first to die: killed by a bullet in the head before he even knew what was happening. Shots echoed off the rocks as the British scattered, seeking defensive positions. Amongst the gunshots there was also the strangest whining sound, like an engine's hum. A line of invisible destruction tore across our narrow path. It cut through a number of Sherpas and British and Afghan soldiers, slicing them in twain like a monstrous blade. Their severed torsos fell in ragged, bloody ruin to the ground. I dropped my pack and ran to huddle against the cliff, hoping its steep angle might act as a shield.

Roxborough, Walton and Sergeant Bishop had each, in their own manner, marshalled a number of men and the British returned fire on their mist-shrouded enemies. The platoon's mortarmen had planted and loaded the repeating mortar but the mysterious whining weapon cut them down before they could fire. The corporal's head vanished into red pulp and vapour, the private taking a wound to his leg. As much as it irks me to praise them, there is no doubting the British discipline under fire: their rifles maintained a constant rolling volley against those above us. It did them little good, for I could see that both soldiers and our Sherpas – the Russians did not discriminate – were being quickly picked off.

As I pressed into the cliff for safety, I sank a foot or more into packed snow and, in that, I grasped a fool's hope of saving us all. The repeating mortar, set up and ready to fire, was a scant fifteen feet distant and nearer to myself than any other,- saving the mortarman's private, who was clutching his wounded thigh and of no use to anyone. I ran for the mortar, slid to my knees, raised the barrel to a high elevation and depressed the brass button trigger.

As the coiled spring inside unwound, mortar after mortar dropped through the hopper and launched into the air. I have since learned that the Elswick Ordnance Repeating Mortar can deploy its entire twelve mortar load in just over ten seconds. It was a long ten seconds: I expected a sniper's bullet or that invisible death weapon to find me at any moment. The first mortar exploded as the fifth was launching, a muffled boom against the rocky reaches. The others followed in quick succession. I could hear no screams or shouts from above but the private beside me produced an almost intelligible stream of abuse, amid which all I could hear were the words: "Too high! Too high!"

In fact the mortar barrage had done exactly as I had hoped, although I almost had cause to regret it. I had intended to run for the shelter of the cliff but there was no time: first there fell a shower of fist-sized clumps snow, followed by a torrent of ice and dislodged rocks. The hard-packed snow covering both the cliff and the ledge from which the Russians attacked cascaded to the ground. I threw myself face down and readied my soul for death.

Debris rained down. A single rock could have cracked my skull or broken my back but ice and snow were all that fell on me, albeit painfully bruising. I was struck countless times; the fear of a sudden and violent death gave way to the horror of being crushed and suffocated by the weight of snow above me. I locked my elbows beneath me, forming and protecting a chamber of air around my face.

There are those who know me well who might think I am a fearless individual. That would be far from the truth. In dusty torture pits, in the airless dark at the bottom of the Thames, in the fiery wreckage of a doomed airship, I have known utter terror. I am not fearless but fear is not my master. In the darkness of what might have been my tomb, I ignored the tendon-ripping pressure on my back and a pulsating tightness around my ankle; instead, I counted the minutes and focused my mind on shallow and economical breaths. In and out, in and out.

4.

A sudden increase in the crushing weight of snow and ice almost ripped my shoulder from its socket. I yelled aloud. Just as quickly the weight was gone; I felt the snow above me shift and loosen. There was a glimmer of light and then there were hands on my back and shoulders. I pushed against the ground and raised myself up. My eyes and mouth were full of snow. I spat and coughed.

"Up you come, lad!" said Captain Walton, brushing the snow from my face.

I looked about. My ankle was still held fast and I could not turn over, but I saw a field of uneven snow, dotted with grey rocks and the bodies of half-buried Russian soldiers. An occasional crooked arm or bent leg jutted from the avalanche.

"I killed them all," I said. It was a bald statement, empty of emotion or judgement.

Captain Walton cocked an ear to the shouts of his countrymen a little way off. "They've taken a prisoner. One, at least. Come. Let us get you out of there."

I tried to move again; the grip on my ankle tightened at once. "There's someone holding onto my leg!" I cried.

Captain Walton called for help and a Pathan sepoy swiftly dug away the snow, ice and stone that almost buried me. I came free and, seconds later, so did the wounded private, screaming and panting as he was brought up.

"B_____ killed me!" he squeaked in shock and anger as he waved an unsteady finger at me. "Damn near b_____ killed me!"

"Private Fuller, by bringing down that ice shelf, our friend here might have saved all our lives," said Captain Walton. "Wazir, help me with this man."

Captain Walton and Sepoy Wazir carried the private to more even ground where Walton could examine and treat his injured leg. I brushed myself down, explored the aches and strains that my brief ordeal had given me and then found a boulder behind which I could check my camera, pistol and the general state of my disguise.

By this time, the British party had regrouped and were able to assess their own losses. I joined them to find that eleven Englishmen lay dead beneath the snow and, more alarming to me, mine was one of only three non-white faces left in the expeditionary party. I heard more than one soldier say he had seen several Sherpas fleeing down the mountain path but I doubted the truth in that.

Against our losses, we had gained a prisoner, a lean and handsome man in a high-collared coat, with his hands bound behind his back. His jaw was clenched tight in a quiet fury and spoke only to answer direct questions. He identified himself as Grand Duke Alexei Mikhailovich.

"A flaming Russian prince!" exclaimed Sergeant Bishop.

"'Iron lungs' Mikhailovich?" said Roxborough. Answering his own question he struck the man in the chest with the grip of his pistol. There was a muffled metallic clang beneath the grand duke's coat.

Roxborough shook his head. "This man was cousin to the late Tsar Alexander III. I think that makes him related to our own dear Queen."

"So we can't kill him?" said Bishop.

Roxborough, gun hanging loosely in his hand, seemed to give the notion some serious thought before holstering his weapon. "He lives," he said. "As long as he gives us no cause to change our minds. What were you doing out here anyway?"

"A geographical survey," said the grand duke in clear English.

76

Roxborough ordered the two surviving Pathan sepoys, the sly-eyed Wazir and a heavy-set fellow by the name of Inzar Gul, to scout the way ahead while the remaining troops salvaged their lost gear. Sergeant Bishop asked the major if they could have some time to search for comrades trapped and possibly still alive beneath the snow. Roxborough was indifferent.

"We move on with or without them. I want us back on the trail within the hour."

Captain Walton approached, wiping another man's blood from his hands with snow "We are not going on," he said.

"You spoke, captain?" said Roxborough.

"Sir. We have lost nine men. Our entire baggage team is dead or fled. We have encountered a platoon of the *Lieb Guard Jäger* battalion barely fifty miles from Gyantse. We have wounded men. Private Fuller cannot walk. And we have a prisoner of great value. Your Highness." Captain Walton acknowledged the grand duke with a bow. In the circumstances the gesture was faintly ridiculous and the Russian returned naught but a stony glare in reply. "It is obvious that we must search for survivors and then return to make our report."

"Obvious?" said Roxborough. "You are, of course, saying you know better than me?"

"Sir, I offer you clear-headed advice. Heed it."

Roxborough stared up at the cloud-wreathed mountaintops for a while and I could see his anger pulsing through his face. "Here is what will be done," he said at last. "You, captain, along with the wounded private and your little bunkmate, take charge of our prisoner and take him to the colonel."

"Colonel Younghusband made me second in command for a reason. This mission does not continue without me. Besides, Fuller *cannot* walk."

"Then, as our sawbones it is your role to put him out of his misery. Laudanum or a bullet, I do not care."

Captain Walton trembled but with what emotions I could not say. "Sergeant," he said, quietly.

"Sir!" replied Bishop.

"Search for your men and for our lost supplies. Take your time."

77

"Captain..." growled Roxborough.

"I have a patient to *treat*, sir," said the captain. "This conversation is not over."

I followed the captain dutifully, seeing a grimly amused smirk on the Russian prince's face as I went.

While Captain Walton sewed up Fuller's leg and Sergeant Bishop directed the search for survivors, I gathered the recovered supplies and sorted through them. Whether it was up or down the mountain, the British had no pack-bearers but myself, and I could not carry tents, equipment and food for nineteen men (twenty, counting the captured Grand Duke). I surreptitiously set aside a smaller pile for Walton, Fuller and myself, because I could see no breaking of the impasse between the captain and the major.

However, that matter changed when the two sepoys returned in an unlikely manner. They were heralded by an eerie growl, like many low voices humming in chorus. Everyone looked up and several rifles were raised in alarm. The noise came from a line of six small engines mounted on caterpillar tracks, chained together in a train with a long but narrow carriage at the rear from which Inzar Gul steered the whole by means of a long pair of reins feeding through hoops atop each engine. The engines, each the size of a clothes trunk, were self-powered, six little funnels releasing fine puffs of grey smoke. I had not seen such a thing before; there was something both amusing and disturbing about the vehicle. I could not decide if it resembled a monstrous black centipede, or the eager pack of huskies it was no doubt designed to emulate.

"What is this?" called out Roxborough cheerfully.

"The Russians' transport, sir," replied Inzar Gul. He pulled on the reins and drew the whole train to a halt. "There are four of them half a mile up the mountain."

Roxborough gave Grand Duke Mikhailovich a questioning look; the Russian said nothing. The men, now nearing the end of any fruitful search (in which no further survivors were found) crowded round the curious transport.

"And look at this, sir," said Inzar Gul, brandishing a long-barrelled weapon of bright steel and toughened glass. Its bore was a flat oval into which I could have slid my entire hand.

"Is this the weapon that sliced our men in two?" he asked the Grand Prince.

Alexei Mikhailovich said nothing.

Roxborough took the weapon from the sepoy and toyed with its trigger and the other confusing controls on its side, all to no avail. "How does it work?" he demanded.

"There is no more ammunition," said the grand duke. "It will not work."

Roxborough cursed and tossed the weapon back to Inzar Gul. "Never mind. We have the transport and that is all we require." He turned to call to Captain Walton. "Captain, you can save your bullet. Put Fuller on the back of this carriage. We'll load ourselves and our gear onto the others. Fortune has smiled on us."

Captain Walton approached his commanding officer. "Sir," he said calmly, "I would ask that you still reconsider this course of action."

Roxborough nodded slowly. "I understand your reticence; your fear."

"I am not afraid, sir."

"Good. Then get to it."

Captain Walton just about managed to say "sir" before wheeling away and shouting at me to help him move Private Fuller.

5.

I rarely marvel at the devices men make, for nine times out of ten they are tools of oppression rather than emancipation. However, the Russians' steam sleds were remarkably suited to the terrain we faced, allowing us to cover more than forty miles in the next two days. With four men to a sled, the only challenge we truly faced was keeping our inactive bodies warm in the increasingly inhospitable climate.

The snow came down in gusts and swirls and the path was invisible to all except the sled drivers, who were issued with the only Michelson-Morley goggles we possessed. Shapes appeared and vanished in the air. I thought I perceived high peaks ahead of us at one time but they vanished from sight. Figures and forms slunk alongside the train; yet these amorphous mountain men were also naught but illusion. For the most part, I hunkered down in the back of the sled with Captain Walton and Private Fuller, helping the captain administer Fuller with regular doses of laudanum and Salvarsan and listening to Fuller's rambling, drug-addled recollections of growing up in the city of Bristol.

By the afternoon of the sixth day, Roxborough and Walton concluded that we were within five miles of their destination, however the encompassing blizzard and vertiginous terrain made further progress hazardous. The resourceful Inzar Gul located a large narrow-mouthed cave in which the whole party could shelter. With some assistance, Private Fuller hobbled into the cave, where we sat him by one of the Ever-Heat stoves warming and illuminating the space.

I was placed on kitchen duty, involving little more than doling out portions of bully beef and hardtack and making tea from melted snow. Roxborough would not permit Grand Duke Mikhailovich's bonds to be loosened and so I fed him myself, spooning crumbs of beef from the tin plate into his less than grateful mouth.

"Your mechanical lungs," I said. "I've heard it said that you can hold your breath for over five minutes."

The grand duke mushed his lips together and said, in Russian, "Your food tastes like s___." Mikhailovich had been placed at the deepest part of the cave and, although Wazir was notionally guarding the Russian, he was still out of earshot.

"I would not feed this to my dog," I agreed with a smile, also in Russian.

The grand duke stared at me, chewing. "Ten minutes, not five," he said, eventually.

"Extraordinary," I said.

"They are extraordinarily heavy," he agreed. "If I fell into water, I would sink like a ship's anchor."

"What are you doing in Tibet?" I asked.

"Will no one believe that I was simply exploring? Seeing the wonders of the world for myself?"

"With a platoon of heavily armed soldiers?"

"The imperial household likes to protect its own."

80

"You lied to the major," I said. "Those weapons of yours work, don't they?"

He smiled. I remember thinking that he had a fine smile, the kind a fool could fall in love with. "It's a teleforce ray," he said. "Invented by one of *our* scientists – a Serbian, would you believe it, and a deserter from the Austro-Hungarian army to boot! – it fires a stream of tiny tungsten missiles at over thirty-six thousand miles per hour by means of electrostatic repulsion."

"Impossible," I said.

He shrugged as well as any man with his hands tied behind his back. "When I was nineteen years old, they told me that my tuberculosis was incurable, that I would be dead within months. There was no hope for me. And then the doctors in San Remo replaced my lungs with this contraption and my life was saved. Are you going to tell me what is possible?" His eyes looked through and past me and, in that moment, I saw not a prince, or a Russian soldier, but a young man who was far from home and living a life he could not have imagined or expected.

I placed my hand on his iron-cased chest, feeling its solidity through his coat. "And your heart," I said. "Could your armour deflect the path of an assassin's bullet or—?"

I stopped. The grand duke's gaze had returned from its distant wanderings and now fixed on me. For one wonderful, awful second, I utterly misread his expression.

"Take your hands off me, *svoloch*," he said vehemently.

"I'm sorry," I said, snatching my hand away, embarrassed.

"I have had enough of your food and your impertinence, boy."

I turned away and hurried up the cave, collecting the troops' plates and mugs as I went. I cleaned them with snow and stored them away before curling up silently by the cave wall alongside Captain Walton.

"Are you all right, lad?" he asked.

"Fine. Just tired, sir," I said but I could not keep the unhappiness from my voice.

"Nitish?" he said.

"Just tired," I repeated.

Captain Walton shuffled over and placed his hand on my upmost shoulder. He sat like that until I fell asleep.

Seventeen of us descended into the valley the next day, abandoning our steam-sleds. A lance corporal and the recumbent Private Fuller remained in the cave to guard the grand duke. Roaring winds battered us, alternately pinning us to the slope or threatening to pitch us off. However there was little snow in the air and, after an hour of walking, we were able to see our destination clearly. In the shadow of the mountain opposite, on a large plug of rock edged by deep chasms, was a complex building of incredible size.

"Look!" exclaimed Roxborough, pointing out that which we could not fail to see.

Behind high white walls towered square block buildings, arranged in step-like ranks. Their wide roofs swept out to enormous horned gables and fat cylindrical towers. At the very base of the wall stood a tall double gateway capped by an enormous carved lintel. A stone bridge, twenty feet wide and twice as long, ran across the chasm separating us from the entrance. The buildings were undeniably old, but they were no ruins. The roofs had not caved in. No walls had collapsed. They appeared as sturdy and whole as any mountain fortress; although I felt the whole had more of the temple or monastery about it than it did castle.

We gazed down on that magnificent sight for uncounted seconds. Only when the snow and cloud began to descend, threatening to shroud our view, did Roxborough stir his men into action: demanding they unpack the box camera brought to document their findings. Private Yates, the appointed daguerreotypist, exposed plate after plate, using the camera's telescopic lens to capture the finer details. I longed to take just one image with my own camera but I was forced to keep it hidden.

"Look at the relief carvings by the gateway," said Roxborough. "I have seen stylised deer-creatures like those on Mesopotamian pieces in the British Museum. So much for Younghusband's cynicism!"

I have had the privilege of seeing the ancient temples of Mars (which are not temples at all) and the sense of wonder and foreboding I felt at that moment was a grim reminder of those dark edifices. I said nothing, nor was my opinion sought but, on Mars, many had seen similarities in the writings and art of disparate cultures where truly there were none. The closest Roxborough got to any agreement was a grunt from Sergeant Bishop, a man who possibly didn't even know what a relief carving was.

"Sir!" yelled Private Yates. "Down there. I saw movement."

"What did you see?" said Captain Walton.

Yates shook his head at himself. "Men. All in white furs." He looked again through the camera's viewfinder, even though the snow had come down on the valley and the buildings were practically invisible to us. Slowly he straightened. "I am sure I did."

"How many men?" said Captain Walton. "Were they Russians?"

"I couldn't say," said Yates.

"Well, they will not stop us reaching our prize," said Roxborough and at once led us on a hasty descent towards the bridge and the temple.

We reached the bottom in a ragged line. Whilst the mountain skies bellowed distantly above those in the lead, they were at least sheltered from the worst of the winds; the obscuring snow meant that those of us towards the rear of the line could barely see the front. When a shout rippled back down the line that *they* were not men, I had no clue as to what was meant.

Roxborough ordered the soldiers to fix bayonets and I ran with the other stragglers to re-join the group. A row of men had already taken up rifle positions on bended knee and a second, standing rank, was forming behind. I realised that the roaring I could hear was not merely from the stormy skies above. Out on the bridge were more than a dozen figures, white and furred as Yates had said.

I was instantly put in mind of the Sumatran Orang Utan which I have glimpsed in the wild. These creatures had the jungle ape's shaggy aspect, powerful arms and large faces. However, these ape-men stood taller, on bowed legs in the manner of a chimpanzee, and there was a glowering and ugly intelligence in their eyes which was disconcertingly human (reminding me very much of the Portuguese smuggler who had helped me to escape from Phobos last year).

"Yeti," I gasped.

The creatures puffed out their chests, bellowed and flung their arms about. They advanced to the edge of their bridge, baring their teeth, and then scuttled back to safety. I had seen the exact same behaviour before in wild apes.

"They're trying to scare us off," said Captain Walton, mirroring my thoughts.

Roxborough drew his pistol and fired a shot above the creatures' heads. The yeti screamed and fled a little way before mustering. One of them picked up a chunk of cracked masonry from the parapet and flung it with such ease and apparent lack of consideration that we did not appreciate the immediate danger. The rock struck one of the front rank privates squarely on the forehead, killing him.

Roxborough took more than a second or two to collect his wits. When he did, he ordered the men to open fire, rank after rank. Three or four of the yeti went down in the first volley. Others remained upright, some sustaining wounds that would have felled a man. The yeti, retreating back along the bridge, threw further stones, some as large as their heads, and more than one missile found its target.

"To the rear!" warned Captain Walton.

I turned to see another band of the ape-men loping down the mountainside towards us.

"To the bridge!" yelled Roxborough. "Charge!"

The men leapt up and advanced, shooting as they ran. Several of the surviving yeti met with them on the bridge, succumbing to bullet and bayonet. One grabbed the arm of the soldier who had impaled it and, with an effortless motion, flung the poor man over the parapet and into the chasm below. I do not know how deep the chasm was, but the man's trailing scream sounded endless.

Another scream from behind told me that the second group of yeti were on us. With the bridge parapets guarding our flanks, the men of the First Somerset Regiment formed two lines, front and rear, and resumed ordered firing. One yeti crashed through the ranks, dashing a man's head against the ground but the lines held. Within a minute, all of the beasts lay dead or dying.

After a prolonged, nervous silence, Bishop was the first to speak. "Why did they attack us? What had we done to them?"

"Just defending their territory," said Wazir.

"I'm not so sure," said Captain Walton. "It felt as though they were trying to warn us of—" He did not finish his sentence but that in itself articulated the unease I too was beginning to feel about the place.

"There's a light inside," said Inzar Gul, pointing into the huge gateway at the base of the temple wall.

I looked, narrowing my eyes against the distracting glare of the snow and the white stone. I was on the point of rejecting his claim when I saw it: a pale anaemic light, green in colour, shimmering in the dark distance.

"We go inside," said Roxborough. "Inzar Gul, you lead. Shingler and McElwee, you are the rear guard. Keep your eyes open."

And so the ten of us who remained moved through a doorway built for giants and into the darkened interior of the temple.

7.

It was only now, by the light of the soldiers' galvanic torches, that I had the chance to view properly the architecture and artistry of this mysterious building. Much of the stonework was crumbling and worn, in places run through with the petrified remains of some creeping vines, an inexplicable sight in this frigid region. Roxborough was once more keen to point out the wall carvings: the humans caught in poses of supplication and meditation, the long-necked ruminants, the flower-tailed birds and the bountiful trees. He prattled on, comparing them to Indus Valley artefacts, Minoan pottery and Babylonian friezes but not one man in his party was interested; all either awestruck by the encounter with the mountain apes or downcast by the loss of their comrades. Besides, I felt Roxborough's excitement made him blind to the scale of this place, that the proportions were far greater than those of any other ancient site throughout the world. As I gazed up at the cold almond eyes of a giant statue fifty feet above me, I could not shake the fear, despite the evidence of my senses, that these halls and chambers were beyond the building skills of any pre-industrial civilisation.

Such was my disquieted fascination that I had failed to notice the party was moving on. Captain Walton took a guiding hold of my elbow. "Come on, Nitish. No need to be afraid."

I nodded and on we went, with the two privates cautiously bringing up the rear.

The pale green light grew as we approached; soon enough we passed through another colossal archway and into a narrower but even higher chamber. Above us, the storeys rose, tier on balconied tier, to a belfry-like level that, judging by the skeins of fine snow and the distant fluting of wind high above us, was open to the elements.

The floor was primarily taken up by a square pool of water and it was from this well that the green glow emanated. I stared into the pool, looking for a source of the light, but I could see none; besides, staring into that liquid caused an inexplicable queasiness.

The soldiers spread out around the side of the pool: Yates setting up the camera to take more images, whilst more prudent types, such as Inzar Gul and Wazir, took up positions in the corners, rifles at the ready. Sergeant Bishop's foot caught against something: a shallow metal bowl attached to one wall by a chain. As the metallic clatter echoed about the chamber, Roxborough's attention was caught by some decidedly different carvings on one wall. They were not, I imagined, created by the temple builders, but scratched into the soft stone by later, less skilful hands: works of ancient vandalism.

Roxborough ran his hands over a triangular arrangement of vertical lines. "You see this?" he said, beckoning Captain Walton over. "One mark. Then one and one. Then one, two, one."

Captain Walton nodded. "Binomial coefficients."

"Yang Hui's triangle," I said.

"Pascal's triangle," said Roxborough curtly, attempting to correct me. "Tell me, boy, do you know what this is?" He was pointing further along at some etchings, made in a different, more considered manner.

"It looks like Vedic Sanskrit," I said.

"*Very* good," he said, as though he was the schoolmaster and I his pupil. "And what does it say?"

"It *looks* like Vedic Sanskrit," I said, "but it isn't."

He made a disappointed noise in his throat. "It is as if the men who came here felt compelled to leave a mark of their wisdom and knowledge on the walls. Look here ... and there. What could it mean?"

Captain Walton set down his pack, removed his doctor's case and took out a bottle of surgical spirits. I crouched down beside him. "What are you doing?" I asked.

"Taking a sample," he replied, emptying the spirits onto the stones and then reaching into the pool to re-fill the bottle with the luminescent water.

"I do not like this place," I said, quiet enough for only him to hear.

He looked about, appraising the place for himself. "Nor do I, Nitish, if I'm perfectly honest." He gave me a smile that he likely thought comforting. "Chin up, lad. We'll be out of here soon enough."

"Of course!" exclaimed Roxborough from the far side of the pool.

We looked up in time to see the major bend over the edge of the pool and cup a little of the water in one hand.

"Don't!" shouted Captain Walton. "We know nothing about this stuff!"

"But it's obvious," said the major. "The well. The chalice." He flicked away the water in his hand and picked up the metal bowl instead. Dragging it the full extent of its chain, he dipped it in the pool and drank.

"There may be elements in the water, sir," said Captain Walton. "Poisons."

"Look at the writings." Roxborough gestured to the scratches on the wall. "Early languages. Simple but brilliant mathematics. Men did not come here to share their wisdom; they came here to receive it."

"I do not understand," said Captain Walton, although I grasped the major's meaning clearly enough.

"The wellspring of human civilisation!" declared the major. "Who knew it would be so literal?"

"Sir?" called Bishop. "Sorry, to interrupt but—" The sergeant gestured upwards. I raised my gaze.

Over the past minutes, the sounds of the snowstorm outside had become punctuated by several thunderous booms and the wind (or so I'd thought) taken on a low keening tone. Now, I saw my error. In the galleries above, a number of the white ape-men had gathered: it was their soft moans I could hear. Their manner was no longer hostile, but still, watchful and sombre.

"Order to fire?" asked Bishop.

"No," said Roxborough. "Of course not. Can you not see that they have come to pay homage to this moment?"

"I'm afraid you're babbling, sir," said Captain Walton.

Roxborough gave his captain a savage grin, condescending and merciless. He leapt into the pool and waded to its centre. In response, the mournful vocalisations of the yeti rose in pitch and volume. We nine humans and the audience of yetis watched Roxborough shed his outer garments and plunge his head into the waters to drink.

"He's lost 'is marbles," whispered one of the privates. I could not disagree.

Roxborough stood erect, his face and hair dripping. There seemed to be a change to his aspect which I first put down to the light shining up at him from the waters. "Look at our ape forebears," he cried. "Cave creatures. We were once like them. Wild, dull in wit and spirit. And then one day, one of them came down to this pool—"

Something was happening to Roxborough's outstretched hands. As though the water was leeching the flesh from them, drawing the fingers out into slender wands. A similar transformation was overtaking his face. Slowly but certainly, Roxborough's cheeks grew hollow, his skin taking on a moon-like paleness. The major seemed entirely unconcerned.

"And so man was raised up from the apes, an act of instant transmutation. Not just physically." Roxborough laughed, his mouth shrunken, his teeth reduced to square pegs. "I can feel the knowledge settling on me like a mantle. I can see truth. Facts long forgotten are returning to me. My old Latin lessons. Science with Professor Flowers. But more than that ... I know more than those fools now."

"Sir," said Captain Walton, "I really think you should get out of there. I fear for your health."

"You fear change!" cried Roxborough. "You fear greatness! Man was raised up from the animals in this spring. This is his Eden, this the Tree of Knowledge. Raised up he was, then over the ages degenerated into the timid and weak specimens you have become. You—!" He aimed a spindly finger at me. "You belong up there with the apes. Your degenerate race, how far you have fallen!"

Impossible though it seemed, Roxborough had also grown in height. His entire body was attenuated, made thin and tall and pale. As he flung his insults at me, I backed away. Yes, I was afraid; my hand instinctively went inside my jacket and curled around the grip of the Webley automatic. Several of the soldiers also regarded their transformed commanding officer with fear or distrust. While the likes of Yates dithered, caught in a situation they could not comprehend, I noticed that Sergeant Bishop and the two Pathans had their weapons aimed at the major, casually and innocuously, but aimed nonetheless.

The yetis maintained their pitiful moaning and the thunder punctuated each moment with its dull booms. Roxborough reached down with translucent hands and drank from the pool once more.

"Please stop," said Captain Walton.

"You cannot tell me anything, captain," said Roxborough, shedding clothes that no longer fitted him. "My mind is expanded, opening doors to dusty rooms long since closed. Yes, I can see with the mind's eye, awakened like the *bodhisattvas*—" He groaned suddenly and doubled up.

"What are we to do, captain?" called Bishop, his tone making it clear that, in his opinion, the major was dead to them.

"We get the major out of there and we leave."

Roxborough straightened, a drawn out "No—!" emanating from his throat. Upright, more than ten feet high, he glared at Captain Walton. In the centre of Roxborough's brow a third eye opened: a glowing vertical slit.

"No one is leaving," he snarled.

8.

"Epiphany upon epiphany," sang the thing that had once been Roxborough. "We are not from this world." He pointed up at the spire above. "From the heavens, from Altair, the flying eagle. This well is all that remains of the Great Emissary."

"What do you mean?" said Captain Walton.

"The divine spark within us all, the eternal spirit. It comes to us, a gift from—" Roxborough reached upward, his two human eyes closed but the obscene third orb in his forehead wide and blazing.

"I cannot reach her. She is too far. Lost..." He drew his arms down wearily and opened his human eyes. "But your puny minds are like low-hanging fruit, easily reached, easily peeled." He gazed at Captain Walton and chuckled. "Oh," he said, playfully. "The little invert with a wormy mind of dark desires."

"Enough now!" shouted Captain Walton. "Step out of the pool, sir! Enough, I say! You have drunk too deeply!"

"Never enough," tittered the Roxborough-creature. "I can reach out to anyone..." He closed his eyes briefly. "To Colonel Younghusband in his bed in Gyantse, for example. Let me sprinkle his dreams with truths beyond reckoning."

Captain Walton was silently gesturing for Sergeant Bishop and the rest of the men to join him at the pool-side nearest the entrance. The mute instruction was noticed by Roxborough.

"I can hear every insubordinate thought in your head, captain. You think I am poisoned. And sergeant, I know full well what you would like to do with that rifle. Do not. And as for—" Roxborough broke off as his gaze swung across me. "Treacherous sow!" he hissed.

I swore loudly in Hindi and drew my pistol. I was not fast enough. With a speed belying his size, Roxborough leapt to the edge of the pool, grabbing my wrist with fingers as cold and slick as dead fish. Brutally, he twisted my arm. Screaming with pain, I was forced to drop my gun.

"Shoot him!" shouted Captain Walton. Several of the soldiers complied at once.

Roxborough released me as the shots struck home. Great gobbets of bloodless flesh blasted from his chest and shoulders, wounds that would have killed a man. But Roxborough had become something far from human; the attacks only enraged him, triggering an even greater transformation.

It occurred to me, as I lay massaging feeling back into my injured wrist and struggling to regain scattered wits, that with each passing moment, Roxborough was increasingly taking on the properties of the water in which he stood. His glowing body was no longer merely pale but semi-transparent like that of a jellyfish. He was losing his form as he grew, becoming amorphous, boneless even. He was now less a man and more a liquid yearning for human form.

The shifting creature (which was still nonetheless recognisably Roxborough) arched backwards, his spine curved like a rainbow and, with a swelling fist, swatted Sepoy Wazir against a stone wall. The man died instantly, bones pulverised. The creature simultaneously smacked the weapons from the hands of several others, pitching one poor private, who would not relinquish his rifle, into the pool.

I picked up my pistol and joined Sergeant Bishop and Captain Walton in firing at Roxborough, though little good it seemed to do us.

"Barbarians at the gates," spat Roxborough wetly. "You cannot hurt me." His human eyes were nothing more than black pinpricks in the jellied folds of his head. Conversely, the wet and luminous orb at the centre of his forehead was so engorged that it strained the lids which enclosed it, threatening to burst free. I felt the regard of that obscene third eye and I fell to my knees at once. I can barely articulate the feel of Roxborough's attack on my mind. I was overwhelmed by a powerful nausea, composed of and amplified by a deep-rooted comprehension of my own inherent worthlessness which, imposed though it was by Roxborough's rapacious thoughts, felt utterly – utterly! – deserved.

Through dimming vision I saw the other soldiers struck down similarly: Bishop clutching at his temples, screaming silently, Captain Walton curled up as though stabbed in the gut. The only soldier not attacked in this way was the poor private who had fallen in the pool: drawn up inside Roxborough's gelatinous torso, writhing slowly, bug-eyed, as he drowned in the creature's innards.

Darkness closed over me; I was alone in blackness, where only the dulled echoes of the wind and thunder could reach me. I was grist to Roxborough's mental mill; his enveloping mass pressed upon me, bleeding into me. I began to lose myself in the incoherent imagery of Roxborough's thoughts.

Weightless and bodiless, I saw myself lifted up into the æther of deep space, dangled beneath the black and infinite depths. The scattered stars were tiny points of harsh light, distant and uncomforting. Below me stretched the airless surface of an alien world: the fourth planet of the star Altair. On a flat, featureless plain reared a vast construction of stone, its multiple, serpentine limbs twisting like roots across hundreds of miles of grey, frozen earth. At the confluence of the limbs, at the highest point of the monstrous structure, was a round lake, green and glowing., Somehow I knew this was the origin point of the liquid in the Tibetan temple. Just as I knew that the construction was a place of worship and pilgrimage, although it was neither building nor monument, its full purpose and alien geometry beyond my human understanding.

For aeons, it had been abandoned, the priesthood dead or gone. All was still. Except, once every millennia, movement stirred that well of strange light and a fat liquid missile would be ejected into the wilds of space, instantly frozen as it began its journey across the cosmos. I came to realise that the vast thing beneath me was a sentient being of unknowable power; a spirit being of the ancient world. It was one of the *asuras*, the powerful anti-gods who fought against the *devas*, the true gods of my people. The structure below me was simultaneously anti-god, temple and monument constructed in honour of itself; a world-spanning starfish deity, alive yet made, constructed yet older than its worshippers. And, as I looked on repugnantly at its splayed limbs, I knew that this was no *asura* but an *asuri*: an anti-goddess. The green water was her spawn, spat into the aether in a desperate attempt to seed and possess far off worlds.

I found myself on Earth and this very peak in Tibet, thousands of years before my own time. A white-haired ape man was crouched over the waters, lapping at its surface. As he drank, a subtle change came over the creature. If these visions were indeed true, then Roxborough's monstrous worldview was correct. The ape-man, now straight-backed and with a changed countenance, was the ancestor of us all. From this time and place, our first human ancestors – the 'great' civilisation of old – spread across the world. I would have gagged had I any connection to my own body; humanity was nothing but an ape-creature raised up by the transmuting spawn of the vile *asuri*. In my horror, I felt I could hear the echoes of the unholy hymns which the *asuri* had once received from her faithful. Those hymns were in my blood, in all our blood, an alien stain on our souls!

I heard something new: a vaguely familiar whining sound. The booms of thunder, far louder than they should be, returned to my ears. There were further whines and an inhuman scream. A voice shouted: "Get up, *svoloch*, or I will leave you here!"

I opened my eyes – I could open my eyes! – and cried out at the return to the real, the inrush of sensation. I lifted my head with difficulty.

Roxborough, larger and more inhuman than ever, was rearing up in pain and anger. At the base of his legless torso stood Grand Duke Alexei Mikhailovich, the wide-bored and clearly functional teleforce weapon in his hands. As the weapon whined, a stream of inconceivably fast projectiles tore a line through Roxborough's body, slicing away an arm and part of his engorged head. Yet as fast at the Russian prince cut the monster apart, it was rebuilding itself: pseudo-limbs of jelly leaping out to catch the severed flesh and reattach it. Mikhailovich's actions were, at best, merely distracting Roxborough's attention from the rest of us.

I staggered to my feet and helped Captain Walton to do the same. Sergeant Bishop and Inzar Gul were already up and trying to rouse the remaining men. Private McElwee was drawn up in a corner, wide-eyed and screaming, refusing to heed anyone's attempts to stir him.

I grew aware that the ground beneath my feet was trembling, a heavy dust falling down on us along with the drifting snow. Before I could ask what was going on there was a loud concussive sound, not at all distant, and the floor rocked beneath us.

"We must go!" yelled the grand duke.

"They're a day early!" Captain Walton was comically indignant.

I understood, automatically looking up to a sky I could not see: the *Gloriana* platform and its eighteen-hundred pound gun, aimed directly at us. The mind has only a finite capacity for fear: it must either yield or deal in priorities. The horror of the Roxborough-creature and its revelatory visions had almost overwhelmed me; now our imminent deaths from orbital artillery was the spur which goaded me to conscious action.

Captain Walton and I were nearest the exit and I yelled out to the other men to flee with us. Bishop, Shingler and Yates skirted the walls to reach us. Inzar Gul was a short distance behind, having given up on coaxing the catatonic McElwee out of his corner and resorted to knocking the man out and carrying him across his shoulders. Inzar Gul staggered and almost fell as another shell blasted the temple, casting dust and pieces of masonry down from the chamber's spire. It was only then that I realised the yeti had disappeared from their positions above, run off to safety or their doom.

Pieces of stonework knifed through the Roxborough-creature, barely slowing as they passed through the viscous body; but neither did they hinder it. The grand prince began his own retreat, maintaining a stream of fire. Only then did Roxborough perceive we were escaping: the thing reared furiously and lurched from the pool.

"Run!" shouted the grand duke.

We fled, as fast as the uneven ground and our injuries would allow. Roxborough's inhuman bellow behind us was abruptly cut off by another blast. The floor heaved and an irresistible compression wave threw us forward. I rolled with the blow, coming to my feet. Through the archway I saw only a deep crater and blocks of collapsing masonry. The pool was gone and Roxborough with it, the 'great' man blown to the four winds by the explosion.

The grand duke shoved me onward. "We are not safe yet!" he snarled.

"Why did you come for us?"

"I told you," he replied. "To see the wonders of the world."

A slab of stone larger than a church altar tipped out of its position on the wall above us. It fell on Private Yates, crushing him and his box camera before we could even cry a warning.

"Before they're destroyed," added the grand prince.

Six of us sped on towards the snow-bright exit (McElwee still unconscious on Inzar Gul's back). The halls around us were falling; slowly, but with a great creaking inevitability. If not for the petrified vines holding some of the stones in place, we might never have made it.

Out into cold freedom we ran. Great plumes of smoke and dust from artillery shells were visible across the length of the valley. Off to my left I saw part of the great wall come down, spilling gargantuan chunks of stone into the chasm before us. The bridge was still there (I had feared it would not be) but it was damaged: partially collapsed along one side.

Sergeant Bishop led the way across. Inzar Gul, coming up behind, stumbled and fell perilously close to the edge. Captain Walton hauled McElwee from him and, with stones slipping away beneath their feet, all three pressed on to the far side. However, their scrambling had dislodged something vital: sections of the bridge gave way. Next to me, Private Shingler cried out as the ground fell from beneath him. I grabbed his arm but my own footing was no firmer. As I began to fall, I looked down at Shingler and beyond: to a dark-edged chasm without end.

My fall was arrested by strong hands grasping my free wrist. I was swung sideways and driven against jutting bridge supports. The impact was so great that I blacked out for moment, letting go of Shingler's arm. He – thank God – had taken a firm hold of my sleeves. When I came to, a searing pain across my breast, he was still there, holding on for dear life. With my chest aflame and the weight of myself and Private Shingler tearing at my arms and back, I could do little except pray that whoever held us had the strength to pull us to safety. I could not look up at our would-be saviour without tearing every tendon in my neck. My gaze flickered between Shingler's terrified face and the rocks tumbling past him into the abyss.

"I have you," called the grand duke. Captain Walton also cried something. There were others at the lip of the collapsed bridge, hauling us up, close to tearing my arms from their sockets as they lifted us to safety. Someone reached beyond me and raised Shingler. The release on my limbs brought a whole new pain; I coughed and spat in agony. I was dragged onto solid ground and, lain down in the snow, tried to regain my breath.

The pain in my upper torso was excruciating. With a hand that barely obeyed my instructions I felt for injuries. Clothes shifted wetly under my touch. Feeling my gorge rise, I raised my head to see. Blood was seeping through the layers.

"Nitish," said Captain Walton, kneeling beside me. There was a tender worry in his eyes.

"I might be hurt," I whispered. It was the last thing I recall saying before slipping into unconsciousness.

9.

I awoke in the cave in which we had sheltered the night before: lying on my back with two thick blankets over me and an Ever-Heat stove by my side. Across from me, illuminated by the stove's orange glow, sat Private Shingler. He watched me, a small but insistent smile on his face as though he had discovered that life was a joke but that the punchline was one of the best.

"You all right, love?" he said.

My throat was too dry to speak, but I just about managed a nod. His smile widened a little and he winked at me before returning to nibbling a piece of hardtack he was holding. I saw, placed neatly at his side, my Webley automatic and my stereoscopic camera. Only then did I realise that, beneath the blankets, my torso was naked apart from a wide bandage dressing across my chest.

Captain Walton came along the cave and crouched beside me; Shingler shifting aside.

"How are you feeling?" the captain asked, a stiff formality in his voice.

"Water?" I managed to croak.

He produced a canteen and carefully poured some into my mouth. I swallowed, coughed a little and nodded. "It only hurts," I said. "How many survived?"

"The sergeant, Shingler and Inzar Gul here. We have McElwee dosed up with morphine. He screams whenever he awakes and will not stop. And, of course, Private Fuller and Lance Corporal Hind were waiting for us here, nursing sore heads and the general embarrassment of having let His Highness escape their custody."

"And the prince?" I asked.

"He has gone. Taken one of his sleds with him. We were in no position to stop him." He cleared his throat. "And I suppose now is the time for our formal, *honest* introductions, miss." There was a cold, sad look in the good captain's eyes.

"My name is Mina," I said. "Mina Saxena."

"Ah, the seditionist. I have heard of you. I thought you were on Mars."

"I left in a hurry."

"So, not some honest country girl run away to play soldier with the men."

"Sorry," I said.

"I suppose you are pleased with this disastrous outcome." His voice rose with emotion. "Twenty good Englishmen dead..."

I shook my head. "I am pleased you survived. All else is tragedy." The answer seemed to do little to console him. "I have nothing but admiration for men like you, captain," I added.

He stood, hasty to be away from me, unwilling to meet my eye.

"Please," I said. "I have to know something."

"What?" he said gruffly.

"The sample you took from the pool..."

"What of it?"

"Do you still have it? Was it lost?"

"What do you care?"

"It's dangerous stuff. What it did to the major..."

"I am not the major," he said.

"No," I agreed. "You are not."

He turned his back to me but paused before he went. "I liked Nitish," he said.

I raised my head as best I could and watched him walk to the cave entrance, where he stood, staring at the blizzard and the shapeless forms the snow conjured; the things that were not there.

1905 – The Bridge to Lemuria

From the memoirs of Mr J. Cadwallander

1.

In all my travels, from the depths of the Pacific Ocean to the cold airless void of the fourth superætheric plane, I have in general found no more comforting sight than that of the British bobby about his duties. The policeman, raised from his working class roots and made literate and noble by our fine education system, only armed and armoured with his pressed uniform, his galvanic truncheon and his innate English sense of honesty and decency, was our best line of defence against everything that might threaten Queen and country.

However, as our horse-drawn cab drew up outside Professor Morrow's townhouse in Cambridge, directly across the street from the Great Gate of Trinity College, the sight of two police constables standing on guard before the house's open door was a most disquieting one. A small crowd of onlookers had gathered on the pavement.

Professor Erskine Sedgewick leaned forward on the brass lion's head of his cane to better look past me. "This does not bode well, Cadwallander," said he.

I readily agreed, stepped out and held the door for the great man. As I paid the cabbie, Sedgewick spoke to the two constables. I have previously noted that Sedgewick, despite being a man of middle years, had no physical need for his cane. It was my private theory that he carried it as a monarch might carry a sceptre: an unofficial symbol of his status as one of the most respected gentlemen in all England. As he spoke, Sedgewick punctuated each point with a gesture of his cane, seizing the men's attention much as a mesmerist with his dangling pocket watch.

Whatever he might have said, it did the trick, for one of the constables, with a servile tug of his peaked helmet, led us into the hallway. Somewhere, in a distant room, there was the sound of a sobbing woman. On hands and knees, a constable worked his way along the carpeted floor, in his hand a humming device of clockwork bellows and bladders.

"Collecting infinitesimal material evidence," Sedgewick noted with solemn approval of modern policing methods. "We shall have to rely on our own eyes and ears, though."

I nodded my understanding, as a slight chap wearing a Homburg and chestnut gloves came out of the parlour to meet us. "Inspector Wilmarth," he said, shaking our hands with overly familiar enthusiasm. "It is a pleasure to meet you sirs. Did you know the professor well?"

Wilmarth's use of the past tense did not go unnoticed. "We were both Fellows of Trinity College," said Sedgewick. "We had adjacent rooms."

"He worked in a similar field to yourself?" said Wilmarth.

"I am a scholar of theology and natural sciences," said Sedgewick. "Professor Morrow was a noted ethnographer. Is his body still here?"

"We have yet to move him." Wilmarth gestured to the parlour door. "I should warn you that the professor died a violent and unpleasant death."

Sedgewick gave a curt nod and I followed him in.

Morrow's parlour was a riotous pæan to his own life's work. Beneath bell jars, in glass display cases, and arranged on the polished dresser and mantelpiece were masks, amulets, fetishes, carvings and idols from more than a dozen primitive cultures around the world. Hollow eyes and gargoyle faces gazed impassively down on Professor Flinders Morrow's body in the hearth. The poor fellow's throat was a slick and savage mess. A ragged pool of blood darkened the Axminster carpet around his head. A line of droplets ran up through the fireplace, across the mirror above it and even dotted the ceiling. Three feet from his body was an iron spearhead, no doubt one of his ethnographic finds and now the means by which he had been killed.

As I tactfully approached the body, Sedgewick silently assessed the scene. Eventually, he produced a folded letter from his pocket and passed it to Wilmarth. "I was invited to visit Professor Morrow this afternoon."

Wilmarth looked at the letter.

"It is not written in Morrow's hand," added Sedgewick.

"No," agreed Wilmarth, "and yet the housekeeper says you were expected."

There was a wooden statue in the hearth: an ugly thing carved from cracked wood. I could see the spot on the mantelpiece from where it had fallen. I crouched down to inspect it more closely.

"Another visitor arrived three hours ago," said Wilmarth. "A young woman, unchaperoned. She had no appointment but the professor agreed to meet her. They spoke at considerable length."

"What was the topic of conversation?" asked Sedgewick.

Wilmarth frowned. "The housekeeper is still in a hysterical state and we've yet to get much sense from her. She interrupted the professor and his visitor twice: once to bring tea, a second time to pass the professor a telegram. She has been unable to offer much other than that, apart from being quite clear that there were no other visitors or staff in the house all afternoon."

I picked up the idol in the hearth to see it better. It was clearly a representation of some living being but it was not human, nor even remotely so. It was a thing of writhing limbs and plant-like spirals. At its centre, in the place where a face might be, was a flowering protuberance of bulbous fronds, like an obscenely shaped jungle orchid. The twisting limbs and questing fronds were curved in such foul angles that, without conveying any specific meaning, they offended my sensibilities. The piece was simultaneously disgusting and fascinating.

"Excuse me, sir," said Wilmarth firmly. "We have yet to dust that item for dactylographs. Do not contaminate it with your own."

I placed the idol back on the hearth and then held out my right hand for Wilmarth to see. He looked at the burnished brass fingertips and the pneumatic joints of my hand. They gave off the tiniest clicks and hisses as I flexed them. "No fingerprints," I said.

"Of course," said Wilmarth, recalling. "You lost your hand in service to the crown."

"The whole arm," I said, rapping on my metal-sheathed shoulder. "May I?"

"Please," said Wilmarth.

I went back to looking at the hideous carving while Wilmarth continued his explanation to Sedgewick. "Ultimately, the housekeeper heard the sounds of an argument or a struggle: both Professor Morrow and the Indian woman. She rushed in and found Professor Morrow at the moment of his death, stood where he now lies, he and the woman both gripping the blade that killed him, his throat already cut open."

My eye was drawn to a piece of paper in the smouldering grate. I snagged it from the still-hot coals. It was a fragment of thin, lined paper. Written on it in pencil were four block capital letters: *MHHG*. The rest of the writing was burned away.

"The housekeeper ran out into the street," said Wilmarth, "and drew the attention of a passing constable. He came in and arrested the woman. I gather that she put up quite a struggle."

"You said she was an Indian woman?" said Sedgewick.

"Yes, but do not imagine some *dhobi wallah* wrapped up in a bedsheet, professor," said Wilmarth. "This woman was dressed as finely as any Englishwoman."

"What was her name?"

Inspector Wilmarth consulted his policeman's notebook. "Saxena. Mina Saxena."

Professor Sedgewick and I looked at one another. "We must speak to her at once," said the professor.

2.

Professor Sedgewick and I knew Mina Saxena well enough. We had met her in a dusty tomb of horrors beneath the deserts of Mars two years earlier, a gun in her hand and violent anti-colonialism on her mind. Although not fully acquainted with the seditious woman, we already considered her name to be synonymous with trouble.

Inspector Wilmarth willingly took us to the police station in Cambridge and down to the cells. Miss Saxena had refused to answer any of the questions put to her by Wilmarth's sergeant. Her appearance was a work of incongruity. I shall not say that one of Her Majesty's foreign subjects should be forbidden to follow British fashions but, on Miss Saxena, that elegant wasp-waisted dress, those elaborate curls of hair and that small green hat perched on her crown struck me as most improper, as did the sly smile she gave us as we stood before her cage-like cell. "Professor. Cadwallander. You received my invitation then?" she said.

"I don't believe we have been invited to attend a murder before," said Sedgewick without a note of humour.

Miss Saxena placed one hand on the bars which separated us. "I did not kill Flinders Morrow."

Inspector Wilmarth gave a scoffing laugh.

"You were alone in the room together," reasoned Sedgewick. "The housekeeper heard you struggle. You were seen with your hands on the murder weapon at the very instant of Professor Morrow's death." His voice took on a momentarily darker tone. "And he was a close acquaintance of mine."

"I know," she said. "I had invited you so that you might vouch for me. I needed Morrow's help."

Sedgewick gave her a querying look.

"In east India there is a village which was home to sixty-seven people of the Naga tribe," she said.

"Your people?" I asked.

"What a simplistic worldview the Englishman has," said Miss Saxena.

"I'm Welsh," I countered.

"And the Naga are as distinct from the Indian Koli or the Marathi as the Welsh or English are from the Greeks or the Russians. Not my people, Cadwallander."

"The Naga, if I recall correctly, are head-hunters," said Sedgewick. "Their tribal myths are quite fascinating."

"There has been no head-hunting in the region since their annexation by the British colonial forces," said Miss Saxena. "I was in the region, having travelled south from Tibet."

"I heard a wild rumour that you had played some part in Roxborough's ill-fated mission into the Himalayas," said Sedgewick.

"I followed the British expeditionary force into Tibet to catalogue their imperialist atrocities. I was doing the same in the Naga lands."

I felt my temper rise. Though I was often intrigued by Professor Sedgewick's unfashionable assertions that all peoples of the world were of equal worth and potential, I was firmly of the opinion that England's colonial interests were those of a tender and guiding parent, leading lesser cultures to a higher ideal. "The British do not commit atrocities, Miss Saxena," I rebuked her.

"Their atrocities are often subtle things. With the Naga, the British seized control of the production of food and rationed it out to the people according to their own rules."

"Ensuring the bounty of the land was enjoyed by all, I'm sure," said Wilmarth.

Miss Saxena shook her head. "The food is distributed in church on Sundays, after the service. No church, no food."

"Bibles and bread," said Sedgewick. "I've heard allegations of it before. It is neither government policy nor particularly Christian."

"Government or not, the policy in the region is Bibles, bread and bridges. The imperialist goal is conversion, control, and the building of railway bridges to link Margherita with Sylhet. And sometimes there are even greater atrocities. In this instance, the murder of sixty-seven men, women and children."

"The villagers were killed?" said Sedgewick.

"Slaughtered. Cut down by British bullets if I'm any judge. Their carved idols and amulets – their only riches – stolen."

"And you accuse Her Majesty's soldiers of doing this?" I demanded.

"No. Victoria likes to keep her enslaved subjects healthy and productive. The Naga were killed for their cultural treasures. Such things can be sold for considerable sums to the right collectors. I am looking for a treasure hunter, an artefact smuggler, a murderer. The man I seek is undoubtedly English."

"The villain you describe sounds like no Englishman I can imagine," said Wilmarth.

Miss Saxena gave him a hard look. "Though it grieves me to admit it, the English in India have certain qualities that the native Indians do not. Foremost of those is efficiency and organisation. Not one villager survived that massacre. They were killed by British soldiers, or perhaps former soldiers, and their commander has spirited his spoils out of the country. That was why I had come to speak to Professor Morrow."

"You suspected the professor?" said Wilmarth.

"No," interjected Sedgewick, "but she hoped he might help her locate the artefacts and thus the culprit."

"Quite," said Miss Saxena. "Flinders Morrow was a genial host, delighted to speak to someone who had travelled as widely as myself. He spoke excitedly about his planned expedition to Java. I showed him some stereoscopic daguerreotypes of the Naga massacre. In truth, he was perhaps more interested in the architecture of Naga dwellings than the poor dead souls on the ground, but he expressed the keenest of sympathies. The professor had not been to the region himself but did have a Naga household deity on his mantelpiece and proudly showed it to me."

Wilmarth coughed pointedly. "I'm waiting for the point at which you picked up an ancient spear and ripped his throat out."

"I did not kill him," insisted Miss Saxena. "We spoke for several hours. There were two interruptions. The housekeeper, who glared at me as though I might be a thief or a common dollymop, brought tea for us both and hovered in the room until Morrow specifically dismissed her. The housekeeper came in a second time with a telegram for the professor, another excuse to loiter and glare."

"And then you killed him," said Wilmarth.

"No. Less than a minute later, Professor Morrow casually rose to his feet, retrieved the spearhead from its wire hangings on the wall and calmly began to saw at his own neck."

"Preposterous," said I in an astonished whisper.

"A Christian gentleman would not commit self-murder," said Wilmarth.

"Not one who was so excited about a prospective journey to the orient," added Sedgewick.

"It's the truth," said Miss Saxena.

"That kind of *truth* will take you all the way to the gallows," commented the inspector.

Miss Saxena growled in unladylike frustration and began to pace her cell.

"Perhaps there was something in the tea?" I suggested.

"Mind-controlling narcotics?" said Wilmarth. "Evil *juju* dust?"

"I cannot quite imagine why the housekeeper, or perhaps the grocery delivery boy, might wish to poison Professor Morrow so," said Sedgewick.

"Then what about the telegram?" I said.

"Contact poison?" suggested Wilmarth.

"Blackmail," I said. "All men have secrets. Perhaps Morrow had a secret shame that someone was threatening to uncover."

"Words have power," agreed my good friend the professor.

Wilmarth produced the fragment of paper that I had taken from the coals. "*Mhhg?*" he said. "It's not even part of an English word."

"The post office would have a carbon copy of the original," said Miss Saxena.

Wilmarth shook his head. "This is procrastination," he said.

"But the post office is a short ride away," I said.

"And Miss Saxena is going nowhere." The professor regarded the woman as one might a caged jungle cat.

3.

The professor, inspector and I rode together to the post office on Wheeler Street, squashed together in a single horse-drawn cab. I felt compelled to point out to Wilmarth that, in the capital and the industrial sprawl of Birmingham, taximeter steam carriages were much more in favour and horses were now a rare sight.

"They would not suit Cambridge, and Cambridge would not suit them," he replied plainly. "Cambridge is not a city. It is a garden."

"An enticing image," said Sedgewick generously.

"You will find no airship docking stations blotting the skyline here. Even our telegraph wires and pneumail tubes having been buried underground, rather than criss-crossing the streets like the devil's own bunting. My cousin, Turlough Oberlin, is an engineer on a marvellous underground railway that will soon enough run from Liverpool to London. Perhaps one day, all our railways will be so conveniently placed out of sight. Besides, I hear that those steam carriages cannot withstand the robust nature of good British cobble. Wasn't there that awful incident in Aberdeen?"

"That was an experimental phlogiston carriage," said Sedgewick. "I don't believe steam carriages are liable to explode in that fashion."

"Regardless," said Wilmarth, "I like horses."

I uttered a short laugh that may have been a little unkind. "With their dung littering the streets? Their stinking stables on every corner? Half a city's effort seems to go into feeding them and cleaning up after them."

"And thus the city is limited," said Wilmarth. "I read a fascinating paper that proved that the reliance on horses created a specific limit on the size of cities, not unlike how the square-cube rule proves that those *dinosaur* creatures the Academy of Science fellows witter about would have been simply too massive to support their own weight."

"You do not like large cities," I concluded.

"I do not like how man spreads himself across the globe and across the stars with little comprehension of the science and technology that propels him there. You have heard of Francis Younghusband's proposed mission to another star system?"

"Altair," said the professor. "I hear Her Majesty is offering him her patronage."

Wilmarth scoffed. "Reckless. We are children at the controls of our fathers' steam train."

"Indeed, we are dwarfs standing on the shoulders of giants," said Sedgewick and his tone told me he was quoting someone but who I had no idea.

"Exactly," said Wilmarth.

"I can't say I agree," I said. "Technology has made man's lot an easier and happier one."

"You mean that knowledge is the enemy of good honest work and the friend of the lazy," said Wilmarth.

"There speaks a man who well knows the university undergraduate," said Sedgewick, which drew an assenting chuckle from the inspector.

The cab pulled up outside the post office on Wheeler Street. I was glad to be out of that cab and on my feet once more. If public decency had not prevented it, I would have attempted to rub some feeling back into my insensate fundament.

Wilmarth approached a harried looking clerk on the post office steps and introduced himself. The clerk's response was a surprising one. The chap almost wilted with relief and explained that he had sent one of his boys to find a constable not five minutes before.

"Whatever for?" asked Wilmarth.

The clerk swept the three of us with his gaze and in a trembling voice suggested we better come and speak to the postmaster. He led us inside, through the doors beyond the counter and up to the first floor, where a stolid fellow in half-moon spectacles greeted us with a tad more decorum than his excitable underling.

"Peters, one of our telegraphers, locked himself in his office," he explained as he led us down the corridor. "He did not respond when we knocked. I even raised my voice."

We came to a door before which stood another clerk.

"Eventually, I had the door broken in." The postmaster gestured to the splintered wood around the lock. Wilmarth motioned for the clerk to stand aside and cautiously entered the room.

The telegrapher's office was a tiny space. A desk took up half the width of the room. On it sat the telegraph sounder, the ivory-handle telegraph key, the triplicate carbon paper ledger in which received messages were recorded, and a stationery spike for sent messages. The telegraph wire ran to the wall and then up to the ceiling alongside the room's pneumail tube. These, however, were all peripheral details.

Our attention was primarily taken by the sight of the telegrapher, Peters. He sat motionless in his round-backed chair, arms dangling by his side, his head tilted back as though he were asleep at his post or wearily regarding the ceiling. Except Peters could not be regarding anything; not in this world. Where once his eyes had been there were now two gaping and bloody holes. Fresh, glistening blood streaked his face and spattered his desk.

"Saints preserve us!" I gasped.

"Murder!" cried one of the postmaster's clerks.

"No," said Wilmarth, to himself as much as anyone. "The door was locked from the inside. Note the key is still in the lock. That window is painted shut. And look here."

He stepped forward and tapped the ledger with a glove-clad finger. The torn, red-streaked page meant nothing to me at first.

"These are the marks of his fingertips. He tore these pages out *after* the injuries were inflicted. And not once did he cry out, or at least not loud enough to be heard."

There came the sound of heavy booted feet in the corridor outside. The sent for constabulary had arrived at last.

"Where are the papers he tore out?" mused Professor Sedgewick.

Wilmarth crouched and regarded the floor of the small room.

"And where are his eyes?" I said.

Sedgewick, with an uncomfortable set to his lips, pointed at the untidy pile of pneumail canisters on the table with the tip of his cane. Peters' bloody fingerprints were clearly visible on a number of the steel containers.

"Impossible," I said.

"Not impossible, Cadwallander. Just deeply improbable," said Sedgewick. "Come. Let us leave the police to their work."

Sedgewick and I repaired to the Eagle and Child public house a short distance down the road. Over a drink – a small glass of India pale ale for the professor, a large measure of something stronger for myself – we considered the horror we had just witnessed and made our interpretations.

"A causal link between the death of Professor Morrow and the telegrapher seems likely," said Sedgewick.

"I don't see how," I replied.

"If we are to accept Miss Saxena's account of Morrow's death and the recent evidence of our own eyes then two men have, on the same day in the same city, brutally ended their own lives."

"I cannot believe that the telegrapher did that to himself. Your hypothesis is that he gouged out his own eyes and then tore out the carbon copies of the most recent telegrams, including the one that had been delivered to Professor Morrow—"

"I imagine so," said Sedgewick.

"—and then, before shock and pain made an end of him, fed both his own eyes and the incriminating papers into a pneumail tube and sent them off to Lord knows where?"

"It is possible that he simply ate them," the professor said quietly.

This suggestion made my gorge rise. "You may be a better man than I, professor," said I. "But I will not tolerate you uttering such foul notions. I cannot account for what I just saw there, but your explanation is a nonsense. Even if the evidence indicates these are suicides, can you tell me why they killed themselves?"

Sedgewick sipped his beer and considered its golden depths. "I honestly cannot, Cadwallander."

Inspector Wilmarth entered the saloon and approached our table. "It is a grim business and no mistake," said he, wringing hands together as though attempting to rid himself of the gory viscera in that telegraphy room. "However, Peters did not tear the carbon slips as cleanly as he might have done."

I forbore to make any comment about the likely dexterity or thoroughness of a recently self-blinded man.

"Do you know if Professor Morrow had any family or acquaintances in Lowestoft?" asked Wilmarth.

Sedgewick shook his head. "There was a spinster sister in Ely. He had few associates outside Cambridge academia."

"Confound it all," said Wilmarth.

"But I can tell you what there is in Lowestoft," said Sedgewick. "There is a bridge. One end of a bridge, at least."

I looked at Wilmarth. The professor's comments patently made as little sense to him as they did to me.

4.

Cambridge railway station was built away from the city centre, at the insistence of successive university chancellors who had wished to curtail the travels of their students. Wilmarth accompanied us no longer. To him, the business of the telegram was a dead end, a *red herring* to distract him from the true deductive investigation. I couldn't say that I disagreed with him, but I was Sedgewick's man and raised no objections.

We took seats on the Norwich train that afternoon, a two-deck Neilson and Reid *Hyperion*. Sedgewick's associate membership of the Savile Club in Piccadilly entitled us to seats in the Gentlemen's Carriage on the upper deck. We were the sole occupants of the carriage and, had we wished, would have been able to play billiards, peruse the small but well-stocked library and smoke the selection of finest Hispaniolan cigars all the way to the coast. As it was, we sat in the glass-ceilinged fore of the carriage, had our personal steward bring us a late luncheon of Dover sole, and discussed pressing matters as the East Anglian countryside rolled by.

"I would ask you one thing," I said as the steward cleared our plates away.

"Ask, dear friend," said Professor Sedgewick.

"Why are we doing this?"

"I thought I had explained. I believe the answer to the deaths of Morrow and Peters will be found in Lowestoft."

"That I understand," I said. "But why are pursuing this matter? Is it to find justice for your associate, God rest his soul, or to save Miss Saxena from the hangman's noose?"

Sedgewick dabbed at his lips with his napkin. "I believe it is the search for truth. I accept whatever end it takes us to. If Miss Saxena killed Professor Morrow then she will need to answer for her crimes. However, we can be certain that she did not kill Peters, being locked in a police cell at the time of his death."

"Then there were two killers."

"Remember Occam's Razor, Cadwallander. Plurality must never be posited without necessity. Do not look for two killers when there is only one. What do the two men have in common?"

"The telegram," I said. "And yet both the telegram messenger boy and the housekeeper came into contact with it."

"But did not read it."

"So, you believe that the telegram message itself caused their deaths."

"It is a hypothesis. Words have power."

"To drive men to kill themselves?"

"Man does not know all the vectors of death," said the professor. "A hundred years ago, before John Snow proved it, who would have believed diseases were spread by infinitesimally small organisms?"

"But infectious words? A diseased language? Incredible."

"A disease of ideas, of the mind," mused Sedgewick. "Of course, there are two other people who, for certain, saw that message."

"The telegrapher in Lowestoft who transmitted it to Cambridge..."

"And the man who wrote it in the first instance," agreed Sedgewick. "We will seek them out in the morning."

The steward returned with our plum duff desserts and we ate in troubled but companionable silence as the sun settled over the bleak but starkly beautiful fens.

While the second and third class passengers changed at Norwich, the station cranes gently lifted our carriage from its bogeys and onto the Lowestoft train. It was gracefully done and we were transferred with barely a ripple in our postprandial brandies.

*

We reached the Suffolk coast shortly after nightfall and sent a porter to secure us lodgings at one of Lowestoft's many seafront guesthouses. The young man took so long in his errand that I was contemplating not tipping the scoundrel but, on his return, he breathlessly explained that few guesthouses in the town had vacancies on account of the grand opening of the Lowestoft-Zeebrugge Bridge in two days' time. However, he had secured us a single small room in a reputable hotel and, although not ideal, Sedgewick and I regarded ourselves as adaptable chaps and bade him lead us there.

The guesthouse was a short distance from the station. The room was indeed small, but the place was clean, the landlady pleasant enough and our room had a sea view. I looked out into the night. The bridge was not visible in the dark although a line of faint lights could be seen running out from the south of the town and out to sea.

5.

After breakfast the following day, Sedgewick and I strolled down to the town post office. Lowestoft is a fine seaside resort, though not a patch on Pwlhelli, Llandudno or the other magnificent coastal towns of my homeland. There is the busy industrial port to the north yet, regardless, its lapping shores, pebble beach, wide promenade and grand edifice of seafront establishments conspire to refresh and relax the holidaymaker.

Sea airs and a hearty breakfast had put us both in a good humour which was reduced to naught when we reached the post office. Sedgewick requested to speak the telegrapher who had been on duty the day before; the postmaster informed us that particular telegrapher was not at work, but at home, ill. When Sedgewick pressed the postmaster on the matter, making elliptical and not wholly untrue references to his involvement in a police matter in Cambridge, the postmaster drew us into his office and confided that the man had killed himself the previous afternoon.

"Left his post, he did," said the official. "One of my boys saw him go down to the sea front where a musical steam organ was entertaining the little 'uns. According to my lad, he put his hand on the driving belt between the engine and the organ and was pulled into the workings."

"How terrible," I said.

"I can't imagine what effect it must have had on the little 'uns. All that blood and ... it don't bear thinking about, do it?"

Sedgewick agreed and asked the postmaster if he could see the papers for the telegrams sent by the telegrapher before he ended his own life. I found myself unsurprised to hear that those telegram messages had vanished with the telegrapher.

"And so our trail comes to an end," I said.

"Not quite," countered Sedgewick, asking the postmaster if the counter staff kept a ledger of payments made for telegrams.

"They do," said he and, without further prompting, showed us the counter clerks' records.

Sedgewick ran a finger down the list of customers' names until he gave a grunt of recognition, thanked the postmaster for his time and took to the street. I caught up with him as he strode back down the promenade. "So, another poor soul killed by the telegram's contents," I said.

Sedgewick nodded grimly.

"And you saw a name in the post office's books that you recognised," I added.

Sedgewick nodded again but did not speak further.

My friend and companion was clearly deep in thought and in no mood for conversation and so I leaned against the promenade rail and let him pace away with his cogitations. I gazed out to sea, at the bridge that had not been visible the night before.

The Lowestoft-Zeebrugge Bridge is, as anyone who has seen it will tell you, an astonishing work of British engineering. However, in appearance and design, it struck me as little different to the piers one might find at many a seaside resort. The only principal differences are those of scale. The bridge was five times wider than any pier I had visited; certainly wide enough to accommodate four Stephenson gauge railway lines. The piles upon which it was built were correspondingly sturdier. Thirdly, though it is obvious to state, this was not a pier but a bridge. It had no visible end. The bridge simply faded into the sea haze; the furthest point I could see marked by the stick thin cranes against the sky.

When Sedgewick joined me some minutes later, I tested his willingness to converse by asking him to estimate how far out those cranes might be. "The horizon from this elevation is little more than three miles away," he said. "The cranes cannot be any further away than that, a fraction of the bridge's full length."

"I heard it is eighty miles long."

"In nautical miles, yes."

"I still don't understand why we couldn't just cut across from Dover to Calais," I said. "We already have the Bazalgette Tunnel under the North Sea."

"Which can only accommodate two very low mail trains at a time," Sedgewick pointed out. "No, despite the shortness of a Dover-Calais route, French bureaucracy and turpitude have put paid to any such plans."

I laughed. "The French's loss is the Low Countries' gain. Let's see how the Frogs like it the next time they're cut off by foul weather in the Channel."

"I was reading about the bridge in the *Ipswich Evening Star* at breakfast this morning," said Sedgewick. "The chief engineer and architect is a man by the name of Edward Klein. He took over the position two months ago, after the bridge's original engineer and architect were both killed in an accident involving a track-laying machine. Klein was well qualified for the post: only just returned from a five year posting with the Assam Railway and Trading Company in north east India. His name is in the post office ledger."

"Well, that's a dashed queer series of coincidences," I said, surprised.

"Or no coincidence at all. I think we need to speak to the man."

To that end, we took ourselves the short distance along the coast to the bridge construction site. Several small engines hauled construction material off and on the bridge but human traffic was limited and controlled by a foreman in a flat cap.

His greeting to us was a curt, "Opening's not until tomorrow."

Sedgewick smiled at him genially. "We have come to speak to Mr Klein, the engineer."

"He's not giving any interviews," said the foreman.

"And we are not newspapermen. My name is Professor Erskine Sedgewick and I have come from Cambridge to discuss a private matter."

The foreman looked at us shrewdly and then went over to a telephonic voicepipe at the side of the bridge. He talked at length before returning, gave us grudging permission to enter and instructed a rotund chap by the name of Bristow to take us down to Mr Klein.

Bristow had us sit on an open top carriage, a steam-powered buggy on rails which conveyed us at a refreshing pace down the track and out to sea. Within minutes, we were riding high above the swells of the North Sea, and Lowestoft was reduced to a white and brown smear on the horizon. I will be honest enough to admit that I found our sudden isolation moderately unnerving. "Imagine if a man fell from the bridge out here," I thought out loud.

"There are life rings and emergency voicepipe stations every two hundred yards along the promenade, sir," said Bristow. "And lifeboats every quarter mile."

"That is reassuring," I said.

"And do you imagine people walking out this far?" asked Sedgewick.

"Mr Jeffers, him being the original architect, he said that people would come out here on walking holidays. There's a platform every ten miles with space enough for hotels, cafés, shops and whatnot. Those buildings are currently used as lodgings for Mr Klein's navvies."

"This truly is a marvel of the modern age," I said.

Sedgewick agreed and spent much of the next few miles explaining the tremendous forces that the support struts of the bridge would have to withstand at all times.

After nearly an hour's travel, riding that uncomfortably narrow ribbon of steel across an uninterrupted field of blue, we approached the construction site near the bridge's centre. Rail-mounted cranes hoisted girders and pallets of wood into position and, striding between them, there were the hulking ogre-like forms of iron navvies.

I have had the pleasure of seeing one of the Queen's Armoured Hussars' mortar-men close up and his enclosing suit of iron and galvanic motors was a daunting and thrilling one, but these mechanised heavy-lifting suits was almost twice the size of that mortar-man. The navvies themselves were barely visible at the hearts of the trunk-legged giants, their arms and legs pinned against the plates and levers with which they controlled their monstrous shells.

As one strode by, carrying five hundredweight of railway sleepers *in one arm*, I noted that the iron navvies did not emit smoke or steam and had no visible exhaust pipes. I asked our driver what fuel they used.

"Beef," said Bristow with a smile. "Beef for the men. Phlogiston for the machines. And a kind word from Mr Klein. He certainly has a way of getting the best out of the workers."

"Isn't phlogiston dangerous?" I asked.

"Only if you don't treat it with respect," said Bristow, a mite affronted.

Sedgewick pointed out an iron navvy backed up against a high-pressure phlogiston container on the tracks next to ours and the team of boys connecting a heavy refuelling pipe to the navvy's rear. As every schoolboy knows, phlogiston is the refined essence of fire and can be found in every combustible material. Or, to put matters more sensibly, it is the presence of phlogiston that allows materials to burn. Separated from its source material, phlogiston is a volatile liquid which burns fiercely in the mere presence of heat and air.

"Derived from Yorkshire chthonic coal," said Sedgewick, reading from the container's side. "An estimable source of power."

"It would need to be to power those Goliaths," I said.

"Goliath was only nine feet tall," corrected the professor.

"Then we truly are dwarfs on the shoulders of giants."

Bristow slowed our car as we approached the central platform which marked the mid-point of the bridge. The platform, a square two hundred yards across, would one day be home to the hotels and whatnot that Bristow had mentioned and, one supposes, the customs houses and other bureaucratic paraphernalia one might find at any border between nations. Presently, however, space was kept clear for the construction of an impressive iron gateway which arched over the entire platform. The still unfinished gateway was a twisted crown of curved girders, sinuously looping one over another and curving outward across the platform, a hundred yards above our heads. The gateway put me instantly in mind of an arch of trained vines, or a woven garland of roses: flowers, thorns and all. And I could not shake the feeling that it reminded me of something else, something sinister and unsettling.

"All change," declared Bristow cheerfully as he drew to a halt.

As Sedgewick and I stepped out, Bristow pointed us in the direction of the railway carriage Mr Klein had taken for his offices, informing us that he would be waiting to return us to England when we had concluded our business.

We stepped carefully between the construction traffic and climbed the carriage steps, Sedgewick rapping on the frame of the open door with his cane before we entered. The long space within the carriage was filled with desks, files, charts and as much hum of industry as any office I had entered. A clerk rose to greet us, silently indicating that the chief engineer, Klein, was currently busy.

I could see, down the far end of the carriage, in front of a large table strewn with charts, two men engaged in heated conversation. One was a foreman of some variety, the other a sandy-haired and moustached figure who I took to be Klein. The foreman clearly had some grievance and was unable to make his point without raising his voice. I don't recall his exact words but, in his terse yet somewhat colourful language, he asserted that it didn't matter what Klein was offering to pay them, certain workers were exhausted and would not be able to work into the night.

Klein nodded sympathetically and placed a hand on the foreman's shoulder, an unusual move, given that many a gentlemen might have preferred to put such a malcontent firmly in his place. Stranger still, Klein leaned close and whispered in the foreman's ear. The man meekly bowed his head, turned and left.

I nodded in greeting to the fellow as he passed, to which he replied with something along the lines of, *"H'rrnhai dho-na, ia g'htep yrnthlai."*

"Is that a local dialect?" I asked Sedgewick once the man had gone.

"I'm not certain that it is," said the professor.

With the clerk's permission, we stepped forward to speak to the chief engineer.

"Professor Sedgewick," said he, shaking the professor's hand. "An honour to meet you. Edward Klein."

"I hope we're not interrupting your work," said Sedgewick, indicating the departed foreman with a backward tilt of his head.

"Without interruptions, I'd be working around the clock. With the official opening tomorrow, some tempers are running a little high."

"But everything is on schedule?"

"The last pieces of the triumphal entry arch will be put in place tomorrow in front of the eyes of the world. All is as it should be. On time and on budget."

He said all this with a devil-may-care grin and I noted that Klein was an extraordinarily confident fellow, and considerably younger than I expected. He was not the typically grey-whiskered and dour engineer of Victoria's England but a lively chap, barely in his thirties.

"I believe I read one of your papers in *Scientific Opinion*," said Klein. "About the discovery of sea fossils in the Himalayan Mountains and their implication for evolutionary transmutation and the Biblical account of the flood."

"And what was your opinion of the paper?" asked Sedgewick.

"It put me in mind of Agassiz's conjecture that the Deluge is simply a racial memory of the flooding of the Black Sea basin and that a worldwide flood is a physical impossibility."

"A theory that also explains the possible existence and later disappearance of Atlantis," said Sedgewick. "Humanity seems to have an insatiable need to believe in lands lost beneath the waves. Where Plato wrote of Atlantis, Melchior Neumayr's successors now write of Lemuria."

Klein found this quite amusing although I was not educated enough to understand why.

On the wall of the carriage, above the many other charts and plans, Klein had pinned a large elevation drawing of the almost complete gateway, his *triumphal entry arch*. Distance lines, measurements and angles were marked on the plan in a neat hand. Laid out plainly before me, I acquired a fresh appreciation of the complexity of the construction. Though this was a twisting, almost life-like edifice, it was not a random or haphazard structure. It was a thing built to a precise specification; a work of purpose.

The clarity with which I saw it on the draughtsman's plan redoubled the sense of familiarity and deep-rooted unease which the actual gateway had inspired in me. The curve of the girders, their angles and points of convergence struck me as intrinsically unwholesome. This may sound like madness but it was nonetheless true.

I am not of a mathematical bent but, regarding the spiral shelled nautilus, Sedgewick and I had once discussed the golden section. A curve through a rectangle with sides of a ratio of twenty-one to thirteen, perpetuated outward into larger and larger rectangles gives the seashell that perfectly beautiful spiral. The same proportion of features can be found in the divine countenances of Da Vinci's Mona Lisa and the dimensions of the Parthenon. Perhaps, if beauty and goodness can be expressed as a golden ratio, then there may also be some unholy black ratio which conveys naught but vile depravity. If so, Klein's gateway was built to its evil rules.

"The Naga people of India believe that they are descended from the survivors of Lemuria's destruction," Sedgewick was saying, "sheltering from the cataclysm in caves deep beneath the earth created by their gods."

"Is that so?" said Klein. His smile faltered somewhat.

"A neat dove-tailing of flood myths and Hollow Earth beliefs," said Sedgewick. "You were in India until recently, I believe."

"You believe correctly."

"Taking the railway to their isolated lands and connecting them to civilisation is noble work. I wondered, given your time amongst the Naga, whether you would be able to help me in a matter."

"I hardly spent time amongst the Naga," Klein argued gently and went on to explain the details of his work for the Assam Railway and Trading Company.

Though I paid polite interest to the engineer, my gaze was pulled time and again to the drawing of the gateway. Its horrendous dimensions fascinated me, pulling me closer, drawing me like a small boy to the edge of a dark well. Those arcs and points were, in one sense, just lines on paper. And yet, in another, they seemed to reach *elsewhere*, into a space that could not be expressed in two dimensional sketches. Looking upon it, I had an inkling of why the agoraphobic feared the vast and open skies, why Inspector Wilmarth would have mankind's inexorable expansion reduced and contained, why there was much to fear from both the infinite cosmos and the infinitesimal world of John Snow's germs.

Foolish though it may sound, I felt that my very soul was placed in greater jeopardy with each moment that I contemplated those coils, but it had my complete attention. Slowly, I found myself coming to the unshakeable notion that the entwining loops were not vines or thorny branches but represented something much more vital and animalistic: snaking tentacles, questing prehensile proboscises, the pulsating fronds of a sea anemone.

Abruptly, I recalled why this design was so utterly familiar to me. I had seen it in Professor Morrow's hearth scarcely a day before.

"The idol," I whispered to myself.

Klein and the professor glanced up at my unbidden utterance.

"Indeed," said Sedgewick. "I had questions about some Naga artefacts, linked to their fascinating belief systems you understand. I had hoped to speak to the Cambridge academic, Flinders Morrow, but I was shocked to discover that he has died recently. Taken his own life."

"That is shocking," said Klein, "although I can't say I knew the gentleman at all. My work in India was all consuming and I had scant opportunity to consider the Indian culture. Besides, rubbing shoulders with the locals is liable to make a fellow turn native. A chap would do best to keep a healthy distance."

"A shame," said Sedgewick. "I'm sure it would have been most edifying."

Klein made a point of consulting his watch. "I must say, I have enjoyed this brief interruption. I would be delighted if we could continue this conversation after tomorrow's opening ceremony. Here." He reached into a drawer and thrust two cream tickets into Sedgewick's hand. "Two passes to attend the official opening. A train is being laid on for the British dignitaries. Ten o'clock sharp. I hope you'll be on it."

"Neither hell nor high water would stop us," said Sedgewick with appreciation.

"That's the spirit," said Klein. "I'll have one of the men take you back."

"I believe our carriage is waiting outside. Cadwallander..."

I struggled to take my eyes from that horrid image but ultimately succeeded, gave Klein the briefest of nods and left with the good professor.

"He killed Morrow," I said confidentially once we were a short distance from the office carriage.

"You recognised the plans on the wall?" said Sedgewick.

"The stuff of nightmares," I said in confirmation. "The same as the Naga idol."

"He's our man, all right."

"But what did he do? And how?"

"And why?" added the professor, remounting Bristow's railway buggy.

6.

That evening, Sedgewick and I ate at one of Lowestoft's larger hotels and took in a variety show at the Marina Theatre. As we

123

returned through the night to our guesthouse, I asked Sedgewick about his reference to Lemuria in his conversation with Klein.

"The landmasses of the world are primarily composed of enormous continents with vast oceans between them," he said. "Yet, there are land animals of strikingly similar species found on these different continents. How did these animals come to appear in both places? It is clear that some of their ancestors crossed land bridges and earlier continents to get to these different locations. Lemuria is one of these continents, now lost beneath the Indian Ocean."

"What happened to it?" I asked.

"Some cataclysmic event perhaps, struck by a series of seismic shocks."

"Earthquakes?"

"Earthquakes. Volcanoes. Floods. We can only speculate. Whatever it was, all that remains of it is Sri Lanka, Madagascar and a smattering of smaller islands."

We walked on in silence as I imagined what such a world-shattering event would have been like for the animals and, perhaps, even peoples subjected to it. There would have been nowhere to run to, nowhere to hide, their entire world pulverised and enflamed and dragged to the deep, cold ocean floor.

"You recall those strange words the workman uttered as he left Klein's carriage?" said Sedgewick.

"Not exactly," I admitted.

"I wondered if there was a link with that word fragment on Morrow's telegram."

"Part of the same magical language?"

"Magic?" Sedgewick's voice contained a mild chastisement. "Magic is simply the word we give to phenomena we do not understand."

"If not magic, what would you call words that have the power to kill, or the power to turn a truculent worker into a docile sheep?"

"All words and concepts have a power of their own. I could utter a single word right now that would be guaranteed to redden your cheeks or fire up your temper."

"I'll kindly ask you not to."

"I was thinking of the show we saw this evening and, no, not that third-rate stage magician who was quite clearly concealing the dove up his sleeve, but the demonstration of mesmerism."

"You mean the electro-biology chap who made that fellow believe his walking stick was a snake?"

"It was a demonstration of the power of suggestion, carried out through certain words and gestures. Words have the power to unlock hidden recesses of the mind. The Lord Himself brought the world into being with words. So powerful is the Tetragrammaton, the four-fold name of God in Hebrew, that Jews are forbidden to ever speak it. Some Cabbalists aver that even the names of angels – the true names of angels – would kill or drive insane those who heard them."

I chuckled to myself. Receiving a stern look from Sedgewick, I quickly explained. "No, I was thinking of another evening and a far superior show at the Malt Cross Music Hall in Nottingham. There was a skit featuring the *lion comique* and a fellow in the tartan jacket: the piece about a joke that was so funny that anyone who heard it would die laughing."

"I recall something of the sort," said Sedgewick, making it plain that he did not remember it with the same fondness as I. "Let us imagine Klein's telegram is like that deadly joke."

"Are they words ones he has discovered by some arcane study?" I suggested.

"Or did he encounter them, receive them, unasked for in the Naga lands? Whatever the case, we should be afraid."

"I'll say."

"The telegraphy network would allow him to send a deadly message across the globe, but only along a single chain, from person to person. Imagine if Marconi's wireless transmitters became something more than a scientific curio: Klein and his like might 'broadcast' their poisonous messages to many receivers at once. The marvels of modern communication technology could be our undoing."

"Now you sound like that Inspector Wilmarth"

Sedgewick attempted to shrug off my comparison. "In days of yore, knowledge was a precious commodity. The monasteries and secret colleges were the true treasure houses of Europe. Knowledge passed from master to apprentice, from scholar to the novice. Whispers in the darkness. The common man was kept illiterate. It was not his place to read for himself, to think and analyse for himself."

"Surely we have moved on from that," I said. "A world where any man can better himself through education is to be praised."

"I agree. And yet here we have a situation in which dangerous knowledge and an unparalleled age of global communications present a credible threat to us all. What will come on the day when even the most stunted of minds have access to all human knowledge, when any man might summon the combined teachings of Socrates, Newton and the Encyclopædia Britannica without any semblance of effort?"

"We will all be wiser men and better for it," I answered.

"No. Wisdom has to be earned, Cadwallander. Dwarfs on the shoulders of giants. We have not scaled those heights by ourselves but have been lifted up."

"This is all supposition," I said, wishing to put an end to Sedgewick's grim proclamations. "We have no evidence to substantiate our accusations against Klein."

"Pah," said Sedgewick, swinging at the air with his cane, knowing that I was correct. We walked on.

Up ahead a group of men in work overalls and cloth caps stood chatting outside a public house, visible only as silhouettes against the murky lamplight from the windows. Further in the distance were the lights of the bridge and, if one strained one's ears, the sound of metal on metal, girders slotting into position and rivets being driven into place.

"There were giants once. Real ones," said Sedgewick.

"Are you talking about those bones they've unearthed in Nevada?"

"No," said the professor. "I think we'll find the size of those 'giant' corpses have been exaggerated a great deal. I was referring to the Old Testament where the sons of God took the daughters of men for themselves and produced a race of monstrous giants, the Nephilim."

"Sons of God?"

"Angels perhaps. The Book of Jubilees says they were watcher angels whose offspring brought an intolerable wickedness into the world."

I harrumphed at that. The cornerstone of my personal faith was the simple yet unqualified goodness of Christ and our need to emulate it in our own modest ways. The God of Jesus Christ might also be the God of the Hebrews but the Old Testament's obsession with wickedness and cleanliness was as tiresome to me as the prattlings of a village busybody. Besides, talk of angels resurrected unpleasant memories of our time aboard the *Lady Henshall* space-lock.

As we approached the public house, the four men loitering at its door raised themselves up from their slouching positions against the wall. Perhaps, I thought at first, readying to make their drunken way home or simply to allow us to pass. "And what became of those giants?" I asked Sedgewick.

"God destroyed them in the flood," said the professor. "In fact, the Book of Jubilees suggests that the destruction of the Nephilim was the principal reason God sent the Deluge."

"And drown all of humanity in the process. A sledgehammer to crack a walnut, what."

Sedgewick smiled fondly. "Questioning the ineffable Almighty again, Cadwallander?"

I'm not sure which I noticed first, the iron crowbar in one of the men's hands or the muttering of one to another of something that very much sounded like, *"N'gaii fhtagn e'hucunech ia."* Whichever the case, my unconscious mind reacted before I was even aware: raising my artificial arm to meet the first man's downward blow. His fleshy forearm met with my brass one. Beneath his sharp exhalation of pain and surprise, I thought – I hoped – I heard the crack of fractured bones.

Two men came at Sedgewick. The good professor briefly incapacitated one with a savage blow to the gut with the head of his cane, which he dropped instantly to grab the hands of the second, who lunged at him with a long knife. I would have leapt in to help but our final assailant had, like some senseless lunatic, grabbed at my face and throat with his bare hands. His grip was strong and piercing and might have crushed my windpipe within seconds. I took hold of his wrist with my mechanical hand and, with the slightest effort, crushed his wrist bones to splinters. The man fell away, screaming incoherently.

Quick as I could, I scooped up my initial attacker's dropped crowbar and knocked the knife-wielding man senseless with a blow to the crown. Before he had reached the ground, I reversed my stroke and lashed out at the one with a broken arm. I have never been a cricketer, but I am sure that such a swing would have knocked any ball for six. In this instance, it smashed the man's jaw and sent teeth clattering against the pub window.

Three of them were down. The fourth, no longer winded by Sedgewick's cane, ran at us, yelling, *"Humuk dho-na g'yll-gnaii!"*

I grabbed hold of his thick overalls and, bracing myself against the pub wall with my feet (my galvanic arm gives me great strength, not licence to break the laws of physics) drew him close and then threw him: over the nearby promenade wall and into the darkness beyond.

By this time, the shouts of our assailants had drawn the attention of the pub's patrons. Several locals and the landlord, a stout fellow with an equally stout knobkerrie in his hand, emerged. "What's all this commotion?" he demanded.

"We were set upon by four men," said Sedgewick, retrieving his fallen cane and inspecting it for damaged.

The landlord reckoned that he ought to call the local constabulary; Sedgewick and I were only too keen to agree.

"That's John Peasenham," said a local, pointing to the one I had smacked on the head. "What's he ever done to you?"

"I don't know them two," added another local.

"They all work on the bridge," said the landlord. He gave us a sharp look, one leant weight by the cudgel in his hand. "You got a problem with the bridge company?"

I looked at Sedgewick and a certain dismal understanding passed between us.

"I believe the bridge company may have a problem with us," said Sedgewick.

7.

Professor Sedgewick and I did eventually find our beds that night, but not after considerable time spent in the company of the Suffolk Constabulary. A number of communiqués were sent to and from Inspector Wilmarth and, once finally satisfied, the local inspector sent us to our guesthouse and a landlady who did not appreciate her guests keeping such hours.

Nonetheless, the following morning we were up early, breakfasted by nine and at the gates of the bridge in time to catch our ten o'clock train. Though we had hardly discussed the matter, it was clear in our minds that our assailants of the night before had been sent by Klein in an act of desperation. Given that we had no true understanding of his desires or motives this was surprising; we held nothing but fragmentary clues, impossible hypotheses and dark, inarticulate forebodings.

Lowestoft was filled with a carnival atmosphere. Thousands of holidaymakers had come to celebrate the bridge's completion and even though they could neither gain access to the bridge nor see the halfway platform from the shore, they gathered on the beach to celebrate nonetheless. We pressed through the throng of celebrants and well-wishers and waved our tickets at the foremen on the gate.

We joined a train which already contained dozens of dignitaries, the children from the local school, each given an æther-filled balloon for the occasion, and a thirty-piece brass band whose repertoire of patriotic marches and hymnals was interspersed with some seaside and music hall favourites. And so, pressed into a carriage with a vicar and his wife, a local Member of Parliament and the Chair of the Lowestoft Chamber of Commerce, and with the sounds of children's squeals and *Daddy Wouldn't Buy Me a Bow Wow* in our ears, we set out.

Upon our arrival the platform at the bridge's centre was already abuzz with people, presumably brought in even earlier in the day. A marching band of the Suffolk Regiment was already entertaining the crowds with a series of de Souza marches. On the continental side, a Belgian marching band did their best to compete but, despite the cheers of the folk of the Low Countries, their brass and woodwind outfit was no match for our drums and cornets. A great red sash ran across the entire width of the platform, separating our two nations. As I understood it, once cut by dignitaries of both countries, the people would be free to cross in both directions and celebrate the trans-Channel adjoining.

The gateway was not yet complete, as Klein had indicated, and two cranes stood by with the final sections of the arch. A team of iron navvies waited to assist. It is my opinion that the schoolchildren found the iron navvies far more impressive than the bridge itself and crowded against the barriers to watch as one strode by to refuel at the phlogiston tanker.

Even the skies above were filled with spectators. Two large airships of Her Majesty's Air Corps circled sedately overhead. Around them, like dolphins among whales, were a number of private airships. Darting between them all were the tiny forms of steam-powered helipterons but they were too small and distant to identify.

A tall stage had been erected directly beneath the gateway; Sedgewick and I stood directly before it. To tumultuous approbation, senior dignitaries from both countries met on that stage to formally greet one another and make their speeches. Klein stood discreetly to one side as was appropriate in the company of lords, knights and government ministers. As the Walloon dignitary spoke, made audible to all (though not necessarily comprehensible) by a series of voicepipes and trumpet amplifiers, one of the cranes lowered the penultimate piece of the arch into place where it was secured by iron navvies with rivet guns.

Many eyes were on the gateway. From the half-frowns and twitches on several faces, I could see that many were as disturbed as I by the construction's dark ratios and unsettling form. I shivered and drew up my collar. I told myself it was the cold wind that had recently begun to blow.

The Belgians loudly applauded their countryman's speech and we joined them, politely. Lord Medway took the podium and delivered his own speech which, though considerably longer than the continental chap's was also considerably more cogent and rousing. The noise of the final piece of the archway being lowered into position and its securing with rivets did not detract from the effect of the speech but punctuated it, driving home the message of

Britain's unassailable position of mankind's road-maker and empire-builder.

The cold breeze off the sea picked up in force, becoming a stiff wind which whipped away many of the children's balloons. Up above, the thin layer of cloud thickened and swirled and the day grew more than a shade darker, turning the sea from a gay blue into a dark and unsettled slate grey. As men held onto their hats, Lord Medway had to raise his voice above the wind to be heard.

"This is not natural weather," said Sedgewick in my ear.

"Magic?"

"Words and gestures. Perhaps they have the power to unlock more than minds."

At that moment, with the wind escalating to a gale, a dreadful tremor ran through the structure beneath our feet. Lord Medway was forced to abandon his speech, drowned by screams and shouts from all sides. There followed a cracking sound, an awful wrenching of timbers and the centre of the platform collapsed. The stage, with Lord Medway and all the dignitaries upon it, fell away through a maw of broken girders. It splintered as it plummeted, torn by forces I could not comprehend.

Sedgewick and I had been close to the stage and now, with many others, stood at the ragged edge of the devastation. I looked directly down at a sea like none I had seen before or since. Directly underneath Klein's evil arch was a maelström! Steep, churning walls of water circled one another, creating a foam-tipped funnel of liquid ebony descending into an impenetrably dark sea. As each stage fragment or hapless dignitary struck the water, they were whipped downwards, never to resurface.

Along the rift, on both sides of the bridge, onlookers lost their footing and were pitched into that horrible vortex. The crowd slipped into a mindless panic: in the swell and throng of the herd, many more were driven over the edge by those nearest to them. I do not know how many lives were lost in those first few seconds, but certain faces, their terrified expressions frozen by the knowledge of their doom, will stay in my memory until my own death.

"Come," hissed Sedgewick, pulling me back into the crowd and to relative safety.

"What is this madness?" I cried.

Sedgewick pointed to the north side of the platform and at a figure with arms raised to the sky as though in exultation. "It is Klein's doing!" he shouted.

It was not just the howl of the wind which drowned speech. The legs of the bridge, driven into the seabed, groaned and screeched in protest as the maelström cut across them. And louder still were the screams and shouts of hundreds of men, women and children trapped many miles from the safety of shore.

Oh, the children! I would have anyone who hears my tale believe that every one of those schoolchildren found safe passage on the trains which sought to flee the scene of carnage. I would have everyone believe it. I would believe it myself, if I only could.

On the British side, one of the trains which had brought merrymakers to the grand opening was slowly pulling away. People clamoured and fought to be aboard, thrusting themselves at carriage doors and ladders with thoughts only for their own safety. There was no Birkenhead Drill in that sorry scene; I felt nothing but disgust for my fellow countrymen.

With insufficient space on the trains, most attempted to flee on foot, hurrying along the promenades on either side of the bridge. Others thought to pile into the nearest lifeboats, although this struck me as the worst kind of folly, for no sooner had they touched upon the dark than many were caught in the whirlpool's terrible gyrations and pulled into the gulf. Above us, a small number of airships slowly began to descend, lowering rope ladders as they came.

It was then I noticed that, although some of the builders and engineers fled with the general public, many of the workmen stood calmly by, watching the wreckage of the bridge unfold before them.

"The men are under his spell," cried Sedgewick. "We must stop him!"

I would have asked my friend what we were supposed to be stopping, and how, but there was no purpose in heaping my sense of futility on an already desperate situation. We ran around the lip of the shattered platform, towards Edward Klein.

Sedgewick called out to the engineer; Klein clearly heard, turning to face us. There was an almost delirious grin on his face. In that instant, seeing the man smile at the horror he had wrought, my hopeless despair was replaced by righteous anger.

"Stop this, now!" I bellowed, tripping over warped timbers as I attempted to reach him.

"Nothing can stop it. The door is unlocked. The triumphal entry arch is open!" He gestured downwards and I looked down into the vortex. Huge shapes, unconscionably foul, were emerging from the eye of the maelström. Black against black, I could not make out the form at first, but from a writhing and throbbing central mass emerged a mass of tentacles of impossible proportions. Those colossal appendages – scaled on top, pocked by quivering mucous-coated suckers underneath – seemed to coil through the same demonic curves and angles as Klein's gateway, whilst stretching out through dimensions other than the conventional three. The entity was not merely *below* us but indefinably *elsewhere*.

"Lord preserve us!" I breathed.

"These are not your gods!" sneered Klein.

"The gods of the Naga people," gasped Sedgewick with cold realisation. "Drowned with Lemuria."

"Not drowned but sleeping," said Klein. "From sleep to sleep, they spoke to me. Whispers in the dark. The glorious tongues of Aklo."

"They had you construct this." Sedgewick looked up. "This arch. Like the Naga idols but on an industrial scale. Like a Buddhist prayer wheel or an Orthodox icon. Concepts as doorways."

"And now they return in triumph!" cried Klein.

8.

The demonic tentacles thrust up from the maelström and into the sky, thicker and higher than the giant sequoia of California. One punched through the boards on the continental side of the bridge, propelling the wretches from the Low Countries high into the air like scattered toys. Another wrapped itself around a partially descended lifeboat, splintering it and spilling the occupants into the ravenous mouth of the maelström.

There was the crackle of rifle fire. Two dozen soldiers of the Suffolk Regiment, those few who were armed on this day of celebration, had taken up position at the edge of the rupture and were firing at will at the monstrous shapes. I did not see any of their shots strike home or have any measurable effect, but their bravery was unquestionable.

Sedgewick grabbed Klein's arm and shook the man. "You think these gods will reward your service?" he demanded.

Klein spat on the floor. "You have the arrogance to question the minds of the gods? We are ants to them. They will do what they will and we shall pay homage regardless. *Ph'nglui mglw'nafh.*"

A tentacle swept across the rim of the platform, catching many of the soldiers unawares and crushing them under its massive coils. Further tentacles rolled out onto the bridge on both sides, in search of additional quarry. One snaked its tip through the rear railings of a departing train, slowly drawing it back against the engine's valiant efforts. Some of the surviving soldiers fired their shots and even plunged their bayonets into this tentacle, again to no avail.

People leapt from their carriages whilst others simply wept at their plight. I found I could stand by and watch no longer. Leaving Sedgewick to remonstrate with the cataclysm's insane architect, I ran towards the stricken train. I can honestly say that I did not know what I might do to help for I acted on instinct alone. I reached one of the iron navvies, mounted the shallow steps in its tree trunk leg and, before its spellbound pilot knew what I was about, hooked him from his seat with my metallic arm. As the navvy rolled on the floor, stunned, I slipped into the control seat, a perch no larger and no more comfortable than that of a bicycle. My feet slipped into moveable cups in the upper section of the machine's legs, like metal clogs, and my hands found paddles and grips in the arm sections. I had not controlled such a device before and I am sure that I handled it with all the grace of a drunkard on an ice rink; but the iron navvy's engines were already running and all I needed to do was direct the mechanical ogre.

Lifting the foot cups and angling my limbs, I was able to turn around and approach that one tentacle impeding the train's escape. The machine I had commandeered was holding a rivet gun; after some experimentation, I found the correct finger paddle to operate it. White hot rivets, phlogiston-heated and driven, burst from the gun and into that hateful flesh. Each rivet punched through slimed skin with an audible hiss, leaving a ragged hole from which issued wisps of steam and a viscous, moon-pale ichor. The flesh quivered at each attack but the tentacle did not retract; the only noticeable effect was a stench, not unlike that of rotten fish, which assaulted my senses.

Meanwhile, the two Air Corps airships had descended low enough to bring their ranks of large bore Maxims to bear. Those guns howled like a hellish siren, shot merging into shot, puncturing lines of holes along tentacles and boards alike. I cannot attribute emotions to this horrid and faceless creature; I can only describe the tentacles' response as akin to anger. The tentacle let the train go, only so that it might swing up – what power could lift that weight with such speed? – and smash through the armoured gondola of one airship. Metal screeched, glass splintered, and the ruins of the ship and its crew rained down on the sea, leaving the untouched gas canopy to drift willy-nilly in the unnatural winds. Meanwhile, another tentacle reached higher and wrapped itself fully around the second airship, squeezing it in its coils and silencing both its guns and engines.

The tragic deaths of those gallant airmen at least served some purpose: freed from the tentacle's grip, that last train was able to pull away, accelerating towards the mainland and salvation. Hundreds of lives were saved in that act, but around me, among the dead and dying, were those too scared to flee, those who searched against all hope for lost loved ones, and those whose minds had been robbed of all sense and reason by the eldritch being from beneath the waves. And there were still the bewitched workers and iron navvies. Not one of them had moved to stop me or the soldiers.

And then an occurrence gave me cause for optimism. As the giant tentacle crushed down on the second airship, one of its hydrogen compartments exploded in flame. The entire gas envelope ignited. An explosion of yellow flame lit the darkening sky and – of this I was certain – the tentacle at its centre shrank back.

It could be hurt!

Professor Sedgewick had clearly seen this too for, whilst still arguing the case of reason with Klein (long past the point at which a more ordinary man would have lost his patience and resorted to fists), he turned to me, waved and pointed at something to the side of the bridge. The high-pressure phlogiston container on its railway mountings.

I dare say that an improper smile appeared on my face at that moment. In all honesty, my mind was not filled with ideas of righteous intervention or justice, but with a hot-blooded desire for vengeance.

I stumbled to the tanker and the arrangement of nozzles, pipes and thickly insulated hosing by which the essence of fire was pumped into the iron navvies. I fumbled at the hose and levers with the iron navvy's claws – imagine if you will trying to play a piano while wearing a thick pair of winter gloves and you will perceive the clumsiness of my approach – and determined that the unit had been designed so the valve could not be opened until connected to its recipient.

I heard Sedgewick call out my name. A tentacle – one of more than a dozen visible – was slithering towards me. In desperation, I smashed down on the valve locking mechanism with my rock-like fist, wrenching the hose from its housing and forcing the lever. Raw, dazzling phlogiston erupted from the hose, dousing the tentacle and the boards of the bridge under it. Phlogiston is like no other substance in God's universe and brooks no comparisons. It burns but it is not composed of flames, no more than the sun is composed of sunlight. It is a liquid but it is not a combustible liquid like paraffin or alcohol; they are merely fuel whereas phlogiston is fire itself. Furthermore, phlogiston obeys the physical rules of fire not liquid. It does not pool or flow downwards; it reaches outwards and upwards, rising like heat. It is all but uncontrollable.

The tentacle and the bridge, awash with the essence of fire, burst into flames at once. The tentacle whipped up and lashed about as though trying to shake off the flames. There were simultaneous cries from Klein and from the sea beneath us. Klein's was a pained and all too human yell of distress. The roar from the maelström was a many-voiced cacophony that ran from high piercing shrieks to sub-aural elephantine bellows which vibrated up through the legs of my iron navvy.

Now, at last, Klein saw me as a true threat. He gave a shout of, "*Wgah'nagl fhtagn!*" and his ensorcelled workmen turned on me.

A dozen iron navvies and a score of unmounted men with naught but their bare hands, charged towards me. I took recourse in the only weapon I had to hand and, though I deeply wish I could have taken another option, I drowned them in phlogiston. The men burst into flame like wax effigies, collapsing to the ground almost instantly. The iron navvy pilots died just as quickly, their machines mindlessly stumbling on a step or two before crashing to the ground.

There was a creaking sound as the fiery boards of the bridge gave way beneath one of the navvies. It disappeared in a plume of floating cinders and smoke. Much of the platform was afire; although both Sedgewick and I stood on presently untouched boards, the steadily growing lake of fire made our situation an increasingly precarious one.

The approaching inferno jolted some of the cowering or catatonic folk from their frozen positions and they ran; the last we saw escaping that day. It was good that they fled because my assault had only enraged the fiend. Tentacles, now so numerous and densely packed that they constituted a single body, thrashed wildly in search of victims. The frenzied attack was accompanied by fresh noises from the pit: a wild and ecstatic ululation from a hundred inhuman throats; a battle cry, a hymn of destruction.

It was no surprise that I could not hear Sedgewick shouting to me above the discordant and unholy choir combined with the howls of the tempest. However, I caught his frantic waving and subsequent gesticulations. It took me a moment to recognise that the arc he was describing with his arms referred to Klein's iron gateway, a few seconds longer to understand what he wished me to do. The good professor had correctly surmised that though Klein's dark gods could be hurt by fire, it would not destroy them. Whatever necromancy or dark science had conjured them from their lost lands, it was contained within the grotesque archway above us and our best chance of driving those dark gods back lay in the destruction of that archway.

I aimed the phlogiston hose high, projecting the blazing element down on the southern base of the arch. That strange substance fell more like snow than rain, blossoming and multiplying in the air according to its own laws. Much of it fell short or was lifted away by the wind, but enough fell on the girder supports to set the iron alight. Smoke filled the air on all sides and if it were not for the unnatural winds sweeping across the bridge we would have choked to death. As it was, the obscuring haze meant that I did not see the gateway support burn through, although I did hear the howl of stressed metal and thought I saw the loops and arcs above me tremble.

Again, the foul creatures and their deranged servant cried out as one in furious anguish. Several tentacles came at me, intent on swatting me like an irksome fly. I sprayed them with phlogiston but they were too numerous. As they descended, I abandoned my position. Awkwardly, I staggered away, over piles of wreckage and between the dangling ropes of the still drifting gas canopy of the Air Corp ship. Boards splintered around me as tentacles slammed down in blind acts of wanton destruction.

An almighty groan heralded the archway's final collapse. It wavered in the air, slowly pivoted like a closing jaw, and fell on the English side of the bridge. The zenith of the arch swung directly above my head before slamming across the entire width of the bridge. The fallen gateway cut through railway tracks, the promenades and railings and, no doubt, many of the supporting struts beneath.

The gateway's fall was as a mortal blow to the leviathanic entity. If the archway had been the doorway to this world from another, then that door was closing and the entity being dragged back. The tentacles wrapped themselves around whatever pillars and supports they could find, trying to maintain a foothold in this world. Instead the platform upon which we stood was dragged towards the maelström. Professor Sedgewick, Klein and I were on an island: surrounded by fire, cut off from escape by wreckage and ruin on all sides, and that island was tipping, inch by inch, into a deadly sea. I did not expect to survive beyond those few moments but my heart was not filled with despair but delight, for reasons that are not easy to explain.

Ever since our visit to Professor Morrow's house in Cambridge, I had encountered symbols and signs and shapes that filled me with unease and dread. These appalling images had reached their apotheosis with these uncountable and otherworldly beings and it was their otherworldliness that sat at the heart of my fears. They were alien, they were incongruous and they did not belong here. Like finding a tiger in your bath or seeing a painted clown at a funeral, the wholly incongruous is an affront to something deep in our psyche. Our only mental recourses at such sights are humour or terror. The absurdity – and I do not use the word lightly – of this evil manifestation was so great that to die in this world, knowing that those beings would soon be gone from it, was a victory within the soul.

The structure beneath my feet shifted and tilted at such an angle that I could, at some distance from the edge, see the lip of the shrinking whirlpool. To my side, the phlogiston tanker slipped from its brakes, rolled down the platform until it reached the twisted ends of the railway, and tumbled over into the maelström. I had nowhere to flee but, still ensconced in my iron navvy, I made down the sloping surface toward Professor Sedgewick.

Klein had vanished from sight but Sedgewick remained alive and whole, leaning heavily on his stick to remain upright. He saw me and shouted my name. As he did, some vital support below us broke; the remains of the platform spun and began what was surely its final descent. Ropes whipped across my vision and a sudden and foolish bid for survival came to my mind. I seized the thickest rope within the iron navvy's powerful grip and, towing it with me, ran at full tilt for Sedgewick.

I am not sure how I made it across those final yards. The floor beneath us pitched like a ship's deck in a storm, all the while sinking. I held out my free arm and, as Sedgewick leapt for it, the platform beneath us disappeared completely.

There was a jolt, I knocked my head against the iron navvy's casing, slumping against one side of the pilot's cockpit. Up above us were the remains of the first airship, the rope in my hand stretching up to the ruins of the gondola. The weight of the iron navvy, considerable though it was, seemed to make little difference to the altitude of the gas canopy. For now at least, it held us aloft.

I looked down. Sedgewick was held loosely but safely in the curve of my arm. Below that there was nothing but the maelström. The wind had carried us a short distance eastward and we drifted directly over the void.

The whirlpool was turning in on itself, the walls elevating to near vertical, the doorway in the final act of closing. The phlogiston container had clearly ruptured within the maelström, either crushed by a violent tentacle or torn apart by the incomparable forces of the whirl. The sea was on fire; streaks of sun-sharp light ran in concentric loops through the grey water. In the midst of that cyclopean abyss, the Naga god-thing still reached for our world through the narrowing access. At the centre of the diminishing ring of tentacles, where a face or mouth ought to be, there was a repugnant protrusion. On the idol in Morrow's parlour I had mentally compared it to a disturbingly shaped flower; gazing down now at its trembling fronds, its mucosal lips and frilled tongues, I saw it was nothing as passive as a flower; not even one of those carnivorous tropical plants they have at Kew. This questing and sensate organ, this toothless orifice, would have taken our world and consumed it all. I gladly watched it drown in fire and brine.

The waters closed over it, sending a single upward spray high into the air and – God be praised – that was the last of it.

9.

We came down in the sea during the night and, abandoning the iron navvy to the depths, clung to the rope until the gas canopy touched down onto the waters, where we climbed atop that island of double-stitched linen. A *Bellerophon* class ship, *HMS Reckless*, found us the following afternoon.

We were returned to our guesthouse in Lowestoft and each fell into our beds, exhausted. There were nightmares of a nature I neither wish nor need to relate. Suffice that their invasive imagery and impossible geometry held me down in the dark and would not allow me to surface until morning. Those dreams and my memories were the only scars I took from that episode, and I consider them a small price to pay.

The days that followed were quiet. It was the calm after the storm: that brief period before the damage has to be assessed and the cost counted. A moment following a violent and terrible crime in which breaths were drawn; a heartbeat before the first scream. The town of Lowestoft was in shock, not yet in mourning. I gather that people went to the landward end of the bridge, stared in incomprehension and then simply walked away.

Professor Sedgewick and I would meet for meals, barely exchange a word beyond the most formal civilities, then retreat either to our rooms or the parlour with our thoughts. Our first proper conversation of any note came at the breakfast table on the third day. I was reading the London papers, burying myself in its mundane contents with the same ferocity with which a shipwrecked man might cling to a piece of flotsam, when I came across a series of pictures in the *Telegraph*.

I showed them to Sedgewick. Although there had been a number of daguerreotype cameras and even a kinetographic camera on the bridge that day, not one of them had survived the catastrophe. The pictures in the *Telegraph* were lithographs drawn by the young and frightfully talented son of one of the bridge's Dutch engineers. The seven year old, identified only as 'Maurits', had captured the creature's assault on the continental side of the bridge in cleanly sketched detail. Two things struck me particularly about those images. Firstly, they recalled perfectly that dark ratio; those diabolical curves that offended the eye so greatly. Secondly, through artistic techniques that I could not deconstruct, young Maurits had conveyed the very sense of the beast reaching through from *another* space: his images turning in on themselves until up was down, back was front and the fundamentals of reality brought into question. I concluded that the boy was either an artistic genius or driven insane by what he had witnessed.

Despite the accuracy of Maurits' image, the accompanying editorial took the position that the boy's drawings were fanciful in the extreme and merely symptomatic of a fragile European mind struggling to cope with the events of a calamitous day. The *Telegraph*, like so many newspapers, had already concluded that an engineering failure was responsible for the collapse of the bridge's central platform, and any suggestion of supernatural or otherworldly causes was hysterical and distasteful nonsense.

"Have you yourself not doubted what we truly saw that day?" said Sedgewick, pouring milk into his breakfast tea.

"My mind does not want to believe," I said. "That such beings are even possible..."

"And yet you and I have encountered life from beyond this orb before."

I could tell that my good friend was testing me, leading me somewhere, as a schoolmaster leads his class and a shepherd leads his flock.

"Compared to this," I said, "life on other planets is like finding new species on the next island over. This—" I waved inarticulately at the newspaper pictures.

"We lack the grammar to adequately articulate such things," said Sedgewick. "I wonder if there ever was such a place as Lemuria: a physical continent connecting India and Africa. Or was Lemuria—" he touched his fingertips together to illustrate his point "—another world, a hell of monsters, pressed up against our world, a border that was made and then lost in ancient times?"

"Perhaps it also gave rise to those Hollow Earth theories," I suggested. "But, if this Lemuria is not in a geographical location lost beneath the waves, why then would Klein choose to make the opening out in the middle of the sea?"

This question pleased Sedgewick a great deal and I could tell he had devoted some thought to it. "Whatever magic, madness or science lay behind Klein's plan, it is conceivable that water or the seas themselves were a necessary conduit."

"Then others could attempt a similar ... summoning elsewhere?"

"Perhaps," said Sedgewick. "Man hurls himself at the universe with almost no notion of what he is doing. We shouldn't be surprised by what we find. Certainly, poor Edward Klein found something in India—"

"Poor Edward Klein?" I interrupted, exasperated. "That man murdered hundreds of people!"

Sedgewick sipped his tea. "Von Humboldt argued that the structure and grammar of a language both reflect the spirit of a nation and influence its thoughts. I believe it is Klein's contact with that vile Aklo language, a language with the power to control minds and break down the walls between realities, that set him, perhaps against his own will, down his dark path. However, of his own will or not, he refused to be saved at the very end. He threw himself into the whirlpool."

"To die with his d_____ 'gods'!" I said hotly.

Sedgewick put his cup down. "Dead? Death is a function of *our* world, Cadwallander. Klein is with his gods now but make no assumption about his state of being."

The landlady appeared with a telegram for Sedgewick. We both eyed it cautiously before the professor opened the envelope and read the message. He gave a sudden and unexpected burst of laughter. "It's from Wilmarth," he said.

"Oh, yes?" I said, pouring myself another cup of tea.

"Mina Saxena is no longer in custody."

"They let her go?"

"No. She inveigled a police constable into her cell and then walked out of the station in the constable's uniform. She is once again at large and wanted by the police."

I slapped the edge of the table, though whether in indignation or amusement, even I could not say. "That woman is impossible!" I declared.

"Not impossible, Cadwallander. Just deeply improbable," said Sedgewick, reaching for the toast and marmalade.

1907 – The Shadow Under London
From the edited letters of Fabian Wilmarth

"Under the great desert lie buried cities, and there still exists part of the so-called prehistoric fauna. The desert tells nothing, for no man has yet explored it thoroughly, nor can do so, until the air ships and Röntgen rays are made practically useful for exploring purposes..."

Walburga Lady Paget
Colloquies with an Unseen Friend (1907)

1.

There is not a soul alive who does not know a little of the Hatch End tunnelling disaster of July 16th, 1907. The catastrophe contained all the components of a kinematographic shocker, all the fuel necessary to propel it through the gossip-mills of the empire, from the bars of working class public houses to the snooker rooms of colonial mansions in furthest Asia. A titanic subterranean explosion, property damage and subsidence as far afield as Watford and Willesden, the knowledge that so many of the dead were innocent women and children, and (for those with a penchant for outlandish theories) the possible involvement of Irish republican anarchists and even Her Majesty's Secret Service in the matter.

However, a great part of the tragedy's grim allure is that the huge number of lives lost in that calamitous event is both unknown and forevermore unknowable. This, any idle commentator will tell you, is because records of the numbers living in the tunnel at the time of the collapse were not properly maintained. I will add to that a reason of my own: we cannot know how many people died that day, because we do not know how many of the dead were human and how many were *something entirely other!*

There are those in positions of the highest authority who would not wish my singular account of that foul event to become publicly known, but I suspect that they have little to fear. I write this in the darkness of my cell, scribing in the hours during which my rehabilitory orthotic suit allows me some personal freedom and, although I write this account expressly for you, my dearest Rose, I do not imagine that you know of my present whereabouts or, if you do, that Dr Allen will pass it on to you.

That I should have become embroiled in events many miles from my Cambridge home is a matter of deep regret. The blame lies both in my cursed blood and my unseemly professional pride. I believe I never had a hope of escaping the doom I now face, but perhaps I could have delayed it; even remained in utter ignorance, had I not acceded to Captain Dansey's request for help.

On the evening of 12th July of that fateful year, I was to be found at a music recital at the Hoop Inn, lost in personal introspection and enjoying a pipe of Cavendish shag. It was during a duet between a young pianist and a Tabulating Machine Company orchestrette (of which the machine was by far the livelier of the two) that one of my constables slipped into the hall to inform me that there was a helipteron parked on the lawns of Jesus College. I could barely contain my ire: not only was this an infringement of local byelaws but a gross breach of the etiquette and niceties that govern this university city. Imagine, if you will, that a steam locomotive had parked in the flowerbeds of your own fair garden and you might have an inkling of my own indignation and distress.

I had the constable lead me there at once. It was just as he had said (for part of me had prayed it more likely that the man was mistaken); a helipteron sat in the centre of Cloister Court, its two rotor-blades still turning, its black exhaust pipes – its very presence! – polluting the noble college buildings about us. A man in a high collar, stiff suit and black leather gloves approached me.

"Wilmarth?" he enquired, raising his voice to be heard above the vile machine.

"What is the meaning of this?" I demanded, holding my homburg to my head lest the helipteron's powerful downdraft take it.

"*Inspector* Wilmarth?" he repeated.

He regarded me closely, clearly doubtful that I could be the police inspector I claimed to be. It is true that I do not strike many as the policing type. I am not the tallest of men and slimly built at that. Although I consider myself to be spry and athletic, my overall physique and youthful sandy hair gave many the impression that I was far younger than the thirty-five years of age I was at the time, let alone a commander of men.

By comparison, the fellow before me had a distinctly militaristic bearing and indeed introduced himself as one Captain Dansey. He did not identify his regiment and he was not in uniform. I took significance from this but did not mention it at the time.

"You must remove this vehicle at once," I instructed him.

"As soon as we are aboard," he said and, with a hand at my elbow, guided me towards the flying craft.

Naturally, I resisted and, at once, he presented me with a remarkable set of identification papers and a letter which silenced my protests. I was still re-reading it while the helipteron lifted away from the green lawns and bore us towards London.

"These are orders from Her Majesty Queen Victoria herself?" I asked.

"Drawn up and signed by her personal secretary," said Dansey. "But, yes, inspector, these are her orders." He had settled on the plush cushioned seat facing me.

"Does Her Majesty concern herself with such matters?"

"Her Majesty shows a great interest in all aspects of the life of the nation," said the captain. "You do know it is by her own decree that Younghusband's mission to Altair was made possible?"

"Space exploration is one thing but this letter relates to a murder investigation," I argued. "Is that not too ... trifling a matter for her?"

Dansey smiled thinly. "And is murder a trifling matter?"

"I think you understand my meaning plainly enough, sir," I said in a restrained tone.

"Indeed," said Dansey. "We believe the murder of Dr Bourke may have great ramifications for national security."

"Is that so? Then why does it require my attention? I was given to understand that London has many fine police officers. Scotland Yard is full of them."

"Two reasons. Firstly, you are a detective of no small renown." He counted the point on his fingers. "You solved the murders of Flinders Morrow and John Peters and, last year, apprehended the serial murderer, Spinnengewebe."

147

Dearest Rose, I did not point out to Dansey that the Morrow case was solved by your genius of an uncle rather than by my own self. I made this omission not out of vanity but out of certainty that Dansey already knew every detail of that unholy affair. It is true that I did arrest Spinnengewebe but that case was easily solved by cross-referencing optograms taken from the victims' eye against daguerreotypes of foreign nationals living in Cambridge. If I ever was a successful detective, it was through diligence and doggedness, not any brilliant ratiocination.

"And the second reason?" I asked Dansey.

He gently took the letter from me and folded it carefully. "Dr Bourke's body was found in a room that had been locked from the inside. When the men at the works broke the lock to gain entry, there was another man already in the room, wounded but alive. It stands to reason that that man is either James Bourke's killer, or another victim and therefore a vital witness." Dansey replaced the letter in its envelope, adding: "The man found with Bourke is Turlough Oberlin, your cousin."

2.

I had not seen Turlough since the funeral of his older brother some eight years before. It had been a subdued and somewhat furtive meeting, given that the older brother had, after falling into bouts of lunacy, taken his own life by the ingestion of lye. Now my late aunt's only surviving child and unmarried, Turlough assiduously maintained a relationship of letters with the only other family member; to wit, myself.

From his recent correspondence, I knew his career within the Great City Railway Company had led him to become one of the principal engineers on the London, Birmingham and Liverpool deep tunnel railway. The daring project would supersede the underground lines which currently extended from the capital into the Home Counties, ferrying passengers out to the great cities of England at the highest of speeds and in the greatest of comfort. Police work has taught me that murder is rarely predictable and often committed on capricious whim but I could recall no evidence from Turlough's letters that he had anything but respect and

148

admiration for those who worked alongside or beneath him. A gentle soul and a gentleman, Turlough was to my mind the unlikeliest of murderers or murder victims.

Our helipteron descended towards a formally structured complex of buildings in what I calculated to be north west London.

"Hanwell Asylum for the Insane," said Dansey in response to my questioning look. "Mr Oberlin was positively raving at the point of apprehension and is considered a danger to himself and others."

The helipteron landed in the asylum grounds and, in the dusky light of a late summer's night, we were met by hospital staff who led Dansey and I into the asylum proper. We were obviously expected, and I was brought to Turlough's room at once. The very word *asylum* conjures up penny dreadful images of old Bedlam itself, of dark stone dungeons and shackles, and my first impressions of that room did nothing to shake them. My cousin sat in almost total darkness on a simple wooden stool, the gleam of metal around his wrists.

I gestured to the one dim lamp in the room, addressing the attendant doctor, one Dr Allen. "Dear God, can you not afford this man some light?"

"It's at his request, sir," replied the doctor. "The patient turns them down or blows them out whenever they are lit. We were worried he might set fire to the room. That's why we put him in the suit."

I asked to what *suit* he was referring and, to illustrate his answer, Dr Allen turned the lamp up a little. Turlough Oberlin flinched at the illumination. There was a series of brass bands fitted over his clothing at wrist, elbow, shoulder, neck, temple, waist, thigh and calf, each linked to the next by brass rods and hinged with units of interlinking cogs. Rubber piping ran from each of the hinged units to behind Turlough's back, although the purpose of these were not immediately clear.

"A rehabilitory orthotic suit, sir," said Allen. "It limits the patient's movements depending upon the time of day or their location in the asylum."

I approached Turlough; with a series of ratcheting clicks, he stood to greet me. There was a strangeness in the motion, as if his movements were as involuntary as yawning or coughing. I understood then the purpose of the suit. It had made a marionette of my cousin, controlling his gross movements. The suit was more of a prison than the locks on the door or the bars on the windows.

Turlough himself was much changed from when we had last met. His skin, where it was not marked with injuries, was exceedingly pale and had taken on a leathery sheen. His hair, once untameably thick, was thin and receding to the point it was naught but a fine covering that lay flat on his scalp. His eyes and mouth, whether this was his usual appearance nowadays or a result of his injuries and imprisonment, were both withdrawn and reduced to simple slits in his face, as though he were squinting, tight-lipped, through the gloom.

I placed my hand on Turlough's shoulder. His gaze, unfocused and wandering as a drunk's, passed briefly over my face without a glimmer of recognition. I looked at the livid cuts and bruises on his face. "What happened to you, Turlough?" I asked.

"We are hoping you will be able to answer that question, inspector," said Captain Dansey. "Mr Oberlin has said nothing since his arrival."

"Not entirely true," said Allen. "There have been words and phrases, some mumbled, some shouted."

"Some nonsense about darkness," admitted Dansey. "And a repeated reference to the Deep One or *a* Deep One."

Turlough strained against his suit at that and took hold of my arm. For the first time my cousin looked at me directly. "Deep One ... uncovered," he whispered. "From darkness to darkness they came."

"There, the darkness, see?" said Dansey. "Nonsense."

"I see without light," said Turlough. "Beneath the Hill of Truth, Wilmarth. *Cnoc Fírinne.*"

A disapproving grunt escaped Dansey's lips. From that sound alone, I comprehended both the Crown's interest in the matter and a possible reason for my involvement.

I doubt poor demented Turlough, his mind a-wandering in the fields of madness, knew I was there, let alone recognised me. Nonetheless, I took his hand and assured him that I would do all I could to bring him comfort and release from incarceration.

150

Outside in the corridor, shared my honest thoughts with Captain Dansey. "You think this is about the Irish Question," I said plainly.

Dansey coolly examined the sheen of his gloves. "Dr Bourke was an Irishman, Mr Oberlin one quarter Irish. Most of the navvies working on the deep tunnel railway are Irish. This very year marks the twentieth anniversary of the Jubilee Plot to assassinate our dear Queen with incendiary pyrotechnics, and we have hundreds of Irish nationals whose works lie not eight miles from Buckingham Palace armed with digging machines and all manner of explosive munitions. I pray that this murder has absolutely no connection to the Irish Question."

I nodded in appreciation of the seriousness of the situation. "It is true that our maternal grandmother was an Irishwoman. However, you will never find so true or loyal a British subject as my cousin."

"Then perhaps that is why he was targeted," said Dansey. "Or why he and Dr Bourke came to blows."

3.

That night, I read the small number of case notes which had already been compiled. At around eleven o'clock of the 11th July, violent sounds were heard from the Dr Bourke's office at the deep tunnel railway site. The only entrance to the office was via the site infirmary. Bourke's nurse and one of the tunnel workers were in the infirmary at the time and attempted to gain entry. Bourke's door was locked. The tunnel worker forced the door and, within, Bourke was found dead, apparently battered to death with a wooden chair, and Turlough was found on the floor, the chair held in his grip.

Despite Dansey's suspicions, my investigation into Dr Bourke's murder was to be carried out openly and without secrecy. A man had met a violent end and a police enquiry into the matter seemed only natural. Captain Dansey had arranged with the London Metropolitan Police for the investigation to be placed formally in my hands and so, equipped with my dactylographer, optographic materials and other investigative tools forwarded from

Cambridge, I journeyed to Watford on the morning of the 13th July to meet one of the works foremen.

The deep tunnel railway, as its name suggests, does not come above ground so along its route a number of sloping access tunnels have been built for the delivery of materials and removal of waste. It was at one of these tunnel mouths that I met Fitzgibbon. He was cheerful and garrulous type who recognised me at some distance among the navvies, draymen and clerks at the works entrance and waved vigorously to me.

"You'd be the police inspector," he said, seizing my hand once he had reached me. "Joseph Fitzgibbon. This is a nasty business. Nasty, nasty business." The tone of his voice conveyed the suggestion it was anything but.

He led me down toward the tunnel mouth. To the right, a conveyer belt of overlapping metal plates and buckets continually regurgitated mud, rock and slag into a succession of waiting carts. The unending procession of material was quite mesmeric.

"Two and a half thousand tons excavated per hour," said Fitzgibbons, noting my gaze. "The conveyors run along the full length of the excavation."

"Astonishing," I commented.

"That's as nothing compared to the amount of water that we continually pump out of the system. Thirty six million gallons every day, from here into the sewers."

Fitzgibbon directed me to a form of funicular railway cart which ran on cogged wheels down the steep access tunnel. As we rode into the earth in the company of workmen, he gave me a brief overview of the deep tunnel railway. Currently at two hundred and twelve miles of its final two hundred and thirty-five mile length, the tunnel stretched from Bootle in Cheshire to Hatch End in London. It ran at an average depth of five hundred feet, more than three times that of the deepest London Underground railway. At its lowest points, the tunnellers had even been known to suffer from Caisson disease.

"Caisson disease?" I asked.

"The Grecian Bends," said Fitzgibbon. "Bubbles of air that can caused rheumatism or worse in men working at great depths or pressure. We've had the great John Haldane down here, advising us on how best to deal with it. We've adjusted our air pumps to help with the problem."

"Air pumps?"

Fitzgibbon nodded and pointed at thick piping which ran underneath the muck conveyors. "Pumping all the air, good or bad, from the digging face up to the surface, thus drawing the clean, surface air down."

Within a matter of minutes, daylight ceased to penetrate the tunnel and our way was illuminated by a string of Swan light bulbs. The incandescent lights did not provide a facsimile of daylight but gave shape and definition to the gloom. I said as much to Fitzgibbon as we disembarked at the base of the slope.

"You will find that your eyes adjust quickly enough," he replied. "Most of us need light only to work by. We don't revel in it."

The electric illumination was sufficient for me to grasp the awful scale of the construction. Our sloping access tunnel gave out into the deep railway tunnel proper: an arched tube some thirty feet high and of a similar width. Riveters, welders and a number of stonemasons worked on the walls and ceiling in each direction, as far as I could see in the gloom. To imagine that a man might walk through a tunnel such as this, all the way to the banks of the Mersey!

"Here, the men are shoring up and reinforcing the walls," said Fitzgibbon, his voice echoing among the clangs, whirrs and scrapes in that cathedral space. "The chalk is easy to work with, but even down here, we're dealing with London Clay. Treacherous stuff. The digging face is considerably further on."

"And the crime scene?" I asked.

Fitzgibbon gave me an inscrutable look, perhaps surprised to consider what had befallen my cousin and Dr Bourke as a crime. "Yes," he said. "Dr Bourke's surgery is in this direction."

As we walked northward along the tunnel, I commented: "I am surprised that your site doctor would actually have his offices within the tunnel."

Fitzgibbon grunted as though amused. "We have everything we need down here. There are no lodging houses directly above us to house all our men, so they and their dependents have accommodation down here. And that necessitates other facilities: stores, canteens, chapels, schools."

"Schools?" I said. "Surely, there are no children here. No one under twelve would be permitted to work in an environment such as this." I was suddenly put in mind of the writings of Engels (in which I had indulged during my liberal youth) and the horrible plight that the Irish working classes had always endured in Britain.

"Indeed," agreed Fitzgibbon. "Hence the need for schools. Please try to understand the reality of this situation, Inspector Wilmarth. Around you is something that is, in the most literal of senses, a travelling community. Yard by yard, day by day, we move towards our destination. The men at the digging face carve out chambers for themselves in which to rest and eat their victuals. The workers who follow add further sub-chambers and make good what was made before. Then come the electricians who fit the lights and the electric fire alarms; carpenters and other tradesmen. Chambers become rooms: properly lit, fully furnished and fully plumbed. And once the digging face has advanced sufficiently, those places are abandoned. There are more empty rooms in the tunnels between here and Liverpool than in all the palaces and castles of England."

"The workers, yes, I understand," I said, "but the wives and children? This is surely not a suitable domicile for them."

"And where would they go?" said Fitzgibbon in what sounded a perversely cheerful tone. "These are not local people. Do you think the good people of Hertfordshire and Bedfordshire want Irish ragamuffins and harlots in their towns?"

I balked at Fitzgibbon's choice of words.

"They've been called that and worse," the foreman said. "As I'm sure you know."

"But do they not have homes and houses back in Ireland?" I asked.

"And wait patiently for their husbands and fathers to send their wages home instead of spending it on meat and beer; and only meat if there's no beer left? No, inspector. Besides, more than a few of our fellows are descended from the Limerick Hickeys."

This meant little to me but Fitzgibbon was happy to explain and asked if I had heard of the Irish Rebellion of 1798. I had to admit that I knew of it but not the details.

"It was a dismal failure," he said. "Sectarianism, poor weather and even the French conspired against the cause of the United Irishmen. Until the Fenian Rising of '67 – which was quickly quashed by Her Majesty's ironclad mortar-men – it was the single greatest opportunity Ireland had to free herself from British rule." He looked at me askance as he said this and I forbore to comment or give any sign of disapproval. I gestured for him to continue.

"The Irish Volunteers fought the British army throughout the spring of that year. There were victories on the battlefield in Kildare and Wexford but our countrymen were frequently outnumbered and compelled to resort to less than honourable tactics. There was a man in County Limerick by the name of Daniel Hickey who the British claimed had committed acts of murder, torture and outrage in pursuit of Irish freedom, all without an ounce of remorse. True or not, when the rebellion was all but crushed, Hickey and all his family were forced to flee Ireland."

"And, a century on, now live out their lives in this pit."

"Oh, it is not so bad, inspector," said Fitzgibbon gaily. "Look up."

I did as directed and was greeted with what appeared to be an endless passageway of stars, circles and spirals of light, rising directly above me without end. Slowly my perception shifted and I saw it for what it was.

"It's a chimney."

"An air shaft," corrected Fitzgibbon. "We sink one every dozen miles or so. It assists in the drawing down of good air and provides another access point to the tunnel." He gestured to an iron staircase running to the base of the shaft and spiralling up the twenty foot wide shaft until it was lost among the lights.

"And people live up there too?" I asked.

"The penthouse apartments," laughed Fitzgibbon.

I squinted at the dimmest heights. "By God!" I exclaimed. "Are those stars?" I fumbled, astonished, for my pocket watch.

"They are stars," Fitzgibbon assured me, "and it is still the middle of the day, sir. I understand that it's a trick of the light. We look up at the heavens through a narrow tube and the sun's light does not come at us with a directness sufficient to drown the starlight. Beautiful, is it not?"

I could do nothing but agree.

Fitzgibbon led me on further and, as we walked, I had opportunity to contemplate the men working around me. Perhaps it was Fitzgibbon's talk of the Hickey family but I was surprised to note a similarity between many of them. Beneath their hard hats, many had a certain narrowness to their eyes, not like the Oriental but as though each was on the verge of sleep. Their lips, pale and thin, were also universally drawn closed. There was also among many a shortness of the arms and legs and a compactness of physique, like uncooked gingerbread men, although I have heard this trait attributed to all of Celtic descent.

I wondered if all of this constituted a certain Hickey look but, considering I had noted not dissimilar attributes in my cousin the night before, perhaps this was more of a *tunnel look*: a condition brought on by the gloomy depths; or a degeneracy caused by some common nutritional deficiency. These speculations were set aside as I espied a further curious sight: a number of the men, diggers and masons, would pause in their work to pick up stones and place them in their mouths. Some simply held the stones in their mouths, whilst others actively chewed on them.

"Dashed strange habit," I said to Fitzgibbon.

He grunted as though there was not the slightest thing strange about it.

I bent to pick up a stone; it was a pointed spiral shell, its smooth turns coated in blue-grey clay. "Fossils," I said.

"Ancient seas," said Fitzgibbon. "Here we are." He gestured to a doorway in the side of the tunnel.

I slipped the fossil into my pocket and followed the foreman along an electrically lit corridor and into a side chamber that, but for the lack of windows, had the dimensions and aspect of a village school house. In this space were arrange a number of empty beds and store cupboards marked with a red cross. A young nurse stood at one of these cupboards, inspecting the medicines within and making a record of them in a ledger.

"This is our infirmary and this is our nurse, Miss Sedgewick."

The young woman put down the bottle she held and finished her note making before turning to us properly.

"Miss Sedgewick," said Fitzgibbon, "this is Inspector Wilmarth. He has come about the ... about Dr Bourke's..."

"Death, Mr Fitzgibbon?" said she.

Fitzgibbon, who had been all comradely cheer with me, had now adopted an entirely servile tone with Miss Sedgewick. If he had a cap, he would be doffing it and wringing it in his hands. I wondered if this manner was a reflection of her valued position within the works, or because her posture and speech instantly marked her of a higher class and status than Fitzgibbon. Or perhaps it was simply that Fitzgibbon was smitten by her.

Miss Sedgewick was young (no more than eighteen years old by my reckoning), shapely, graceful in her movements and so exceedingly fair of face that it seemed almost blasphemous to have her among the dirt and rough toil of this place. And yet, there was also a shining intelligence in her eyes of a type possessed by few women – at least in my experience.

Yes, dearest Rose, this was how I regarded you on our first meeting. Perhaps if I honestly believed this written account would ever reach you, I would not have the temerity to speak of you in such candid terms. You were a vision of virtue, a woman of obvious charity and faculty and, yes, perhaps I was also smitten by you in that instant.

"Good morning, inspector," she said. "I was expecting you sooner."

"Apologies, miss," I said. "I was flown down from Cambridge late last night."

"Flown?" she said, although the look in her eye made it a clearly rhetorical question.

"Miss Sedgewick was the one who had the authorities alerted," said Fitzgibbon.

"You were the first at the scene of the crime?" I asked.

"Once Mr McNamara had broken down the door," said Miss Sedgewick. She stepped over to a side door where I noted the frame around the door had been forcibly splintered apart. A short plank was nailed over the doorway to seal it.

"Perhaps you would like to see the scene of the crime, inspector. Dr Bourke's corpse has been removed to the mortuary but I assure you it remains otherwise undisturbed." Miss Sedgewick spoke without a tremor of emotion and, far from regarding her as repulsively callous about the matter, I had only admiration for her steely resolve and fine degree of common sense.

The local constabulary had boarded up the door when the crime was uncovered and Turlough taken away into custody. A minute's work with a crowbar had the door open once more. Dr James Bourke's office was, to the untrained eye, most modestly furnished. His desk and chair might as well have once been the dining furniture of a pauper's house. His 'filing cabinet' naught but a number of cardboard boxes on a shelf. However, I also noticed the radionics cabinet, Röntgen screen and patented Hahnemann medicine chest that marked this as a most modern medical surgery. Much of the furniture and equipment was in disarray: a chair flung over here, papers and instruments cast to the floor there and, across the floor and wall in one corner, a violent spray of dried blood, deep maroon in colour.

"Who has been in here since the incident?" I asked, holding fast at the doorway.

"Myself and Mr McNamara in the first instance," said Miss Sedgewick. "There were the three police constables who removed Mr Oberlin and then Dr Bourke, this last under my direction. I seem to recall that Mr Topham was in here, also."

"That he was," agreed Fitzgibbon. "He's secretary to one of the major shareholders in the company. He came to make an account of events for his boss."

"I see." I opened my Gladstone bag, removing my dactylographer and Sprengel-Farmer particle extractor. "And I thought you said it had remained undisturbed."

"We've moved nothing," said Miss Sedgewick primly.

I kept my opinions on this to myself and instructed the two of them to remain beyond the doorway while I entered to salvage what evidence might remain. By means of clockwork driven bellows and the helical mercury pump within, the particle extractor sucked up matter from the floor as I progressed into the room.

"This is the murder weapon?" I asked, pointing to but not touching a fallen chair which had severe indents along one leg and was marked with blood.

"Mr Oberlin was holding it when we entered the room," said Miss Sedgewick. "He was wild-eyed, as though he had been fending off lions or bears."

I nodded, my mind filled with grim speculation. The detective's work is to reconstruct a picture of the past, a picture of a very specific and abhorrent moment in time. In the smashed chemist's jars, in the scrapes of furniture legs on the floor, in the horrible dynamism with which blood had been shed, I held a picture of two men locked in a barbaric and mindless fight to the death.

I took dactylographic images of the chair leg (a remarkable process employing radium-infused steam and sensitive plates) and then crouched to inspect the office door. It had been closed and locked; the key was still in place. "Why would either of the men lock the door?" I mused.

"It was never Dr Bourke's habit to lock himself in, certainly not with a patient," said Miss Sedgewick.

I raised my gaze to meet hers. "Was Turlough Oberlin a patient?"

"Dr Bourke was physician to all of us."

"I meant was Mr Oberlin ill?"

"Not that I'm aware of. He had made no appointment with Dr Bourke."

"And yet," I said, "we may assume from the very evidence around us, and from Mr Oberlin's strange utterances since, that an illness of some kind had come over him."

"Dr Bourke certainly wouldn't have been receiving patients at that time," she insisted. "He does not hold his Monday surgery until midday."

"And yet this McNamara character was in the infirmary," I interjected.

Fitzgibbon, at once, contrived to look sheepish. "McNamara is a somewhat intemperate soul," he said.

"The man is an inebriate," Miss Sedgewick supplied, bluntly.

"He is an old man, ma'am, and drinks to drown out his demons," defended Fitzgibbon.

"He's a fool," she said. "We allow him to sleep off his excesses in here, lest he choose to sleep them off on the railway line. And

160

when he awakens, we attempt to steer him in a more Christian way of life."

"I'd have thought that would the job of his priest," I said.

Miss Sedgewick scowled and Fitzgibbon smirked momentarily at her dour expression.

"Is the priest an inebriate also?" I hazarded.

Fitzgibbon coughed politely. "I think the problem is that Father Kelly is a Roman Catholic and Miss Sedgewick – begging your pardon, ma'am – thinks we papists are all drunkards."

I waved his comment away. "I'm curious how Mr McNamara could be in the room next to this violent tussle but not think to make entry until instructed by you, Miss Sedgewick."

"He was only stirring when I returned from my morning errands," said she. "As I said before, he's an inebriate and had not yet finished sleeping off his folly."

"Nonetheless, I will need to speak to him. Where may I find him?"

"Wandering dangerously close to the digging face as is his wont," said Miss Sedgewick.

"Telling all who will listen that our chthonic excavators are no match for navvies with steam-drills and good honest toil," added Fitzgibbon. "I shall see if I can find him for you, inspector."

My initial survey of the room complete, I snapped my dactylographer shut to preserve the recording plates and suggested that, while Mr Fitzgibbon sought out Mr McNamara, Miss Sedgewick would be able to show me the body of the late Dr Bourke.

Fitzgibbon was glad to be spared the sight of Bourke's remains and so, with him gone, Miss Sedgewick led me along a corridor to a more secluded chamber which served as the site's mortuary. Miss Sedgewick perceived my surprise at the simple room and the two stone shelves serving as mortician's slabs.

"You didn't think we would have need of a mortuary?" she said.

I was honest. "I am not sure. Part of me wonders that, whilst another wonders if it is large enough for your needs."

This drew a small smile from her; despite the morbid setting, I was pleased by this. "You are not wrong," she said. "There are always deaths – tunnelling is a dangerous occupation – and when there are accidents, we are rarely fortunate enough to lose only one or two men."

Bourke's body lay on one of the tomb-like shelves. He was dressed in checked trousers, his shirt sleeves rolled up to silver sleeve garters at his elbows. In life, he had clearly been a healthy fellow, his strong limbs, full cheeks and a bold English moustache compensating for his short stature and balding crown. Now, a full day after lying in this stuffy and surprisingly warm subterranean sepulchre, Bourke's body had moved beyond rigor mortis and was even showing early signs of corpse bloat.

"However," Miss Sedgewick continued, "there is hardly need to keep bodies from burial. Their kin, if they have any, are already here, and cause of death is rarely a mystery. For most, this room is the briefest of staging posts on the journey into eternity."

I regarded poor dead Dr Bourke: the vilely colourful wound in his temple that had finally dispatched him, the absence of two shirt buttons and a tear in his collar, the bloodied fingernails and abrasions on his forearms which spoke of that fateful fight. There was a curious serpentine blemish on the back of Bourke's left hand, the red line of raised flesh caused by something beneath the skin, I took it to be a skin infection and irrelevant to the matter in hand.

"You must see your fair share of injuries, Miss Sedgewick," I said.

"Occasionally, a man will put his hand into the workings of his steam-drill to clear a jam without thinking to switch it off, or stand just a little too close to a goods truck as it rolls by, but injuries in this industry appear to be of an all-or-nothing variety, inspector." She placed a hand of Bourke's leg to smooth out a crease in his checked trousers, and in that gesture I saw that she had held the doctor in some esteem. "If a pocket of firedamp meets a naked flame, the men caught in that explosion and subsequent collapse will likely be beyond any medical help."

"Is there much danger of firedamp down here?"

"Some, but the danger of stinkdamp is of greater concern." She smiled a little at my confused expression. "Stinkdamp, or sulphureted hydrogen to be scientific," she explained. "Heavier than air and both poisonous and flammable, it can pose a terrible threat to life. The one saving grace is that it has an odour not unlike that of rotten eggs and is quite unmistakable. If you can smell the rot, raise the alarm. And be doubly quick if you stop smelling it."

"Why?"

"Because in more lethal concentrations it causes a certain nasal paralysis. It destroys one's sense of smell."

"Sounds awful."

"Safety in the tunnel has been improved immeasurably by the introduction of the air pumps at the digging face," said Miss Sedgewick. "Sulphureted hydrogen, firedamp and other phlogisticated gases are pumped along the length of the tunnel and safely out into the open."

In the clarity of her explanation and the glint in her eye, I saw something I recognised from another time and place. I felt emboldened to ask her something that had occurred to me from the moment we were introduced. "Sedgewick is an uncommon name. You wouldn't happen to know a certain Professor Erskine Sedgewick of Cambridge University?"

Before Miss Sedgewick could answer, Fitzgibbon appeared at the door. He rapped at the doorframe and, standing sideways so as to avoid looking in on the body of Dr Bourke, told us that he had searched all of McNamara's usual haunts and the old drunkard was nowhere to be found.

"This is unacceptable," I replied. "The man is the closest thing we have to a witness."

"I cannot find what won't be found, sir," said Fitzgibbon with an apologetic bob of the head. "Perhaps if you are to finish your other investigations here today, I could bring him to the police station another day."

"I think not," I said. "I will stay until this man is brought before me to give his statement."

"Quite right," said Miss Sedgewick unexpectedly. "Inspector Wilmarth shall stay the night if need be."

"Stay where, ma'am?" asked Fitzgibbon.

"Here in the infirmary, naturally. We have beds and I am sure the inspector will appreciate our good hospitality. Besides," she added, giving me a most perplexing of looks, "he and I have much to talk about."

5

As it was, Miss Sedgewick (that is, *you*, dearest Rose) did know Professor Erskine Sedgewick. The great scientist and theologian was her father's brother. I had come to know the professor during my investigation into the death of Professor Flinders Morrow two years before and, I am not ashamed to admit, he is a far finer proponent of deductive investigation than myself.

I was curious how a girl from such fine stock should come to be a nurse to navvies in this dark and grimy place. Our supper was delivered to the infirmary by a Methuselean serving woman from the works kitchens and, over a supper of boiled meat and potatoes (followed by a superior Keiller's marmalade cake), Miss Sedgewick explained how she came to work there. I remember how she – you – told me that her parents' objections were primarily of a religious nature.

"Although horrified to think of me surrounded by what she describes as left-footers, in all other ways, my mother has somewhat progressive views," she said. "She feels these charitable endeavours of mine are quite laudable."

Miss Sedgewick had enjoyed the fullest of educations and went on to read natural and moral sciences at Girton College, Cambridge. She was, by her own admission, a gifted mathematician but was drawn to medicine out of sense of moral duty. Despite the pioneering careers of Elizabeth Garrett Anderson and her like in the past half century, there were few routes into true medicine for women. However, in Dr James Bourke, Miss Sedgewick had found a true patron and gifted mentor.

"I have run the site dispensary single-handed for the last four months and, under supervision, carried out four amputations and an appendectomy," she said with some pride. "Dr Bourke and I also collaborated in research into the effects of sulphureted hydrogen on the human body, particularly as a potential use in suspended animation."

The phrase was meaningless and alien to me and I asked Miss Sedgewick to elaborate.

"A Dr Roth of the Territorial University of Washington has established that in precise concentrations, sulphureted hydrogen brings about a state of hypothermia and induced torpor in test animals. The mixture of air and sulphureted hydrogen reduced the animals' temperatures to just above fifty degrees and reduced breathing and heart rate to such an extent that the animals' life signs, their anima, were effectively reduced to naught."

"Impressive," I said.

"The implications for mankind, from treating the ill to transporting individuals across the world, or indeed between worlds, are inestimable. We were also composing a detailed paper on miner's anæmia which, if published, would have credited me a co-author. At least," she added with a quiet, self-conscious air, "that was what Dr Bourke had promised."

"What is this miner's anæmia?"

"I saw you observe the inflammation on the back of Dr Bourke's hand, inspector."

"An infection?"

She nodded. "Miner's anæmia, also known as tunnel disease and Egyptian chlorosis, is caused by the parasitic hookworm which latches onto the walls of the intestine with its teeth and feeds on blood from the gut lining. Many of the people here carry the infection."

"I assume it's caused by ingestion of contaminated foodstuffs," I suggested, averting my eyes from my now empty supper plate.

"Not often. The hookworm's method of infection is fascinating, ingenious even." Miss Sedgewick's glee was barely suppressed. "Infection comes about through contact with contaminated soil. The less than perfect sanitation down here and the fact that many of the women and children are entirely barefoot is much to blame. The larvæ burrow through the exposed skin and enter the bloodstream which carries them—" she drew an imaginary line around the edge of her torso "—to the lungs. From there, they ascend to the tracheal-oesophageal junction where they are swallowed by their unwitting host. What you saw on Dr Bourke's hand was the trail of a larva that had failed to locate a blood vessel and had migrated along and beneath the skin."

"Fascinating," I said, without much enthusiasm.

"It is," she said. "Fascinating and ingenious but, do not mistake me, Mr Wilmarth, utterly abhorrent. In sufficient numbers, the hookworms' consumption of host blood will bring about anæmia, malnutrition and death. There are also, I believe—" She hesitated, stopped altogether before standing to stack our plates.

"What is it, miss?" I said.

"Later," she said. We ate our cake and drank our tea in silence until the ancient kitchen hand came in and cleared the dinner things. Miss Sedgewick watched her leave, then closed the infirmary door and prepared a fresh pot of tea. Only once the tea was poured, did she speak freely.

"You may think me mad, Mr Wilmarth," she began, "and I do not suggest that this has any bearing on the death of Dr Bourke, but my uncle has spoken to me of you and, in his words – take it as a compliment if you will – you are a 'thoroughly modern policeman' and there are queer goings on here that perhaps require a policeman's eye."

"Queer goings on?"

"A shadow hangs over this place—" She paused, silently but visibly chastising herself; perhaps for the melodramatic turn of phrase. "I shall be plain and stick to facts where I can, discrete and unrelated though they may appear. Inspector, I believe a number of the people here are deliberately infecting themselves with hookworms. Some consume the earth from the tunnels as a matter of daily habit."

"I saw this as I arrived," I said. "I thought it an old miner's trick, a way of gauging the composition of the rock. Or something more akin to superstition, like the hunter daubing himself with the blood of his kill."

"Inventive suggestions," said she, generously. "Geophagy – the eating of earth – is a not uncommon practice in primitive cultures. In some, it is believed to enhance male potency. Others believe it may ease women's discomfort in pregnancy, although this may more likely be a reference to the unnatural cravings experienced by some pregnant women. Burton writes that, in Haiti, so-called *bon bons de terres*, made with salt and fat and cooked in the sun, are a staple food of the poor."

I smiled in recollection of an almost forgotten memory. "My grandmother sent peculiar little biscuits to my mother while she was carrying me. *Cácaí cloiche* she called them. My mother tried one and spat it out. It was made with clay. Old Irish recipe, I understand."

"Bentonite clay has digestive properties," agreed Miss Sedgewick, "but there is more. These people, these earth-eaters, are changed people, physically and mentally."

"How so?" I asked.

"They crave the darkness, claiming to need no light."

"A man adjusts to life in this gloom..."

"...But should not crave the dark. I've heard them speak of it in revered, even sacred tones. They—" She fixed me with a fierce stare and I could see that this woman, this self-assured and wilful young lady, was quite afraid. "They *see things in the dark!*"

"Ghosts and ghoulies?" I said, attempting the lift her state of alarm with a jovial tone.

"Do not mock me, sir!"

"I do no such thing," I assured her. "Perhaps what they are seeing is—"

"I am aware, sir," she said, interrupting loudly, "that there is a documented phenomenon called the prisoner's cinema in which protracted periods of darkness cause the individual to see a veritable magic lantern show of lights and shapes. In fact, such shapes and designs have been seen in the cave paintings of the Asian troglodytes."

"I was actually going to point out that, in complete darkness, sensitive individuals are able to see the electromagnetic Odic force that emanates from all living things. Perhaps you have a clutch of sensitives here."

Miss Sedgewick shook her head. "You mean well, Mr Wilmarth," she said, "but though you might rationalise every one of my trepidations, I cannot shake the queerness of it all. Strangeness abounds in this place and I feel a terrible, *terrible* foreboding."

At that moment, I remembered that my cousin, in his ravings, had spoken of darkness and of seeing without light. Had I not also noticed the remarkable tunnel look which some of the workers shared, and which poor Turlough appeared to be acquiring? "Miss

Sedgewick," I said, "when I spoke to Mr Oberlin yesterday he was quite out of his wits but he did mention something called the Deep One. Does that mean anything to you?"

Miss Sedgewick treated me to the most disdainful look. She had evidently decided that, since I had not taken her anxieties seriously enough, my questions would for now go unanswered. "It is late, Inspector Wilmarth," she said, coldly. "I shall make up a bed for you and, perhaps tomorrow, someone will show you the wonder and majesty that is Deep One."

6.

Sleep eluded me that night.

Miss Sedgewick had retired to her own apartments a short distance away and I was alone in that subterranean infirmary, a room away from the office in which, according to all the available evidence, my cousin had bludgeoned to death an innocent physician. This was not a locked room mystery; the mystery lay in what knowledge, fear or compulsion had driven Turlough to slay another man.

Furthermore, Miss Sedgewick's concerns, disparate and unmarshalled though they were, preyed on my mind. In my short time below ground, I too had sensed a queerness among the tunnel-folk and this alone warranted investigation.

There was no means of gauging time in those lightless catacombs but by my watch. It was one o'clock in the morning when I rejected any hope of sleep and decided to explore the tunnels. I took from my bag the pair of Michelson-Morley goggles I had the foresight to bring with me. Once out in the gloomy half-light of the great tunnel, I was able to see well enough via the Michelson-Morley glass's detection of changes in the ætheric wind as it flowed around bodies in the earth's atmosphere.

With no day and no night to govern them, it was not surprising that navvies worked on the tunnel around the clock. The flow of men, materials and waste was unending. My night-time explorations were without specific aim but remembering that the drunkard, McNamara, was often to be found at the digging face, I chose to head south, walking in the opposite direction to the endless conveyer belt of spoil. Navvies tipped their hard hats at me as I passed, or murmured a greeting of sorts. I saw several chewing on the local stone and many with the narrow-eyed, close-lipped and short-limbed tunnel look. I was a stranger in this place and I felt it keenly, but I was not challenged or questioned. I also passed a number of women – ragged and filthy they were – with their guttersnipe children in tow. These offspring, I saw, were as bright and well-proportioned of limb and as *normal* as any urchin above ground, whilst their mothers had more than a little of the tunnel look about them.

I have such understanding of the natural sciences as a good detective requires. I am given to understand that Karl Pearson has done some sterling research into hereditary deformities and such social inadequacies as might be passed along the familial bloodline, but if the tunnel look was a product of defective blood (de Vries' *pangenes*) then it did not manifest in these people until adulthood.

Within half an hour, I had moved beyond the leading edge of the tunnel dressing works. Smooth masonry and gleaming steel supports gave way to rough stone walls and temporary support braces (between which bands of white stone and blue clay pressed against one another) and it was shortly hereafter that the strings of incandescent Swan lights stopped. Ahead lay only tracks on the ground, waste conveyors, air-pumping pipes, the darkness of the rock and, in the far distance, the sound of great engines.

I was not then nor have I ever been afraid of the dark (I write these very words in near total darkness) and pressed onward, seeing only by the ætheric wind made visible by my goggles. There were as many workers in this part of the cavernous tunnel as in the illuminated sections behind me and their toil was not impaired one jot by the lack of light. The only difference was that there was far less talk among the men and, when they spoke, it was either in Gaelic or with accents so thick that I could not decipher a single English word. I would also add that the tunnel look seemed far more pronounced among these folk, that their faces were almost featureless, their eyes, mouths and even noses quite subsumed into the pale leathery skin. I supposed that this was some artefact of the Michelson-Morley glass.

It was as I passed a trio of these unusual men, regarding them with evident curiosity, that a voice, slurred with drink and speaking in a heavy Irish accent, although nonetheless in English, spoke to me. "He was one of them – one of us – and could not bear the truth of it."

I considered the man slumped in a niche in the uneven wall. He was grizzled and unshaven, and his lined face, etched as it was with dirt, made him appear perhaps older than his true age. There was nothing of the tunnel look about this fellow.

"Mr McNamara?" I ventured.

He pushed himself up from his resting place with many an impolite noise and stood unsteadily before me. "Come to see the gateway to Yoharneth, have we?" he asked.

"Yoharneth?"

"The great city beneath the Hill of Truth," said McNamara, as though it was obvious. "Ah, be off with you!"

This last was directed at the three tunnel men who had stopped pushing their rail cart of what appeared to be blasting powder and turned to look at us. McNamara waved his hands at them (one of which clutched a large toddy flask) and growled some dismissive gibberish at them. The pale little men shuffled off reluctantly.

"They know you and I are no threat to them," said McNamara, mystically.

"The Hill of Truth is not in London," I said. *"Cnoc Fírinne* is a hill in County Limerick; according to legend, at least."

McNamara shrugged. "This Truth'll be one of them universal truths, copper. As true here as it is there. Come." He began to walk in the direction I was heading, with the deliberate and focused gait of a man who spent most of his life at some level of insobriety. I walked beside him towards the ever growing thunder of the machines ahead.

"What is making that noise?" I asked.

"Deep One," McNamara replied. "Deep Two is some two hundred miles north of here, currently burrowing its way under the Mersey. Irishmen working that end of the tunnel too, but not like us. You know we are all Hickeys here. Every man, woman and child.

Our mams may have married men with other names but Hickeys we are and our blood has drawn us here. There. Deep One."

McNamara pointed ahead and I could see a hundred yards distant, a colossal shape taking up the entire height and width of the tunnel. From this rear aspect, it presented as a slow-moving wall of iron and steel. An iron staircase ran from the ground to gantries at two levels, giving access to bulkhead doors. Great exhaust pipes dotted the wall, several feeding flexible hoses that led to the air pipes. An endless regurgitation of rock and sludge poured from a letterbox-shaped opening high up on the machine, diverted along a steep funnel down to the waiting conveyors. However, it was only when I saw the rear aspects of two great caterpillar treads – each as high as a man and twice as wide as they were high – beneath the outer edges of the machine that I finally grasped the reality of it all.

"It is a digging machine!" I exclaimed. "A vehicle that bores its way through the earth!"

"An unrefined mechanical behemoth," said McNamara with some rancour. "One hundred and fifty feet long and nearly five thousand tons in weight. We could have done an equally good job with a hundred men and good honest steam-drills."

I did not respond to McNamara's Luddite remarks; I was awe-struck by the great machine. I saw that, in the space immediately behind Deep One, stockpiles of other resources stood waiting: railway lines and sleepers to extend the track in Deep One's wake; a neatly stacked arrangement of conveyor belt units to add to the existing chain; the rolls of rubberised tubing to further lengthen the air pipes which contained and ultimately carried away the firedamp and sulphureted hydrogen of which Miss Sedgewick spoke.

We passed beneath one of the great air shafts that punctuated the tunnel roof. This one, freshly dug, was not yet dressed with stone or equipped with stairs. McNamara gazed up.

"That's Hatch End up there," he said. "A quiet little suburb I hear. Folks in their beds, not knowing there are monsters beneath their homes and hearths." He stood in silent contemplation of the distant night sky for a minute, swaying slightly. "I suppose we should count ourselves lucky to be here."

"In what way?" I asked.

"Hickey sacrificed a number of his children to Donn."

This statement, so absurd and shocking and unexpected, left me dumbfounded.

"If Hickey and his followers had offered up your great grandpappy or my great grandpappy to the Lord of the Dead then neither of us would be standing here," said McNamara.

I shall break off this narrative momentarily to explain what I understand of Donn and his place in the rich tapestry that is Celtic mythology: the lies, truth and poetry that have, like the physical geography of our land, been laid down on us across untold ages. Known as the Dark One or, more precisely, the Brown One, Donn was one of the sons of Mil who came and fought with the tribes of Danu but was later slain after slighting the goddess, Ériu. The dead god (and alleged father of the entire Irish race) was granted dominion over the dead. *Cnoc Fírinne*, the Hill of Truth, is one of several places in Ireland that are said to be Donn's domain. However, neither then nor now (after devoting my time to some limited research) have I found evidence of Irishman, ancient or modern, making child sacrifices to Donn or any other god. Nor have I found any reference to the city of Yoharneth of which McNamara spoke. At the time, I thought he was dissembling or taken by some personal delusion.

McNamara beckoned me onward, towards the rear of the great boring machine. He took a swig from his flask and proffered it to me. I waved it away. "Did Fitzgibbon give you his little potted history of Daniel Hickey?" he asked, a foolish grin on his face as though he was taking me into his confidence. "Some tomfool nonsense about the Irish Rebellion one hundred and wotnot years ago? I bet he painted Hickey as an essentially good man whose atrocities against the English and Limerick folk alike were the result of a surfeit of patriotic zeal?" He grunted to himself in satisfaction, even though I had not given word or gesture in answer. "And I suppose that Mr Fitzgibbon also conveniently forgot to mention old man Hickey's deal with the devil too?"

"What deal would that be?" I said, humouring the man (It is from experience of handling the intoxicated laymen and undergraduates of my home city, that I hold that a drunkard is more easily led through kindness than driven with harshness).

"Up here," said McNamara and began climbing the stair at the base of Deep One.

"Are we allowed to do this?" I asked, even though no man around had shown the slightest interest in our activity.

"Do you want to see their changes to the plans or not?" said McNamara irritably and climbed.

The moment I laid my hand on the stair rail, I felt a deep thrumming vibration through the metal. From the tunnelling machine's engines, I felt rather than heard a *basso profundo* note, deeper than human ears could hear. I felt as though Deep One was an organ of titanic proportion and I was experiencing its music through senses beyond the ordinary.

I hurried to catch up with McNamara. "What changes to the plan?" I asked. "Do you mean the plans for the tunnel? Is this something Mr Oberlin did? Something he noticed?"

McNamara paused at the first gantry. "Truth is, Daniel Hickey was an indifferent herder in possession of a blasphemer's soul. He had no love of God. His view was, if Christian folk were taught to value poverty, modesty and chastity and expect naught but hardship and adversity in return, then they should go find themselves some better gods. No one was sure when he began the rituals up near Templeglantine, and him digging holes in the ground, but it was not long after that his fortunes began to turn."

He climbed the second set of stairs to the higher level and I followed. The exhaust pipes and cascade of expelled waste were now beneath us. McNamara had to raise his voice. "Hickey had been involved in a dispute over grazing rights with a neighbour and, quite conveniently, that man died of apoplexy. Hickey won two pounds and six shillings from a Cork man in a game of shove ha'penny. Furthermore, a local lass who had fallen pregnant by Hickey – or, to be certain, that's what the rumours were – she disappeared from her home one night while Hickey was at the local tavern in the company of three impeccable witnesses. All this was within the space of a year or two. After that, a number of folks who shared Hickey's distaste for Christian piety, and the stoic acceptance of life's ills, were drawn to him and his ways. And they got to make their own pacts with the devils under the hill."

McNamara had to accept my help in turning the wheel of the bulkhead door on the highest gantry, not because he lacked the strength but because he steadfastly refused to put down or pass over his flask of spirits to free his hands. Beyond was a companionway of riveted iron, much like I had seen in an *Illustrated London News* piece about the submersible *HMS Serpentine*.

"Now some the lads are in here are true Hickey folk," McNamara warned me. "Not long before they'll be returning to the earth and their own kind. You understand that they'll take no exception to you unless you choose to make something of it?"

I understood little of his nonsense but it did spark a comment from me. "Many of the men down here have a certain aspect to them," I said, "a peculiar ... tunnel look."

"That's them," agreed McNamara.

"But you seem to be unaffected."

McNamara grinned widely, with a mouth of mostly broken and missing teeth. "A wise man watches what he eats and drinks," he said and waved his flask at me. "I may be old but eternal life in Yoharneth is not for me. Not yet."

McNamara said no more and I did not press him as we entered the machine together. The power of the engines, distant yet close, throbbed all around us. I could also sense – only just – the slow forward progress of this locomotive mole, driving us foot by foot into the heart of London. The companionway was fitted with lights throughout but none were lit. Still my goggles enabled me to see the shape of things.

"I do not know if it was Donn himself or his children that Hickey and his followers struck a bargain with," said McNamara. "Perhaps an ounce of Donn's blood still ran in those Irishmen's veins and it was more of a family reunion. I was not there and imagine that I would have fled had I been, but my great grandpappy didn't. He shook the devils' hands, or what passed for their hands, and their deal was struck."

"You still haven't told me the nature of this supposed deal," I said, my exasperation at his absent-minded circumlocutions finally showing.

"Hickey would provide three things for Donn. First, he promised to uncover the city of Yoharneth and release the Dark One from his earthy tomb."

"But you said Hickey had met with Donn," I argued.

"Meeting and freeing are two different things," said McNamara. "There is whole lot of difference between where things are and where they *are*. Secondly, Hickey and his followers would give over children in blood sacrifice to their new god."

"That is a vile notion and I refuse to believe it," I said firmly.

"Then you won't like the third, inspector," said McNamara, licking his lips. "Hickey's folk handed over their womenfolk to Donn – or Donn's children perhaps – so that they might have congress with them and give birth to their unholy, miscegenated half-breeds."

I recoiled from McNamara's profanity. I did not care whether these notions sprang from his madness, his filthy imagination or from some third source; McNamara deserved to be shunned for such offensive impropriety.

He gestured to a doorway, indicating that I should go in.

"And, tell me, what did Hickey get in return for these repugnant offerings?" I asked, despite myself.

McNamara chuckled foully. "He got the god he deserved," he said.

7.

How best to describe Deep One, dear Rose?

Several newspapers carried images of it in their reporting of the Hatch End disaster. Those diagrams give a better perspective of that great machine than I had as, seeing it in operation, its exterior was concealed from me on all sides but one by the earth itself. It was an earth excavator, though not like those mechanical shovels one might see in mining quarries or on the wider thoroughfares of the city (and which, to my eye, are an unimaginative mechanical replication of the Indian elephant or the African cameleopard). It moved on wheeled tracks like one of Diplock's pedrail tanks and was powered by the same locomotive power which drives trains or traction engines. However, these analogies fail to create the overwhelming impression of its form, scale or function.

In my estimation, Deep One was like nothing so much as one of those spacefaring ships which venture beyond the sub- and superætheric planes of our solar system. Essentially bullet-shaped and built to withstand enormous exterior pressures, Deep One ploughed a course through England's earth as a superætheric ship ploughs the luminferous planes of space.

Continuing the metaphor, the rooms to which McNamara led me might best be described as the bridge or wheelhouse. Two men stood at what I would call a viewing panel but there was no forward porthole or window through which to look (for what would there be to see?). Instead, they monitored the progress of Deep One via various displays and gauges. I recognised a compass, a barometric dial, a thermometer and a liquid filled gauge which appeared to relay the machine's speed. There were other instruments, including a brass gyroscope and a matrix of tiny Swan bulbs, but I cannot speak to their function.

As McNamara pulled me over to a central table laid out with maps and charts, one of the two crewmen plucked a voicepipe from its bracket on the wall and with an outlandish bark of greeting – "*Iä! Iä!*" – relayed orders to the engine room, I assumed, using terminology and language that was quite beyond my comprehension.

I was about to asked McNamara in what Irish dialect or other tongue the men spoke but was silenced by the sight of the man's hand as he replaced the voicepipe. In truth, it was a further extension of the tunnel look I had previously seen, but one can only accept so many increments of grotesque, physical abnormality before concluding that one is in the presence of something wholly unnatural and *entirely other*. The hand looked to be wrapped in a pale leather mitten. There was no thumb and the other digits had withdrawn into the body of the hand, becoming little more than round nubs of flesh.

I barely restrained myself from crying aloud.

McNamara tugged my sleeve, drawing my attention to an open chart. "This is the deviation from the plans," he whispered, tracing his fingers over the draughtsman's chart.

176

With difficulty, I pulled my gaze from the perversely formed men to the papers. McNamara's meaning was clear. I could see that certain pencil marks had been erased and that the path of the great tunnel now moved five or more degrees further north than originally planned. I tried to relate what I was seeing to my knowledge of the city above, immediately thinking of the enigmatic Captain Dansey and his fears of Irish seditionists.

"This new line would take the tunnel close to the Palace of Westminster," I said softly. "Even directly beneath it."

McNamara chuckled at that and took a belt of spirits from his flask. "These lads aren't interested in your earthly palaces. In the lightless city, Donn's own country, there are mighty spires and towers such as would paralyse your city leaders with awe and terror. I've heard it said that if a man looks upon some much as a single pillar of the cruel architecture of Yoharneth, that he would be robbed of sight and mind at once."

"Rot and nonsense," I said, annoyed and, if I am honest, unsettled by his words. Even so, I kept my voice low so that the queer fellows at the controls would not hear me. "What I see here is plain enough: a plot is afoot. Whether the enterprise is criminal or political in nature, it seems probable that Turlough Oberlin uncovered it. Did he confront Dr Bourke regarding what he had learned or did he seek him out as a confidante? Was the good doctor a Fenian plotter, hiding his anarchist tendencies behind his bedside manner?"

McNamara hawked up a gobbet of phlegm and gave me a fiery glare. "You've not listened to a word I've said, boy," he hissed. "A plot is afoot – I told you so myself – but Oberlin, Bourke, you, me and every soul down here is a part of it. Donn awaits us all. He's sleeping in his tomb, a frozen god in – what does that pretty nurse call it? – *suspended anima*. The Dark One's day is coming. and right soon."

I had heard enough of McNamara's nightmarish fantasies. I hurriedly folded up the chart so that I might take it with me as evidence. At the rustle of the papers, one of the crewmen turned to me, waving his malformed arm.

"*Cuir G'flar! Ní féidir rh'yd a chur xlen.*"

I have transcribed the sounds he made as best I can but do not know what specific meaning they conveyed. However, from his tone and the downturn of his lipless mouth, this ugly subhuman was not happy with me taking their maps.

"Do not think to impede a police officer in pursuit of his duties," I said firmly and gave the jacket pocket containing my Webley break-top revolver a meaningful pat.

The man did not take kindly to this and raised his voice in further gibberish speech.

"There's naught to worry about, friend," said McNamara to the engine driver, holding his hands out in a bobbing, calming motion. *"Gye sé ar sholg fineáil. Gye sé dho-na cheann hyu dúinn."*

His attempts to reassure them were unsuccessful; the two tunnel folk rounded on him as one, spitting and growling. A change came over McNamara's face, becoming fearful. Whereas I had felt like a trespasser, an interloper, ever since my arrival, McNamara had brought me here with the self-assurance of a lord touring his own manor. No longer. He gave me a sideways look that suggested he had walked me into a lion's den.

"I told you not to rile them!" he said, his voice strained by anxiety.

"Do they not understand who I am?" I said, putting my hand in my pocket but not yet drawing my gun. "Do you need to translate?"

"They know you are one of us," said McNamara. "But they are—"

One of the man-creatures growled and lashed out with his stunted arm.

"Out! Out!" hissed McNamara, giving me a shove towards the bulkhead door.

A policeman acts with unimpeachable authority in the service of justice and should never need to retreat from the threat of violence. However, the alarm in McNamara's voice propelled my feet from that room. I clutched the plans in one hand and my pistol in the other.

Beyond the door, a bark of exclamation drew my attention along the companionway: a half dozen figures were coming at me. Fleetingly I thought – oh, how I wished – that these were more with the tunnel look deformity, but my baptism into this realm on horrors was not yet complete!

The unclothed beings were whiteish in colour, with shades of intestinal grey and light fleshy pink shifting beneath their skin as though they were translucent, rubbery sacks of butcher's offal. Their skin was coarse and thick, apparently arranged around their heads and bodies in bands. As they approached, these segments shifted and rolled over one another, profoundly varying their height in the manner of a concertina or – God in heaven – the ambulation of a worm!

This sickening revelation rocked me on my feet and near drove me to madness. The most human aspects that they retained were their limbs: stubby arms and legs, without distinct hands or feet and no longer than that of an infant child. I saw that these limbs were more impediment than aid to their movement. Furthermore, the horrors had no eyes to speak of except pinpoints in the folds of their hides where their human eyes had once been (for I understand clearly that these unholy entities are the final stages of the vile tunnel look). Their mouths too had degenerated into lipless holes filled with sharp, triangular teeth. However, they had retained some facility for speech: their baying howls of fury conveyed all the animosity that their faceless countenances could not. I recoiled from these blasphemous worm-men, unwillingly accepting every truth McNamara had spoken about these fiends and the devils who had spawned them.

I raised my pistol and shot the nearest of them in the place where a man's heart might be. The creature fell to the metal floor, milky ichor splashing freely from the mortal wound. The one immediately behind arched over its fallen brother and came at me. I made to flee. I did not know where McNamara was (and it shames me to say, Rose, that neither did I care). My mind, sharpened to singular purpose by fear, was set upon escape. As I turned, the worm-man lashed out at me, snagging the leather strap of my Michelson-Morley goggles and dislodging them from my eyes.

I was plunged into complete darkness. I did not see where the goggles fell but I knew that the exit onto the higher gantry at the rear of Deep One was straight along the companionway. I ran with devils at my heels, the clang of my shoes pursued by the relentless slither and calls of the worm-men. I slammed into the bulkhead, jarring my outstretched wrist, and turned the wheel with a fury and strength I have not possessed before or since.

Propelled by fear, I felt that the worm-men were but inches from my back as I barged the door open. Perhaps they were, for no sooner was I on the gantry above that gloomy tunnel than one of the creatures drove into me: its loathsome mouth against my throat, its unnatural hide against my body, pinning me to the low safety rail. Below us, the expelled soil tumbled from the mouth of the machine in a continuous irregular tattoo. I screamed, I yelled. Oh, dignity and reason had abandoned me completely and I roared like primeval man locked in deathly struggle with a wild beast. I thrust my revolver in the demon's maw and pulled the trigger.

The worm-man slumped against me further and our combined weight tipped the pair of us over the gantry. I fell, having no time to flail or scream for salvation. My head struck hard metal and darkness overtook me.

8.

It would be appropriate to say that I was surprised to awake, albeit slowly, alive and whole. It would also be appropriate to say that my surprise was deepened by the fine furnishings of my surroundings. However, I was surfacing from a complete and terrible blackness and any normality was seized and welcomed as an old friend. The only surprise was the presence of Captain Dansey in the room.

He sat at a table by the window, drinking tea in the light which fell through the ribbed silk drapes. I levered myself up onto an elbow, wincing at the instant pounding in my head. I had been undressed, my head bandaged, and put to bed in the first and only four-poster bed I have ever slept in.

"Dr Walton said you ought to come round today," said Dansey, placing his cup on its saucer. The chink of china on china drove through my head like a gunshot. "I believe you might have been lost to us if not for his restorative tonic."

I asked Dansey where I was. The man gave a grunt that, in his type, was the closest he would approach to a laugh. "One might be more interested in where you were, inspector," he said. "You were found by some young lads, unconscious and waist deep in a spoil heap in Watford. I might speculate that you had fallen onto one of those muck carrying belts in the tunnel and been transported most ignobly out from the works."

I thought of the waste-diverting funnel at the rear of Deep One. Wide though it was, I was more than lucky to have struck it in my descent and, as Dansey suggested, slid down to the conveyor belt. "I must have been carried miles." Another thought struck me. "Was there another ... thing, a man of sorts, beside me in the spoil heap?"

"Buried five feet beneath you," said Dansey, nodding. "Another hour's muck on top of you and you'd have been buried too."

"You saw the creature?" I asked, scarcely believing that my encounters in the dark had been real.

"The creature and the fragments of paper still clutched tightly in your grubby fist, Wilmarth. I think I can piece together much of what happened from those facts. However, you will be called upon to give your account before you lead us back there."

"Back there?" I said, a tremor in my voice. I at once felt weak and – so unlike an Englishman – tearful. I had met with true dread in the pit beneath our capital and I think, right then, I would have sacrificed all else to spend the rest of my days in the daylight. The rectangle of grey light that came in through the silk drapes was beauty and life itself to me.

"You'll be accompanied by a platoon of my own men," said Dansey. "Force of arms and God himself will be on our side."

"Still, I cannot," I said.

Dansey's gaze hardened. "These are orders from Her Majesty, man."

"Forgive my impertinence," I said. "A brush with death and dark spirits might have addled my sense of duty but I do not think I could obey even if those orders came from her own regal lips."

"Get dressed then," Dansey said with a grunt. "She's expecting to see you downstairs within the hour. I'm sure she'll be most taken with your newfound insolence."

"She?" I murmured. "Her Majesty is—?"

Dansey exited the room without further word and at that moment I saw that the ancient spiral shell I had found in the tunnel stood on the cabinet next to my bed. It had even been cleaned. I was a far from perfect specimen, pitted by the ages and scored with mineral deposits.

Fresh clothes had been laid out for me. They were of fine material and cut to my exact measurements. A homburg from Lock & Co. of St James's Street had even been placed to one side to replace that which I had lost.

As I dressed, I opened the drapes wide and looked down upon narrow, distant streets, and what I took to be the Thames beyond. I found the view familiar and yet, for the moment, quite unplaceable. As I knotted my tie, realisation struck me. The scene was familiar because I had once, on a summer's outing, stood in those streets and looked upon this very building. I was taking my convalescence in Windsor Castle, one of Her Majesty's residences!

A footman appeared a quarter of an hour later to escort me to Her Majesty. As we descended stairs and crossed a gallery with windows overlooking one of the central lawns, I could not help but comment upon the vast airship tethered above the lawns. The servant informed me, politely and without elaboration, that Emperor Wilhelm II of Germany, Her Majesty's eldest grandson, was visiting England; although was at that moment in London.

I was brought to what I later learned was the Crimson Drawing Room. I was not in any state of mind to appreciate the fine ceiling mouldings, the inlaid floors or the many trophies of conquest on the walls. Ahead, sitting to one side on plush seats, were three men and a single, heavily veiled woman. Captain Dansey I knew, whilst the two men I recognised from the illustrated news: the Queen's physician Dr Herbert Walton and, that most curious of pets, her personal advisor, Chioa Khan. I have read that the two men met shortly after Chioa Khan's ill-fated attempt to climb Kangchenjunga in the Himalayas, at a time when Dr Walton was posted with Colonel Younghusband's Tibetan Expedition. I have also read, in the less reputable papers, that Her Majesty's continuing good health is due to a mystical elixir Walton had found on the high Tibetan plateaux, further imbued with restorative powers through Khan's secret magicks. Dr Walton was a pale creature with a wide-eyed gaze of a man recently awoken from a troubled sleep. Chioa Khan looked, as I very much imagined him, like a cat which had had all the cream.

As to the veiled woman, I could not see her face, but she sat with the grace of aristocracy and had the bony and liver-spotted hands of an elderly woman.

More centrally, on a significantly higher armchair, sat Her Majesty: Queen Victoria of the United Kingdom of Great Britain and Ireland, and Empress of India and Mars. I shall not bore you with a description of that most famous and celebrated woman of the age save to say that the Queen appeared far younger than her eighty-eight years and somewhat slimmer than I recall from pictures of her. She gazed upon me with a piercing intelligence that fair turned my legs to an impossible combination of lead and jelly.

The footman announced me in a clear voice. I approached with footsteps as awkward as a newborn foal's and, at what I prayed to be the correct distance, bowed as deeply as a Chinese mandarin and croaked, "Your Majesty."

"Come closer," said she with a beckon of her gloved hand. "I am told that you have performed great service for your country."

I replied that I had only performed my proper duty. The Queen commanded that I relay the story of my adventures in the tunnel; with an exhortation from Dansey to be bold enough to speak the truth and omit nothing, I proceeded to do just that.

My audience showed no surprise as I detailed my encounters with the perversely formed worm-men and McNamara's claims of their ridiculous plot to unearth what I understood to be some sleeping prehistoric god. Strange to say, in the telling of the tale, I could rationalise the whole and reconcile it within my mind. Indeed, by the end, I had convinced myself that there was no devilry or ancient sorcery at work in the tunnels below our feet, only shared delusion, the kind of fear which darkness encourages, and the unfortunate effects of the worst kind of disease (brought on by the hookworm, no doubt).

"Your Majesty," I concluded, "when Captain Dansey and I first met, I did at first question your interest in this matter. I now understand that this is a most concerning matter. The social ills faced by the tunnel workers and their families need addressing and the ... the wicked and pernicious superstition that may have led to both Dr Bourke's death and Mr Oberlin's slip into insanity needs to be weeded out."

The veiled woman motioned silently with her hand, a gesture that the Queen noted. "Lady Paget?" she said. "You wish to comment?"

The veiled woman, Lady Paget, sat forward slightly but did not lift her veil. "The earth is a hollow orb," she said, speaking in a fine English accent but with a certain precision of enunciation that suggested she was of European birth. "There are sunless lands and ancient cities beneath our very feet."

"I did not know, My Lady," said I politely.

"The survivors of Atlantis and of sunken Lemuria took refuge beneath the earth in those ancient cities."

"They did not build the cities themselves?" I asked. "Then there were people of even greater antiquity living there?"

Lady Paget paused and somehow I sensed that she was smiling. "Not people. Some might call them gods."

"The titans of old," suggested Chioa Khan, speaking for the first time.

Lady Paget inclined her head slightly in mild agreement. "Those who fell from the stars, from heaven, and wait beneath the earth for their dark day to come. These are not true gods."

"And must be destroyed," agreed the Queen.

I mentally stumbled. I had come to disbelieve my own account as I told it and, here I was, in front of our glorious head of state who not only believed every word but was happy to accept the further, baseless utterances of her peculiar lady-in-waiting.

"Excuse me, Lady Paget," I said. "Begging your pardon, but how do you know the truth of these things?"

The slightest wrinkle in Her Majesty's brow told me that my question was impertinent but Lady Paget answered nonetheless. "An unseen friend speaks to me," she said (which was no answer at all). "Daniel Hickey's descendants conspire to uncover Yoharneth and to free the exiled Son of Mil. It is vital that they be stopped."

"Your men are ready, captain?" said the Queen.

Dansey nodded. "Yes, Ma'am. We can leave at once."

184

Queen Victoria's gaze returned to me. "And you will show the captain's men the way and identify those who are complicit in the plot."

I heard my own voice utter the word, "Ma'am..." but I had no question or plea with which to follow it.

"Your redemption is at hand, inspector," spoke the Queen, her voice as soft as any mother's, yet underlaid with a core of steel. She gave me a look that was perhaps intended to inspire conviction and bravery, but I could not help but compare it with the pale and permanently startled expression on the face of Dr Walton. I have been in Crown Court many a time. When men are sentenced to the gallows, the look of fathers and mothers about to lose their son, of women soon to become widows, was the mirror of that etched on the doctor's face.

9.

Captain Dansey's platoon consisted of twenty-two men. They wore a black uniform without insignia or denotation of rank. None of the men were particularly young and I surmised from this, along with a hardness of eye and a variety of scars that Dansey's private platoon was composed of veteran soldiers.

At nightfall, we rode north to Watford in three helipterons, though every fibre in my being willed us not to. As we travelled, Dansey presented me with a weapon to replace my lost pistol: a compact carbine, worn over the shoulder and designed to be fired from the hip. It was manufactured from a body of steel and surmounted by a frame of hardened glass inscribed with a plethora of sigils and symbols, none of which I recognised. All of Dansey's men were equipped with the same weapon.

"A teleforce gun," explained Dansey. "A charged particle beam accelerator based on Tesla's original design. Fires two thousand rounds a minute. These are British prototypes but already an improvement on the Russian model."

I took it from him reluctantly. I was a policeman, a copper, not a soldier. To accept the weapon was to place myself alongside men who had known battle and carnage. In my heart, I felt that to accept it was also to accept I was potentially going to my death.

Dansey guided my hands to a detachable bolt and reel of wire underneath the body. "Slide this into the barrel and the weapon fires a grappling hook and two hundred yards of line. It tenses against a coiled spring within, immediately retracing with a pulling power of three hundredweight."

I held the weapon unhappily and stared at the engravings. They were not pictographic hieroglyphs but they struck me with such profundity that I felt I could read their meaning full well. They spoke of power and distance, of the twisting of things out of true, of the perversion of the world as I knew it. The weapons' innards glowed a faint blue, perhaps with the electric forces that powered them, and the light seemed to imbue the symbols with an eldritch energy. Nauseated, I looked at Dansey.

"And what are these?" I asked.

"Think of them as prayers inscribed on bullets," he said. "Talismans from the other gods."

"What gods?" I said, thinking I had misheard.

"Other gods," he repeated.

We landed sooner than I would have wished.

By lights, both gas and electric, the work at the site in Watford went on. Though our black craft were near invisible against the night, they were not silent. Many stopped in their work to watch us descend. Dansey's platoon disembarked rapidly and followed him to the tunnel entrance.

Dansey's principle tactic was one which has served the middle and upper classes of England well for centuries: he simply marched in as if he owned the place. Striding ahead, with a *V* formation of his men in his wake, Dansey ignored all greetings and waved a piece of paper authoritatively in the faces of any who sought to question him. He commandeered a number of the cog-wheeled funicular trains to take us down to the tunnel base.

At my suggestion, the men had all been issued with Michelson-Morleys; during the descent they slipped them on. In the growing gloom, the soldiers were bathed in the watery blue light of their teleforce guns. I sat in the foremost of the carts beside Dansey and, on his copy of the tunnel charts, outlined once more the most recent location of Deep One.

"We take control of Deep One," he said. "Any of those ugly goblin creatures we encounter shall be subdued or killed."

"And the innocent bystanders?" I asked as we disembarked.

Dansey's expression was hidden behind the goggles, but I suspect he placed little store in the notion of innocent bystanders. Nonetheless, he stepped to the nearest firedamp alarm box, opened the tin cover and pulled on the cord within. At once, the sirens high up on the walls emitted a piercing and discordant whistling. In a wave, the sirens along the walls took up the call. Men downed tools, jumped or climbed from their scaffolding and ran.

"Fair warning to get out of our way," he shouted and waved his men on.

We marched southward, slipping through a tide of fleeing men, women and children. I could not help but think of you, Rose, and wonder whether you had taken to the nearest exit, or had nobly gone to assist in the evacuation of the young and the infirm.

We were perhaps half a mile from the digging face with the dissipating throng of people still dashing past us when the sirens stopped. Dansey grunted to himself, tugging at the cord within the nearest alarm box. The alarm remained mute. "Then that is how they wish to play it," he said, shifting his teleforce weapon in his grip. "Anyone left down here is an enemy or a fool."

"And fools get what they deserve," spoke a broad-shouldered Yorkshireman beside me. Clearly, in pursuit of demons, these men had no interest in the application of law or justice.

A band of women and children scurried past us, the last of the crowd. Only when one stopped before me and spoke did I realise it was you, Rose.

"Inspector Wilmarth," she said, astonished. "What happened to you?"

I first thought she was referring to the peculiar weapon that I held, before it occurred to me that I had disappeared from my infirmary bed without warning and she might have imagined I had come to some foul end.

"You must get out of here, Miss Sedgewick," I said.

"Aye, clear out of here, lass," said the Yorkshireman.

"These men—" she began, gesturing to Dansey's soldiers.

"Agents of the crown," I said.

"And so the alarm—" She unconsciously glanced up to where the nearest alarm horn might be and frowned.

With the sirens silenced, we could all hear the distant but throaty roar of Deep One's engines and the constant rumble of the waste conveyors. I realised I could also hear another sound, much closer. I had not paid any heed to it before but, following Miss Sedgewick's gaze, I perceived that the clinks, knocks and creaks were all coming from high above. The soldiers raised their weapons. There was a set of linked girders by one wall, acting as a floor to ceiling brace for the incomplete tunnel; perched at the top, his legs wrapped around the girder, was one of the tunnel workers. He held a package in his hand and was busily but awkwardly working to fix it to the top of the brace.

"Hold still or we shoot!" shouted the Yorkshireman.

The man above us, turned his pale face towards and spat. *"Fhtagn ar g'yll Béarla! Críostaithe e'hucunech!"*

Behind me, Miss Sedgewick asked, "Is that blasting explosives?" just as I had come to the same conclusion. An instant later, one of the soldiers fired his weapon, someone else shouted "No!" and disaster was unleashed upon us.

I saw the miniscule bullets of the teleforce gun rip through the man on high like a scalpel. As they touched the bundle in his hand, the ceiling instantly became a fiery cloud of dust. Dansey was yelling orders that I could not hear. The men were falling back or frozen in shock. The Yorkshireman shoved me roughly aside. I stumbled against Miss Sedgewick and, acting without thought, grabbed and propelled her away from the scene. The Yorkshireman raised his weapon to fire, at what I am not sure, when with a single, short groan of warning the roof fell in.

A ton of earth collapsed onto at least five men. The buckled brace fell across the width of the tunnel. I heard a scream among the chaos of falling rock. I stumbled forward blindly, Miss Sedgewick before me; then the entire tunnel arch above us collapsed.

A clod of earth bigger than a man broke across my back. I staggered, pitched forward and threw myself to the ground, shielding Miss Sedgewick's body with my own.

10

Death did not come. I waited it out, breathing dust and soil while the noise of falling earth echoed around me for what seemed an age. Beneath me, Miss Sedgewick clung fiercely to my arms. I could feel her breathing: ragged and fearful; but, by God's grace, she was breathing.

Once I was confident the last of the earth had fallen, I raised myself up, shifting aside the layer of stony earth which had settled on us. Miss Sedgewick sat up and gave a single cough to clear her lungs.

"We are buried," she said simply.

The explosion had robbed the lights above of all power and, without my goggles, I would not have been able to visually assess our situation. As it was, the deep railway tunnel lay ahead; above us the roof remained in place, but behind was only rubble and ruin. A great slope of earth blocked the tunnel from floor to ceiling, sealing the southward section of the tunnel completely. There was no knowing how much had been buried; it might be twenty yards, it might be two hundred. What I did comprehend, with a faint heart, was that we were quite alone. There was no sight or sound of Dansey or his men. The Yorkshireman's shove and our subsequent stumbles had taken us beyond the forward edge of the collapse. I wondered if he and the others were safely on the other side of the cave-in, but I could not bring myself to believe it. Some or all of Her Majesty's men were entombed scant yards from me, their military assault on the tunnel thwarted before we had even reached our target.

We were alone and, I reasoned, unlikely to be rescued for considerable time; if at all. The Hickey folk – worm-men, twisted worshippers of the dark god, Donn – knew that we had come in force and now Miss Sedgewick and I were all that remained to challenge them. There was no escape to be had behind us and five hundred feet of London earth above us. The only escape route I could conceive of was the freshly dug air shaft just aft of Deep One. Our options were reduced to proceeding along the tunnel, facing whatever lay before us, and making good our escape.

The prospect was appalling to the point of insanity. If I did not regard self-murder as an unpardonable sin, I might have put the teleforce weapon to my temple and ended my misery there and then. But there are moral boundaries that a decent man will never cross and I now had Miss Sedgewick in my charge. "We must go on," I said grimly.

"I cannot see," said Miss Sedgewick who lacked the benefit of Michelson-Morleys.

"I am with you," I said, with far more conviction than I felt. Hand in hand with Miss Sedgewick, I proceeded into the pitch black.

I thought it my imagination but the air in that space seemed abruptly foul. A smell of decay, like that of rotten eggs, permeated the air. I walked towards the noise of the giant excavator's engines but, as I approached, I heard another sound, confounding and utterly chilling; it was the sound of singing. "What is that?" I asked.

"I have no idea," said Miss Sedgewick.

It was no earthly song, not of English or any other language I have heard. It had a certain atonal quality, of half and quarter notes that one might find in the music of the Indies, and the ponderous gravitas of a hymnal or a religious chant. Apart from the faint glow of the teleforce gun, there was no light in the place, and I doubt Miss Sedgewick was able to perceive much of the horror laid out before us both. That, at least, was a blessing. For the music was rising from the mouths and throats of two hundred or more individuals, gathered in the cavernous space behind the excavating machine and beneath the very air shaft which was our only route out of this Bedlam.

The Great Book speaks of lions lying down with lambs, of the leopard and the lamb eating together. In the moment I beheld that host, that choir, I understood that such Biblical metaphors, though well intended, are wholly repulsive and abominable. The lion and the lamb are never meant to lie together; they do not belong side by side, neither in harmony or peace. Each has their place in the world, in the order of things. To put them side by side is to create horrible incongruity. The world should rebel at such categorical incompatibility, as two magnets will resist efforts to thrust them together.

Before me was a crowd of incongruous beings. Here were all of Hickey's surviving offspring. Here were the workers of the tunnel and their wives, each in varying stages of their diseased metamorphosis. Here – my stomach and soul rebelled to simply look upon them – were the worm creatures themselves, taken beyond the frontier of what could even be called human. And, here – the sense of vile absurdity and irreconcilability of it all striking most keenly – were children and young adults as yet utterly untouched by the taint. Lions and lambs. Every one of those individuals, human and *other*, was singing in full voice, even though I saw the fear in the eyes of the children and young folk: terrified, yet singing in exultation and worship. Here was Hickey's perverse cult, a religion whose apotheosis – whose rapture – was upon them even as its members feared the world that was to come. I noticed too that the intensifying smell of decay I had noted shortly beforehand had taken on a new tone; the chamber was filled with a sickly sweet odour: incense for this diabolical choir.

Miss Sedgewick's hand tightened on mine.

At the front of the crowd, I saw McNamara. He rolled on the ground, bound hand and foot with rope, singing – nay, bawling and yelling – the words of the unholy hymn. His eyes and his mouth were smeared with mud and, in the filth that coated his few teeth, it appeared that he had been feasting, willingly or unwillingly, on the tunnel earth. He wriggled blindly, like the infesting worm he had resisted for so long.

The front ranks parted and Fitzgibbon stepped out to meet me. He was barely touched by the tunnel look but he wore the beatific smile of those who were truly at home. He stopped singing to greet me. "Oh, to be certain, it is by Donn's blessing that you have come to us, inspector," he said, hands outstretched to clasp me.

"Fitzgibbon?" said Miss Sedgewick, recognising his voice. "What is the meaning of this? What is going on?"

Fitzgibbon turned his gaze on her. There was a disdain and a hunger on his crazed face. How different this expression was to the servile adoration with which he had once regarded her! "You brought an outsider with you," he said to me. "A lamb brought to the altar?"

191

I took a step back and readied my gun. Fitzgibbon's smile only widened at this.

"What will you do, Wilmarth? You intend to stop us, to fight us? What can you do?" He spun in a circle, almost dancing, to indicate the gathered people. "Will you kill us all? Will you batter yourself against our machines or against our god?"

On the ground, McNamara screamed in his unholy ecstasy. Tears streaked his muddied cheeks. The old drunkard seemed to be having trouble breathing. Miss Sedgewick pulled away from me, her instincts urging her to go and help a man she could barely see. I held her close.

"The Dark One is almost here!" cried Fitzgibbon and raised his hand high as though reaching to the stars in the night sky far, far above us. "From darkness he came, travelling across unimaginable gulfs of space, like his brothers and sisters, cast out into the void. Explorers of the unknown! Pilgrims!"

"There are others?" I gasped.

"None so great as Donn, our father, who came to this New World to settle it in the name of the gods. But what colonist will accept rule from afar? You know this, Wilmarth. Our own history tells us this. Donn and his siblings rebelled against the Ancients. War was joined even though the children, the new gods of earth, were not yet the equal of their parents."

A foul dizziness was coming over me. I was finding it harder to concentrate. I found myself wondering if this experience was my mind's final and willing descent into madness. Of course, Rose, I believe you had already recognised what was befalling us both but it took me a few moments further to work out the truth.

"Those who were not destroyed, consumed, were forced to flee and hide," continued Fitzgibbon, shaking his head sadly. "From darkness above to darkness below. Donn slept in the ruins of Yoharneth. For untold æons he has lain in torpor, awaiting this day. And we, *his* children, will be here to greet him."

Fitzgibbon held out a hand to me. In it was a clod of earth and, just visible within it the wriggling white bodies of hookworms. "Take his benediction, Wilmarth. Be what you were born to be. Live forever in his city!"

"This is insanity," cried Miss Sedgewick, appalled.

I stared at the mud in Fitzgibbon's hand. On the floor, McNamara was coughing and choking, not on the earth he had eaten but on something else. None but me paid him any attention.

"We break through the final barriers now," said Fitzgibbon. *"Gnaii Duinn, leanbh na sho mháthair humuk!* Rejoice, son of Hickey! Son of Donn! Eat the flesh of the Great Worm, the Lord of the Dead and be one with him!"

Fitzgibbon's hand was on my shoulder, pushing me to my knees so that I might take his blasphemous holy communion. For an instant, the stench of cloying sweetness about me was overpowering, and then gone completely. In my dazed state, I grasped the truth.

"Stinkdamp," I coughed.

"Yes, inspector," said Miss Sedgewick, with the exasperated tone of a schoolmarm coaxing the times tables from her slowest student.

The sulphureted hydrogen gas was flooding the chamber. The pumps of Deep One vented all noxious gases up the wall-mounted pipes, but the cave-in would have blocked or ruptured those pipes. The poisonous and flammable gas, heavier than air, was pooling around our knees. If the dark cavern these monsters were drilling towards was filled with the life-suspending gas, then it would be flooding into our current space in ever increasing quantities.

McNamara was drowning in the poisonous air as inevitably as a man drowns in water. Forced to my knees, I took a single breath and almost fell into a faint. That my sense of smell had abandoned me was a frightening indicator that I was close to being utterly overcome.

"Take it!" commanded Fitzgibbon. "Be one with your kin!"

"Stop this!" said Miss Sedgewick. "This is madness. We must get out before we are all killed."

Fitzgibbon laughed. "You will know madness, its sweet caress, when we present you to the sons of Donn," he said. "But death? Death will not find you even if you wish it."

In those threatening words I found my moment of strength. I rolled back on my heels and stood. Retreating two light-headed steps – Miss Sedgewick safely behind me – I fired my gun at Fitzgibbon. The teleforce weapon had almost no recoil, yet the chain of invisible bullets thrown from it punched a hole of such a size through the Irishman that I might as well have fired a small cannon. Soundlessly, he fell.

Even if I had not been dazed by the sulphureted hydrogen I am not sure if I could say the killing of Fitzgibbon brought a halt to the congregation's singing. They were a crowd possessed unholy song and I doubt they could have stopped if they wanted. However, the psalm took on an immediately different tone and many voices were raised in a wail of hatred and condemnation. Worm-men, and those with the most profound tunnel look, pushed towards me. It was clear that if I was not a willing convert then I would be a sacrifice alongside Miss Sedgewick.

I fumbled with the teleforce weapon, clumsily detaching the grapple rod and sliding it into the barrel. "Hold onto me," I commanded Miss Sedgewick. "Now!"I aimed up at one of the high inner walls of the airshaft and fired. The line unspooled with astonishing speed; in a moment it was taut and pulling at me. If I had not worn the weapon's strap over my shoulder, it would have been ripped from my grasp. Miss Sedgewick clung to my shoulders and I held her firmly around the waist. As hands that were not hands grasped for us, we were lifted off our feet at speed and, swinging on a rapidly shortening pendulum, were hoisted roughly up the air shaft. It was by chance alone that we did not dash our heads or smash our bodies against the underside of the tunnel roof. Some hundred feet up however, I did strike the air shaft wall with enough force to knock the wind from me and rip the front of my trousers. Though my muscles screamed in agony, I did not lose my grip on Miss Sedgewick.

But, by all that is holy, how sweet the air had suddenly become! I hauled in breath after breath, feeling life and reason return to me. Far below, the inharmonious choral continued, projecting their hatred and their deviant religious zeal up at us.

Rose, I write this knowing that you will never read it. I do not know if you understood the act I was about to commit.

Perhaps I only hastened the inevitable. Deep One had an engine which, complex though it was, was a thing of coal and fire and steam. Surely, the flammable gas would have found flame soon enough. Perhaps I should not blame myself.

We hung above that abyss. I stared down at that unholy mass, seeing what you could not. I saw the young and the old, the tainted and the untouched. I looked down at them and saw the weeping children. I looked down and thought of the horror they believed they were soon to unleash.

Rose, forgive me.

Battered and hanging onto life by only a canvas strap and the grappling wire, I told you to reach for my ferrocerium pipe-lighter in my jacket pocket. I took it from you and opened it. I regarded its flame solemnly for a moment and then dropped it down the shaft.

11

Many months have since passed.

The Hatch End tunnelling disaster was the newspaper sensation of the season and, in addition to unprecedented column inches, the catastrophe led to questions in the House of Commons, further changes to British labour laws and a flurry of purportedly ingenious inventions which would make such accidents impossible in the future. Certain accusations were thrown at the Great City Railway Company (I heard mention of the suicide of one of the senior company clerks although I do not know if this was related) but the company retained its licence to complete the works. The finished tunnel, running all the way from Liverpool to Marylebone Street station in London, was completed in the cold February of 1908. The final few miles of the London end took a noted detour around the entombed wreckage of the destroyed mining machine. The decision was taken to leave the dead where they lay and erect a modest memorial to them on the Uxbridge Road above.

All this is a roundabout way of saying that the true nature of what occurred in the deep railway tunnel was never publicly released. Captain Dansey and an undisclosed number of his men survived the cave-in and vanished back into the dark regiment from whence they had come. I was not summoned back to Windsor Castle or received word from any of Her Majesty's servants and the Crown's involvement in the affair remains secret and unverifiable. The only possible link between myself and my employers in this affair is the supply of monies which pays for my continued recuperation at the Hanwell Asylum.

I have not seen you since that dark night of terrors. We were hoisted up to the surface by local men drawn thence by the terrible explosion. We came up into a confusion of people: workmen, policemen, the curious and the startled. I found myself attempting and failing to explain myself to the local constabulary when I realised that you were gone from my side.

I was brought to the hospital with minor but notable injuries but even the flintiest of souls would have also recognised that the terrible visions I had witnessed and the mental traumas these caused required medical attention. My initial progress was slow but upward and soon my days were spent in the hospital library and the perusal of such books of national and local history that the hospital possessed. Lured perhaps by some subconscious disquiet, I began a small but earnest study of my own family's history. My one living relative, Turlough Oberlin, still resided in the hospital (the death of Dr Bourke never came to the attention of the magistrate's court) and I felt that, once Dr Allen permitted us to meet again, it would be good to present him with some narrative of our shared heritage.

I knew much of my father's family but little of my mother's. I have already pointed out that my maternal grandmother, Margaret Solkirk *nee* Enright was Irish by birth, although discussion of that branch of our family was not heard at the dinner table while my parents lived. Dr Allen aided me with my research, seeing the value of mental exercise and endeavour to my convalescence. A copy O'Neill's *History of the Irish* was acquired from a bookseller in Knightsbridge and certain papers were loaned by the Home Office. Margaret Enright, I learned in the fullness of my research, was born at a Magdelen institute in Dublin, the daughter of an unwed mother; a fallen women. There was no initial answer as to who Margaret Enright's mother had been but after some significant correspondence and the brief employment of solicitor in Dublin, the Sisters of our Lady of Charity who run the institute sent to me the child's birth record. It transpired that, although my grandmother was raised in an orphanage under the name of Enright, she was born as Margaret Hickey, daughter of one Mary Elizabeth Hickey of County Limerick. Daniel Hickey, I discovered, had been my great great grandfather.

I state this plainly for it did not come as a shock to me. Both Fitzgibbon and McNamara had intimated as much, though how they knew this I could not say. I wonder now if Turlough had not taken knowledge of his ancestry less calmly and had sought reassurances from Dr Bourke. Perhaps Turlough, faced with the truth (and this coming from the lips of another of the Hickey folk), lost his mind in that instance and turned to violence.

Indeed, I took the news with an unseemly calm but, from that day, I began to study myself in the mirror above my room's mantel. My skin had taken on a pallorous colour during my hospital stay (a fact I had put down to a lack of sunshine and my preference to spend hours inside, often with the curtains drawn against the light). Also, I had developed an increasingly debilitating rheumatic ache in my hands and feet and now found myself wondering if my fingers and toes had once been longer. Oh, the slow transformation that was overcoming me, the disease of the Hickey folk, was alarming to behold, and yet I also found in it a puzzling sense of contentment, a progress toward some end purpose.

I wonder what my cousin Turlough looks like these days.

Last week, I had a troubling dream in which I met with my maternal grandmother in a grand and terrible metropolis that could only be Yoharneth. Stalagmite towers, neither built nor grown, loomed over us, reaching for a sky that had no stars. Without sound or motion, I sensed the movement of our one great ancestor, Donn, moving through the earth beneath us. Limbless, white, one great, toothed maw that consumes the earth.

I woke screaming and raving. After a week of such dreams, Dr Allen had me confined to this rehabilitory orthotic suit. A clockwork ensemble at the small of my back divines and directs my movements according to the instructions on the Hollerith punch cards the doctor inserts (curious, the suit is from the same manufactory as the orchestrette I was listening to on the night this whole episode began).

I do not care for the suit. I do not care about it. They can constrict my limbs while I still possess such things. Rose, dear Rose, I am moving towards glory.

I prefer the darkness now, making a cave of my asylum cell. Be it the Prisoner's Cinema or a developing acuity for Odic forces, I see without light. The dreams of Yoharneth persist but I do not fear them any longer.

Perhaps one day I will step, no, wriggle from my cell, having abandoned the need for limbs, the suit that constrains all men. Perhaps I will free my cousin and we will find our own way down into the shadows under London. There we will travel to the splendorous spires of Yoharneth and we will dwell in the house of the Lord of the Dead forever.

1908 – The Herald of the Ancients

From the memoirs of Mr J. Cadwallander

A tale told simply and well should be told from the beginning. However, the nightmarish events which saw the fall of the *Afrikanschen Himmelaufzug* and, in the dark years that followed, the fall of nations and empires, is a tale without a beginning. I am sure that my dear friend Professor Erskine Sedgewick would agree wholeheartedly and tell us that this story is one with roots in a time before time itself in which *beginning* and *end* are words without meaning; a time in which life and death are equally meaningless. But it is not in this sense that I speak of a tale without beginning; I am not the good professor and I am not inclined to the metaphorical or metaphysical.

Yet, I can say in all honesty that my tale began near its conclusion. We were aboard the *Afrikanschen Himmelaufzug*, more than two hundred miles above the surface of the Earth. Professor Sedgewick and I, along with the seditionist adventuress Mina Saxena and the Grand Duke Alexei Mikhailovich, were held at the utter mercy of those who would surrender our world to *beings beyond imagining*!

The first of these beings – a creature of fiendish proportions, encased in coal-black chitin – stepped forward from the summoning circle and it was in that frantic moment that I looked fully into the hideous heart of that artefact which Chioa Khan had christened the *Aleph*.

Surmounted by a stone setting and furthermore held in position by an arrangement of clamps, the Aleph would initially appear to any observer to be a glass crystal, the size and shape of a goose egg. This appearance, Sedgewick has since instructed me, was the opposite of the reality. Glass appears as it does because it has no light of its own but simply reflects and refracts the light of elsewhere. The Aleph, far from having nothing at its heart, possessed all things in its unholy facets. In Lewis Carroll's Alice stories, it was a rabbit hole that connected our world to the nonsensical Wonderland. This Aleph too was a hole between worlds but, instead of connecting to a singular fantasy land, the

Aleph's magic writhed and wormed a connection to all places and all possible worlds.

I did not mean to gaze deeply into that crystal egg (which was, one must repeat, no such thing) but a point of light caught my eye and drew me in. I can only suggest that as I looked at it, it returned my scrutiny, for I can think of no other reason why I was immediately struck with such specific visions. I stared and saw a scene that took place over four thousand miles away and nearly a year in the past!

"Maurits," I said.

I could see it with a vividness that no daguerreotype or kinetograph could emulate. I can only say although my body, mind and memories were left so far behind that any notion of self was lost to me, my senses were transported to a high-ceilinged cell and the three figures passing through the door from the main hospital corridor.

"What is it, Cadwallander?" The professor's voice was distant, but his presence, like the momentary recollection of my own name, slipped quickly from me and I was entirely elsewhere.

"Arnhem."

1.

The local physician, Dr Kipp, clicked his fingers to gain the boy's attention and gestured to the man and woman who accompanied him.

"Maurits. You have guests."

The boy did not look up from his drawing. A procession of neatly spaced black bees crawled across the sheet, marching towards and tessellating perfectly with columns of white toads proceeding in the opposite direction.

"Maurits," said Dr Kipp, "this is Dr Zwaardemaker and his secretary, Miss—" He cleared his throat and waggled his fingers as memory failed him.

"Miss Capelo," supplied Zwaardemaker.

"Of course. My apologies, *senhorita*," said the physician with a tiny and unnecessary bow to the brown-skinned woman. "Maurits, will you say hello to your visitors?"

The ten year old boy steadfastly ignored his doctor. (I automatically knew his age through means unknown, just as I understood the Dutch language in which they conversed; and just as I knew that not only was Zwaardemaker no doctor but the supposedly Portuguese amanuensis was also no such thing – borrowing her name from a Martian smuggler of her acquaintance.)

"I would describe it as a form of catatonia," said Kipp to his visitors, "except, of course, for the level of industry and active intelligence on display. The poor lad—" he tapped the side of his bald head "—is locked away from the world, communicating only through his ... art."

Miss Capelo surveyed the pictures which had been pasted up on the wall above the boy's bed, removing a compact daguerreotype camera from the satchel she carried. "Do you mind, doctor?" she asked.

"Be my guest," said Kipp.

As the woman took images of the boy's drawings, Kipp outlined certain details to Zwaardemaker. "You will see that many of his sketches are of sea monsters. This monstrosity, this Kraken, is the most common subject. Though we try to discourage him, he draws it at least once a day. I do not need to be a respected psychotherapist such as yourself to see that this creature represents the Lowestoft-Zeebrugge Bridge disaster which robbed him of his family. Do you subscribe to Freud's theories?"

"Hmmm?" Zwaardemaker's thoughts were elsewhere.

"I read his *Three Essays* recently. I am sure that Professor Freud would have his own interpretation of those thrusting tentacles, that toothless ... mouth."

Zwaardemaker said nothing, mesmerised by the image on the table.

"Whatever the case," continued Kipp, "this monster is his muse, his inspiration. It squats at the centre of all his thoughts, a spider in the web of his mind." He smiled in embarrassment at his own florid metaphor. "This century seems to breed monsters of the mind."

"It's horrible," agreed Zwaardemaker, pulling himself away from the image with difficulty, as though connected to it by powerful elastic. "Yet fascinating. Horribly fascinating."

"I sometimes wonder if there is meaning in those curved limbs," said Kipp.

"Meaning? Meaning, how?"

"A philosophy, conveyed in image not words." He shook his head. "A baseless fancy of mine, sorry. But I cannot otherwise explain the allure of these pictures. I am certain that if you decide to take him on at the clinic in Leiden, you will unlock the secret meaning of his art soon enough."

"These other pieces are very good," said Miss Capelo. Her Portuguese accent had clearly been copied from a native of Oporto.

Kipp re-examined the drawings on the wall before the woman: impossibly looping pathways; an artist drawing a figure who was, nonetheless, in the room with the artist; an interior room of a castle that was simultaneously a stone-paved courtyard.

"Tricks, *senhorita*," said Kipp with a condescending smile. "There's a certain rudimentary cleverness to it, but no real skill. Any student of art could render something equally good."

Zwaardemaker could see irritation flare in the woman's eyes. "That is what they said to Brunelleschi," he interjected smoothly.

"Sorry?" said Kipp.

"The Florentine architect," explained Zwaardemaker. "To win a commission to complete the cathedral, he told the city fathers that he could stand an egg on its end. Brunelleschi took an egg, smashed the end flat and thus stood the egg upright. Anyone could have done the same but no one else thought to do so. I'd say this boy is a genius."

"You'll take him on?" said Kipp hopefully.

Zwaardemaker stroked his beard, turning to Miss Capelo. "Do we have everything we need?"

She nodded and, from my omniscient vantage I observed, in the slight creasing of her eyebrow and the tiniest upturn of his lips, the unspoken communication which passed between man and woman.

"We do what we can here but our resources are so limited," Kipp was saying. "I am sure an ambitious doctor could make his name in the exploration, the interpretation, of this monster-mania. Cases of it abound across the continent. Castruni, Shapp, Wilmarth, Machen. My housekeeper swears that it is a result of galvanic residues but I—"

"Wilmarth?" interrupted Miss Capelo. "The British policeman?"

"Fabian Wilmarth," nodded Kipp. "Until recently a resident in a London hospital."

"Until recently?"

"He escaped, miss. By means unknown."

Miss Capelo hastily fastened the buckle on her satchel and gave Zwaardemaker a fierce glance.

"Time to go," said Zwaardemaker.

Young Maurits continued to draw bees and toads and shapes that were both and neither.

*

A voice called out to me, a voice that was not with me, but in another place entirely.

"Cadwallander."

My gaze and perspective shifted and my senses whipped away to a different location and time. Yes, I thought.

I heard my name repeated but whether it was by me or another party, I did not know.

2.

In short, I found myself.

I saw myself sat in the Knightsbridge study of Mr Braintree, the surgeon who had not only made good Professor Sedgewick's hasty amputation of my right arm aboard the *Wakefield* in 1902 but also was the principal designer of the artificial limb of brass, wire and leather that I have made use of ever since. My prosthetic arm was removed, lying across the wide blotter board of Braintree's desk, while the surgeon examined the stump of my arm in the light of a banker's lamp.

I recognised the scene as our last meeting some months earlier. Recalling it well yet simultaneously observing it from outside, I felt a momentary crisis of identity: vacillating between the man in the room and the external observer; an electric light flickering between two states. On and off; on and off—

Eventually I settled on identifying with the man before me, not as the ghostly spy in the room. Nonetheless, I could not prevent facts that were previously unavailable to me bleeding through into my comprehension of the scene; not least the realisation that I had evidently eaten *very* well in the last few years and that, if I was not careful, I would one day be an exceedingly rotund old man!

"Pink and puffy," Braintree was saying. "Does it hurt?"

"Not that I notice," I said, which was the socially acceptable lie.

"You are still using the powder?"

"Yes."

"And wearing the arm for no more than eight hours at a time?"

"Perhaps not," I admitted.

Braintree grunted good-naturedly (he was, I must say, one of the most personable and even-humoured fellows I've had the pleasure to know), turning his attention to the four socket tubes embedded in my stump and the clustered wire heads which ran through to the nerves of my shoulder. The flesh around the tubes was sensitive to his touch.

"I hear the army are interested in the designs for your prosthetics," I said, to distract myself from the discomfort.

This drew a darker grunt from him. "Prosthetic arms and legs. With those clever mechanical hearts and lungs those Italian chappies have developed, all we need is someone to build an artificial brain and we'll have metal soldiers fighting our wars for us." He sat back and tapped his fingertips together. "Six years," he said, "and still your body has not fully accepted the implants."

"Man and machine, an unholy union," I said, a jest that had ceased to be a joke and instead become my personal motto.

"I have a fresh powder you might wish to use," said Braintree, swivelling his desk chair. He produced a bottle with grey contents from a cabinet.

"What is it?" I asked.

"The active ingredient is a Norwegian mould. Its main function is to suppress the body's defences against infection."

"Suppress?"

Braintree nodded. "This tenderness around the implants is caused by your body attacking the implants as it would an invading bacterium, although achieving nothing other than irritation and pain to yourself. Your body is, in essence, being an overly zealous defender, unable to distinguish friend from foe. This medicine should bring a certain balance to your system. But do use it with care and inform me of any untoward side effects. You are the first amputee to whom I've given it. Until now I've only prescribed it as treatment for Dogger Bank Itch."

I gave the man a playful frown. "That sounds like some dashed awful .... *sailors'* disease."

"Indeed it is," he smiled, "but not *that* sort of sailors' disease, you scandalous knave. It afflicts the divers working on the trans-Atlantic pipe network and, like the reaction you suffer is caused by the body's over-sensitivity to an external agent, in this case the sea chervil."

"What is that, some sort of fish?"

"A moss animal actually or, to be more exact, a colony of moss animals, rather like—" Braintree broke off with a click of his fingers. "I knew there was something I wished to show you!"

Without further explanation and pausing only to enquire if I would care to take tea with him, Braintree left the room. He returned minutes later, followed directly by the maid with tea and a plate of macaroons. Braintree placed a heavy apothecary jar on his desk. The action sent ripples through the water, stirring an inch-deep layer of sand at the bottom and causing the trunk and fronds of a strange purple-white organism within to wave. I have enough of an education, whilst spending time in the company of better men, to know that this was not a plant, even though it had the gross shape of some seaweed. It was an animal: within there was a brain and a nervous system and a will to act.

"Sea anemone?" I said.

"Very good," said Braintree. "Incorrect but a very astute guess, nonetheless. It has the appearance of an anemone or similar but is, like the sea chervil, a colony animal. I found it at Shepherd's Port on the Norfolk coast whilst spending Christmas there with Ada and all the little Braintrees. I had thought I had never seen its like before and believed that your naturalist friend, Professor Sedgewick, might help me with its identification and classification."

Then, as now, I heard the emphasis in his words. *"Had thought?"* I said.

"Indeed. I took samples, made slides..." As he retrieved a pair of photographic plates from his desk drawer, I placed two coconut macaroons on the edge of my saucer. "Here."

The silvered plates clattered on his desk, next to the jar. I looked at magnified images of the sea creature's interior structure. The creature's hide – that is, the many creatures which made up the structure's hide – was a thick rind with a furred inner wall. Needle-thin walls of furred pith ran buttress-like throughout the structure: faintly geometric lines that held the whole in place. I quailed at the sight, recognising it as surely as I would recognise my own face!

"I have seen this before," said Braintree heavily. "As have you."

"The angels," I breathed.

He nodded. "Anatomically, this sea creature is all but identical to that queer infection which consumed your arm."

I – that is, the man in the room – was stunned. My perspective – that is, my omniscient viewpoint – reeled in sympathy.

A voice cried out.

3.

"Siberia!"

*

There are landscapes on the worlds of our solar system which are made astonishing by their vastness and uniformity. The great deserts of central Asia, the ice sheets of Europa, the American grasslands – like the sea, their trackless homogeneity creates a sense of wonder in some, an animalistic terror in others.

The Siberian taiga is of a size that defies comprehension. The British Isles, heart of an empire, would fit in it a hundred times over. The Podkamennaya Tunguska river cuts through the taiga forests, running a course from the Mongolian heights to the Arctic Ocean. A rare landmark, it is an anchor for the psyche in that measureless land. Several miles off from a bend in the river there was an area cleared of trees and the only visible signs of human activity for several hundred miles.

There were fifty-seven individuals at the expedition site. Eight of them were Evenki huntsmen, lured away from their reindeer herds and tent villages with the promise of St Petersburg gold. Five were scientists, explorers and soldiers, including one prince of the imperial family. The remaining forty-four figures moving about the site were maybe not people at all, being dead or in a state very much like it.

At the centre of the site, all trees had been removed and a pit, twenty yards across, had been excavated. Deeper than three yards the soil was, even in late spring, frozen and compacted to the consistency of stone. The lateral tunnels fanning outwards from the pit had required considerable effort and some ingenuity in their excavation.

At the furthest reach of the south tunnel, Grand Duke Alexei Mikhailovich placed an oscillator unit at the base of the impenetrable soil face. "Ready?"

Kirill the archaeologist spat whilst Vasiliev the geologist wrapped arms about his abdomen. The grand duke took both as signs of agreement. He crouched beside the oscillator and twisted the valve on the phlogiston pump.

The Tesla-designed oscillator was of unexceptional appearance. It consisted of a reinforced piston tube within a metal case containing inlet and outlet valves and an attached phlogiston reservoir. Powered by pure phlogiston, the oscillator piston was, within moments, moving at a frequency which set vibrations running the length of the tunnel and beyond. The oscillator was potentially a very dangerous machine: the piston pressure could easily rise as high as five hundred pounds per square inch and the internal temperature exceed four hundred degrees Fahrenheit.

Originally designed as a means of generating electricity, five of the devices had been brought on the expedition for their other, notable ability. Alexei lowered the intake valve a fraction; the vibratory hum of the device calmed a little. He was searching for just the right frequency; with the experience of several weeks' practice, he soon found it.

The oscillator created a sympathetic reverberation within the earth. The ground hummed. It also affected the three men in the tunnel: the tremors rose through their boots, numbing the sensation in their legs. Even the air seemed to purr in response. Alexei felt his metal chest plate sing in resonance, turning his iron lungs into the equivalent of a giant tuning fork. The tingling sensation, the sound of his artificial innards singing, was wholly disquieting. However, he reflected, he was probably better off than Vasiliev who had, more than once, suffered uncontrollable bowel movements in the presence of the oscillator.

The reverberations built, wave on wave, until dusty soil was drifting down from the tunnel's low ceiling. Up above, the Evenki would no doubt be trying to calm the horses. A number of the *automatichesky-chelovek* would have toppled over, their punch card instruction wheels jammed.

"Enough," said Alexei and closed the valve entirely.

The dust settled. The men took deep breaths and wiped their brows. The tunnels, humid and warm despite the frozen ground around them, became hotter still after the oscillator's use.

Vasiliev stepped past the Russian prince and pulled loosened, frozen sods from the digging face. By the light of Kirill's lamp, all three could see what lay beneath.

"Another wall," grumbled Alexei.

"Fallen masonry more like, Your Highness," said Kirill. "I would suggest we are looking at a higher level of the original tower."

"Because that would confirm your hypothesis that it fell in a north-easterly direction?"

"Precisely," said Kirill, grinning. "I will fetch the *automatichesky*."

Vasiliev pawed at the rock and soil, muttering unhappily to himself.

"Stomach upset?" suggested Alexei.

"No, Your Highness. This strata worries me."

"Only a geologist could be worried by rocks."

"This layer is more than ten thousand years old. Ten thousand."

Alexei picked up a clod of earth and brushed away its crumbly outer layers. "So, it is old."

"Ten thousand years," said Vasiliev. "That's before the time of Moses; of Abraham. A tower that, even if this stonework represents its top, must have been more than a hundred feet high. Such a thing is ... incomprehensible."

"Then maybe this is the tower of Babel," grinned Alexei.

The sound of whirring *automatichesky-chelovek* echoed along the tunnel. The puppet slaves marched in unison. The engine-driven, punch card-controlled braces on limbs and back orchestrated their every action, robbing the suits' occupants of all free will. The men, each convicted of various terrible crimes, had been alive when shackled into the mechanical apparatus and pricked with the hundred or more galvanic wires which directly controlled their muscles. Work without end and imprisonment without release had killed most within weeks. Not that it mattered: the men's bodies, alive or dead, provided structure and strength for the unit. Until their muscles lost all integrity and their bodies began to decay, the dead could dig as well as the living.

Alexei stepped aside to let the first pass (clearly dead, given that his lower jaw was entirely missing). The *automatichesky* gathered armfuls of earth from the digging face, the suits' powered joints and the galvanic muscle controls giving them more brute strength than any ordinary man.

A change of texture under the grand duke's fingers made him look down. Within the lump of soil he held was a pale and twisted thing of fragile stone. "What is this?"

Kirill touched the mass of intertwined strands in Alexei's hands. They crumbled at his careless touch. "It's not a carving. A fossil?"

Vasiliev was shaking his head. "Too recent for that, but I do think it was once alive."

"Are they worms?"

"A single sea creature," said Vasiliev.

"Sea creatures here?" said Alexei. "Five thousand miles from the coast?"

"Arnhem."

*

It was not a warm day, but an open air café in Klarenbeek Park offered reasonable views of the parkland where Zwaardemaker could be rewarded for his efforts with drink. While he poured himself a generous glass of red, Mina Saxena turned up the collar of her coat and cradled a cup of coffee.

Zwaardemaker drained his glass in one go, poured himself a second and began to pull away the strands of false beard glued to his chin. "I think I make a very good doctor," he said. "I could set myself up in practice somewhere, somewhere no one knows me."

Mina simply looked at him. Jan Zwaardemaker was a gifted young actor, but self-knowledge of that fact, coupled with the exuberance of youth and his intemperate drinking, caused him to confuse his own abilities and shortcomings with those of his characters.

"What?" he said. "With you as my able and beautiful assistant, I would be sure to make a success of it."

"You would kill a patient in your first week," Mina replied. The Indian woman had dropped the Portuguese accent. "And I only lower myself to act as your secretary to gain access to places where a lone woman cannot go."

Zwaardemaker shrugged, his idiotic dream gone as quickly as it had come. "And you evidently found something of interest in that mad boy's cell," he said.

"I did."

"I see. No elaboration? No explanation of what this is all about?" He gave her a look, eyes half-hooded, just the faintest of smiles on his lips. The man was undoubtedly handsome and she was sure that look worked on the hearts of many a weak-willed woman: the bankers' daughters and businessmen's wives whose money funded his drinking habit.

"After all we've been through, Mina..." he said.

Twice, Zwaardemaker had made unwanted amorous advances on her. Mina had solemnly promised him that she would break his wrist if he tried it a third time. An uncharitable part of her wanted him to try, just so she could teach him the difference between figurative and literal threats.

"I could tell you," she said briskly, "but you wouldn't believe me."

"I have a broad mind and a generous spirit," said Zwaardemaker. "You never know."

"Very well," said Mina. "You have heard of the British space expedition to Altair and Colonel Younghusband who is to lead it?"

"Only in the most cursory of details."

"He was stationed in Tibet a few years ago. I was there also."

Zwaardemaker raised an eyebrow as he drank.

"I had my own agenda," said Mina. "I travelled into the Himalayas with a platoon of British soldiers and, in a roundabout way, with a Russian prince."

"A Russian prince?"

"The Grand Duke Alexei Mikhailovich. You would hate him."

"I am a republican, true," agreed Zwaardemaker, smiling.

"And he's prettier than you. Anyway, we had a miraculous ... encounter in the mountains."

"Yeti?"

"No. Well, yes, but more than that. We found the remnants, the ... seed of a being from deepest space."

"An alien creature."

"A god. Or, I think, a goddess. An *asuri*." She held up a hand swiftly. "Don't think I mean some Olympian or some Titan. Think—" Involuntarily, she raised her eyes to the sky as though to gaze at the depths of space which lay beyond the scattered clouds. "Imagine that the blackness of space is the home to nightmares without measure or number. Monsters the size of worlds."

"You've been listening to too many space-sailor yarns."

Zwaardemaker was being a fool, and a rude one at that. Mina could have stood that very moment, left him to his wine, and caught the first train to England without saying another word to the man; but it felt good telling it to someone. Even if that someone was an ignorant fool who refused to take it seriously. She had kept half a decade of horrors to herself – dreams, suspicions and discoveries – and had not shared them directly with anyone before.

"It's not a yarn," she said. "I experienced it. The emissary of the *asuri* spoke to us in our minds; to me and the other soldiers. Even to Younghusband in Gyantse. I saw into her mind. I glimpsed their history. I've spent the last four years following its trail across our world."

"Oh, they've been here before, have they?"

"The *asura* – the gods from the stars – came thousands of years ago. They colonised this world."

"I can see why you hate them."

"They were worshipped by South Sea Islanders, by the Naga tribes of India and by the ancient Lapps. Perhaps others too. But then something happened."

"What?"

"I'm not sure." Mina was thoughtful. "Some great cataclysm. Floods, earthquakes. The link between the star gods and their colonists broken. Lemuria and Mu sunk beneath the sea. Ancient civilisations tumbled. The gods on earth hid themselves away, buried themselves deep, deep down."

"Underground?"

Mina frowned. "I have read scientific papers that I've barely understood which tell us our universe has more than the three physical dimensions we all know. These deep gods might be buried in a sense other than the obvious."

"I see," said Zwaardemaker, taking time to reflect and refill his glass. "And what has this got to do with a crazy ten-year-old in Holland?"

Without looking Mina took her gloves from her satchel and began to slip them on. "The Lowestoft-Zeebrugge disaster was caused by one man's attempts to bring a deep god back into this world. The bridge's very shape formed the arcane symbols, a summoning circle for the ritual. The sea was the conduit through which the monster would return."

Zwaardemaker pointed off in the vague direction of the hospital. "Those drawings? That squid thing?"

"One of the deep gods," nodded Mina. "And, at the same time, Francis Younghusband is leading a mission to one of the homeworlds of the star gods."

"All the old gods returning, eh?"

"I hope not. And now I must go to England to see what can be done to stop it." She interlaced fingers to push her gloves into place and stood. Zwaardemaker raised a glass to her.

"Well, you were right, Miss Saxena," he said. "I don't believe you."

Mina looked away across green parkland and the quiet city beneath a cold blue sky. It was, in a complacently dull European sort of way, quite idyllic.

"I don't blame you," she said.

5.

Another sky, another time. This one I recognised.

The landscape of the north Norfolk coast and the Wash was flat and of limited charms. Behind us were fenland fields and the hamlet of Shepherd's Port, ahead the treacherous Ferrier Sands, stretching out to meet the sea more than a mile out. But for one hedge and a trio of farm buildings there was nothing to impede my view of the horizon in any direction.

My good friend Professor Sedgewick viewed matters on a different scale. He crouched beside the shallow and sandy Wolferton Creek, leaning on his lion's head cane for balance and stroked the brackish water's surface. "Here is another one," he said.

I brought a jar to the professor; taking care to ensure the plant-like creature remained covered by water at all times, he scooped it up from the creek bed. He passed the jar to me, wiped his hands on his outer coat and marked the find on the map he had brought with him.

This last action brought a look of satisfaction to the professor's face and, by turn, caused me to smile also. Even though we had lived together as friends for more than a dozen years, there was a distinct separation between us. Sedgewick's brilliance, his unparalleled grasp of the world around him, was greater than mine by an order of several magnitudes. I was in all matters of the mind a child to him. Yet, ignorant of them though I might be, I took a vicarious pleasure from his intellectual pursuits and discoveries.

At least here, in the search for Braintree's false-anemones, I understood some of the purpose of our work although not the apparent importance of this latest find. "What is it, professor?" I asked.

"Lunchtime," was his perverse reply.

We sat on tufts of grass (which were sharply uncomfortable but at least drier than the sand) and ate the haslet sandwiches, boiled eggs, tomatoes and fruitcake our guesthouse landlady had made for us that morning. Sedgewick was quiet while we ate, a mannerism that I knew full well. He was gathering his thoughts and would, in his own time, put forth on the subject to hand. I was entirely unsurprised that five minutes later, as I peeled a hard-boiled egg, Sedgewick spoke without warning, saying:

"The sea anemone is a master of the symbiotic relationship."

"Is that so?" I said.

"Many sea anemones form symbioses with single-celled algae. The algae, through heliovorous action, provides oxygenated water for the anemone. In turn, the anemone provides protection and access to sunlight for the algae."

"An amicable trade."

"And other anemones have been recorded as forming mutually beneficial relationships with hermit crabs. The hermit crab, a fascinating creature which must find the discarded shells of other creatures in which to live, will sometimes seek out a shell with anemones attached. The anemone benefits from crumbs of food the crab might overlook and the crab is protected from predators not only by its shell but also the anemone's toxic tentacles."

"But this is not an anemone," I said.

"It is not, dear chap," said Sedgewick, regarding the jar by our feet "One cannot help but wonder if some convergent transmutation or design has prompted the creature to adopt this form."

"You have thoughts on the matter?"

"I do," said the professor. "Five specific thoughts to conjure with. May I share them with you?"

"I'd be delighted if you did."

"First," said Sedgewick, facing me directly, "I recall what happened when we removed our first sample from the water."

"It died."

"Yes. Not *drowning* in air as a fish or mollusc might do, but shrivelling and dying almost instantly, as though it could not survive for any time outside its element. If so, it is a fragile creature at best; which leads me to my second and third thoughts. Braintree suggested that this is the same lifeform that attacked us aboard the *Lady Henshall* space-lock, yet how did it come to be here? Has it been spawned from the remnants that came to Earth on your arm? If so, how...?"

"Braintree said that the arm is in the collections at the Academy of Science..."

"...Or did this variant arrive from space at another time and by some other means? Whatever the case, I think this creature is somehow different to the 'angel' strain."

"How so?"

"You will recall that it took only a touch from the space creature's tendrils to infect you."

I shuddered at the recollection of the flying creatures' cold and slippery strands enwrapping their victims. "We've been careful in the handling of these things," I noted, nudging the jar at our feet with the toe of my shoe.

"But may we assume that anyone else who has encountered them was equally cautious? Was Braintree?"

I had to profess that I did not know.

"Although it might be the wildest and most dangerous reasoning," said Sedgewick, "I would suggest that the contagiousness of this parasitic lifeform is diminished in this incarnation. So, my fourth point of conjecture, is that this is some secondary, degenerate lifeform which, like the mule—"

"Mule as in donkey?" I said, confused.

"The offspring of a horse and a donkey, yes. It is an aberration from the norm, and, tellingly, is utterly infertile." He rapped the jar with his cane. "The geographical spread of this animal, limited to the area fed by this particular creek offers some small support to my theory."

"I see," I said. "I think."

Sedgewick smiled. "Doubt and honesty are two qualities I've always admired in you."

I tipped my hat. "Your fifth thought?"

"Concerns tomatoes." He picked one out of our lunch basket as an example. "Did you know that wild tomatoes grow in abundance on the riverbanks at Beckton in East Ham?"

"I did not."

"Do you know why?"

I shrugged. "Can't say I do."

"May I suggest you consider what Beckton is principally known for."

I thought for a moment. "Little of note. All I can think of is that it is where the Bazalgette sewerage treatment system re-joins the Thames."

"Exactly," said Sedgewick.

I pondered on this further and, soon enough, understood the professor's meaning. Our picnic tomatoes remained uneaten!

6.

A strange sense of unease: coming upon a scene that one did recognise, would not approve of, yet which was still familiar and personal. Miss Mina Saxena, a tubular map case in her hand, standing in the hallway of the Cambridge apartments shared by Sedgewick and I. Mina Saxena gazing at the knick-knacks, ornaments and detritus on our hall table. Mina Saxena inspecting herself in the scallop-edged mirror next to the hat stand. I can only describe it as being akin to discovering someone watching you while you sleep.

Cecily the maid reappeared and invited Mina to follow her. I would have cried at this further invasion of our home, but, disembodied, I had no mouth and could not scream!

In the drawing room, Cecily announced the guest. Mina stepped inside and was taken aback to find neither myself nor Sedgewick, but a young lady she did not recognise.

Rose Sedgewick appraised Mina at length, drawing a narrow-eyed stare from the Indian woman. "Do you know," said Miss Sedgewick, "I had somehow expected you to look ... wilder."

Mina smiled in realisation. "Miss Rose Sedgewick, I assume. I can see an unfortunate family resemblance."

"The eyes?"

216

"The arrogance. Niece, I suppose? I can't imagine any woman giving him children. So, would you have me dress like a savage rather than in the most fashionable French skirts?"

It was Miss Sedgewick's turn to smile. "Wilder of expression, I meant. Cadwallander's description of you could equally have been that of a rabid jungle beast. And I understand hobble skirts are the *latest* French fashion."

"Jungle beasts can't run with their legs tied together. I do a lot of running."

"I'm sure you do. But I don't think you're a beast."

"No? What then?"

Miss Sedgewick frowned, but it was a gentle expression, quizzical and amused. "I do not know. Shall we decide over a cup of tea?"

Tea was brought and, while Miss Sedgewick poured, Mina outlined her investigations and discoveries of recent months. From the Himalayas to India, to England and then to Holland, Miss Sedgewick followed Mina's account with interest and spoke only to seek clarification on certain points. Why didn't the British arrest her when they identified her in Tibet? What linked the prehistoric temple in the Himalayas to the barbaric religion of the Naga people? What had she hoped to learn from visiting poor Maurits in Arnhem? Mina answered all questions without hesitation, mildly surprised that Miss Sedgewick accepted everything she said without any note of ridicule or scorn.

"But now you need my uncle's help," said Miss Sedgewick.

"Help he would gladly give," said Mina.

"Oh, you know his mind that well?"

"I know that he is a man driven by love."

Miss Sedgewick laughed discreetly. "Then you know a different man to most of us. My father has described him as a cold fish on more than one occasion."

"Sedgewick is nothing but love," insisted Mina. "He loves his God, he loves the natural world around us, he loves his country and he loves his fellow man, particularly that roly-poly valet of his. Now, he and I might have different opinions about England's rightful place in the world but there is much we would agree on. Terrible events are circling towards us."

"Aren't there always?"

Mina opened the map case she had brought with her and slid out the rolled up prints of Maurits' drawings held within. "I am sure there is some meaning within these pictures," she said." They play on the mind. I cannot help but look at them and think that there is something I am not quite seeing – like one of those trick paintings in which faces appear from the stonework or topiary."

Miss Sedgewick canted her head slightly as though giving the matter some thought but little credence. "And you thought my uncle could find that meaning for you."

"He would at least take me seriously."

"Well, my uncle and Cadwallander have gone on a vacation of sorts, to the coast. I don't know when we are to expect them again." Miss Sedgeick stood abruptly. "However, there is something I might show you."

She led Mina out of the parlour, along the hallway and to a small study at the rear of the building. Pinned to three of the walls were papers, charts and – much to Mina's astonishment! – further copies of young Maurits' sketches, many of them identical to the ones Mina had brought with her.

"Sedgewick visited him too?" she said.

Miss Sedgewick shook her head. "My uncle wrote to the hospital and the eager Dr Kipp sent us copies by pneumail. He was only too happy with any supplementary questions I had."

"*You* had?"

"Oh, yes. This has very much become my project of late."

Mina approached one of the pinned sheets. It was an enlarged reproduction of Maurits' drawing of the tentacled monster rising from the sea. Mina had the same image among her collection but she still had to suppress a shudder at seeing the vile twists of limb reaching out of the depths, seemingly out of the picture itself. On the wall next to it were what appeared to be architectural designs for the central section of the Lowestoft-Zeebrugge Bridge where the diabolical titan had emerged, wreaking havoc. Above and between the two pieces was a sheet of mathematical curves, notations and complex formulae.

"There is meaning in those images," said Miss Sedgewick, "meaning in the creature's poses, just as there was meaning in Edward Klein's evil designs for the bridge."

"Can a bridge be evil?"

"I think you can see that for yourself. Cadwallander, when trying to explain it to me for the first time, made a canny reference to the golden ratio. There is goodness and beauty in mathematics, provable beauty. The bridge and the monster are expressions of true repulsiveness in numbers, what he called 'dark ratios'. It's an apt name."

"These are your calculations?"

"I have an affinity for numbers. These encrypted messages are certainly fascinating, and I have been without valid employment since—" Miss Sedgewick stopped and looked pointedly at Mina. "You saw ... evil in the Himalayas. Not an entity like this but another horror."

"I did."

"Has there been a night since when you did not see it in your dreams?"

"No," said Mina slowly, sensing Miss Sedgewick had a similar experience to share.

Miss Sedgewick briefly recounted the events in the deep tunnel railway that culminated in the Hatch End disaster. She could only offer fragments of information regarding the final encounter with the "Mad tribe of Irishmen" and the disease of mind, body and soul which had come upon them. She had seen almost nothing in the pitch black of the collapsed tunnel, but there were images she had dimly perceived which time could not erase. For certain, full sight of them had entirely robbed Inspector Wilmarth of his sanity.

"This," she said, indicating the walls of pictures, diagrams and scientific notation, "has become an obsession of mine. An understandable one I hope."

"And have you drawn any conclusions?"

"Several. Do you know what a waggle dance is?"

"Can't say I do."

"Maurits has created a number of drawings of bees, alone and in groups. Structured patterns and tessellation. He has a mathematical mind; perhaps it is only that rational core holding the rest of his mind together. Bees are mathematical creatures."

"Hadn't noticed. Educated English bees perhaps."

"Really? Not many creatures fashion their homes out of perfect hexagons. The waggle dance is how the bee tells the others in the hive where the best flowers are. With turns and duration, the bee pinpoints the location of the pollen-giving flowers."

"I see," said Mina, not at all sure what the younger woman was on about.

"These," said Miss Sedgewick, tapping one of the pictures emphatically. "These are not randomly vulgar tentacular poses. These dark ratios are a waggle dance of sorts."

"They show where the pollen is?"

Miss Sedgewick pouted at Mina's obtuse remark. "That may be a more worrying analogy than you could possibly imagine. The numbers and equations expressed by these curves and lines represent – I *think* they represent – a form of celestial coordinate system."

"You will need to explain that," said Mina.

Miss Sedgewick proceeded to do so. Using terminology with which she herself was not wholly at ease (being a mathematician rather than an astronomer), Miss Sedgewick spoke of the vastness of the void beyond our Earth and the spatial relationship between the stars within our galaxy, the Milky Way. Expressing the direction and distance between two objects relies on commonly understood points of reference. On Earth, we have the magnetic poles as our initial starting points. The measurable lines of longitude and latitude allow us to describe any location on the globe. In the whorls of space the solar ætheric plane's gravity provides us with our own immutably fixed position, but there is little evidence that it extends beyond the Solar System. In a universe without a centre, without an up or a down, describing position and direction is a more complex affair.

Taking in astronomy, astrology, numerology and a willingness to discuss more dimensions than I would like, Miss Sedgewick attempted to make clear her theories regarding the information that Maurits captured from his brief observations of the creature Klein had attempted to summon. Her account concluded with two drawings as explanatory tools, one on the table, the other held directly above it, facing down. She made a show of carefully angling it.

"With two patterns in alignment," said she, "the equations balance and the two termini are instantly made aware of the position of the other."

"So, the deep god was—?" Mina's mouth twisted uncomfortably at the thought. "It was calling out to some other point in space? To what end?"

Miss Sedgewick brought the two pieces of paper together, one laid on top of the other. She took a loose drawing pin and pinned the two sheets together on the table. "Space folds, two points become one. A gateway is formed."

Mina felt a tightening in her chest, a dreadful foreboding.

"Or not," said Miss Sedgewick cheerily. "The further we move from what we know for certain, the more pure conjecture takes over."

"But you believe this to be true."

As though taking Mina's willingness to believe as permission, Miss Sedgewick drew her over to another selection of wall-mounted papers. Miss Sedgewick betrayed her youthfulness when excited; she spoke to Mina with the wonderment of a child at Christmas: fast and without pause for breath.

"My uncle shared your suspicions regarding Younghusband's mission to Altair and so suggested I make my calculations on the assumption that the furthest end of the line of travel starts there."

"And you were successful?"

"Indeed. At least, I suppose. The calculations gave a solution and, due to the continuous but nowhere differentiable nature of the functions I had developed – thanks to some kindly advice from a Dr Poincaré at the Sorbonne – I was presented with an increasingly accurate position for the other end of the line of travel."

"Earth?" said Mina.

"As we might have suspected and feared."

Mina took a physical and mental step backwards. "So this ... squid-devil, abandoned here ages back, was calling to the star gods, inviting them to our world once more."

"Not just to our world but to a very specific point, an unusual point, and to a specific time." Miss Sedgewick placed a finger on one of her diagrams. "Directly over the equator. Two hundred and fifty miles above the Earth, just beyond our planet's own atmosphere."

"And the time?"

"When the Earth is at aphelion."

"And what is that?" asked Mina.

"When the Earth is at its furthest distance from the sun. Which, this year, would be on the second of July."

"Less than a week from now," said Mina.

7.

Alexei lowered the field glasses, considered matters for a moment, and raised them to his eyes once more. "I don't know whose it is," he admitted. "I don't think we have any airships of that size."

"Who knows what the Tsar has commissioned in some far off manufactory!" said Kirill, squinting through his telescope.

"Russia is full of secrets," added Vasiliev sourly. "Why should we worry about one more?"

Alexei adjusted the focus minutely. "And there are those rotors on the very top of the canopy. Six of them in a row, like helipteron blades."

"Half airship, half helipteron," said Kirill with a carefree shrug of indifference. "Invention moves ever on."

"I'm not sure," said the grand duke. He put down the field glasses. The airship was five or more miles distant but surely heading towards their camp. "Gentlemen, I do believe we are about to be attacked."

"Please, Your Highness," said Vasiliev. "There's no need for melodrama."

"No, it's a good thing," said Alexei.

"How so?" said Kirill.

Alexei gave him a look that contained enough of his determination and exhilaration to wipe the ever-present smile from Kirill's face.

"Dear Kirill, it means we have found something worth fighting for."

Until recently, the weeks of digging had brought nothing but stunning, maddening, appalling repetition. Along the main tunnel's length they found new ruins; regular blocks of stone, some whole, some pulverised beneath the weight of others. What they had at first considered to be the ruins of a tower or fortress now extended more than half a mile across the taiga. Alexei had tried to suggest that it was a long wall, not the remains of a tower – a frankly impossible tower! – but Kirill spoke at length about stone compression and angles of descent and insisted that this ancient find had once been entirely upright.

A tower a half mile high! Alexei knew Kirill was prone to jokes but not wild speculation. Kirill had countered not with compromise but with hyperbolic embellishment; when towers collapse, he had explained, they mostly fall in upon their bases, leaving ruins far shorter than the tower's overall length. In his opinion, they were only exploring a fragment of the archaeological site about them, ants crawling up the spine of a fallen giant and hoping hubristically to grasp the entirety.

For the sake of their collective sanity, Alexei was pleased when they had uncovered what they all unconsciously thought of as the tower's apex. Not only had it marked the end of the trail of fallen stone but also presented some unique finds. There was a greater proliferation of the desiccated remains of wormy sea creatures. Veins of green and black ran through the stonework here, putting Alexei in mind of both marble and quartz, although clearly being neither. Vasiliev caused a stir when he declared in miserable exasperation that he had never seen such stone before and could not identify it at all. Thrilling though this might prove to be in geological terms, Kirill and the grand prince could not help but be more taken with the singular object that they had found in the midst of those ruins.

The glittering object, hoisted out by *automatichesky-chelovek*, wrapped in cloths and now stored in Alexei's tent was, he assumed, the reason for this mystery airship's arrival. The only thing of value or interest within a hundred miles was his own royal personage and he was prepared to wager that these interlopers, be they domestic or foreign, were more likely interested in their strange find. The object in his tent was, as far as Alexei knew, entirely without equal; whereas Russian princes were hardly in short supply and, if one listened to the whispers of malcontents, too numerous by far.

"We must prepare for the worst," said Alexei, regarding the airship with a decisive finality. He turned to the two Cossack soldiers who had accompanied the expedition and instructed them to fetch the black cards and command box from his tent.

"Is that truly necessary, Your Highness?" asked Vasiliev as the soldiers ran off in obedience.

Alexei grunted and told him in clear terms that it was. "I have bowed to your experience and expertise in all matters geological," he said. "I have looked to you and Kirill as my superiors in that and have allowed you a degree of autocracy."

"I know, Your Highness," said Vasiliev.

"Now, you will bow to my expertise. I am your superior once more, as I ever was." The grand duke rested one hand on his teleforce pistol in its holster. "Until this matter is resolved, you will not question me again."

Vasiliev gave a shuddering nod as though his whole body was stammering in surprise. "Yes, Your Highness," he said hoarsely.

Alexei looked to Kirill.

"Oh, absolutely, Your Highness," nodded the archaeologist.

*

As the airship continued its approach, Alexei had the Cossacks run round the *automatichesky-chelovek*, replacing their various white instruction cards with the simpler and more frightfully specific black punch cards. Meanwhile, Alexei opened the wooden command box. It contained three command whistles, each of different length and tonal pitch, plus ten magnetic amulets on chains.

Alexei passed three amulets to Kirill. "For you and the Cossacks."

"And the Evenki huntsmen?" said Kirill.

"No. Maybe you should tell them to saddle up and ride into the forests."

"Your Highness," said Kirill and left.

"And not to return for at least a day!" Alexei shouted after him.

Alexei passed an amulet to Vasiliev and slipped another over his own head. The round magnetic disk stuck to his iron chest with a small clang.

"Have these things been tested in battle?" asked Vasiliev.

Alexei thought for a moment. "No," he said, taking up the command whistles and leaving the box on the ground. "But it may not come to that."

"And if it does, Your Highness?"

"I'd stay out of the reach of the *automatichesky* just to be on the safe side."

Nearer now, Alexei could see the airship more clearly. Its canopy, rough canvas skin over a steel skeleton, was at least six hundred feet long and seventy feet in diameter. It was grey, like a shark, the three tiered gondola sections hanging like dorsal fins from its underside. On the upper surface, two rotors not quite obscured from view by the curve of the canopy, turned faster.

"It's British," said Alexei.

"How can you tell?" said Vasiliev.

"I've seen a Vickers company ship with the same lines. It's either British or a blatant copy."

The rotors on top of the canopy lifted and peeled away, revealing themselves not to be part of the ship but a twin-rotor military helipteron carried on its back.

"That," said Alexei reflectively, "is something I've not seen before."

The helipteron, leaving a faint black trail across the white sky, descended in a spiral towards the camp. Alexei saw guns (probably Maxim machine guns, he decided) slung below the nose of the vehicle.

He rolled the smallest command whistle in his hand. Around the site, forty-four *automatichesky* would be standing dormant, their black cards inactive until their clockwork units detected the resonance of a specific whistled tone. Alexei had not lied when he had said the *automatichesky* black cards had not been tested in battle. However, he had seen twenty-six seconds of kinetographic footage of them being tested in the *Nerchinsk katorga* prison yard.

He doubted the *automatichesky* would ever be of value on the true battlefield, but they could be counted upon to provide a distraction, and a particularly violent distraction at that!

The helipteron dipped below the trees some distance away. Alexei shifted from foot to foot to try to get a view of the men disembarking on the ground. He looked round at the sound of Kirill's return. The archaeologist had a heavy bundle of cloth in his arms.

"What did you bring that for?" said Alexei, irritated. "I told you to give the amulets to Razin and Krasnov."

"They won't need them, Your Highness," said Kirill.

Alexei's brow twitched. There was the click of gun being cocked behind him. For a man who had spent ten years in the army before devoting himself to geology, Vasiliev looked decidedly uncomfortable holding a gun. Maybe he had never pointed one at royalty before.

"Why?" said Alexei, regarding the gun.

"Get his weapon," hissed Vasiliev to Kirill.

Kirill put down the bundled artefact and approached the grand duke. He pulled back Alexei's coat and took the pistol from his belt holster. Alexei did not resist. Kirill shoved the pistol into the waistband of his trousers and then snatched the magnetic amulet from Alexei's chest and the command whistles from his hand.

Men in black military uniform and great coats approached from the tree line.

"So, you are traitors then?" said Alexei.

Kirill looked amused. "Shall I tell you that Vasiliev here has seen too much corruption, brutality and lives carelessly wasted in Russia's military bureaucracy? Maybe I could reveal that one of these *automatichesky* is my own brother, Pavel, and that I've had to watch him die, day by day, in the service of inbred fools who are the true criminals in Russia."

Alexei stared at him. Kirill shrugged. "Or maybe we're simply doing it for the money. Pounds, not roubles, are today's currency of choice. Isn't that right, sir?"

This last was directed in fair English to the high-collared officer leading the half-dozen soldiers towards them. The rifles they carried were Lee-Enfields: British soldiers.

"Captain Dansey," the officer introduced himself, holding out a gloved hand to Alexei. "It's a pleasure to meet you, Your Highness."

Alexei ignored the hand and addressed Dansey coolly. His English, unlike Kirill's, was perfect and well-practised. "Captain, we are on Russian soil and this is an act of military aggression. Are Britain and Russia at war?"

"No, Your Highness. Britain and Russia remain the firmest of allies. I have nothing but respect for the noble house of Romanov. Her Majesty, Queen Victoria, Empress of India and Mars, would no doubt wish her fondest regards passed to her distant cousin except of course—" Dansey gestured at himself and his men, at the aircraft in the trees and in the sky, no doubt referring to the lack of national or military markings on any of them "—we are not here and this is not happening." He took a deep, cleansing breath. "Your death will be a tragic accident."

"Not planning on shooting me then?" said Alexei.

Dansey spoke to Vasiliev. "Your plan will work?"

"It will be as if we were never here," said the geologist. "They will have to dig for months if they wish to find his body."

Dansey looked to the bundle at Kirill's feet. "And is that the Aleph?"

"It's what we found," said Kirill. He unwrapped the covers slowly, not out of caution but out of a sense of showmanship and jokey self-importance. Within the protective cloths was a flat stone carving, broken and eroded to the approximate size and shape of a circular serving tray. There were other carvings in the ruins, several in better condition and with fragments of cuneiform lettering that academics across the globe would have killed each other to merely glimpse, but only this piece of stone had a fist-sized gem set in its centre. A gem of brilliant white, of all colours and none—

*

I felt a horrible vertigo in that moment as Kirill the archaeologist uncovered the Aleph. I viewed this scene through the gem – this omniscient crystal ball, this demonic scrying pool – and in this scene was the gem itself. A magic mirror viewed in a magic mirror. My mind reached out and comprehended the terror that would come if these two mirrors aligned and pitched me into an infinite recursion of images: loops of representation like the strangest of little Maurits' strange drawings...

8.

My mind recoiled from the abyss of the infinite and snapped back to that which was most familiar.

*

I came back to my own self and the heartfelt sentiment that a two week stay on the Norfolk coast – despite any of the rustic attempts of our guesthouse landlady to make us comfortable and welcome – was more than enough for anyone. Shepherd's Port might have curative airs, a bracing easterly wind and the kind of light certain painters might kill for, but it held few points of interest (unless one has a passion for wading birds and rock pool creatures) and nothing to excite the spirit (apart from the potential for drowning in shifting sands).

Thus, even though I did not know the reason for the excursion, I was more than pleased to be accompanying Professor Sedgewick aboard a steam-brougham to Anmer Hall in Sandringham, some miles to the south. The gates opened as we arrived and the driver took us to the front of the wide house. But for the white Tuscan columns and arch over the door it was a large but unimpressive building.

"Amner Hall," said Sedgewick. "The summer retreat of Lady Walburga Paget, the Countess von Hohenthal. The house was a personal gift from Her Majesty the Queen."

"Then I shall be on my best behaviour," I replied.

"Her late husband, Sir Augustus Paget, was a patron of the Academy of Science," said Sedgewick. "His last visit to the collections was five years ago."

I admitted I did not see the connection.

Sedgewick smiled. "He died eleven years ago."

"Then that makes him a dashed clever fellow."

"And since Lady Paget agreed to this audience without questioning its purpose, I suggest we keep our wits about us."

To underline a point already made perfectly clear, Sedgewick tightened his grip on his cane. In reply, I flexed the fingers of my powerful brass hand to the accompaniment of tiny taps and pneumatic hisses.

A butler opened the brougham door. I stepped down from the rumbling vehicle and saw that nearly half the windows on the property were in fact bricked up and painted a leaden grey to resemble glass. Such remnants of the Georgian window tax were not uncommon but, here, I felt I was looking into the dead and lifeless eyes of the house.

The butler greeted us cordially, directing us into the house and to a large parlour. What gas lamps there were in the room cast little light and much of the space was shrouded in gloom. At the far end of the parlour, in a nook formed by two bookcases and a Venetian screen, sat the room's sole occupant. Lady Walburga Paget was a slender and frail looking figure; this much I could tell even though she was fully clothed, her arms encased in elbow-length gloves and her face shrouded by a heavy lace veil. I would have taken her for a woman in mourning except that her wardrobe was grey and muted green, like lichen on tombstone. A book lay open in her lap.

Sedgewick stepped forward and made the formal introductions.

"Professor Sedgewick. Mr Cadwallander," she said in perfect, unaccented English. "You are most welcome. Sit, please."

"Thank you, My Lady," said the professor. I mumbled something to a similar effect.

The butler was already presenting us with glasses of sherry. Lady Paget regarded us without a word, her expression masked by the veil. I sipped at my drink, finding the silence increasingly uncomfortable.

"I have read your book," said the professor.

Lady Paget inclined her head in acknowledgement. "I don't believe *Colliliquies* is widely read," she replied.

"There is certainly an appetite in some quarters for books of a spiritual or theosophical nature."

"And your appetites?"

Sedgewick smiled in an attempt at politeness. "I receive my revealed wisdom from a different book, My Lady."

"Ah." It was a single syllable, heavy with meaning and condemnation. "You are a Cambridge man, professor, of some singular note. What endeavour brings you to our sleepy corner of the country?"

"My concern for your health, My Lady."

"I did not realise I was sick. Has Dr Walton been lying to me?"

"With the deepest respect, I believe you are quite unwell and have been for some time."

Shadows shifted in the room, as though a drape had moved in front of the light, but there was no breeze in the room.

Sedgewick tapped his cane. "My dear friend and I have been spending some time on the shoreline, studying the local wildlife. We have developed a recent interest in sea anemones. I had explained to Cadwallander here about the symbiotic and mutually beneficial relationship struck up between some sea anemones and the hermit crab."

"Oh?"

"The host provides food and movement to the best feeding grounds; the other protects the host. But there are other relationships between animals, more one-sided. Tell me, My Lady, have you heard of the pea crab?"

"I am not a student of crustacea, professor."

"It's a tiny thing, insignificant in size, hence the name. It lives inside the mantle of certain molluscs. Lodged in the mucous and fleshy folds, the crab shares the mollusc's food and is carried within its protective shell. However, it offers the mollusc no benefits in return for free food and lodgings; furthermore, if the mollusc becomes diseased or is attacked, the pea crab has no qualms in abandoning its host. These relationships, both parasitic and commensal, are so deeply entrenched that one wonders if the host is even aware of the other creature, let alone able to determine if the relationship is a positive one or not."

"I was informed you do nothing but speak in metaphor," said Lady Paget.

"What is interesting in your case," continued the professor, "is that there is a definite balance between yourself and whatever resides within you."

"You overstep the mark." Lady Paget spoke coolly but, remarkably, with no anger.

Sedgewick turned to me. "Lady Paget wrote a book in which her *unseen friend* revealed to her secrets regarding life on this world and others; details of lost civilisations and of science beyond our time." He turned to the countess once more. "I do not think that your *friend* would have necessarily wanted you to publish such things. There is still a semblance of your true self within." He edged forward to sit on the lip of the couch we shared. "Is it still Lady Paget I speak to now?"

The professor's questions were bizarre but less bizarre than Lady Paget's willingness to entertain them.

"What science or intuition led you here?" she asked.

"My reasoning involves notions of a most vulgar sort, My Lady," he replied. "May I simply say that the sinks and drains of this house empty into the brook which ultimately forms Wolferton Creek. And – again, forgive me – like rats fleeing a sinking ship, your offspring have attempted to take up root where the creek meets the sea."

"Steady on, old chap," I said, mortified.

"May I?" He held out a hand to the countess.

Lady Paget, understanding his intentions entirely, removed one of her gloves, peeling it down from her elbow. She hissed in pain at one point and then persevered to the end. The hand revealed was, at first appearance, simply that of an old woman; skin, mottled with age, hung in wrinkled folds from almost fleshless bone. And then I saw that there was much wrong with that hand. Lines running along joints and fingers were not merely wrinkles or varicose veins but actual cracks in the surface of the flesh; jagged fissures that ran deep. It was as though Lady Paget's hand and arm were those of a badly painted wax mannequin which had cracked and ruptured with the passage of time.

"It hurts?" Sedgewick enquired.

Lady Paget nodded beneath the veil.

The professor carefully took her hand in a shocking breach of social etiquette. "Is this thing mindless? Do you know its intentions?"

"They come again," she said. "To reconquer and to eradicate the degenerated barbarians they left behind."

"Barbarians? The monsters beneath the sea? So, what does that make you? What does that make the angel creatures?"

"I am the herald of the true gods," said Lady Paget. "I am the emissary of the ancient ones, come to prepare the path. The Aleph is being recovered as we speak and—"

"*That* is quite enough," said a voice from behind the screen.

I should have recognised that voice:. those false, plummy tones, that audible sneer. We had last encountered the man, and thought to have left him for dead, beneath the deserts of Mars.

The shadows in the room shifted once more and the self-styled Chioa Khan emerged from behind the screen, dressed in a starched grey suit and white gloves. This last item struck me as most fitting; the man would have the world take him for a wizard or mystic but this provincial charlatan had more of the music hall magician about him.

"Lady Paget was just about to reveal something of interest?" suggested Sedgewick, unsurprised by the man's appearance.

"I was more interested in what you might have to say," said Chioa Khan. "You're only alive because of what you may already know."

"Is that so?" said the professor. "And would you do away with me with one of your magic spells?"

Chioa Khan dipped into his jacket pocket and removed a silver tube, etched with strange sigils and emitting the faintest blue glow.

"A magician's wand," I said, allowing an impertinent smirk to appear on my lips.

"My blasting rod," said the ridiculous man. "Would you like a demonstration?"

"I don't think we could stomach your theatrics," said Sedgewick. "So what is it that you fear we know?"

"You know of Lady Paget's sacred affliction and I gather you know that, chalice to the divine though she might be, she cannot contain it for much longer."

"It is killing her," said Sedgewick and, perhaps reading something in Chioa Khan's expressive dark eyes, added, "And she is killing it? Ah, yes. There is something about her or this world that simply does not agree with it."

"Go on," said the magician.

Sedgewick cleared his throat and settled in his seat. He was being tested and would not rush. "Air," he said simply. "Or something in it. My good friend will recall that the winged creatures we encountered aboard the *Lady Henshall* space-lock seemed to struggle in the denser æther within the space-lock itself. I would posit that æther has some detrimental effect on this organism *except* the specimens we found on the coast are, after a fashion, thriving in water. It was only when we removed them from that medium and exposed them to air that they died."

"Very good," said Chioa Khan.

"Ætherated air as poison. I could see how that might be a barrier to any invasion of our world by beings from beyond the stars." There was a slender trace of mockery in the professor's voice.

"But inside a willing host—" Chioa Khan indicated Lady Paget.

"Who is dying," said Sedgewick.

"Transforming," said Lady Paget.

"Dying," insisted the professor.

"Then how would you suggest the ancients be protected?" asked Chioa Khan

"Of course, I wouldn't," said Sedgewick. "But, if a solution was required, one might think about how man protects himself in environments hostile to mortal flesh. Spacefarers and deep sea divers wear protective suits." He laughed suddenly.

"You are amused?" rumbled Chioa Khan.

"Gods in spacesuits. Clumsy and pathetic."

"Their majesty will be undimmed by whatever vessel they occupy. And, in time, they will adapt to Earth's airs just as their rebel brethren have adapted."

"Adaptation is the province of mortals. If your star gods can change then they can die. You have given me nothing but courage and hope."

"He will come with us," spoke Lady Paget.

"Are you sure?" Chioa Khan was uncertain.

"I want his courage and hope brought before the Aleph. I want to see it melt into despair at the procession of the glorious and deathless into this world!"

I had had my fill of their insane nonsense; my fists clenched in restrained anger. However, the professor remained quite calm. He turned to me and spoke in light, conversational tones.

"So, would you wager there is a link between this Aleph thing and Rose's astronomical calculations?"

Miss Sedgewick's star maps and sheets of mathematical scribbling on the walls of our Cambridge rooms were as much an esoteric arcana to me as Chioa Khan's mumbo-jumbo. Miss Sedgewick, as precociously intelligent as she was beautiful, made me feel quite the dunce when explaining her theories at the dinner table. I could offer no word of agreement or understanding to the professor.

"A gateway from one point in space to another," said Sedgewick, "mediated by some ... device?"

"Which will soon be recovered from the ruins of the first tower," said the countess.

"My Lady," murmured Chioa Khan, "do not make him privy to all our secrets."

"Frightened?" smiled Sedgewick.

"I simply wish to savour your surprise," huffed the magician. "You have no idea what wonders you will bear witness to."

"Wonders?" said Sedgewick sourly. He raised his cane, slowly, quite casually and tipped Lady Paget's hat and veil from her head. Her hands flew to her face. I stared in horror at the devastated visage. My comparison to a time-ravaged shop dummy was hideously apt. Had someone taken an iron bar to a mannequin's head, it would have looked not unlike the diseased Lady Paget. Her temple, brow, her left eye socket and cheekbone were all gone, collapsed inwards into the seemingly hollow cavity of her skull. There was no blood, no livid wounds or colourful scars, only a ragged hole and the deep fissures radiating across her face, slicing her nose in two and touching her top lip. Strands of thinning hair dangled into the dark hole, over a lip of skin composed more of fungoid pith than of anything human.

"Blasphemer!" screamed Chioa Khan, raising his blasting rod.

I launched myself from the couch, my mechanical arm already drawn back and ready to deliver a bone-shattering punch to his nose. In the instant before I reached him, he angled the silver wand towards me and depressed a stud in its barrel.

I felt rather than saw the blue bolt of power which struck me. It froze my chest. Instantly I could not breathe. I fell heavily to the carpet, unable even to lift my arms to slow my fall.

As I struck the floor, as Professor Sedgewick turned to aid me, I heard both of the doors open. Through dimming vision I saw men rushing in, pistols in hands. I saw black military uniforms, undecorated and without markings...

9.

From blackness to blackness. The cold tunnels beneath the taiga forests.

*

"The grand duke."

*

Alexei was certain there were worse places to die but, at that moment, was unable to think of any. A pair of British soldiers had methodically and with a peculiar degree of silent deference marched him to the end of one of the shorter tunnels radiating from the original dig site and chained him to one of the metal support struts keeping the roof in place. Any Russian soldier worth his salt would have spat on him before leaving him. Alexei felt almost insulted that they departed (taking the lamp light with them) without any comment at all, neither prayer nor condemnation.

He tested his bonds and found them to be utterly secure. He explored the dark, frozen floor around him with his feet and made contact with an object which turned out to be a wooden hammer handle, not the pick or spade he hoped for.

As he contemplated his chances of escape, two closely-spaced sounds reached his ears. The first was faint and high-pitched, almost beyond the cusp of audibility. Alexei cursed in earthy Russia. The black cards of the *automatichesky-chelovek* had been activated. The machine-controlled men were preparing to mercilessly bludgeon any person not wearing one of the protective amulets. Alexei hoped, without much optimism, that there were still unprotected British soldiers on the ground.

The second sound, by contrast, was so deep that he felt more than heard it. One of the oscillator machines, perhaps in one of the other tunnels, had been turned on. By the feel of it, Alexei guessed it was the largest of the five they had brought on site and the phlogiston valve had been fully opened. Vibratory waves, building up to many hundreds per second, would work through the ground in all directions. Alexei recalled the Serbian inventor had allegedly boasted that an oscillator small enough for a man to carry in his pocket could producing resonating frequencies of sufficient power to cause large buildings to collapse.

Alexei cursed again. Given the structural integrity of the tunnel about him and the unpredictable efficacy of the *automatichesky* black card, it was quite debatable which would kill him first.

The oscillator's hum intensified as the earth took up in resonant vibration. Alexei could feel the ground beneath him quivering. Dust and specks of dirt fell on him. He had concluded that he was to be buried alive rather than ripped apart by mechanised prisoners when he heard the whirr and clunk of *automatichesky* moving in the tunnel ahead of him. God had not yet decided his fate.

Alexei decided to take the decision out of God's hands. Acting on the vaguest of plans brewing in his subconscious, he swivelled round, bringing his feet up to the strut to which he was bound, and began to kick at it. At any other time a futile activity, the soil loosening power of the oscillator now made it dangerous in the extreme. He had little doubt that if the strut gave way, the ceiling above him would collapse. Depending on the terrain under which the tunnel passed, that would mean anything between five to twenty feet of soil coming down on him. If it didn't crush the grand duke, it would smother him in moments – or perhaps not. As he kicked, he dragged breath after breath into his lungs, holding them down in the pressurised mechanical reservoir of his chest.

Automatichesky clanked and banged towards him in the darkness. Alexei did not understand their workings as well as he would have liked; he did not know if they were drawn by sound, movement, heat, or simply bumbled their way closer through some mechanical Brownian motion. Nonetheless, the thought of those tireless bodies of plates and wires, and the claws of steel rod and bone, spurred Alexei on to more desperate kicking.

With one final strike, the support strut jolted from its position, pivoting and freeing Alexei's hands. A horizontal roof brace, now unsupported, fell down. With something like a sigh, the entire roof collapsed. Beneath the inescapable bass hum of the oscillator, Alexei heard the groans of *automatichesky* suits crumpling under the weight of the falling earth. Alexei dragged himself into an upright crouch, his hands above him, before the earth hit. It was soft but unyielding as it fell, coming down like the unstoppable hand of a giant. It enfolded him, crushing him. Alexei fought to hold his position, doing his utmost to create a supporting frame with his body in which to maintain some form of airspace. It was a desperate gambit and without success.

A second or two after the initial fall, the grand duke found himself pinned into position, cold soil pressing in on him from all sides. It weighed down on his head, compressing his neck and spine. It lined his forehead, filled his ears, sealed his eyes shut and pressed insistently against his lips. His arms were locked into position. His legs were fixed and useless. In the silence of his skull, he screamed.

Another man would have been dead within seconds; Alexei had the dubious blessing of his iron lungs and the minutes of air stored within them. As he tried to restrain his panicked mind, Alexei felt and heard the oscillator once more. Its vibrations fed through the earth encasing him and, sickeningly, his entire body. The soil resonated with a powerful intensity, dancing against his skin.

Alexei did not instantly grasp what was occurring about him. It was several moments before he realised that the vibrations were sending waves through the solid earth, bringing a qualitative change in the earth, transforming it from a solid into something more like viscous liquid.

Fingers steepled, Alexei pushed upwards and, through the thixotropic mud, was able to extend his arms towards the surface. He attempted to straighten his legs and stand. It was a slow and gruelling task. With much of his senses overwhelmed by the ever-present soil and industrial blare of the oscillator, he could not tell if he was raising his body or simply lowering his legs further into the wave-excited mire. He did not think about it; hope did not occur to him.

His body burned through the air in his lungs. He worked his way upwards in an action that was not unlike swimming. He could only move slowly, fighting as he was against the soupy earth, the not inconsiderable weight of his body, his clothes and his metal chest. He quashed the fear that it was a futile effort; that he was simply thrashing about like a pinned bug.

When his left hand pushed up into cold, open air, he almost froze in his excitement, sinking back into the ground. Recovering himself, he dug upward with a suddenly reckless conviction that he might, after all, survive. He breached the soil with both arms, blindly pulled himself up and, as sweet air touched his face, roared. It was a roar of pent up fear and mindless exultation. He tore the mud from his eyes and stared about at a landscape transformed.

Although the vile experience had seemed much longer, Alex guessed that he had been entombed for no more than five minutes. In that time, the unchecked oscillator pump had wrought a bizarre and incredible change on the dig site. The pump had broken up and homogenised the ground, destroying the natural barriers to its vibratory waves. With the forest enslaved to the rhythmic pounding, there was little to stop the waves of resonance – escalating! harmonising! – from growing in magnitude. The ground rippled, as though it was a millpond and the oscillator a rock thrown into its surface time and again. Rolling waves spread from the centre, trough and peak a foot apart but growing, ever growing! And the trees – Alexei gaped – the trees were swaying like the undulating spines of some gargantuan crawling beast!

Alexei stumbled as a wave rolled beneath his feet. He saw now, around the site, *automatichesky* on their backs and sides, some even sinking into the unstable earth. They lacked the physical co-ordination to stay upright in this shifting terrain and were no longer a threat. He was far from safe, though. If he remained still for more than a moment, the ground began to suck on his boots; the waves, mounting in size, threatened to knock him from his feet.

Alexei ran from the fearsome epicentre of that living quicksand. He pushed through the trees. Steam (or was it smoke?) rose from their trunks as the mighty pulsations heated the woody atoms within. A cloying heat filled the air, compounding the sickening and unnatural sensation the vibrations drove through his body. If he ever found time to stop and breathe, Alexei was sure he would be thoroughly sick.

A wave rose behind him and the grand duke found himself running down a small hill that grew beneath his feet. It raised him up at least five feet before passing before him. He staggered in the trough and ran on, waiting for the next wave to hit him. Somewhere off to his side there was a flare of light as one of the trees spontaneously burst into flames.

The British airship hung surprisingly low in the sky ahead of him. From the brief, trembling glimpses he had of the huge craft, Alexei believed it to be in some trouble. It listed slightly as though it struggled to veer away through the shaking air.

10.

From one airship to another. My point of view slid with increasing ease from one person to another.

*

The most direct route between two points on the Earth's surface was not always the quickest. Likewise, the quickest route between two such points was rarely the cheapest. Mina Saxena had not objected to the expense (it was other people's money she was spending after all) and the planning of the route had the attraction of some intellectual problem-solving exercise. However, she had felt some concerns over the dangers of passing through English, then French, then German border points with forged papers. She had travelled most of the way under the Maria Capelo identity; a European passport and identity were far less troublesome than any other. From cross-channel passenger helipteron, to ætheric orbital flyer, to the train from Cairo to Dar-es-Salaam, she changed her story, documents and clothing to suit her needs.

Less than four days after leaving Cambridge, she was on the final leg of her journey, via Zeppelin from Dar-es-Salaam to the *Afrikanschen Himmelaufzug*. Like others who had not seen it before, Mina sat in the forward gondola café-bar and watched the Skylift emerge from the haze of the African sky, first as a faint grey line rising straight up from the lonely and majestic peak of Mount Kilimanjaro. As the distance narrowed, the airship docking station became visible just above the mountain's peak and the line of the Skylift solidified, becoming a needle-like rod running from the mountaintop into the invisible blue. Hundreds of miles up, in the transitional space between Earth's atmosphere and the æther of the void, was the orbital docking station. The orbital station, where cargo and passengers travelling to and from Earth were transferred on and off spacegoing ships, acted as a spinning counterweight, keeping the Skylift cable taut and aloft through centrifugal force. Indeed, the main stresses placed on the tower was not the weight of the cable bearing down but the upward force of the cable straining against its tether.

Such forces were beyond the tensile strengthen of earthly materials, and so the Skylift had been constructed with Cererianium from the asteroid belt. The scarcity of the metal and the technical challenge of Skylift construction meant that, although there were Skylifts throughout the Solar System, on lower gravity worlds such as Mars, Titan and Europa, the *Afrikanschen Himmelaufzug* was currently the only complete and functioning Skylift on Earth.

The Skylift's impact on the local region, and indeed the world, was considerable. Germany had joined its rivals – the British, the Belgians, the French – in the disorderly and brutal scramble to build an empire through foreign colonies and had, for the most part, come up short. On Earth, three lumps of African territory, a handful of Pacific islands and the tiniest of toeholds in China could not stand shoulder to shoulder with Britain's command of India,

Asia and a strip of African territories which ran uninterrupted from Cairo to Capetown. Similarly, Germany's ownership of Titan, Rhea and a smattering of asteroids in the third subætheric plane was nothing beside France's control of the Jovian moons or Britain's dominion over Mars. However, the Skylift, this dagger of space-iron stabbed into the Equator, had given Kaiser Wilhelm a fast and cheap conduit to space and an imperial swagger that he had not previously possessed.

As the airship drew nearer, Mina could see the train tracks radiating out from the slopes of Kilimanjaro. Tiny puffs of smoke marked locomotives hauling in the coal, iron and other resources destined for space, and those transporting the spoils of solar empire away to His Imperial Majesty in Berlin. Putting her own detestation of all emperors aside, Mina could not help but think those railways lines made Kilimanjaro look like the centre of a vast spider's web.

Once docked, Mina disembarked with the other passengers, passed through the lightly guarded checkpoint and into the docking station proper. The station was a circular platform built around and hanging from the central Skylift spire by a conical web of iron cables. Six elevators (which, in function, were six vertical funicular steam trains) powered up from the peak of Kilimanjaro, sometimes stopping at the airship station on their way to the orbital station, taking passengers and cargo with them. The airship platform was home to several small warehouses, stores, a number of bars and two uninviting guesthouses. Though this staging platform was modest in size (far smaller than the railway stations of any of the world's great cities), it bustled with life. Merchant seaman of all nations rubbed shoulders with trade agents, traffickers and clerks. Silent teams of African labourers, cleaners and service staff moved through the crowds, flowing around the patrolling Prussian officers who oversaw the whole affair. In such a glorious gallimaufry of nations, with a babble of Swahili, German, Kirundi and English swirling about her, Mina passed entirely unnoticed and unchallenged.

She made straight for the guesthouses. The two establishments were only distinguishable from one another in that one was slightly cheaper and the other slightly cleaner. Mina checked into the cleaner of the two, not out of any sense of fussiness or propriety but for the marginal improvement in privacy that a higher tariff might bring. She specified an outward facing room which provided a view to the north. In her room, Mina unpacked her small valise and hung up what little clothing she had before reviewing her weaponry situation.

She had two pistols: a Webley Top-Break and a Schofield Revolver. She unwrapped them from their leather roll and laid them on the bed. There was no knowing who or what might come, or if the Earth's aphelion would pass without incident. Indeed, there was no knowing if the two pistols would be unnecessary or woefully insufficient in the days to come.

11.

Cadwallander was waking and I woke with him.

*

I immediately attempted to sit up but Professor Sedgewick laid a hand on my chest and insisted I stay down on the thin mattress on which I had been placed. I did not resist. I felt weak, as though I had been struck down with influenza. That damnable Chioa Khan and his blasting rod! With a dry cough, I cursed to that effect.

"A nasty and cowardly weapon," said the professor, as he fed me a little water from a canteen. "Not magic of course but, I believe, an adaptation of the electrostatic force weapons carried by some of our captors."

I tried to ask how long I had been unconscious but did not get beyond the first syllables before a coughing fit took me again. Sedgewick gave me a further drink.

"A day and a half," he replied, guessing what I had intended to ask, and explained we were prisoners of Chioa Khan and the forces with which he and Lady Paget conspired. He remained coy as to who and what those forces exactly were.

I angled my aching head from one side to the other, taking in the room we occupied. From its size and coolness, I might have thought it some sort of pantry but the walls were of riveted metal and, as the grogginess ebbed, I felt a slight but definite sensation of movement.

"We are on an airship," said Sedgewick, "and have been progressing in a southerly direction for the past day."

"Where are they bally well taking us?" I asked.

"My best guess is that we are making for the *Afrikanschen Himmelaufzug* in German East Africa."

"The Skylift?"

The professor nodded but would not answer further questions until he had fully tended to me. Chioa Khan's device had attacked every muscle and fibre of my body and I could almost feel my body creak as I reasserted control over my damaged limbs. I realised that my artificial limb was not responding: it hung from my shoulder, elbow locked, fingers curled into a frozen fist.

"The internal workings are damaged, I shouldn't wonder," said Sedgewick with a nod.

I sat, with assistance, and together we inspected my arm. Fortunately, Braintree had designed it so that I could conduct much of the maintenance myself and had – God bless him – provided me with the tools to do so. With my sleeve rolled up, I opened a brass door on my upper arm and removed a small screwdriver from the cavity within. My still-numb fingers, like those of an arthritic old woman, weren't up to the job of fine repairs and I had to ask Sedgewick to unscrew the plates which covered the workings of my arm. As he worked on inspecting and repairing my arm (which mostly consisted of replacing or re-tightening the galvanic valves) the professor spoke once more.

"As best I understand it," he said, "we are to be witnesses at some unholy summoning ritual."

"Like the one Klein performed on the bridge," I said.

"Except this is not to draw forth one of the god-creatures that lives beneath our world but to open a gateway for their kin, their elders perhaps, from across the void of space."

"And this requires us to go to the *Himmelau*—" I stumbled over the tongue-tying German, "—the Skylift tower?"

"So it appears, or at least so they believe. You are familiar with the story of the Tower of Babel."

I frowned. "The Bible story?" Sedgewick was the theology professor not I and, although I had an unshakeable Christian faith, it did not come with a fraction of the theological knowledge

243

Sedgewick possessed. "Let's see. Man builds a tower to reach God but God confounds him by making everyone speak different languages."

"There was a real tower," said Sedgewick, "although its exact location is debatable. The name *Babel* gives its name to the city of Babylon and many erroneously think it originally comes from the Hebrew *balal*, meaning a jumble or confusion. In truth, it comes from the Akkadian *babi-lu* which, more tellingly, means 'the gate of God.' It was built by Nimrod."

The only Nimrod I knew was part of the musical work by Elgar (which we had the pleasure of hearing the composer himself conduct at a Regent Street concert hall the year before) and said as much.

"The piece is named after the man," said the professor. "The Bible describes him as a mighty hunter but he was more, and less, than that. He was king of Shinar, the land between two rivers. Josephus tells us that he was a tyrant and an idolater and sought to challenge God. He commanded a tower be built, this Babel, this gate of God. The Sumerians called the tower *Etemenanki*, the Temple of the Seven Lights of the Earth."

"Was it a temple then?" I asked. "A place of worship?"

Sedgewick spoke slowly, choosing his words well. "There is some troubling uncertainty in the early Bible stories. God – Jehovah, Yahweh – speaks of other gods in Genesis. He is not alone. Babel might have been a temple, but to whom? Jewish Midrashic texts give one account in which the tower builders fire arrows into the heavens which return tipped with blood, perhaps showing that a war against God is at least possible, if not winnable. Nimrod's intentions were not good."

"And Chioa Khan needs a tower for his ritual," I said.

"If my Rose's calculations are well-founded and correct then it would appear he needs a tower of astonishing proportions and one built on the Equator."

"The Skylift."

"The Skylift indeed. A tower over two hundred miles high."

"But surely," I said, "if there was any truth in this Biblical story, the ruins of a tower even a fraction of that size would have been found and identified."

"Perhaps, but let us not fall into the trap of associating this story with a limited period of history. If, as our past encounters with unearthly horrors have suggested, man's history and origins lie far further back than the six or seven thousand years previously thought, then we must consider that those ruins could be buried deep, or utterly destroyed."

"And yet, if one made a methodical exploration of the lands along the Equator..."

The professor stopped me with a smile. "The Equator is not a fixed thing, Cadwallander. The earth changes. There is compelling evidence to suggest that the build up of polar ice, particularly during past Ice Ages, has caused the Earth to topple from its axis, for north and south to become east and west. The ancient kingdom of Shinar might easily be buried in some higher or lower latitude. In fact, there are ruined pyramids in Cholula in Mexico which a Swiss archaeologist has suggested—" He broke off, in thought.

"What is it?" I asked.

"The pyramids of Cholula were probably temples dedicated to the serpent god Quetzalcoatl. I recall reading a piece about the Aztec priests. They would ... commune with their god through items called *wind jewels*."

I grunted in understanding. "Chioa Khan, that jumped up son of a brewer, mentioned something called the Aleph. What could that be?"

"*Aleph* is the first letter in the Hebrew alphabet and denotes the number one. It is, according to cabbalists, the number that contains all other numbers, the one from which all other things come. Cantor used the symbol *aleph* to describe infinite sets of numbers. The one thing with all else inside it. Conceptually, one might draw links between it and Leibniz's monadology."

"His what?"

Sedgewick shook his head, smiling. "Ignore me, dear chap. I do waffle on."

"I'm not going anywhere right now and there are far worse things to listen to than your 'waffle,'" I said with no small amount of affection.

The professor had replaced the blown valves in my arm but a number of the piston rods had jammed and required freeing. I directed my friend to the relevant panels in my forearm and hand.

"A gate of the gods," he said as he worked. "A single artefact that has the power to contain all other things within it. Chioa Khan would open a door to admit abominable hordes into our world. I fear a *physical* intrusion of the worst sort."

"We have seen our share of monsters, Erskine."

"Physical as in physics. Whatever dimension these things crawl from may bring its own mad science and logic with it. Reality reordered, life and death overturned. Hell brought to our world."

"Why would anyone want to usher in such horrors?" I said, incredulous as always in the face of the unreasonable. "The fraud Chioa Khan is as mad as a March hare, but Lady Paget...? Dash it all, she's blue blood and should know better. She was lady in waiting to Her Majesty. What would dear old Queen Victoria have to say if she knew?"

"Oh, she knows," he said. "She knows full well."

Sedgewick was silent after that. I thought at the time that it was because the repairs to my arm required his fullest attention (three of my fingers still did not function). He worked without word for several minutes. The only sounds were of the wind at our tiny window and the faint burr of the airship's engines.

Sedgewick eventually gave a deep sigh and said, "Of course, it was destroyed in the end."

"The tower?" I said, barely keeping up with his mercurial mind. "I thought the people just sort of stopped building.

"The Book of Jubilees tells us it was destroyed by a mighty wind. The top third was burned, the bottom third swallowed up by the earth and the middle left to ruin. And those who had ordered it built were punished."

"This King Nimrod fellow?"

"Well, the builders were transformed into beasts – dogs, demons or somesuch – and banished to another dimension. Nimrod himself was enraged by the failure of his tower and waged war on the good and virtuous who stood against him. It is said that he faced Abraham on the battlefield and that the Lord Almighty sent a plague of insects to destroy Nimrod's army."

"And that was the end of Nimrod, eh?"

"No. *Quos Deus vult perdere, prius dementat,* dear friend. A gnat crawled in Nimrod's skull and drove him mad."

"Ah," I said appreciatively. "I think Chioa Khan has a fair share buzzing around in there already."

I flexed my mechanical hand and although two of the digits moved with a graceless stiffness, my arm was fully functioning once more. "That's good then," I said. "I wouldn't want to face mad gods and wizards without both hands."

"Quite so," agreed my friend, tucking the screwdriver in my jacket pocket.

1908 – The Gears of Madness

From the continuing memoirs of Mr J. Cadwallander

1.

In the sense that all experience is valid, however it is mediated, I was there with Mina Saxena when the British attacked the *Afrikanschen Himmelaufzug* on the morning of the first of July.

Mina did not initially identify them as British, but the larger craft was obviously a warship (even through the glassless Chwolson pocket-scope she was using, gun emplacements along its gondola and a stubby airstrip bearing three helipteron on top of its canopy made its purpose unmistakeable) and she concluded that if there was to be some *situation* in the next twenty-four hours then this marked its beginnings. The second airship, following in the first's shadow, had the lines of a luxurious passenger craft. Mina might not have thought the second was in league with the first but for the fact that, quite conspicuously, neither carried any identifying blazes.

"A covert attack then," she said to herself.

She sat at her open hotel window, wrapped in a blanket against the frigid air, and munched on a crust of black bread while she considered her options. Though she would not be the only person at the Skylift aware that a military airship was approaching there was no sound or sense of alarm within the airship station. The two craft had been visible from a dozen miles away and Mina had the luxury of time in which to observe and reflect, and see the airship's evasive Morse code replies to the station's requests for identification.

Only when the airships were within a mile of the Skylift did Mina shut her window, cast the blanket aside and slip into a short jacket that neatly covered the twin shoulder holsters in which she carried her pistols. She exited the hotel, ignoring the hotelier's warnings that there was some worrying commotion outside, and stepped into the broad concourse in time to see the brief exchange of gunfire between the platform's small contingent of German troops and the invading forces. The Germans had taken up positions behind the support bollards and stanchions on the docking platform and, in the instant that they gave warning for the airship to clear the platform, riflemen picked them off from positions within the armoured gondola. There was no battle; most of the Germans died without firing a single shot. Everyone else dived for cover: merchant pilots, cargo handlers and transients all seeking personal salvation.

The first men to step from the airship were a pair of mortar-men, goliaths of armoured plates, galvanically-assisted limbs and shoulder-mounted artillery. They strode into the heart of the platform concourse and gave the order in English that everyone should remain exactly where they were. Most people were attempting to flee before the mortar-men had finished speaking. Mina hunkered down in the doorway of a supplies store and waited. A scrawny dockhand squatted down next to her, clutching his cap to his head as though it would afford him some measure of protection.

"*Piraten!*" he hissed.

"They're British soldiers, you fool!" she hissed back in German.

Two platoons of black-uniformed troops, perhaps sixty men in all, marched out into the concourse, peeling off into units which seized control of the Skylift elevator machines, the communications rooms and the administrative offices. In all this activity, only three shots were fired: a small pistol and two rounds of rifle fire in immediate reply. Within five minutes, a dozen German naval staff, various office boys and the crew of the one civilian airship already docked at the Skylift were brought into the centre of the station platform to join those already corralled there.

The second British airship docked soon after and the infantry officers from the warship went to meet the contingent from the more luxurious vessel. Mina scowled as she attempted to discern what was taking place.

"More troops," she muttered to herself.

Several large crates were wheeled from the docking platform, across the concourse and toward a commandeered elevator. Through the wooden slats, Mina glimpsed flashes of glinting material: tubes and panels.

"Machines?"

"We must find a way out of here," said the young dockhand and attempted to take Mina's hand in his.

She slapped him away and drew one of her pistols. "Do what you like but just do it quietly," she told him sharply.

"But this is no place for a—" He trailed off in contemplation of the gun in her hand. "What *is* happening, miss?" he asked.

"I don't know," she replied, both to him and her own internal questions. "Soldiers and machinery and—"

The party from the second airship was not entirely composed of military personnel. Five figures drew her eye. Only one she did not recognise: a veiled woman in grey who walked with geriatric rigidity. Of the others, Professor Sedgewick stood beside his doughy chum Cadwallander, both with the unhappy and uncertain stance of those who were there against their will. Ahead of them, talking volubly to an army officer was the b_____ sorcerer Chioa Khan who Mina had met, shot and the left for dead on Mars several years ago. The fifth, surrounded by officers and attendants, looked upon the work of her soldiers with considerable pleasure. It was Queen Victoria.

"God in heaven!" breathed Mina in disbelief.

*

The gaze of the Aleph swung about, not in a great leap through space or time but from one viewpoint to another. Like a baton tossed between jugglers, my perspective flipped and I had not a moment to consider Mina's offensive suggestion that I was 'doughy' before I was submerged into the mind and senses of Cadwallander and utterly oblivious to the Indian woman crouched in a nearby doorway.

*

I am not always a rational man and perhaps this makes me quite normal. My mind should have been focused on any number of concerns. I should have been consumed with fear for the nightmarish beings these fools wished to unleash on our world. I should have been stunned with unalleviated horror at the discovery that this was all being co-ordinated under the aegis of our monarch, Queen Victoria. I should have been fretful for what this attack upon Germany's colony would mean for the stability of Europe. But no, at that moment my thoughts centred mostly on how much I wished to smack the smug look of self-importance from Chioa Khan's face. He was a ringmaster and this was his circus.

He raised an arm in the manner of a Roman emperor to greet the appearance of an officer and two bearded civilians, one of whom carried a wrapped bundle in his arms.

"You are to be congratulated on your success, Captain Dansey," said Chioa Khan.

It was clear in the look this Captain Dansey gave Chioa Khan that congratulations were neither welcome nor his to give. Chioa Khan either did not see or chose to ignore it.

Sedgewick leaned close to me and whispered in my ear. "I would wager that is the Aleph," he said, with a nod to the wrapped package.

"It looks awfully small to be a gateway of any sort," I replied.

As Chioa Khan brought the two civilians – Russians, it transpired – to meet and kowtow to our Queen, we were bustled by soldiers to the nearest lift. Among the Skylift employees and travelling folk held prisoner on the platform, a number of faces looked up as we passed.

"Do you think the Germans know what's happening here?" I asked.

"Undoubtedly," said the professor. "I shouldn't wonder that their local armies are being mobilised as we speak."

"Then this could become a sticky mess of a situation."

A soldier jabbed his rifle butt in my ribs to silence me. I gave the young lad a stern glare but held my tongue nonetheless, as we stepped through the concertina gate of the lift. This lift was not a dissimilar affair to the Phobos Skylift that the good professor and I had used in our travels to and from Mars. The gate led into a square space with perhaps the same capacity as a railway goods container. A stairway to the side led up to an upper floor and passenger compartment where a much-simplified form of a locomotive's controls against the wall allowed a driver to direct the vehicle up or down the tower.

We sat at gunpoint while a soldier stood at the controls and prepared to take us up. Below us in the hold were great boxes whose contents I had had sufficient opportunity to scrutinise in order to establish their purpose.

"Gods in spacesuits!" I exclaimed. Despite the violence this mad enterprise had brought to German East Africa, despite the terrors that might await, and despite the betrayal of all that was reasonable and human by our own monarch, Professor Sedgewick and I shared grim smiles with one another.

The soldier at the controls spun a valve wheel, depressed a clutch lever and we began to rise towards the heavens.

2.

Mina found herself presented with the ridiculous but nonetheless tempting opportunity to assassinate the British Queen. She was not so ill-educated or unaware of the ways of the world to imagine that the death of Victoria would end Britain's vile colonialism. Nonetheless, with Victoria within twenty yards of her while she held a gun in her hand, Mina was compelled to weigh up the possibilities before sitting tight and watching the Queen and much of her retinue enter one of the elevators and ascend.

As best she could discern, a dozen British soldiers remained at this level, plus whatever crew remained aboard the two airships. A handful of them were intent on supervising the prisoners sat on the open platform, who for the most part had their heads low and huddled together against the cold wind. The other soldiers, she surmised, were divided between guarding key positions and searching the platform buildings.

It would only be a matter of time before she and the young dockhand were found in their meagre hiding place, but Mina had no intention on staying there long.

"I am going to make for that elevator," she said to the dockhand.

She received an insultingly shocked look in reply. "They'll shoot you, miss," he said.

"Not if you provide a suitable distraction," she replied and outlined her limited plan.

And so it was that, while a young German man who was either fearless, unnecessarily gallant or simply easily led ran around the side of the stores and stumbled onto the platform proper, noisily knocking aside the seats, Mina slipped from her position and moved in the opposite direction towards one of the unoccupied elevator carriages. The plan relied on more than a modicum of luck and, although she reached the gate door without being shot, she heard a shout of "Hey!" as she stepped inside.

Mina ignored the cry and dashed for the stairs to the upper compartment, and the controls.

"Hold there!" came a voice behind her.

She stopped and turned on the bottom stair, hiding her pistol behind her skirts. At the elevator gate stood a soldier and what she took to be, from the peaked cap and ridiculous sabre at his side, an air corps officer. The soldier's silvered rifle was aimed directly at her; the officer's pistol was drawn but not aimed.

"Come here!" commanded the soldier as though speaking to a disobedient dog. "There is nowhere for you to go up there, lass."

The officer was giving her the most curious gaze. For her part, Mina thought there was something more than a little familiar in that lean and handsome face.

"Miss!" the soldier warned, gripping his rifle tighter.

At that, the officer turned, pushed the soldier's barrel aside with his free hand and, with his other, slammed the soldier's head against the elevator wall with the pistol grip. The soldier fell without a noise, the officer slipping the rifle from his grip as he went down.

"Last time I saw you, you were a Russian prince," said Mina.

"Last time I saw you, you were a man," replied the Grand Duke Alexei Mikhailovich.

"These are strange times," she said.

The grand duke cast a look back over his shoulder to check they were not yet discovered and then looked at Mina. "I take it you have a plan."

"Barely any," she said.

"You can drive this thing?"

"I intend to."

"Then get to it," he said and went to close the gate.

*

The Indian woman had the vehicle in motion before Alexei had locked the gate into place. Drawn by the sound of the elevator engine, two British corporals ran over to the elevator. Alexei gave them a salute as they vanished from sight. No shots were fired. Alexei took that as a promising sign and hoped that the British were sufficiently stupid to give no chase.

Alexei ran up to the passenger compartment and found the Indian woman operating the controls with apparent confidence. "How fast does this thing go?" he asked.

She tapped a glass dial. "Maximum upward acceleration of twenty feet per second per second. Overall speed?" She glanced about. "I do not have the faintest idea."

"Well, as long as we don't blow the boiler."

"Or forget to stop when we reach the top." The woman stepped away from the controls. Their course was set. She picked up her pistol from the shelf on which she had set it and holstered it.

"So, my prince," she said lightly, "is this meeting of ours fate?"

"The proper term of address is *Your Highness*," said Alexei.

"That is not going to happen."

He set aside the deputy officer's cap on a nearby table. The man he had stolen the uniform from aboard Dansey's nameless airship had a rather small head (and a thin skull, it had transpired). "I don't even know your real name," he said.

"I'm Mina Saxena," she said, in a tone that indicated he should have heard of her (which he hadn't).

"And what brings you here?"

The woman, Miss Saxena, smiled and then told him her tale. It was a wild concoction of anecdotes, thinly linked, that raced from their first meeting in the Himalayas, through barbaric Indian religions, some nonsense about the plots of an English bridge-builder and the scribblings of a mad Dutch boy. All told, the woman was possessed by the belief that she, and only she, could avert some form of apocalyptic magic ritual that would herald the end of the world.

"Forgive me," said Alexei, "but that sounds like a lot of Hindoo nonsense."

"I'm sure your reasons for being here are far simpler," she said hotly.

"Indeed," he said. "I am pursuit of two treacherous Russian thieves and a gemstone the size of your fist."

She sniffed dismissively in response and went over to the observation windows.

"I would have probably given up the chase several days ago if I had been able," he said. "But, having stowed away on the airship that came to kill me, I've been forced to hide amongst gas tanks and cow intestine balloons ever since."

He walked over to join her at the windows. His feet felt heavy under the constant acceleration and he trod without grace. Outside, the sheet of white cloud which lay across the Earth was several miles below them. Beneath it, Africa was golden brown. The further they sped away from the Earth, the more pronounced the curvature of the horizon became and the blue sky around them took on a darker, purplish hue.

As Alexei understood it (he had not taken to any of the tutors his tyrannical mother had put before him, and his education in the natural sciences had not been a particular success), soon the true atmosphere of Earth would give way to the substantially different but nonetheless life-giving æther of space.

"She's family of yours, isn't she?" said Miss Saxena.

"She?" said Alexei and then understood. "Distantly. My cousin, the late Tsar was the Prince of Wales' brother-in-law. Or, alternatively – additionally – my late cousin's son, Tsar Nicholas, is married to her granddaughter." He looked at her. "What are your intentions, Miss Saxena?"

"I was just wondering the same," she said. "Go up there and bring a note of chaos to proceedings?"

"You intend on shooting anyone in particular with those pistols of yours?"

She mulled it over and said, "There's a man who claims to be a holy man or mystic. Chioa Khan. I should imagine a bullet through his weasel's heart might put paid to things. I have no particular designs on the Queen."

"Good," he said. "Ours is a large family and both Her Majesty and myself have lots of distant cousins to spare – there is no particular love between us – but I know the ruinous effect of royal assassinations on the state of nations."

"Then, my prince, I think our individual objectives might not be mutually exclusive. We each have deaths to deal out; and there are two English fools I might stoop to saving if they don't get in my way," she added.

(Dear reader, I shall not draw your attention to the woman's inability to recall that I am, and always shall be, a *Welsh*man. I shall let her character defects speak for themselves.)

Alexei nodded at Miss Saxena. "There is a platoon of British troops at the top of this tower," he said. "You do know they won't let us simply walk in there."

She gave Alexei a sly glance and he found himself, against his better judgement, thinking this woman was quite handsome – in an unrefined sort of manner. "So this will require a degree of subterfuge," she said. "That soldier downstairs. I'd say he wasn't much larger than me."

Alexei shook his head. "You are too swarthy and, to be blunt, too shapely to pass for an English infantryman."

"Details, dear prince. Now, uniform. Hop to it."

"Me?" he said, hand on chest.

"Of course. What kind of lady would I be, stripping unconscious men of their clothes?"

He was certain she was playing with him – almost entirely certain – but, nonetheless and with a peevish sigh, he made for the stairs.

"And you will give me some privacy while I change," she called. "I know what you men are like."

"*I* am a member of one of the grand royal houses of Europe," he replied with equal fervour.

"I know," she called down. "The worst kind of man."

3.

The scale of the *Afrikanschen Himmelaufzug* defied belief, at least for me. I think part of my personal disbelief was that such a grand feat of engineering was the product and property of the German peoples. To my mind, the natural order inherent in human society applied to not only men but to nations. Germany was a powerful country but it was a young one. It did not have the weight of history or culture of Britain, France or Russia to be considered one of the great nations of the world. To build the Skylift was an act of

257

impertinence, hubris even. That Germany was capable of building it was irrelevant. Just as a greengrocer, however rich, shouldn't take it upon himself to buy a stately home in the country, so Germany should have known better than to flex its might and resources in something as ostentatious as this.

The orbital space station atop the *Afrikanschen Himmelaufzug* was a massive, cylindrical drum fixed onto the tether cable like the world's largest conker. From the central area, where the lifts rose up into the structure at cable-top, the station was spilt into a number of wedge-shaped sections; some taken up with offices, passenger areas and stores, but most consisting of large warehouse spaces where cargo could be loaded or unloaded from the ships docking at the huge outer doors. Never passing out of the solar ætheric plane where breathable æther was at its densest, the space station did not need any of the pressurising machinery or air locks required by spacegoing vessels.

Naturally, the station was manned. The Germans at the airship station miles below had managed to relay a warning to their comrades above before they were either captured or killed. The professor and I arrived to the sound of sporadic gunfire. With dozens of well-disciplined British troops on the offensive, the fight was soon over.

Prisoners were rounded up and brought to join us in a large and empty cargo chamber. This cathedral space was two storeys high, with gantries circuiting the upper level. The cargo doors were flung wide to the starry majesty of the heavens; through them, we could see the ships circling the station. The only merchant ship to be docked at the station (a fat bulk-carrier under an Argentine flag) had hauled away and retreated at speed before the British could board it and was now among those remaining in the vicinity, either out of bravado or simple curiosity. I saw a French freighter loitering at a safe distance and a trio of phlogiston-driven orbital coasters: nippy little craft too small or distant for me to read their markings. Whatever happened here, the world would know.

A British warship, a four-funnel coal-burner called the *Prospero*, hove into view, and our captors prepared their rituals. Sedgewick and I, honoured captives, were stood to one side, like ushers to an unholy wedding. The two Russians, looking decidedly uncertain, stood not far away in whispered conversation.

Soldiers brought various crates from the lifts and, under the direction of a pair of officers (who referred constantly to paper schematics), the boxes were opened and the materiel of horror laid out in position. I have read enough penny dreadfuls and seen sufficient music hall representations of witchcraft to recognise a magic circle. Five raised oil lamps were placed evenly around the circle and, at its centre, a tall contrivance of wooden rods and screw clamps. Chioa Khan carried the bundled Aleph to the centre of the circle, removed its covering and set it down in the cradle of clamps which he then tightened around it.

*

Once more, my vision of past events (though I was now reviewing events that were only minutes in my past and to which I was already privy) caused me to look upon the Aleph through the medium of the Aleph. The vertiginous terror I had felt before returned but with far greater intensity. The past unravelled before me as the eye of the Aleph drew towards the present. Knowing without knowing, I feared the worst would come when those magic mirrors aligned, when the present reality perfectly overlaid the present as vision...

*

I flinched at the sight of that brilliant gem set in a fractured wheel of ancient stone. For some unknowable reason, I felt sickened when I looked upon it.

"Fascinating," said Sedgewick, apparently impervious to the object's unnatural glamour.

"What is it?" It was part question, part declaration of my revulsion.

"I would suggest that the Aleph, the one thing containing all else, is a means of connecting to distant places, perhaps a beacon, a lighthouse." He grunted to himself. "Actually, I am put in mind of a pinhole camera. An aperture, tiny in size, and yet able to admit and capture an image of the infinite."

"I do not like it," I said simply.

"And I am glad you do not," said the professor.

In an act that contained equal measures of blasphemy, pantomime and lunacy, red carpet had been unrolled across the floor from the doorway to the edge of the magic circle. Her Majesty Queen Victoria – I cannot express fully enough how shocked and appalled I remained to see our Queen, *my* Queen, involved in this abominable charade – stood at the far end of the carpet, flanked by the diseased Lady Paget and Captain Dansey.

"I'm not sure the carpet is for her," said Sedgewick quietly. He nodded towards the Aleph in explanation.

On the far side of the chamber, soldiers had finished unpacking and assembling the contraptions they had brought up with them. There were four in all and none of them alike. They did indeed resemble the most cumbersome of spacesuits, but nothing into which any man could step. Interconnecting pieces were constructed from fabric and rubber, but the bodies and plate sections were of a glistening black material that, to my eyes, resembled volcanic glass or the shiny carapace of some gargantuan insect. The largest of the suits was at least fifteen feet tall and of vaguely anthropoid outline. Where the helmet might have been, squatted a swollen dome of burnished black. A mass of rubberised tubes ran from this headpiece to connect back into the suit at various points, giving the helmet the overall appearance of some beached cephalopod. Four fat limb sections jutted awkwardly from a bulbous torso composed of overlapping scales, and each of these limbs terminated in prodigious black claws, crawling with etched symbols and ideograms. I realised there was no visor or eye-holes in the suit; the only egress was a hinged porthole of thick glass in the torso.

"What is that black material?" I whispered to Sedgewick. "Ceramic? Glass?"

"Perhaps. It appears to have a chitinous quality," he mused. "Chitin, the substance that forms the linings of certain fungi and the shells of animal exoskeletons."

"Insects."

"And crustaceans, yes. But why, I wonder, are these particular shells not made from metal? See: the lamps and the supports. None of it metal."

"Their august majesties have chosen what shape they shall take," said Lady Paget, following our gazes. "They showed me in a dream what robes of raiment we should prepare."

"A dream?" There was a shade of mockery in Sedgewick's voice.

"You do not believe in dreams and visions, professor?" sneered Chioa Khan as he finished his preparations. "There is such wisdom to be found in the mysteries and portents of your own timorous faith. Would that Daniel had visions of beasts as beautiful and terrible as these!"

Sedgewick riled at that. "Do not attempt to sully my faith by comparing it with these petty ... magicks!"

Chioa Khan strolled over. "This is your new faith, professor," said he. "You refused to believe when I told you that Aiwass had called me to herald in the age of Horus -"

"That mirage led you out into the Martian desert to die," said Sedgwick.

"It led me here!" crowed Chioa Khan. "You would not listen to the whispers of gods. You did not heed their subtle signs. But, today, you will hear their roar and tremble at their footfalls! Today you will believe!"

*

Elsewhere, a voice bleated repeatedly from a nearby telephonic voicepipe.

Mina wore her borrowed soldier's cap low in a poor attempt to cover her face. The two soldiers who had met and challenged them at the lift now lay hidden alongside the man whose clothes she now wore.

Grand Duke Alexei Mikhailovich, who had taken a teleforce rifle from one of the soldiers (complaining all the while that it was an inferior copy of a Russian design), picked up the voicepipe trumpet while Mina rooted through some weapons cases by the soldiers' station.

"Orbital station. Go ahead," said the grand duke. Mina could hear how the Russian had tempered some of the plumminess in his spoken English whilst maintaining a deliberate air of arrogant officiousness.

"Has the lift reached you yet?" asked a voice, carried from miles below at the airship station.

"Yes. The lift is here. The deputy flight officer has arrived with a message for Captain Dansey."

Mina clicked the latches on a long case and flipped up the lid.

"There have been no orders to that effect," said the voicepipe.

"Then I'd suggest the orders were not relayed via you, *sir*."

"We're sending a section of troops up to check on the situation."

"Belay that order," said the grand duke. "Her Majesty has commanded that all other troops stay at their post."

"What? Give me your name and rank, soldier."

Mina saw the grand duke grimace before ripping the voice pipe from the wall and casting it to the floor. "What a dull little man," he said and turned to Mina. "We're going to have company soon enough. What's that?"

Mina held a fat tube with mounted sights and gyroscope. "Wire-guided stovepipe rocket."

"Yes," said the grand duke doubtfully. "That would certainly bring a note of chaos to proceedings!"

*

Her dark skirts gliding across the cargo bay floor, Queen Victoria approached Sedgewick and I, Dansey at her side. Be it a treasonous thought or not, I saw there was something strange and unnatural about our Queen. For certain, she did not look like a woman approaching her tenth decade and little like the daguerreotypes I recall from my youth. There was a smoothness to her complexion and an ethereal leanness to her frame. Whatever potions or quack tonics Chioa Khan had plied her with, they had perhaps allowed her health and life beyond what nature intended.

"Gentlemen," she said. "Imagine, if you will, what it was like to be present on the morning when Christ rose from his tomb. Could anyone who witnessed it fail to be awestruck? Here – here and now – the true gods return to us. Surrender your doubts."

"I implore you, Your Majesty—" the professor began but Chioa Khan cut him off.

"The optimal time approaches, Your Majesty," he said, consulting a pocket watch in his gloved hand.

Next to us, one of the Russians tugged nervously at Dansey's sleeve. "Captain, much obliged as we are by this honour, Kirill and I would be happy to take our payment and depart."

"Soon enough," said Dansey curtly.

A section of soldiers hoisted the largest of the malformed suits onto their shoulders and carried it into position before the Aleph. Chioa Khan took a leather-bound notebook from his pocket, opened it as he approached the edge of the summoning circle, and began to read: intoning a string of nonsense words with all the pomposity of a third-rate Shakespearean actor.

"Ph'nglui mglw'nafh. Wgah'nagl fhtagn..."

Lady Paget and Queen Victoria, mad or ensorcelled, stood expectantly at his side.

Sedgewick and I have experienced phenomena which might all too readily be described as magic. The good professor has always held that, although the Almighty himself has the power to deliver miracles, the seemingly impossible acts we have been witness to should be regarded as the product of sciences and technologies that are simply beyond our current understanding. As Chioa Khan's ritual reached its bombastic climax, I reminded myself that, just as a South Seas savage might mistake the action of Röntgen rays or radionics cabinets for sorcery, I should recognise that what was unfolding before my very eyes was simply science that we had yet to comprehend.

The Aleph was ablaze with light, flashes of sickly yellow and violent purple flickering within the painful brilliance. And then, like a thread being drawn through the eye of needle, a chain of green, semi-corporeal material passed *out from the centre of the Aleph* and directly into the monstrous suit of armour's open porthole.

"Whether it is æther or air that is their true poison, the star gods are able to tolerate a short passage from the Aleph's mouth," observed Sedgewick.

I was agog. "That ... that *goo* is the star god?"

"Think in terms of potentiality, my friend. Some suggest that living things on Earth are the transmuted descendants of a primordial slime."

"We must do something!" I said and rocked angrily on my heels.

"Violence is not the solution here," warned the professor. "We are outnumbered and outgunned."

"Then what?"

There was a disconcerting creak as the arm of the suit now housing the emerging star god flexed an inch or two.

Sedgewick bowed his head. "I do not know."

A voice shouted from on high, cutting across the sound of that abominable chanting: *"Khan!"*

We looked up at the gantry over the inward door. Rifles were raised. The Russians swore. Even Chioa Khan broke off his incantation. At first glance, two British soldiers appeared to be up there, one holding a rifle, the other with a rocket weapon on his shoulder. And then I saw that *he* was a *she* and that she was well known to me.

*

"Mina Saxena!" spat Chioa

"I'm going to blow it up!" she yelled.

Captain Dansey stepped forward. "Your Highness," he called, his voice all frosty politeness. "How did you manage to survive the blast in Tunguska?"

Alexei allowed himself a small smile but kept his teleforce rifle aimed at the conjurer-cum-priest. There were two dozen guns trained on him and Mina but, if the British army could be relied upon to do anything, it was to hold their fire until the order was given.

"I'm surprisingly persistent," replied Alexei. "It's the hallmark of good breeding."

"And cockroaches," said Miss Saxena as an aside, quiet enough that only he could hear.

Rather than flee from the stovepipe rocket's aim, the British Queen and the strangely veiled woman with her placed themselves in front of the Aleph, and the ogreish suit of armour at the centre of the circle. Alexei wanted to doubt the evidence of his own eyes but the suit of armour was moving, joints bending minutely: a giant slowly stirring from its upright slumber.

"Move aside, Your Majesty," Alexei called. "She's going to destroy it."

The look Victoria gave him seemed to be one of pity more than anything else. "Surely, Alexei dear, you don't think you can escape from this situation?"

"We don't have to escape," replied Miss Saxena. "We only have to stop you."

"I was actually planning on surviving this," Alexei whispered.

"And the two of you are willing to kill all these people to do it?" said the Queen.

Miss Saxena tilted her head and gave it a moment's thought. "Some," she said.

Alexei fired. The supersonic tungsten needles ripped a bloody wound across Chioa Khan's abdomen. The man dropped to the ground.

Queen Victoria and her lady-in-waiting did not flinch. Behind them, the grievously injured Chioa Khan lay, making mewling whimpers and soundless screams. They did not spare him a single glance. The British soldiers held their fire.

The veiled woman made a dry sound that took Alexei a moment to realise was laughter. "Yes," she said. "Throw your bombs and rockets." She gestured to the nearest soldiers. One pulled two young German prisoners into the central circle. Another grabbed the stout Englishman with the mechanical arm and thrust him to his knees in front of the Aleph.

"Yes," continued the woman. "Make a libation of blood to welcome the ancient ones. Kill us all. The Aleph is open, a gateway to worlds beyond your wildest imaginings. You are too late to stop it now and your weapon far too puny."

"Do it, Miss Saxena!" shouted the fat Englander.

"Yes. Do it," said the faceless woman.

4.

I had often thought Miss Saxena lacked the common decency and moral rectitude that sets the civilised man apart from the savage. And now when a little indecency and moral blindness might have saved all mankind, she confounds it all by showing empathy and compassion for the innocent.

As she lowered the rocket launcher, Dansey's soldier ran to the upper gantry to take them prisoner. They were dragged down to join the interrupted ceremony. An officer was crouched beside the wounded Chioa Khan, stripping away the clothes over his wound. Though the man had brought this ignoble end upon himself, I was disgusted to see that Lady Paget and the Queen seemed not to care one jot. The officer tended to a undoubtedly mortal wound and I, knelt an arm's length from him, watched the fool gasping for breath, his eyes wide and staring specifically at me. His mouth struggling to form words but only managing to produce a string of gulping *G*s.

Miss Saxena and the Russian prince were brought forward and, I noticed, the two bearded Russians, Kirill and Vasiliev shrank back. There was clearly a connection – and not an amicable one – between the men, though I had no idea what and had no time to dwell on the matter. Queen Victoria reached out and touched the prince's chin with thumb and forefinger as though admiring his countenance and then sighed.

"Alexei. The prodigal son." She turned her gaze on Miss Saxena, who might have scratched Her Majesty's eyes out if her elbows weren't securely held by two soldiers. "And is this one of our subjects?"

Miss Saxena spat at the Queen's feet. Victoria blinked slowly. "If I am in some way not worthy enough to rule over you, think of the Kings and Queens who are coming now and to whom even I must bow. Smile, my dear. This is a moment to rejoice."

The god-filled suit of armour, which had been twitching and stirring for several minutes, now *came to life*. It is hard to describe how I now apprehended that this black suit was inhabited as all I can say is that I now perceived the presence of a malevolent being within.

The Church speaks of evil as something discrete and material, a force as real as gravity, *odic forces* or *élan vital*. But, although I am willing to describe certain thoughts and acts as evil, I struggle with the concept of evil as a thing. Furthermore, I cannot explain to my own satisfaction why this armoured god, this squid-headed troll, should not strike me as evil though *no physical change had been wrought upon it*. I regard my own recollections as horribly illogical, as foolish as a man rejecting one fork, one pen, one cigar for the sake of another identical one on the grounds that the first was somehow morally deficient.

Nonetheless, I trembled at the arrival of the evil one and, for sure, that presence was felt by all others in the room. Grown men cried out and covered their eyes in fear. Many fell to their knees, some involuntarily and awestruck, others in deliberate and perverse adoration. I heard more than one voice cry out in pitiful prayer. I heard Sedgewick himself muttering the Lord's Prayer. On the floor by me, Chioa Khan stirred from the edges of unconsciousness, gave a wordless groan of pleasure and slipped away.

The beetle-black squid god stepped forward. Its three-toed elephantine foot came down with a flat echoless thump. Lady Paget, graceful and evidently unafraid, stepped forward and delicately closed the glass window in its torso.

"W'heyl riagn, Shle'k Tset-dhon." She backed away, bowing like a Chinese mandarin.

"Bring the next!" shouted Dansey and a team of soldiers prepared to bring the next suit into position.

But I did not watch them. My eyes had drifted back to the Aleph. In hauling me out as a bargaining chip to use against Miss Saxena (clearly they were unaware of the general antipathy Miss Saxena and I had for one another) I had been placed directly before the Aleph. I looked now into its pale and sinister glare.

Through means I could not grasp, my vision and all my other senses besides were channelled through the hideous eye and transported to distant times; to past events in far off places. In the orbital station cargo chamber, my body swayed as my mind roved. I mumbled words, paltry commentary on the visions that poured over me.

"Maurits."

"What is it Cadwallander?" the professor called to me.

"Arnhem," I muttered in nonsensical reply.

Sedgewick said my name – once, twice – calling me back, but he was drowned out by the rush of memory and experience.

"Siberia! Arnhem. The grand duke."

*

Here, I must pause and seek clarity in my recollections. My account of these events began with my looking into the light of the Aleph, and the visions which followed. Now, I come to the point at which those visions include the moment in which what was happening in reality and what was seen in the vision were the same: the present.

The accounts of past events had been presented to me at speed, visions of events ranging across more than a year impressed on my mind in mere moments, but I was abruptly launched into the very *now-ness* of things. If you will forgive my metaphors, I was put in mind of the maelström that I was unfortunate enough to see envelop the Lowestoft-Zeebrugge bridge back in '05. My hallucinatory review of the past had been the appraisal of a flat scene, shifting, fascinating, but as ostensibly level as the surface of the sea. Previous glimpses of the Aleph in my visions – at the grand duke's camp in Siberia, at its unveiling in the cargo hold – had been squally dips in the sea, premonitions of the whirlpool ahead; but the present moment had opened up a yawning pit into unfathomable depths, a funnel of horrible experience with the naked and unmediated Aleph at its heart. My perspective descended now-into the dark eye of the maelström on a journey that could only end in insanity and death!

But there was an end to that tunnel. In a fall that was both infinite and yet over in an instant, my consciousness passed through the Aleph, beyond an impossible singularity, and came to that place from which the star gods had set out for Earth. I saw the landscape of an alien world and knew that this was one of the planets orbiting the distant star, Altair. But, simultaneously, I understood that this place was beyond the reach of physical travel; that I had passed through a great folding lens and moved into a realm where the rules governing space and all its dimensions were something altogether *other*.

In a hollow before me was a mass of all shapes and yet none. Limbs, bony digits, boneless tentacles and pulsating extrusions boiled from the surface, reaching out to touch and take. I was looking on the *asura* and the *asuri*, the anti-gods, the star gods, the beings who would take control of our world. They were of a colour I cannot describe for it does not exist within our universe. I comprehended further that this inconsistent soup of horrors was not the actual selves of the star gods. This was a membrane, a curtain against which the star gods were pressing themselves and throwing representations into our space. I was not gazing upon the star gods any more than a primitive looking at the flags of the nations of Earth would be looking on the countries themselves.

I had travelled beyond all rational comprehension and, still, there was a gap between myself and the star gods: a physical gap, a gap in meaning; what Professor Sedgewick would later call an epistemic gap. For me to step across that distance would require a further transformation of myself, one that would rob me of all sanity and, perhaps, make me more like the star gods than the human I am.

And, in that, I found in my final revelation. These powerful beings were not intrinsically horrible and terrible. It was distance and difference that made them monsters to us. Forged on the anvil of the infinite, these beings (who, do not misunderstand me, were nonetheless consumed by the desire for acquisition and destruction) emerged into our universe as perverted and obscene titans. I don't know if they understood this fact. Perhaps, it changed nothing. They were intent on taking Earth and putting all that we hold dear through a contortion of magicks that would destroy us all; bringing upon us a hell in which future, past, life and death would be unpicked and made as one.

There was no timescale to that vision. I saw all that but, whether I tarried for a moment or an age it does not matter, I was not to stay in that place forever. The travelling eye of my visions had passed into the infinite pit of the present but was now moving on.

I was hauled out of those incomprehensible and distant scenes but the Aleph was not finished with me. I had been presented with a number of specific visions of the past but now, moving beyond the present, I was shown certain visions of the future. I was privy to events that I was yet to live through and subsequently endured in the knowledge of what was yet to occur. I am sure my companions thought my actions in the minutes and hours that followed (guided as they were by my temporary clairvoyance) were peculiar in the extreme. Nonetheless, I shall recount them as they occurred, beginning with that which happened immediately after the Aleph released its hold on my mind.

5.

Alexei considered himself to be a simple creature with simple desires, and understood without delusions that the simplicity he sought was only available to a man born into a world of wealth and privilege. He craved fine company, fine hospitality and the kind of high adventure which came with few surprises and little personal discomfort. He had no time for trifling and distracting matters like politics, religion, business or, worst of all, work. He had been brought to the *Afrikanschen Himmelaufzug* by two very simple matters: his anger at the thieves Kirill and Vasiliev (who had sloped off to hide in some corner) and the fact that he had been unable to exit the Englanders' airship earlier. This business with alien creatures from distant space and arcane rituals was not only incredible but also none of his business, and far too *involved* for his liking.

The fact that Cadwallander, the provincial Englishman with the mechanical arm, was babbling like a gypsy fortune-teller did not improve matters. However, matters did take a dramatic turn when Cadwallander gave a sudden shout of "Gimlet!" drew a small pointed object from his jacket pocket and stabbed it into the Aleph.

At once, a tremor ran through the whole room, as though a mighty hand had grasped the Skylift tower and shaken in. Simultaneously, the Aleph's light recoiled and twisted liked an injured snake. Great, lightning-bright shafts forked out from the stone. Many of those present were instantly blinded. There were screams. As one soldier cowered, a blade of light lanced through his midriff, throwing him across the floor and killing him instantly. Those not blinded flinched and covered their eyes. Alexei felt the hands pinning him loosen their grip.

He turned and elbowed one of his captors in the face and then, completing the turn, laid a wild punch on the jaw of the man next to him. He snatched the man's rifle as he fell. Beside him, Miss Saxena, similarly freed, had already laid her hands on an officer's pistol and coolly shot the man from whom she had taken it.

A great shout of panic went up in the room. Prisoners cried fearfully and tried to flee. Some of the soldiers fled with them. Others – and there was no distinction between troops and officers – called for order or shouted commands. Victoria and the veiled woman were frozen, stunned. Dansey, lips curled in anger, had his pistol drawn. The armoured monster stumbled and staggered, a great groan of alarm issuing from within its shell. In short, the room had descended into bedlam as surely as if Cadwallander had set off a grenade.

Alexei, despite the confusion (or perhaps because of it), had only one clear aim in his mind: to find and punish the traitors Kirill and Vasiliev. He cast about for them but there was no sign.

The floor shifted under another tremor.

"Alexei!" shouted Cadwallander. "Shoot it!"

The Aleph, having spat out its violent energies at Cadwallander's attack, had died to an ordinary gem-like lustre. Whatever diabolical bridge it had forged to far off hells was now closed. Alexei could hardly claim to be able to read the emotional state of the faceless demon-god but, by the manner in which it swung round, swatting aside a hapless British soldier who happened to be in its way, Alexei judged that it was not best pleased.

"Shoot it now!" yelled Cadwallander, pointing frenetically at the monster one last time before his friend the professor hauled him out of the way and behind the shelter of a packing crate.

*

The demon stormed forward across the room. Next to Mina, the grand duke raised the teleforce rifle high and fired. A line of needles sliced across the creature's wrist and severed its claw hand. Dansey yelled at his men; a number of soldiers regained their wits sufficiently to shoot at Mina and the grand duke.

Mina ran in a crouch for cover. She found herself sliding into a position beside Sedgewick and Cadwallander, the second staring wild-eyed as though on the edge of hysteria.

"Miss Saxena," acknowledged Sedgewick, as though greeting her at table.

Mina peered over the edge of the crate offering them some small protection. The alarming vibrations in the station structure,

271

initiated by Cadwallander's assault on the Aleph, grew. That, and the gunfire, had driven most of those able to move from the room. Besides the scattered bodies on the ground, there were no more than a dozen. Apart from herself, Sedgewick, Cadwallander and the grand duke (who was firing blindly as he ran to the Aleph) there was the British Queen, the veiled woman Lady Paget, Captain Dansey and a handful of his black-clad soldiers. Dansey was pleading with Victoria to seek cover, but the woman was steadfastly refusing despite the dangers about her and was desperately making for the injured black *asuri*.

Green slime, like so much compacted pond algae, oozed from the fiend's stump. Where it emerged it instantly lost its colour, becoming dry and brittle as though it were ash.

"The suit is breached," said Sedgewick. "The air is killing it."

"Good," said Mina. Aiming swiftly, she took down another soldier.

Though the *asuri* appeared wholly ignorant of her presence, Victoria reached up and attempted to staunch the wound with her hands. As the alien flesh slipped over Victoria's fingers, the Queen thrust her arm elbow-deep into the cavity. Mina had a moment to wonder what madness had seized the woman before the entire arm was sucked in.

"It's a parasite," said Cadwallander. "But too large to hide in her body—"

Pulled by whatever incomprehensible powers that star-god possessed, Victoria was hauled further in through that wrist opening and – I can speak of Miss Saxena's horror in witnessing this and of my own quivering disgust and loathing in relating it – with a bone crunching rend, the British monarch's upper body folded in to pass through into the creature's arm. It did not stop there! By all that was sacred, it did not stop there! It hauled in her entire body, legs spasming as they were lifted up and, as Mina at last hid her eyes in horror, the Queen's head was drawn in, green ooze dribbling *out* of from her mouth and nose, her eyes wide and beyond human expression!

"God save us!" whispered Sedgewick in shock.

Once she found her voice, Mina's choice of words was far more earthy.

Dansey screamed. Alexei glanced up from the stone tablet containing the Aleph (which he was simultaneously using as cover and trying to free, so that he might reclaim what was his). The British captain was howling at the demon-god incoherently and firing at it. The veiled Lady Paget was being forcibly bustled from the room by the remaining soldiers. There was no sign of Victoria but the wet bung of bunched up dress material plugging the monster's injured hand made Alexei wonder what had happened while he had been looking elsewhere.

Regardless, the enraged monster was rearing at the preoccupied Dansey, none of the remaining soldiers had their attention on Alexei, and the anarchy in the room provided him with the opportunity to release the remaining clamps holding the Aleph in place. The stone was awkward rather than weighty and scraped against the supporting frame as the grand duke lifted it free.

"Alexei!"

The shout came from Cadwallander. Alexei looked up to see the demon-beast charging across the chamber towards him. He understood immediately: it was drawn to protect the Aleph. However, understanding didn't bring solutions. Faced by a thundering juggernaut, coming at him like an enraged bull elephant, Alexei had wits only to raise his rifle and take several hurried backward steps.

Gunshots, presumably from Miss Saxena, exploded off the creature's shoulder plates, doing nothing to slow it. Alexei feinted to one side but the demon-god's arms swept wide to grab at him. He retreated further. The great cargo doors were wide open behind him with only the starry heavens and the drop to Earth beyond. Another time, he might have marvelled at that vista: the Earth was itself a great gem, banded in a curve of indigo horizons, light and colour playing across its cloud-streaked surface. At that moment it only spoke of fear and death to Alexei.

In the last instant, Alexei threw the Aleph aside. The demon-god turned its octopoid head, but the thing had too much momentum. Alexei dived to one side, though not far enough to avoid the creature. A limb with the weight and solidity of an oak tree knocked from his feet.

He spun through the air, felt his feet bang once against the demon-god's chest, and then twisted round. Æther air rushed about him. Tumbling, he saw the Earth, laid out like a vast, mist-shrouded dome, and the cold and uncaring stars above him.

6.

Howling, the *asuri* collided with the grand duke. They both tipped through the cargo doors and fell from sight.

Mina swore in vehement Hindi and stood up.

Professor Sedgewick started to ask what had happened and then, standing too, understood and said nothing.

A quiet of sorts had suddenly descended on the scene. The British had fled, leaving only the dead behind. The monster and the grand prince were falling to their doom.

"A fall from this height will kill that thing, surely," said Mina.

"Perhaps not the fall," said Sedgewick, "but when the suit rips apart on impact, exposure to the air should finish it off. Her Majesty—" The professor put thumb and forefinger to the bridge of his nose and bowed his head.

"No one should die like that," said Mina.

Sedgewick gave her a most complex look and said, "Whatever devil had possessed her in recent years, it chose this path."

"Devil?"

"I don't know," said Sedgewick, his strained voice indicating his general mental weariness. "My niece spoke with Fabian Wilmarth while he was in Hanwell Asylum. He mentioned that the Queen – God rest her soul – fell under the influence of both Chioa Khan and a Dr Walton, who treated her ailments with a mystical tincture he had acquired in the Far East."

"I told him to destroy that stuff," said Mina.

Sedgewick, in the act of helping Cadwallander to his feet, paused, frowning. "Told whom? Walton?"

"It is a long story," said Mina.

"One you might have to save for later, then."

The orbital station shook alarmingly. Mina suspected that did not bode well. "We need to get to an elevator," she said.

"Assuming they have not all gone," said Sedgewick.

"No," said Cadwallander. "The Russians took one. Station workers and some of the soldiers took a second. Dansey and Lady Paget are in a third. There is one left up here."

"How could you possibly know that?" asked Mina.

"My man clearly has hidden talents," said Sedgewick with an amused air. "I say we descend as fast as we might before catastrophe takes the Skylift from beneath our feet."

The three of them hurried from that unholy place. Cadwallander, regaining his wits second by second, was soon leading them through the short corridors to the lift stations clustered around the central tower spine. There was indeed one elevator left.

The three of them sprinted through the entrance into the lower hold and up the stairs to the control room and passenger lounge. Mina made for the controls and inspected the dials. Although gravity would do most of the work in powering the elevator's descent, the wheels were geared to the engine and they could only descend once the boiler pressure was up.

"We'll be away in a minute," she said.

Cadwallander reached past her, spun a brake release wheel and opened the engine valve. The lift carriage dropped instantly. Mina's stomach flipped unpleasantly and she grabbed a handrail for support. With the brakes off, it was only the engine resistance which prevented them from descending in free fall, with furniture, fittings and more besides floating up into the air.

"That was queer!" declared Sedgewick. "A bit of warning next time please, dear fellow."

"Sorry, professor," Cadwallander replied. "But we have to be quick if we are to meet the grand duke at the airship."

Mina threw her arms out in a gesture that was meant to be emphatic but possibly came across as merely petulant. "Damn it, Sedgewick. What's happened to your valet? He's turned into a babbling lunatic."

"Perhaps my *friend* has become a latter day Daniel, touched with insights of things yet to come."

She smiled bitterly. "My mistake. You are both loons. Alexei is dead. He's gone."

"No," said Cadwallander. "You have to consider the lower gravity at the orbital station, the recoil action of the Tesla weapon he was holding and his speed relative to that of the fastest lift."

"Madness!" spat Mina.

7.

Alexei's situation, outside the confines of the Skylift and falling to Earth, held little beyond the promise of imminent death. However, like a man savagely wounded and holding his own innards in his hands, Alexei could either stare in disbelief and terror, or attempt to do something – anything – however futile.

The demon-creature was falling beside him, scant feet away, clawing at the air in fury or desperation. Alexei had the teleforce rifle in his hand, the strap slung loosely over his shoulder. There were no other tools, no other physical objects within range. Through blurring tears brought on by the cold slipstream, Alexei could see the tower itself moving past at such speed that to make contact with it would tear him apart. Far below, and descending at such a rate it too seemed to be falling uncontrollably, was one of the elevators.

The unconscious mind is frequently wiser than the conscious mind. Alexei, fighter by birth, soldier by training and fencer by choice, had long since learned to surrender control of his body to instinct and reflex. Purposefully, without coherent thought, Alexei brought his knees up, turned in the air and, finding the right moment, kicked out against the tumbling demon-god. The action flattened the grand duke's uncontrolled spin, nudging him in the general direction of the Skylift cable.

With his legs and free arm spread to provide stability, Alexei pointed the rifle off to his side. He fired a two-second burst of tungsten rounds. His knowledge of weapon recoil was only as much as a man need know to fire straight and true. If only he had paid attention to his dull tutors, he might have more finely grasped the mechanics of what he was attempting. He knew there was some law about actions and their opposing reactions; beyond that, all he comprehended was that he was attempting to control his lateral position by firing in a variety of directions.

A sharp glance down told him he was still falling towards the descending elevator (he was vaguely worried that it had accelerated beyond the speed at which he was falling). The roof of the elevator was mostly taken up by the steam engine which drove it: tender, boiler, chimney, the pistons and driving wheel feeding the cogs, all clustered together in a tower formation. What remained of the roof was roughly twelve feet square; it was towards this that Alexei aimed himself. If he drifted too close to the Skylift, he would be dashed to death or fall into the engine workings. If he strayed too far adrift, he would miss the roof entirely and plummet to an inescapable death. Even if he struck the flat of the roof directly, there was still the all too real possibility that the impact would kill him, or he would bounce or slide off the edge.

The dangers and the odds were immaterial: this was his only chance of survival. After two controlled bursts, one to draw him closer to the Skylift, another to correct his position in relation to the roof, Alexei cast aside the rifle to reach out and brace his fall with both hands.

He struck the roof squarely. The impact jarred his outstretched hand – he felt joints pop, something snapped in his left wrist – nearly ripping his shoulder free of its socket. His face smacked against the iron surface; he almost blacked out. If not for his iron chest, he would have suffered broken ribs and a punctured lung. Alexei pitched forward and rolled to the edge. His legs slid over the roof's outward rim; he grabbed for any sort of handhold, wanting to scream at the pain shooting through his left arm. The fingers of his right hand dug into the roof-edge's up-curved lip. He hung by one hand, knees knocking against the windows of the passenger lounge.

He caught a glimpse of the demon-god as it dropped away, continuing its unstoppable descent to the airship station, and the rocky slopes of Kilimanjaro. He looked through the elevator carriage's window. For a moment he hoped the two men inside might open the window and help him; until he recognised them. One was fumbling at his belt for a pistol.

There was an emergency access ladder running up beside the window to the roof, too far away for Alexei to reach. He cursed and, with a strength born of frantic urgency, swung a foot over the roof lip. By the time Vasiliev fired, smashing the window, Alexei was pulling himself up and out of sight. He rolled into the shadow of the engine. There was another gunshot and a dull clang. Had Vasiliev tried to shoot through the solid metal roof? Alexei hoped the fool had killed himself or Kirill with the ricochet.

Alexei lay on his back, staring up at the orbital station (already almost too distant to see). He sucked in the sweet and cold air, reflecting on his ridiculous good fortune in surviving the fall. Admittedly, he might have done better to land on the roof of a carriage not occupied by men who had left him for dead in Siberia.

As this thought passed through his mind, the carriage beneath him accelerated rapidly, powering downwards with such speed that he felt a sudden weightlessness. He might have drifted off the rooftop if he hadn't wedged his boot in between the tender and boiler, and grabbed onto a extraneous pipe. The engine pitch rose in volume; the carriage accelerated further. Alexei found himself being lifted as the concepts of *up* and *down* reversed. Soon he would be standing on his hands, clinging to the roof by whatever grip he could maintain. Vasiliev and Kirill would be experiencing something similar inside the vehicle, but they at least had the carriage ceiling to act as the new 'floor'. To kill him, all they had to do was withstand the discomfort until Alexei's grip gave way and he fell up from the carriage. They had many miles of track in which to do so.

Directly in front of Alexei was the intake pipe to the reciprocating cylinder, and on it a centrifugal governor valve. It spun slowly, weighted arms relaxed. Reaching down awkwardly with his injured free hand, Alexei drew his sabre. The instant, searing pain in his arm almost made him drop it. Gritting teeth against the agony, he thrust the sword into the governor mechanism, twisting it, forcing the lever arms upward. The valve opened fully; steam meant for the cog wheels vented out in a powerful jet.

Deprived of steam, the engine instantly lost power. The carriage slowed, gravity returned and Alexei fell back onto the roof, taking care to avoid disembowelling himself on the sword jutting from the governor. The carriage decelerated further, its power dissipating in clouds of steam. Alexei could imagine Kirill and

Vasiliev in the room below: futilely stoking the boiler, opening the drive valves, trying to raise the boiler pressure. Even they might not take long to realise that the problem was not fixable from within.

Indeed they did not. Alexei was still regaining his composure: attempting to assess the damage to his pink and swollen left hand (which throbbed as though it had been plunged into scalding water) when a head and hand appeared over the roof of the elevator. The head was Vasiliev's; in the hand was a Mauser pistol.

Alexei tried to crawl for what little cover there was amongst the engine. A side wind blasted across the elevator roof; it tipped him face down, his feet once more dangling over the edge. Vasiliev opened fire. The first shot pinged off the boiler; the next ricocheted painfully off Alexei's iron chest. He cried out at a sudden pain in his legs. It was Kirill: hanging onto Alexei's feet, almost breaking his legs against the lip of the roof.

Seeing Alexei trapped and held in position, Vasiliev took his time in gaining a sure footing. Alexei grunted in pain, awkwardly looking round. Vasiliev was less than five feet away, gun levelled. Alexei's sabre was still thrust into the jammed and steaming governor valve.

"One bullet left, Your Highness," Vasiliev shouted over the constant gale around them. He was savouring the moment.

"I doubt you're going to get paid now," called Alexei.

"Someone will pay," said Vasiliev. "The British don't break their word."

"Not like Russians. You left me to die in that Siberian pit."

Vasiliev made a vaguely contrite facial shrug that seemed to say that this was the way of the world.

"And how many others?" said Alexei, groaning as Kirill, leaning out of the window below, continued to haul down on his legs. "My soldiers. The Evenki. You killed them."

Vasiliev's expression became abruptly colder, more hostile. "No, Your Highness. Do not think to bring them into it. You never cared about them in life. What prayers have you offered for their souls?" He peered closely at Alexei. "No, none. You only care about yourself, my prince. It's *all* about you."

"You're right," said Alexei. He reached out, grabbed the hilt of his sabre and ripped it out of the governor mechanism. The ball-weighted lever arms dropped, allowing steam back through to the engine. Following its own momentum, Alexei's sword swung at Vasiliev's knees. Vasiliev stepped back out of range, firing just as the elevator – once more under power – accelerated downwards. His step back was transformed into an effortless backward leap: he rose in a low arc sufficient to carry him over the edge of the carriage. The terror on Vasiliev's face was tinged with deep indignation at the unfairness of it all. He fell, a thin scream escaping through clenched teeth.

As the elevator accelerated ever faster, his growing lightness gave Alexei greater freedom of movement. He sat up, bringing the sabre down on one of the hands which hauled blindly at his foot. Bloody fingers went spinning off in the wind. Alexei heard Kirill shriek in surprise; the weight on the grand duke's feet vanished.

Alexei did not pause. He swung himself over the access ladder and clumsily made his way down. Alexei didn't think about the drop at his back, or how many miles above the Earth he was dangling with a broken wrist and near useless fingers. He stepped off the ladder and swung through the open window which Vasiliev had used. It was a gamble: Kirill might be armed and waiting. But the archaeologist was sat at one of the passenger tables, attempting to bind the bloody ruin of his right hand with table napkins.

A bitter, crazy smile flickered on Kirill's face. "Would you believe me if I said I was happy to see you alive, Your Highness?"

Alexei approached slowly, sword raised. "Believe, maybe," he said. "I'm not sure that I care, though."

Kirill swallowed hard, his face pale with shock. "For God's sake, Your Highness, have mercy."

"I've had enough of gods for one day. But I will give you one mercy. I'll give you a choice."

Alexei looked from Kirill to his drawn sword, to the open window and back to Kirill once more.

Miss Saxena made a perfectly competent engine driver – the visions of the Aleph had shown me this – but habit and my own reasonable prejudices made me keep an eye on her nonetheless: overseeing her as we slowed towards the airship docking station. An alarming vibration ran through the entire carriage, although I knew that it was neither the carriage nor Miss Saxena's driving at fault.

"What's happening to the tower?" she asked, her thoughts mirroring mine as the shaking became more noticeable.

"One might say that God is once more showing his displeasure," said Professor Sedgewick, sitting at a passenger table with a restorative glass of sherry in front of him (the lift bar was well stocked – even if it was mostly sticky German drinks) "But that may be flippant. And yet—! What was it that you did up there, Cadwallander? I can't help but be put in mind of Baruch's Apocalypse."

"To hell with that!" snapped Miss Saxena, ever passionate. "If this damned tower is falling, why are we stopping off now?"

"We meet Grand Prince Mikhailovich at the airship," I said.

"But we could just carry on down to the mountaintop."

I shook my head. "The tower will crumble at the base first. If we continue downwards we will dash ourselves on the wreckage. At least here we may board the last airship."

For the final furlongs of the descent, Miss Saxena applied the brakes without mercy. Sedgewick picked up the sherry to avoid it being spilled before drinking it down. "Are there not two airships?" he said.

"Her Majesty's airship is gone. Most of the soldiers and prisoners too. I expect some officer chap made the wise decision to evacuate them all."

The lift came to a halt. Miss Saxena made quickly for the stairs.

Sedgewick and I followed her down "I would have thought they would take the warship, out of choice," observed the professor.

"It was damaged by that alien god monster as it fell. But it's still airworthy – just."

I allowed Miss Saxena to lead us across the station platform. It was empty of all who might oppose us, as I had foreseen in the Aleph (for this, I must be clear, is a series of events which I was shown in the Aleph's visions and which I *then* experienced with full foresight). Apart from the bodies of those German soldiers killed in the first attack by Dansey's troops, there was no one to be seen until we reached the docking platform of the nameless warship.

The huge airship was indeed damaged. The armoured star god had clearly torn through the rigid canopy as it fell: not only ripping the envelope but damaging the skeleton of girders beneath sufficient to bend the entire ship into something akin to a banana. The many-tiered gondola hung miserably from this skewed canopy. Although it still had some buoyancy, and its rotors spun yet, the ship was not going to fly far.

Two dockhands (including a scrawny, boyish fellow who I had seen in an earlier vision of Miss Saxena), were casting the last ropes off a docking stanchion. We hurried past them to the gangplank. There were people crowded in the open companionway of the airship – prisoners who had descended from the orbital station before us – with one notable figure standing at the hatch, a voicepipe held ready in one hand. His other hand was bound against his chest in a makeshift sling.

"How the hell did you survive that fall?" demanded Miss Saxena. Her voice was harsh but there was a smile of pure delight on her face.

"Guts, determination and noble breeding stock," said Alexei Mikhailovich, giving her an indecorous look that did not go unnoticed.

"People of noble stock rarely hang around to rescue ordinary folk," observed Miss Saxena.

"Indeed. But ordinary folk know how to fly airships. We have a German crew familiarising themselves with the controls as we speak. Our British passengers have all been disarmed and confined to quarters."

There was a sudden groan from the tower. The two dockhands ran for the gangplank. The airship appeared to shoot up a dozen feet, but in truth it was the tower collapsing, crumbling on its base. The scrawny dockhand, bringing up the rear, leapt for the gangplank. He managed to grasp its trailing edge, thrusting his fingers desperately into its grilled surface. The grand duke yelled into the voicepipe in fluent German. Although my German is all but non-existent, I understood his meaning well enough.

As I helped a rough fellow haul the lucky young dockhand on board, the airship veered slowly and decisively away from the Skylift. The *Afrikanschen Himmelaufzug*'s final descent into calamitous ruin was not something anyone wished to observe closely, but such was the scale of the structure that even as we made directly away, it felt horribly near.

Nonetheless, in the midst of such destruction there were formalities to be observed. Sedgewick coughed politely. "Miss Saxena," said he with mild reproach in his voice. "I don't believe we've been introduced to your acquaintance."

"Oh," said Miss Saxena. "Professor, may I introduce Grand Prince Alexei Mikhailovich of the House Romanov; dilettante, wastrel and a relic of the old world order."

"Your Highness," said Sedgewick, bowing his head.

"And this is Professor Erskine Sedgewick of Trinity College, Cambridge; keeper of dusty books and lackey of the imperial oppressors."

"Sir," said the grand duke. "I assume you can explain all—" he waved his one good arm "—this. Perhaps over a drink or two."

"I'd be delighted," said the professor.

"I'm afraid it's not over yet," I said.

The professor looked at me questioningly.

"Captain Dansey is on board with Lady Paget. They are making for the helipterons on the upper level."

"How could you possibly know that?" asked the grand duke.

"My companion is possessed of an unerring clairvoyant at the moment," said Sedgewick. "I say let them flee."

"Fleeing is not their plan," I said.

The grand duke glanced at his wounded arm and nodded. "Never let it be said I am not up to a challenge," he said, making for the narrow stairway which led out under the canopy and up the exterior of the airship.

"You'll need my help," called Miss Saxena.

"No, we're needed elsewhere," I said, waving the grand duke on. "And not you, professor," I said to my friend. "Carl will need your help to steer us down to Lake Chala."

"Carl?" said Sedgewick.

9.

During his five day confinement in the hold of the dirigible, hiding from the British crew and pilfering rations from stores when he dared, Alexei had listened and come to appreciate the rhythms of the airship. It was a sturdy ship, more lumbering and less elegant than its German equivalents perhaps, but it was as dependable as any vessel, in air, water or æther.

The stairs Alexei climbed were bolted directly onto the duraluminium superstructure through the canvas material of the envelope, zig-zagging across its surface. Although they were as secure as any stair, Alexei nonetheless wished he had the use of both his hands; or that the guard rail was a little higher. To have survived a fall from a collapsing Skylift only to trip from this ship would be less of a tragedy and more of an embarrassment.

Near the top of the envelope, the stair leaned into the curve. Alexei could hear the sound of an engine above the swirling winds: one of the helipterons was in motion. The British ship had a platform fixed to its dorsal surface, sitting on the balloon like a long, low trestle table, constructed from wooden panels overlaid with riveted metal plates. Light but strong. Stretching the full six hundred foot length of the airship, and over forty feet across, it was as large as the deck of an ironclad and could have hosted a military tattoo if so desired. Presently it was housing three twin-rotor helipterons: hulking and unlovely devices with multiple barrelled machine guns slung under their noses. To Alexei's eyes, they looked like fat, armoured wasps.

The middle helipteron, nearest to Alexei, was listing sharply to its side, undercarriage sunk in the broken deck. The helipteron had nearly been thrown overboard as the demon-god crashed through the envelope. Only the ropes securing the machine to the deck had prevented it toppling off. Beyond the crippled vehicle, the rearmost helipteron sat with its rotors spinning. A black-clad figure moved in a scuttle around its base, untying the mooring ropes. On board, through the forward windows, Alexei could just about make a second figure: the pilot, he guessed. Lady Paget and Captain Dansey stood nearby, waiting to board.

Alexei drew his sabre and made his way across the deck. Lady Paget raised her arm and spoke to Captain Dansey. The captain turned. Alexei imagined him contemplating whether to meet the grand duke with sword or pistol in hand.

"Planning on running like a coward, captain?" Alexei called.

"Withdrawing, Your Highness," said Dansey. "Lady Paget assures me that this is merely a setback."

Alexei rolled his shoulders and looked across at the Skylift. From a mile distant it still dominated the sky. As best Alexei could judge from the imperceptibly fine angle, the Skylift appeared to be falling away, to the west. He tried to imagine the damage that the hundreds of miles of tower would cause across central Africa. "I would be more inclined to describe this as a catastrophic failure. The Aleph—" Alexei allowed himself a momentary scowl "—is lost. Your space-god is dead. Your Queen—"

"Also dead," said Dansey and drew his own sword. "Long live the King."

"Edward?" Alexei was incredulous. "I think you'll find he's more interested in fine food and fine tailoring than in these satanic follies. And I should imagine that when his nephew, the Kaiser, declares war on England in response to this outrage, he will be far too busy."

"War?" said Dansey, taking a practice swipe with his blade. "You have no comprehension of the war that awaits us. You think I want to give our world to these monsters?"

"The evidence suggests so, captain."

"We are in an impossible position Your Highness. Gods above and gods below. We unleash one to stave off the other; create a war to end all war."

Dansey's nose twitched, a revealing tic; Alexei was ready when the captain came at him with an opening jab towards his shoulder. Alexei flicked it aside with his sabre and riposted.

*

Mina followed Cadwallander up the access ladder, through a wheel-locked hatch and into the airship canopy structure.

"What are we looking for, Cadwallander?" she asked.

Cadwallander stepped off the ladder and held out a hand which Mina did not take. "The *asuri*," he said. "Victoria."

"The Queen is dead and ... what?"

Cadwallander was shaking his head. "The star god did not kill her. It absorbed her. And neither are yet dead."

Mina looked along the gantry on which they stood. The interior of the airship's gas canopy was a metal frame wrapped in cloth. The scores of gas bags which provided lift were each as high as a man and secured to the outer frame by rope nets. Plumbing and pumps dominated the central areas. The bulging gas balloons, the faint background hiss of shifting vapour and the stuffy air put her in mind of an industrial laundry. Three levels of metal walkways and connecting stairs ran throughout the structure: narrow tunnels through the press of balloons. The crowding paraphernalia made it impossible to view the entire length of the airship but Mina could see the huge gash in the centre of the canopy which had knocked the whole construction out of shape.

"It landed *on* the airship?" she said, angry more than surprised.

"It is wounded," said Cadwallander and then shook his head. "The *asuri* cannot be wounded while in its protective suit. But the suit is damaged."

Mina checked her pistol. Cadwallander looked at it meaningfully. "You are aware, miss, that we are surrounded by dozens of bags filled with highly flammable hydrogen?"

Mina pursed her lips and counted to five in her head. "Actually, they are filled with dephlogisticated hydrogen. Entirely safe. Now those—" she used her pistol to indicate a fat boiler-like cylinder bolted to a central walkway "—are the phlogiston collectors. If I shoot one of those then neither of us will live long enough to regret it." She smiled briefly. "I shall be careful."

*

With a grunt of pain, Alexei pulled his injured arm from its sling. He parried two successive blows as he freed it and then pushed Dansey back towards the helipteron.

286

The deck beneath their feet was not stable: it tilted with every ship's movement. The winds cutting across the deck, although not powerful enough to knock the men off their feet, were ceaseless. Alexei's hand might be useless, but bound as it was it affected his balance.

Dansey was clearly no stranger to the blade but his experience was limited, his moves confined and unimaginative; as though he had learned to fence from a manual. Given time and barring surprises, Alexei would beat him soon enough. Dansey knew it too: he had made a grave error choosing sword over pistol.

Dansey launched a series of attacks, designed to distract and dazzle rather than strike. Believing Alexei to be off-guard, he drew his pistol. The Russian anticipated the move and was already forcing Dansey's blade wide as the man's pistol cleared its holster. Alexei slipped his blade past Dansey's guard, stabbing him in the forearm. Dansey dropped the gun with a bellow of pain and frustration.

"Regrets, captain?" smiled Alexei.

Flushed with anger, Dansey came at him savagely. The Englishman was evidently unaccustomed to losing.

*

In our search, Miss Saxena and I took to separate walkways but stayed within sight of each other. There were several emergency oxygen stations along the ship's length: canisters and face masks hung on posts for those caught in a catastrophic hydrogen leak. It was as I stopped beside one of these, I recognised the very moment from my visions of future events. I heard Miss Saxena call my name and then her voice being cut off by an ear-splitting rend of metal. Ahead of me, not far from the ruinous gash in the airship's outer layer, a huge arm thrust out from between clustered balloons: the star-god pulling itself onto the walkway. It rolled as it hauled itself up, coming unsteadily to its feet. Upright, the suited abomination filled the entire walkway, its shoulders pressing into the gas bags, its black and eyeless head nearly touching the gantry level above.

I took a down long sailmaker's hook and readied it defensively. There were gunshots and the abomination's head twitched as Miss Saxena's shots pinged off the black headpiece. The beast turned, distracted, and I jabbed at it with the long hook. I snared one of the tentacle-like pipes beneath its chin and pulled at it.

If it had possessed a mouth, the star god might have cried out at our attacks; instead it vented its silent fury through violent response. Later, the vile thing's movements would put me in mind of a gorilla I saw once at the zoological gardens in Regents Park; at the time my mind was overwhelmed by the demon's aura of pure evil. It was lumbering and bulky, true, but there was a poise and dexterity that one would be foolish to ignore. As yet another bullet ricocheted harmlessly off its armour, splitting an overhead steam pipe, the star god grabbed the shaft of my hook. Before I could let go, it flicked me easily aside.

I crashed against a metal upright and, with a groan, fell back.

Miss Saxena called out to the star god, continuing to fire. Though it had no eyes, I swear it regarded me for an instant before dropping the hook – a mere twig in that gargantuan fist– and shambled off through the billowing steam in search of Miss Saxena.

*

Alexei could not only see but also feel, with every thrust and parry, that Dansey was weakening. Uninjured, Dansey had been the stronger of the two, but Alexei's nonchalant defence – hurt as he was – elicited ever harsher and more desperate attacks from the captain.

Perhaps guided by recklessness and instinct rather than his textbook technique, one of Dansey's attacks slipped past Alexei's guard: a savage horizontal cut at neck height. Alexei tilted his head aside, losing an epaulette rather than his life. But the captain had over-reached himself and was utterly exposed. They were too close for Alexei to turn his blade on the man without losing the advantage; instead he jabbed Dansey in the gut with his sword pommel. As the captain staggered, Alexei slammed the flat of his blade into Dansey's face.

Dansey sat down hard on the deck. A shallow cut from eye to lip bled down his face. Dansey blinked, aghast that he had been beaten. Alexei kicked the sword barely held in Dansey's limp grip across the deck.

"Lady Paget," called the grand duke. "Your flight has been cancelled."

The woman, grey and veiled, stood on the runners beneath the helipteron's whirling rotors. She held a peculiar gun with a duelling pistol handle and a trumpet-like bore in her hands. It was shakily aimed in Alexei's direction. He realised it was a flare gun, most likely one she had found amongst the helipteron's emergency equipment.

"Now, let's not do anything silly," Alexei heard himself say. "That's a big gun for a fine lady such as yourself and I'm sure I don't need to remind you that we're stood on top of a giant hydrogen b—"

Lady Paget fired. A line of fire shot from the barrel, leaving dazzling trails across Alexei's vision. The ball of flaming magnesium, slower than a bullet but still too fast for the human eye, struck Alexei squarely in the chest, welding instantly to his uniform. The flare burned his face; he instinctively threw back his head.

If he had been an ordinary man, he would already be dead, his internal organs cooked, but his artificial chest shielded him. Even so the molten heat conduct outward across his torso to meet his all too human flesh. Gasping in fear and the growing, soon to be intolerable pain, Alexei batted away at the flare. In white hot panic, he dropped to the deck, rolling in an attempt to extinguish the flame. He rolled and thrashed, until he tipped himself off the edge of the deck and down the side of the airship.

His earlier fears of an embarrassing but deadly fall about to be realised, Alexei was too preoccupied to care.

10.

Mina ran with little thought other than of staying ahead of the armour-clad titan. Repeated attempts to shoot it had confirmed the worst; her bullets annoyed it, no more. She had managed to draw it away from Cadwallander – Damn it all! The man had tried to poke it with a stick! – but that was the limit of her success. She would need far more powerful weaponry if she was to fight back. One of those teleforce rifles which had sliced off its hand would be more than handy. Or, while she was fancifully wishing, one of the English's mortarmen suits might stand a fair chance. A galvanicallypowered armoured suit – or even one of those unwieldy iron navvies – might have given her the height and power to wrestle the thing down.

Her only recourse, escape, was about to run out. The port and starboard walkways followed the inward curve of the dirigible's nose and would soon meet in the middle. She was all but trapped at the prow of the canopy with nowhere else to go.

There was a crunch of metal. Behind her, the *asuri* (she had decided that this was an anti-goddess, not an anti-god), stumbled on stairs that were far too narrow for its frame. It clutched at supports, crushing railings as it thumped up the steps. The confined space did not suit it, fighting against its environs as it moved, and Mina ought to have taken comfort from seeing the *asuri* so fallible and flawed. She did not; its hateful and unnatural movements underlined its alienness all the more. This beast did not belong. Its very presence jarred against her psyche like an unshakeable nightmare.

As it climbed, she saw the translucent green matter swimming behind the glass porthole in the armour. Loose scraps of material drifted within, churned by the tides of the *asuri's* movements. A jagged fragment washed up against the porthole: a crescent of smashed bone held together by skin, remnants of a face. An eye, with eyelids skewed across it; part of the upper jaw, flapping with tattered lips.

Mina opened her mouth to utter an unbidden prayer. It died in her throat when the eye swivelled to look at her! Mina's legs very nearly give way. Queen Victoria's lips twitched in a terrible ravaged smile. Cadwallander had been right: she was not yet dead! This monster from another world had consumed and joined with her. Fleeting though the sight was, Mina saw only hate and desire in that floating eye. The two were now one.

Slowly, too late, Mina regained control of herself and made to flee the little distance she had left, but the hybrid thing thrust out its one good arm and snagged Mina about the waist. She fired, striking the porthole; cracks spread across its outer pane. The *asuri* shook its head in rage, rubber pipes undulating, and it enclosed its fist about Mina. Her ribs burned at the pressure. She coughed painfully.

The alien-Queen lifted her like a doll, bringing her face level with its blind helmet. Mina could see her own reflection in that black, insectile carapace: a distorted reflection, eyes hidden in shadow, her mouth a frozen *O* of fear.

Tears pricked the corners of Mina's eyes. She had failed. Her bullets and bravado had done nothing to hurt the creature. She was as insignificant as a fly, nothing more than an irritant. This thought, most likely her last, brought a dismal smirk to her face. Surely this was a fitting metaphor for her personal battles against the British Crown: she the irksome insect that the imperial monster – with the Queen at its heart – could so easily swat if it had troubled to catch her. Had she ever believed she was more significant than that? Vanity! All was vanity.

The *asuri* drew back its arm, Mina helpless in its grasp. With all its strength it threw the woman across the airship, to crash into the port walkway.

*

Alexei did not fall immediately from the airship. As he tumbled from the deck, it was not the rocky slopes of Kilimanjaro beneath him, but the fat, curved outer shell of the gas canopy. Alexei rolled, elbows and knees braced to protect his body and slow his fall. He bounced against the canvas as the curvature increased.

His shoulder slammed into something painfully hard and unyielding. For a moment his fall halted. He flailed with both arms. His injured left hand clutched a rail. He pulled instinctively, screaming with pain, and fell – inward – to land clumsily on the stairs which zig-zagged up the side of the balloon. A leg folded underneath him, a stair ground into his back, his left arm was nothing but white hot pain, but he had stopped. He was no longer falling, he was alive.

The flare had fallen from where it had lodged in his chest, leaving a hole that had burned through all of his clothing and melted into his chest plate. Within the black, scorched metal glowed a dull red, fingernail-sized spot. There was an unpleasant wheeziness in his lungs, a sense of uncontrollable weakness. He realised with alarm that his mechanical lungs had been punctured. Every breath he took was leaking through that tiny, molten hole.

"You're falling apart," he muttered to himself and attempted to get to his feet.

A distant clang and a vibration in the metal stairs caused him to look up. It was Dansey, gun in hand, blood flowing freely down his face. Alexei stood, wincing. He had wrenched his ankle in the fall and could barely put any weight on it.

Hand, wrist, chest, and now ankle. "Truly falling apart, young man," he said.

There was a manic set to Dansey's countenance. The man was consumed with rage, clearly beyond rational thought. Alexei was beaten and not worth the effort of pursuing. If Dansey had wanted him dead, he could have taken Lady Paget and the helipteron and merrily shot Alexei with the aircraft's machine guns.

Ultimately, it did not matter. Alexei did not have the strength to run away or the means to fight back. If he had possessed even the tiniest blade, he might have attempted to cut through the canvas envelope and climb into the canopy interior but he had nothing, nothing at all.

*

I heard the last of Miss Saxena's shots, the crash of metal bending under the *asuri's* implacable weight and then silence. I knew what had happened. I had seen this before, and seen that I had known it would happen. I felt the most terrible burning guilt that I had brought her here and to this most unhappy state. Yet I also knew where I needed to be to meet the star god. I made my way from one walkway to the other, doing my utmost to ignore the crippling ache in my side. Net-covered balloons obscured much of the view and steam clouded the air. Even though I was expecting it, I did not see the beast until it was almost upon me.

Having satisfied itself that Miss Saxena was no longer a threat, the *asuri* came for its other attacker: myself. Though I had been cursed with a limited omniscience by the Aleph's all-seeing eye, I had no insights into the mind of the star god. I imagine that doing so would be to court total insanity. Perhaps Professor Sedgewick (who was even now busily talking to the German pilot and urging him to land the airship) would have suggested that mind and thought were concepts as alien to this entity as life, death or moral decency. I do not know if the star god came for me with a plan or, like an enraged tiger, sought me with nothing more than a dim animal recollection that I was a source of pain and annoyance.

The *asuri* burst from the miasma of escaped steam, its shoulder plates snagging and pulling apart the balloon nets through which it barged. Its vicious claw was held out to grab me. I scuttled sideways, out of its reach, back across to the portside walkway. The star god turned and pursued me. As I stumbled towards the stern of the vessel, I was convinced that any delay on my part could spell my doom.

I struggled up the final set of stairs. It was there that the star god almost had me. Its hand reached out for me – so close – and brushed heavily against the rear of my tweed jacket. It was enough to throw me off balance. I staggered forwards, tripped and fell clumsily into an emergency oxygen station with sufficient force to knock the thin oxygen cylinder from its duraluminium housing. I fell to the floor.

I am sure the monster would have crowed victoriously if it had a mouth. I rolled myself over to face it as it bore down on me. Armoured plated like a knight of old, as heavy-footed as a rhinoceros, the monster could simply crush me with its bulk.

It charged in the last few yards, titanic feet trampling dents in the walkway. I lifted the only weapon to hand, the oxygen cylinder. With my pneumatically powered hand at the base, I thrust it before me like a spear. The canister's valve found the glass porthole in its torso and the cracks which Miss Saxena's bullet had made. I pushed with all the power my mechanical arm could muster, even though much of that power simply propelled me back along the floor. The star god's momentum did the rest. The gas cylinder broke through the porthole glass and impaled the monster.

A second before its bulk would have squashed me utterly, the *asuri* reared back in whatever passed for pain. Its slimy vital fluids oozed along the edges of the cylinder, drying and dying as they came into the air.

I threw myself to my feet as I knew I must and hurried away. "Mina!" I shouted. "Do it now!"

There was a gunshot and the sound of a ricochet. I pressed on towards Miss Saxena, whom I saw lying on the walkway ahead of me. One of her legs was bent most unnaturally. Her hair was matted with blood, a strand of it obscuring one eye and half of her face. She held a pistol out in front of her, the butt resting on the walkway, her hands barely able to keep it level.

Another shot went past me; another miss. "Get out of the way," she growled.

I shifted to the side of the walkway. Miss Saxena squinted with her one good eye. "Smile now, you b_____!" she said and fired. Guided by skill or God's will, the bullet found and struck the pressurised canister embedded in the foul *asuri*.

*

Fifty feet along from where Alexei clung, a powerful, flameless explosion ripped out from the side of the airship canopy, splitting the outer canvas in a roaring cloud of steam and debris. Dozens of bags of lifting gas destroyed, the airship heeled to one side. As the stairs tilted some thirty degrees from vertical, Alexei clutched desperately at the handrail.

Above him, Captain Dansey had done the same and was staring down wildly at the grand duke. From his position, Alexei saw what Dansey did not: the helipteron sliding off the landing deck and over the side of the airship. The machine, its rotor blades turning, would fall straight past both men, well clear of the gas envelope and the gondola beneath. Alexei could also see that the ropes which had previously tethered the helipteron to the deck still gathered loosely around its undercarriage.

Perhaps Dansey interpreted something in Alexei's expression. Perhaps he heard something. Whatever the case, he looked up and saw the semi-tethered helipteron, saw the ropes go taut and the machine flip over, swinging like a pendulum towards the airship canopy, the stairs and the captain himself. Something like a large bundle of grey cloth pitched from the helipteron interior and was cut to arid strips in the blades.

Dansey might have leapt to his death rather than be met by the whirling mass of metal. At the last moment, Alexei looked away and did not see what choice the man made.

*

In the cockpit, Carl Menckhoff (who had until a few hours ago been employed as a menial dockhand on the *Afrikanschen Himmelaufzug*) grabbed the control deck as a second shudder ran through the ship. The airship's temporary captain, Brunner, was slower to react, slamming against the pressure and altitude gauges he had gone to check. Brunner slid to the floor, unconscious.

The English professor was already moving to help the fallen man when Carl yelled at him. "Grab the wheel!"

The professor leapt to obey with an alacrity Carl did not expect from the British well-to-do. "We have to descend!" the professor shouted.

"We're doing that already!" replied Carl darkly. "To starboard!"

The professor spun the wheel into the airship's list, trying to steer the massive craft *upwards*. "That's the lake!" he cried out, pointing off towards the south.

"Lake?" said Carl, nonplussed and then understood. "Well, as long as there aren't any crocodiles," he added.

11.

The airship came down in the marshy shallows of Lake Chala, burying the lowest of the gondola levels in the mud, with the fore section of the gas envelope resting against the rocky embankment which ran around the entire lake. There were shouts and screams in those uncertain moments, when the vessel threatened to roll over onto its side before it settled. The survivors of the *Afrikanschen Himmelaufzug* disaster made their way onto the shores, wet and shaken but grateful to be on terra firma.

There were casualties of course: broken bones and concussion but, among those who had boarded the airship, there were no deaths. I dragged Miss Saxena ashore in the most undignified manner, ignoring the delirious curse words she uttered as I hauled her broken body to safety.

We found Professor Sedgewick in the lee of a rocky overhang, counting survivors and making a list of names on the notebook he habitually carried in his pocket. His list included those who had yet to be accounted for. Assuming fire did not break out aboard the airship, a search party would need to be formed, to go back into the downed vessel to search for any further survivors.

I do not blush to recount that the expression on Sedgewick's face, when he saw that I was hale and whole, fair filled me with joy. I am not one for unnecessary and uncontrolled expressions of sentiment and emotion, and I would not have tolerated the same in my good friend; but there was a glint in his eye and a set to his lips which told me clearly enough that I was loved and my continued survival meant the world to the dear chap.

I lowered Miss Saxena onto a blanket that a young fellow laid out for her. She said something as I laid her down but she was drifting into unconsciousness and the faint syllables could have been thanks or insult. Either seemed equally likely.

Sedgewick clasped me on the shoulder and gave it an affectionate squeeze. "I think there is much we have to tell each other, Cadwallander."

"Erskine," I said, "I think I would rather forget it all. It has been the most bewildering affair."

The professor nodded, amused. "But one burning question," he said. "It was you who disrupted the Aleph and halted the star gods' plans."

I looked up to see if I could observe the Skylift. There was a distant ribbon of white, curving westward across the sky, hundreds of miles of metal artifice falling to Earth. It looked so slow, almost imperceptible in its movements. "I shudder at what I've done," I said.

"No," said Sedgewick. "I imagine you saved us all. But I must ask, how did you know what to do? What drove you to act?"

"It was you," I replied. "You mentioned Baruch's Apocalypse."

"But that was *after* the event, when we were in the lift."

"Which caused you, now, to relate your theory."

Sedgewick frowned. His eyebrows, grown to be quite magnificent in his middle years, bunched together in thought. "The Apocalypse of Baruch is an obscure text but it does discuss the Tower of Babel," he said. "And I simply recalled that it speaks of the tower builders. Let me see... *And they took a gimlet, and sought to pierce the Heavens, saying Let us see if the Heaven is made of clay, or of brass, or of iron. When God saw this He did not permit them, but smote them with blindness and confusion of speech, and rendered them as thou now seest.*"

And, with that, the last vision of the Aleph came to an end. I returned to my own senses in the cargo chamber atop the Skylift. I was on my knees before the Aleph, Miss Saxena off to my side, the bleeding and dying Chioa Khan in front of me. His hand was outstretched to point at me, his mouth struggling and failing to make words. I knew that he wasn't trying to speak to me; he was trying to warn the others. He may have been an insufferable fool, but he was a well-read fool.

I understood fully what I must do, what I already knew I would do.

"Gimlet!" I said.

I reached hurriedly into my jacket pocket, withdrew the screwdriver with which Sedgewick had repaired my arm aboard Victoria's airship and jabbed it into the Aleph, piercing its otherworldly light.

12.

I shall not bore you with the details of what is known to anyone who can afford a penny for a newspaper or tuppence for a kinema ticket. The coronation of King Edward VII in 1909 was a cause for only the most muted of celebrations. Those of us who had fought to protect the world from ethereal and eldritch horrors simply saw them replaced in the following years with the man-made horrors of war.

However, I will recount that Professor Sedgewick and I (after some difficult weeks and by the most circuitous of routes) made it back to England. Miss Saxena travelled with us, although only after we had smuggled her out of a hospital in Dar-es-Salaam, beneath the noses of her German guards. Grand Duke Alexei Mikhailovich also travelled with us for a way, although he left without a word in Cairo. He did leave a letter for Miss Saxena but I know nothing of its contents and would probably not reveal them if I did.

London did not welcome us as heroes. None knew what we had done. Miss Rose Sedgewick, the professor's precocious niece did meet us at the docks and, impulsively improper though it might have been, the fierce hug of greeting I received from her did more for my spirits than any festive bunting or marching band.

We returned, all of us, to our house in Cambridge. I was surprised that, in the following weeks, Miss Sedgewick and the convalescing Miss Saxena became friends. I would have thought they would hate each other on sight, but I don't profess to understand women one iota.

In those weeks, I myself was to be found, more often than not, in the parlour with a sketching pad in my hand. Drawing is one of my few talents (far more serviceable than my workmanlike attempts at journalism, for which I must apologise to you all) and I attempted then, and attempt now, to exorcise my nightmarish memories through my drawings of them. I hope I do not become obsessive, but as day draws to evening and Cecily comes in to light the lamps, I can remain fixated upon the paper: correcting details, finding the angles of evil to represent those terrifying visages, reshaping the sigils and etchings, divining the meaning present in the gears of madness. All this is a mostly futile attempt to cage those demons within the pages of my book. Would that I could pluck those memories from my brain and be done with them!

And then, dissatisfied with my efforts, I might look up from my drawing and see that Professor Erskine Sedgewick is there too, sat in the lamplight in his high-backed armchair, perhaps perusing his copy of Chambers' *Vestiges*. He will perceive that I am looking at him and he too will look at me and, in his eyes, I see understanding and compassion.

God be thanked for the gift of friendship. God be thanked.

Appendix: Notes on Historical Figures

I have included this short appendix for two principal reasons. Firstly, I wouldn't want the reader to go away thinking I invented all of the characters in this book; there are some very steampunk and downright queer characters who are nonetheless entirely real. Secondly, this is the only place in which I can properly apologise for my abuse of some frankly blameless real-life individuals.

This list is by no means exhaustive. There are numerous historical figures who get a mention in the story that I have not included here. You'll just have to look them up yourself.

Joseph Bazalgette (1819 – 1891)
One of the great – if not *the* great – civil engineer of Victoria's Britain, Bazalgette is best remembered for the construction of the London sewer system which was not only epic in scale but also massively cut cholera deaths in the city. His other works include Hammersmith Bridge, Victoria Embankment and early plans for the Blackwall Tunnel.

J. Cadwallander (1868 –)
Sedgewick's batman, Cadwallander, is an entirely fictitious character.

George Curzon, Marquess of Kedleston (1859 – 1925)
The one-time Viceroy of India was a rather controversial man who was seemingly liked and loathed in equal measure. He suffered a painful spinal injury as a youth and his apparent arrogance and diffident manner as a man was only enhanced by the metal corset he wore at all times thereafter to alleviate his suffering.

Claude Dansey (1876 – 1947)
Claude Dansey was until World War I a career soldier, son of a disciplinarian father and an alcoholic mother. He was a veteran of the Boer War, an intelligence officer in South Africa and, once World War I started, played an increasingly important role in the organisation that would become MI6. During World War II, when

Nazi spies compromised MI6, it was Dansey's *Z Organisation* that continued much of the important intelligence work for the British. As far as I'm aware, Dansey never met Queen Victoria, let alone worked directly for her. Similarly, although some accounts say Dansey was "spiteful, vindictive, [and] short-tempered," my portrayal of him as a villainous character is entirely fictitious and without historical basis.

Bramah Joseph Diplock (1857 – 1918)
Diplock was the inventor of the pedrail wheel, a system of 'feet' on the wheels to allow it to cross uneven ground. Although ultimately replaced by the caterpillar track, Diplock's pedrail was influential on early designs for tanks in World War I.

Maurits Cornelis Escher (1898 – 1972)
Escher was born in Leeuwarden in the Netherlands but spent some of his childhood in Arnhem. His father was the civil engineer, George Arnold Escher. The lithographs and woodcuts he produced as an adult would bring him lasting fame and acclaim. Obviously, almost everything that happens to Maurits in this book is made up.

Iain Grant (1974 -)
Grant was born in Lincolnshire but now lives in south Birmingham with his wife and two daughters. He writes a lot. Although he loves steampunk, he does not own a pair of goggles or anything with cogs on.

Inzar Gul (d. 1915)
Inzar Gul was a sepoy with the 40th Pathans. The 40th Pathans, nicknamed *the Forty Thieves*, accompanied the British Expedition to Tibet in 1904 and then, at the outbreak of World War I, joined the fighting in France. Inzar Gul died on 20th April 1915 and is remembered on a memorial at Meerut Military Cemetery in St Martin-les-Boulogne. I'm sorry that I know no more about Gul than this.

John Scott Haldane (1860 – 1936)

Haldane was a bold pioneer in the exploration of the effect of gases and pressure changes on the human body. He visited the sites of industrial accidents, tested toxic chemicals on himself (and on his son!) and even visited the front line in World War I to investigate the composition of chemical weapons. His efforts resulted in life saving inventions such as the gas-mask, pressure chambers for deep-sea divers and, through innumerable discoveries, reduced the health and safety risks posed to many industrial workers.

Chioa Khan (1875 – 1947)

I'm unsure if I owe Aleister Crowley an apology or not. I have portrayed him as a sorcerous agent of mysterious gods and, of that, he might have approved. Born into a wealthy brewing family in Warwickshire, Crowley had the resources to devote much of his life to his aesthetic and spiritual pursuits. Whilst on his travels, Crowley was said to hear the voice of Aiwass, the messenger of the god, Horus. At this time, he took on the name of Chioa Khan, a title he claimed to have been granted by a foreign potentate. He travelled to the Nepalese Himalayas to make an ill-fated attempt on Kangchenjunga at a time when Captain Herbert Walton was in Nepal with the British Expedition. However, there is no evidence to suggest the two of them met.

Carl Menckhoff (1883 – 1949)

As a Westphalian youth, Carl Menckhoff has a fascination with engines and aviation, and participated in balloon flights with his older brother. Menckhoff enlisted for army service in 1903 but suspected appendicitis put paid to this first attempt at a military career. Several years after the events in this book, Menckhoff enlisted in the German Air Force and became one of the most persistent and successful fighter pilots of the First World War.

Albert Michelson (1852 – 1931) & Edward Morley (1838 – 1923)

Michelson and Morley were American scientists (although Michelson was Polish-born) who are perhaps most famous for the Michelson-Morley experiment of 1887. The experiment attempted to detect the *æther wind* produced by the movement of the earth through the luminiferous æther by measuring the speed of light travelling in different directions. Finding no notable variation in the speed of light, Michelson and Morley presented the first major challenge to the then-prevalent luminiferous æther theory. In my alternate history, their experiment was a success and led to practical applications of the knowledge gained.

Grand Duke Alexei Mikhailovich (1875 – 1895)
One could cheekily argue that the Alexei who appears in this book is identical to his real-life counterpart but for one small fact: the real Alexei succumbed to his tuberculosis and died in San Remo at the age of 19. He was, according to accounts, a handsome and intelligent youth with great promise. Writers like to play God from time to time and I have relished giving Alexei a second chance of life in these pages.

Walburga, Lady Paget (1839 – 1929)
The Lady Paget portrayed in this book is astonishingly close to the real life version. Sure, the real-life Lady Paget had no dealings with alien beings (that we know of). However, Lady Paget was indeed a close personal friend of Queen Victoria. She did believe in Hollow Earth theory, claimed to have a spirit guide and indeed wrote about cities beneath the earth where the survivors of older civilisations still lived. The book and quotation attributed to her at the beginning of *The Shadow Under London* is genuine.

Cecil Rhodes (1853 – 1902)
Rhodes was the archetypal British colonialist and as such can be viewed from a historical perspective as either a great man or as a despicable man. Twain's quote about Rhodes in *The Pearl of Tharsis* perhaps encapsulates this. In this book, I took Rhodes to Mars instead of South Africa. On the subject of the wider universe, Rhodes said, "I would annexe the planets if I could; I often think of that. It makes me sad to see them so clear and yet so far."

Mina Saxena (1877 –)
Mina Saxena is entirely a work of fiction. More's the shame.

Professor Erskine Sedgewick (1863 –)

Professor Sedgewick is a fictitious character. However, I stole his surname (and a smidgeon of his character) from Adam Sedgewick, the Victorian geologist, and also from the later Adam Sedgewick, great nephew of the original and a respected zoologist.

Nikola Tesla (1856 – 1943)

Nikola Tesla is a staple of steampunk-era science fiction. He was an inventor, a genius, a shameless self-publicist and, quite probably, an incorrigible liar. The inventions he is credited with in these adventures – wireless power transmission, teleforce weapons and earthquake-causing oscillators – are genuine inventions (or genuine Tesla lies).

Queen Victoria (1819 – 1901)

In writing this book, I have been entirely unfair to one of Britain's most famous monarchs. Giving her seven extra years of fictional life is hardly a fair exchange for transforming her into the catspaw of alien gods. I shan't patronise the reader with a potted biography here since you probably already know more about her than I could possibly convey in this short space.

Laurence Waddell (1854 – 1938)

Regarded by some as the inspiration for the fictitious Indiana Jones, Waddell was an explorer, archaeologist, army surgeon and recognised scholar of chemistry, pathology, Tibetan, Sanskrit and Sumerian. Waddell believed that the Sumerians (who he equated with the Aryan race) were the originators of all human civilisation. His adherence to a belief in hyperdiffusionism and the associated racial theories meant he became increasingly marginalised by his peers in later years. The book he completed in the year of his death was never published.

Captain Herbert Walton (1869 – 1938)

Herbert Walton was the medical officer and naturalist attached to the British Expedition to Tibet in 1904. Mina's fictional observations of his medical ministrations to the native population are based on fact. Although Walton never married, Roxborough's accusations regarding his sexuality in *The Well of Shambala* are entirely without historical basis. Furthermore, his career post-Tibet was far less exalted and far less sinister than that I have invented for him here.

Inspector Fabian Wilmarth (1872 –)
Inspector Wilmarth is a complete work of fiction. I stole his surname from a HP Lovecraft story, just one of many things I have affectionately "borrowed" from Lovecraft for these adventures.

Colonel Francis Younghusband (1863 – 1942)
Younghusband was a career soldier and explorer who led the British Expedition to Tibet in 1904 almost exactly as described in *The Well of Shambala*. According to his biographer, in the retreat from Tibet, he had a divine revelation which ultimately led him to posit beliefs regarding cosmic forces and alien super-beings on Altair. The book with the ridiculously long name quoted at the beginning of *The Well of Shambala* is a real book and quite reflective of Younghusband's spiritualist philosophy.

Acknowledgements and Thanks

Acknowledgements first. I don't believe there's such a thing as an original story. Well, maybe one original story. Okay, two. Perhaps three original stories. But no more than that. Everything else is a blend of copying and narrative trickery.

The Gears of Madness is not a pastiche of or homage to any one writer but there's a particular literary shadow that looms large over this novel, that of HP Lovecraft. Without his mythos or his philosophy of cosmic indifference these stories just wouldn't exist. And, let's face it, *The Shadow under London* is an unsubtle retelling of one of his most famous tales, just in a wholly different setting.

But if I'm going to acknowledge the brilliance of Lovecraft then I'm also going to have to give a nod to those other writers of short stories, novels, TV shows and films, who I've either fondly homaged or cheekily stolen whole scenes from. So, thank you, Benchley & Gottlieb, Buchan, Cameron, Conan Doyle, Greifer & Holmes, Kasdan, London, Lucas, MacLean, Moore, O'Bannon and Poe (and probably many, many others).

Now, thanks. Thanks to those people who offered opinions during the writing process. Particular thanks to Martin Sullivan who suggested I rewrite Wilmarth as a republican spy (I just couldn't do it) and helped me when the physics of skylifts became too much for me. Thanks to the Mikes: Mike Chinn for his skilful editing of this particular volume and Mike Watts for his wonderful covers for all the Sedgewick Papers. Thanks to Heide Goody, my publishing partner, for supporting me in this when I should have been writing more *Clovenhoof* books. And, as always, thanks to my wife, Amanda, who puts up with me and complains whenever she thinks I've made up a word.

www.ingramcontent.com/pod-product-compliance
Lightning Source LLC
Chambersburg PA
CBHW031251170626
46807CB00001B/95